THE NANNY GOAL

AINSLEY BOOTH

Copyright Ainsley Booth, 2025.

All Rights Reserved.

www.ainsleybooth.com

for everyone who hasn't felt seen

ABOUT THIS BOOK

When I first met her, I was just her brother's best friend and a hockey player. Then I was the secret fling who broke her heart. Now I'm a single dad … and her new boss.

On the best and worst night of my life, I left the perfect girl alone in a hotel room, confused and angry. Since then, Emery Granger has ignored me, despite the fact that our families are friends, and I would do anything to have a second chance with her.

When we're thrown together again, it's in the worst way possible—with me needing an emergency nanny, and my daughter immediately attaching herself to the last woman I got to third base with, making Emery the reluctant best candidate for the job.

No matter what happened in the past, I will always put being a good father first. My feelings for the nanny? Irrelevant. Impossible.

Which is a challenge, because the nanny herself? Irresistible.

GLOSSARY

This is the first book I've written in this series that doesn't have a Canadian protagonist, so there are fewer Canadianisms in this book than the first three novels. (But it is still written in Canadian English, due to setting and series continuity—and scene-stealing Canucks.)

So instead, this book's glossary will focus on hockey and chef terms!

Also, it's possible that some of the hockey slang defined below are regional, too, and not used everywhere hockey is played. But they are definitely used in my corner of the hockeyverse.

Dash - *I'm not pulling nearly as many hot supermodels now that I'm a dash eight on the season* - hockey slang for minus, as in the wrong side of the plus/minus stat for scores against your team

Dub - short for W, or a win in hockey jargon

Zip, Nothing - variations of saying zero in a score. *It's already two nothing for the home team, and this goal would make it three zip before the end of the first period.*

Stage - an unpaid internship in a restaurant kitchen. It's pronounced *stah-j*, not *stAge*, and it comes from the French word *stagiaire* which means trainee or apprentice.

CHAPTER 1
ALEXEI

At the top of the list of key lessons I've learned about being a single father is that the safest time to stroke one out is really fucking early in the morning.

File that under "things nobody tells you".

Of course, nobody knew I was going to be a father before I was suddenly thrust into the experience with an hour's notice.

Two years later, I'm still figuring out how to balance my pro hockey career and raising a toddler—and finding reliable personal time remains a struggle.

You might think it would be late at night, but half the time I'm too fucking wiped, either from a game, or pushing myself too hard through workouts, or simply managing the complicated mess that is my new life. And the rest of the time, there's a solid chance my parents will barge in because they're night owls with zero sense of personal space.

Middle-aged Russian parents do not understand that a guy needs his privacy because he's not getting laid, he might never get laid ever again, and the only thing that would get him off anyway is a memory he feels fucking guilty for indulging in.

Another reason I take care of business at dawn... this is when I'm weakest. This is the time of day I can't stop myself from getting hard for an off-limits woman.

My best friend's younger sister.

The woman I was with when—

I don't think about that part of it, the part that means it will never happen again.

In hindsight, it should never have happened in the first place.

I'm not proud of how much I enjoyed the way she looked at me, like I could build sandcastles in the sky for her.

And when I give in, like I am right now, and shove my shorts down to wrap my fist around my erection, I desperately reach for any fantasy but that one.

I imagine her fingers on my cock, something that never happened. Her breath, warm and sweet, against my most sensitive flesh. Licking at my tip with her pointy pink tongue.

Something else she never had a chance to do.

Most of my fantasies are basically alternate endings to that night. What if I hadn't checked my phone? What if she'd gotten my zipper undone and her slim fingers into my boxers?

She'd been so fucking willing. So eager.

I stroke myself harder than she would have, punishing myself, jerking roughly. I never pretend my hand is hers, probably couldn't even if I tried. But in my head, I see it play out. She climbs on top of me, curious fingers exploring my length. Teasing me. Making me buck into her touch, needing more. Needing so much more.

I would make her hold my gaze as she brought us together, replacing her hand with her entire body, her sweet pussy, that tight, wet—

Fuck.

It's a good thing it's just a fantasy, because I just prematurely jizzed at her entrance like a teenage boy.

Chest heaving, I pump the last of my seed into the pooling puddle on my abs and shut my eyes.

"I'll take that as a compliment," my fantasy of Emery says. *"I'm so hot you couldn't hold it."*

Real life Emery wasn't that cocky. She was sweet and innocent, and the adoration in her eyes as I took that innocence was headier than any drug.

I put us both in a terrible position that night.

And right on cue, as the blood pounds fast and heavy in my ears, a rustling sound comes across the baby monitor on my bedside table.

The fantasy dissolves as quickly as that night did.

From now until late tonight, my time belongs to others.

I take a deep breath and remind myself of the daily goals: getting through the day without snapping at anyone, and being grateful for what I have.

The nearest thing I can find to clean myself off with is

the t-shirt I took off last night. After wiping myself off, I dump that in the hamper in my bathroom—laundry I've made it clear to my mother I can do myself—and quickly wash up before pulling on a fresh shirt.

Then I head to the nursery at the opposite end of the hall, across from the spare bedroom where my parents sleep. A shared bathroom is in between the two rooms, and often my mother beats me to the task of getting Inessa out of my bed, but not today.

My tiny tyrant of a daughter is sitting up in her toddler bed, rubbing sleep from her eyes. I just built the white princess frame a week ago, after I found her climbing out of her crib. But she's still not sure what to make of it, and when she wakes up in the morning, she waits for someone to come and get her.

A princess with tyrannical tendencies.

Silently, she holds up her arms, wanting to be picked up.

"Good morning, little one," I say in Russian.

She presses her face into my neck.

"Can you say, good morning, Papa?"

A slow little sigh warms my skin before she mumbles a half-hearted *Dobroye utro, papochka* that runs together.

"How about some breakfast?"

That gets a silent nod.

"How did you sleep?"

No answer.

Inessa is not a morning person.

I change her diaper, but she whines at the idea of getting dressed, so I leave her in her PJs for breakfast.

As we step into the hallway, my father opens the bedroom door. His hair is standing on end. "Dobroye utro."

And then he mumbles something about coffee.

None of us are morning people.

If I didn't have some basic adult needs that couldn't be met any other time of the day, I'd probably be as silent as the two of them, but orgasms have a way of kick-starting me better than caffeine.

My dad opens the baby gate at the top of the stairs, and we file down to the kitchen. Inessa doesn't let go of my neck until I get her a sippy cup of milk. Then I find some blueberries for us to share. Yesterday, raspberries caused a meltdown for being *wrong*, so I don't want to risk those again.

"She needs bacon," my father mutters as I put three blueberries on Inessa's tray.

I love my parents.

I am grateful to my parents.

I am tired of explaining toddler food preferences to them when they spend as much or more time with her as I do, especially to my dad. My mom at least can read my body language and tries to keep the peace.

Also, she has the magic ability to talk Inessa into trying new things, or having a bite of something she doesn't enjoy, like bacon. I do not have that ability and neither does my father. And a day that starts with a tantrum is twice as long as one that starts with a quiet, peaceful breakfast.

Tension crawls up my back as the coffee maker hisses its way through an espresso.

But when my father goes to the fridge and pulls out the bacon and eggs, I need to say something. "Maybe wait for Mama, yeah?"

"She's sleeping."

I frown. My mom never sleeps in. "What's wrong? Is she sick?"

This is terrible timing if she is. I have a home game tonight, and then tomorrow we get on the team plane and fly out to St. Louis and then Detroit for two road games.

He shrugs. "Indigestion," he replies in Russian. "She was up all night. I can cook."

He can, but in his own way.

Not to my nutritional needs and not to my daughter's preferences.

"I'll make eggs," I offer. "If you want some bacon, go ahead, but none for us."

Hopefully my mother is feeling better by the time I need to leave for morning skate at the arena. My dad is a doting grandfather, but he doesn't know how to care for a toddler the same way my mother does.

So, we'll let her sleep in and hope for the best, but plan for the worst. Like tiring out my tiny tyrant girl. "Maybe I'll take Inessa out for a walk this morning, hmm?"

My daughter's eyes light up. "Walk?"

My dad mutters something else in Russian under his breath, and again I restrain myself from engaging.

He doesn't think I should speak English to Inessa. But

she gets enough Russian from them, and I want her to be fully bilingual.

I want them to speak more English as well, but that's a harder fight.

They've been in Canada for two years, and they don't believe me that this is the hardest part. I've been here for ten years, since I was eighteen, and to them, my English is beyond reach. I know it's not, because I remember just how much my vocabulary has grown in the last two years by being really conscious about using it more and no longer relying on teammates to translate for me.

And in the last year, it's been supercharged because I don't have a Russian teammate, unlike in Calgary. The team does have a Russian-speaking trainer on staff, but the only conversations where I've allowed myself to rely on her to translate have been very technical discussions with medical jargon.

My dad puts an espresso in front of me, then makes one for himself. I sip at it as we eat blueberries, then Inessa finally starts talking. "Papa make toast?"

"Of course." I pick her up out of her highchair and set her down. "Do you want to help?"

When she nods, I prompt her.

"Get the bread you want."

She opens the bread drawer and swings a bag of sandwich loaf at me with the enthusiastic aggression of a rookie D-man, whacking me on the leg. "This one."

"Gentle," I remind her.

She laughs, an out loud cackle.

We definitely need to go to the park. As soon as she

has toast in her little belly, she'll be zooming upstairs looking for her babushka.

I sweep her into my arms and spin around before depositing her back in the highchair.

"Papa," she chastises.

I grunt at her, unswayed. I need her confined while I cook.

That gets another laugh, and I distract her with more grumpy dad noises until there's buttered toast on her tray.

I've also managed to cook some scrambled eggs in the same time. They're basic but good enough. I'll eat again when I get to the arena for morning skate.

Once we're both fed, I get Inessa changed into warm clothes. They don't match, and she keeps her unicorn nightgown on underneath, but nobody at the park will care about fashion choices.

Outside, it's brighter than it has been maybe all winter, and Inessa throws her hands up at the sky in delight.

"It's sunny," I say in English.

She doesn't repeat it, and I don't prompt her. I'll save my Dad voice for when she needs to listen to me for safety reasons on our walk.

Learning to pick my battles has been another frustrating curve as a single parent—especially when the people who parented *me* are actively watching and judging.

And getting traded at the same time as Inessa discovered her attitude was a challenge.

After spending almost ten years in the Calgary organization, from getting drafted to slowly developing in their farm teams, I honestly thought I might spend my entire career there.

The trade calls blindsided me.

"We appreciate everything you have done here in Calgary…"

"Welcome to Hamilton, son. We understand you have a young child and your parents live with you? We have people in the organization who can help them get settled. We need you to fly out today…"

The next three weeks were the longest stretch of Inessa's life without me. She was used to seeing me on a video call on Baba's phone, but road trips are rarely longer than a week, and the team would keep me at home if they knew I wasn't going to play.

From the second I landed in Hamilton, I was playing, and playing a lot. Plus, I needed to find a vacant house we could buy immediately, and I had a laundry list of requirements. Walking distance to a park, a separate suite for my parents, and a space that could be customized for a gym.

I had help from the team, but by the time we found it, the season was well under way. I only had one free day to pick them up from the airport and bring them to our new home before I had to get on the team plane again for a few days.

When I finally returned, Inessa clung to me and refused to sleep in her own bed for the next three nights. My parents abandoned their plan to live in the separate suite, and moved into the spare room across from the nursery instead.

It was a long, dark winter of trying to find a new normal like the one we'd had in Calgary. My parents, too, are struggling.

Inessa stops and squats down, looking at a patch of frozen ice on the sidewalk. In ten minutes, we've gone about two hundred metres. I shove my hands deeper into my pockets and my thoughts about my family into the back of my mind.

We have a game at home tonight, and I'm the starting goalie.

After a rollercoaster of a season, the Hamilton Highlanders are on the cusp of making the playoffs again for the second straight year, only their second year in the league.

Last year, though, they bombed out in the first round.

Everyone in the locker room is painfully aware of the internal pressure to be better this time. To make the playoffs handily, and excel once we get there.

And our biggest acquisition at the trade deadline—veteran defenceman Luca Carter—was injured in his second game with the Highlanders. He's now on long-term injured reserve, and we'll be lucky if we get him back for the second round of the playoffs, if we make it that far.

"Papa, come on," Inessa urges, as if *I'm* the slow one.

Taking off at a terrifyingly unstable run, ignoring my stern reminders to be careful, she laughs and leads me the last fifty metres to the park, then immediately climbs to the top of the slide and waves down.

Fearless little girl.

I sigh in secretly proud defeat. "Show me how you slide down. But be—"

She flings herself into the plastic mouth of the slide and catapults down it, somehow landing on her feet.

Bouncy is in her genes, I suppose. "Careful," I finish saying, laughing with her.

She climbs up and goes down again, and then again, until her cheeks are pink and she's out of breath. While she recovers with the speed of a professional athlete, I do some pull ups on the climber.

"Me do it, too, Papa."

I pick her up and she holds on to the bar, mimicking me and giggling.

When I suggest it's time to go home, she protests and runs back to the slide.

I hear my mom's voice in my head. *You can't ask her, Alexei. You must tell her. Or better yet, let her think it is her idea.*

I scoop up a handful of wood chips from the edge of the playground and start juggling them, a habit I picked up from a coach in the minors. It's good for my hand-to-eye coordination, and also for tricking my daughter into coming closer.

"Me juggle, Papa."

"Sure thing, little one." I put her on my shoulders and hand her a couple of the wood chips, stashing the others in my pocket. They're light enough that when they fall on my head, it's not a problem, but I don't need them all raining down on me at once.

She tosses the ones I gave her up, and I catch them, my hands snatching them mid-air…one, two, three.

"More juggles."

I give her those three back, and we repeat it as I walk back home.

We're halfway there when she realizes she's been tricked.

"Papa!"

"I know, I know."

She kicks her feet, protesting. I just hold on tight and put up with the complaining, because when we're not going at her speed, it's a pretty short walk.

And then she sees a bunny rabbit on the edge of our lawn, and all is forgiven.

We look at the rabbit until it darts away, then climb the stairs and head inside.

As we take off our coats and boots, I hear my parents talking in the kitchen, so I hope that means my mom is feeling better.

"…Granger road trip," my dad says, laughing.

My pulse turns sluggish at the heavily accented way he says Emery's last name. But it's not about Emery, of course. My parents don't know Forrest's sister. They know of her, of course, but they've never met because Emery Granger won't come within a hundred miles of an Artyomov.

My fault.

"Baba!" Inessa calls out.

"We're...in the kitchen."

I frown, not liking how tired my mom sounds. But when we find them, she has a bright smile for my daughter. "Why are you still wearing your nightgown?" She clucks as she quickly, deftly works the pyjamas out from under Inessa's sweatshirt. "That's better, isn't it?"

"No," Inessa says, scowling.

I close my eyes and count backwards from five.

When I open them again, I see my mother rubbing her chest.

"Papa says you aren't feeling well," I murmur after kissing her forehead.

"I'm fine, don't fuss. It's just heartburn."

"Do you want me to take Inessa with me to the rink?" It wouldn't be ideal, but I don't need to skate this morning, and she can come with me to the team meeting and to get the scouting reports.

But my mother shakes her head. "No, of course not. My sweet girl is no trouble."

"She's an Artyomov. She's nothing but trouble."

"Shush." She laughs, though. "I'll be careful about what I eat today. And I won't let your father talk me into drinks with our friends tonight."

"The Grangers?" I ask, as casually as I can, pretending I'm barely interested.

I've already put the pieces together. My buddy Forrest, a former teammate in Calgary, is one of five kids. Emery is his younger sister, but he has three older brothers, who also all play in the NHL.

Out of the 82 games a year I play, at least ten percent

are played against a Granger. Tonight is no exception—Minnesota is in town to face us, and the oldest Granger, Camden, is their captain—and Forrest's parents love to watch their kids play hockey.

"They asked about tickets," my father explains.

Discomfort squeezes my chest like a fist. "How many do you need?"

He shakes his head. "Our regular seats are fine."

Someone from the team helped arrange four season tickets for my family. Sometimes it's just my parents who come to the games, sometimes they invite Russian speakers they have met through local community groups. Last week it was a Ukrainian professor from the university and his daughter.

Tonight, it will be Emery's parents. Two people only, to fill the two empty seats. But nobody else in their extended family.

The discomfort fades to something that feels like irrational frustration.

I like the Grangers. They stayed in Calgary when I discovered I was a new dad, and they helped me through the initial shell shock, taking me shopping for a baby car seat and then a house.

Emery didn't stay, of course. I didn't see her again after that night. She went back to her college team in Boston. Her parents, though, became de facto grandparents until my own parents could get visas and plane tickets. And once the Artyomovs landed, the Granger-Artyomov Hockey Parent Bond was officially forged.

Despite the language barrier, our families have stayed fast friends ever since.

A friendship Emery Granger has pointedly kept herself removed from.

I deserve that.

Doesn't mean it doesn't fucking hurt, but I did that to myself when I followed her to her hotel room and took something that wasn't mine to take.

CHAPTER 2
ALEXEI

two years earlier

ALEXEI

Leaving for the restaurant now

FORREST

Why are you always so fucking early?

ALEXEI

I don't like to be late

FORREST

Not the Granger way, bud… Have a drink
in the bar and we'll be there ASAP

Normally I wouldn't leap at the opportunity to have dinner with a teammate's family, because my conversational English isn't great and loud restaurants make my listening comprehension even weaker.

And we don't get very many nights off during the hockey season.

It is the depth of Canadian winter, and the last time I got laid it was the end of summer in the South of France.

That is the longest dry spell of my entire adult life.

But my New Year's Resolution this year was to make smarter choices when it comes to women.

The smartest choice of all would be to take a break from them, because they are more trouble than they are worth.

On the other hand…I like trouble.

I especially like trouble with a wet, eager mouth.

So, I'm probably not going to keep my dick from getting into *some* trouble, but at a minimum, I can promise myself there will be no more high-maintenance supermodels.

No more international divas who like to tag NHL players on their Instagram posts but have no interest in moving to Calgary, Alberta. Who will dangle promises for years that it *might* happen.

In other words, no more Tatyana.

I may have only dated one woman who fits that profile, off and on over the last three years, but she's been enough of a handful for a lifetime.

Which is why I'm arriving fifteen minutes early at the address Forrest texted me. I can't get into trouble at a Granger family dinner.

I give my name to the hostess, and she gestures for me to wait in the small bar to the side.

The only other customer in that space is a compact little blonde woman who has exploded out of an over-sized puffy jacket, a thick wool toque, and a bright purple pair of fuzzy mittens, all of which are scattered over the barstools around her.

She's on the phone, nodding with an aggressive level of agreement as she listens to whoever she's talking to, so I take a seat at the far end to give her space.

"What'll you have?" The bartender asks.

"Lime and soda," I say.

No drinking the night before a game where I'm getting a rare start. As the third-string goalie, I sit on the bench more often than not, so knowing I'm in net tomorrow is a big deal.

The woman on the phone tips her head back to stare at the ceiling, a dramatic reaction to whatever is being said to her, and her black turtleneck slides down, revealing the delicate curve of her throat and jaw. Her hair is a wild but short mane of sunshine rays.

It would look incredible spread across my pillow.

Alexei Artyomov, at the very least find out if she is local before you jump straight to picturing her naked.

Not that I need her naked for what I could do with her.

That turtleneck is no match for my hands.

And her loose-fitting, high-waisted jeans could be unzipped in a flash.

It's not the sexiest outfit ever invented, but I find myself cataloguing every little piece of it.

As if she can feel me looking at her, she rolls her neck and glances sideways, bringing her bright gaze to lock on my face. Her brows jump in surprise when I don't look away.

And her eyes spark with undeniable interest.

"K, well, I have to go. No, they aren't here yet, but—Why do you think I'd get into trouble?" She laughs, and it rolls through me like thick honey. "Cecilia, go practice. Love you."

She sets her phone down as the bartender slides an Old Fashioned in front of her. She lifts her drink in the air to me. "To anxious friends."

Friends. Not lovers.

I gratefully take the soda the bartender hands me, and salute her back.

"Cheers to that," I murmur, watching her mouth work.

Trouble, I'm sure.

I still get up and circle around the bar.

She holds my gaze again, and holy fuck I like the way she looks at me.

Her lips are wet from her drink, soft and wet and curling up at the edges—

"There's my little sister," Forrest says from out of nowhere.

"Come here, Em Bear," says a matching voice.

Those voices are the reason for the family dinner.

I halt in my tracks, just a few feet away from the *serious* trouble I was about to hit on, as my teammate Forrest and his older brother Connor, two of the four Granger brothers who all play in the NHL, who will be playing against each other tomorrow night in our barn, squish the little blonde between them in a double bear hug.

"Get off me!" Laughing, she pushes them away and brushes a few chaotic strands of hair off her face, all breathless and giggly. "This is why I never visit you idiots. It's dangerous to my health."

Forrest clasps at his chest. "Hurtful."

"Literally," she mutters, but her gaze quickly slides back to me. She shrugs in a universal apology motion, as if to say, *Sorry my brothers interrupted our moment.*

I wince back in my own apologetic way, *sorry it's about to get so much more awkward,* as Forrest pulls me into the conversation. "Emery, this is my teammate Alexei Artyomov. We call him Arty. Don't let his scowl fool you, deep down he's a softie."

Am I scowling? I frown and rub my jaw.

He gestures from me back to her. "And this is my bratty little sister, Emery. We call her Buzz."

"Or Em Bear," Connor adds, grinning as he sticks his hand out. "And I'm the handsome older brother."

"Second oldest," Emery says, rolling her eyes. "First in ego, though."

He shrugs shamelessly.

But I'm still focused on her.

I knew she is a college student in Boston...and that's about it.

She doesn't look anything like Forrest described. *Emery? She's a tomboy. Plays hockey. Gives as good as she gets in a fight.*

All of those things could be true *and* I could have used a head's up warning that his sister is wildly hot, too.

Maybe he doesn't know that yet. Maybe when he looks at her, she's still his pipsqueak little sister.

She's young, after all. But there's something there, under the surface. A hot little thing just ready to burst free.

Fuck me.

Because even knowing she's off-limits, the way Emery Granger is still looking at me, I know she's exactly the kind of trouble I will want to get into at the first opportunity.

CHAPTER 3
EMERY

I love hockey. It's been in my blood since the day I was born, the first daughter to an NHL star after four boys—who all grew up to play in the big game, too. Grangers *love* hockey.

But I've never, ever wanted to bang a hockey player.

Especially not a grumpy one, because life is way too short for that—although Alexei Artyomov's frown didn't appear until my brothers showed up.

Come to Calgary, my mom said. *It'll be fun*, she said. *We'll get to see Forrest play against Connor, and have a family dinner with three of the five Granger kids.*

Never mind that I'm in my final term at college, and since *I* don't have a lucrative pro hockey career to look forward to, maybe I should actually give that my full attention.

Never mind that nobody in the family came to see *my* team play this season. And sure, yeah, we had a shit season that's already over, but Forrest is having a brutal season, too, and here we are in Calgary anyway.

At least my parents always get me my own really nice hotel room. I might be neglected, but I'm still spoiled in my own way.

And they let me pick the restaurant for dinner.

Which is good, because it turns out that our family dinner the night before the game isn't *just* family.

Mom forgot to mention that Forrest has an intensely hot new best friend who doesn't speak a lot of English, but is fluent in eye-fucking.

The hot goalie is off-limits, Emery Granger. He is not *sex on a stick for you to lick.*

Would my family notice if I snuck off to the bathroom and gave my V-card to my brother's teammate?

Coming from a family of pro-hockey players and playing at an elite level myself, I have to say that athletic bodies don't usually impress me.

But the Calgary backup goalie is stunning. Taller than everyone in my family, and broad but not thick. His wing-span is incredible, like his arms go on forever, and his shoulders…

A girl could sit on those shoulders with ease. Maybe rub myself against his face…

I look up at the ceiling, my cheeks heating up. I have never in my entire life had an explicit face-sitting fantasy about anyone, let alone a stranger sitting across from me while my family discusses the wild card spots for the playoffs.

Our food arrives, which helps me re-centre myself and

regain control over my body. In the hierarchy of things I care about, hockey is at the top, followed by food, family, school, music, working out in general, fashion, and *way* at the bottom, sex. So it should be easier than it is to ignore my reaction to Alexei.

I threw a bit of a tantrum until my mom let me pick the restaurant, which is more foodie than my brothers usually like, but the steak here is well-rated. They got their steaks, and I have a really amazing scallop dish with asparagus done four ways—foamed, gelled, pickled...and frozen in an unexpected sorbet, which I'm instructed to eat first, to set the stage for the rest of this course.

If the hockey thing doesn't work out for me, and women's hockey has a way of not working out, I might go to culinary school so I can learn how to make asparagus ice cream that *delights* on the palette.

"Mmmm," I say, savouring the bright, grassy flavour. "Oh, wow."

"It's good?" From across the table, Alexei is staring at my mouth intently. A ghost of a smile tugs at the corners of his lush, elegant mouth. "It sounds good."

I lick my lips and wink at him. "It's delicious. You have to like asparagus, probably, but it's fun."

"Fun?" He waves down the waiter and points at my plate. "I want that, too."

Beside him, Forrest chokes on his first bite of steak. "Man, no," he tries to intervene. "It's *asparagus*." He gestures at the pickled slices draped perfectly over my scallops. "Look. Green shit. You don't like green shit."

Alexei frowns. "I don't like *salad*. She says it's good. You heard her."

Forrest narrows his eyes at me. "Oh, I heard her. She's a shit disturber."

"What does *shit disturber* mean?"

"She's tricking you." My brother changes his voice to sound like Admiral Ackbar from Star Wars. "It's a trap."

"Oooh." Alexei looks back at me. "You try to trick me?"

"No trick," I say with a straight face. "But yes, vegetable."

He shrugs. "I still try. I like the way you sound when you eat it."

Someone really should tell him it's indecent to say things like that out loud. But I'm not going to, because I'm enjoying how uncomfortable my brothers are right now. When you're the youngest of five and your four older brothers are all pro hockey players, it's not that often you get to shock them.

I let my gaze linger on Alexei's interestingly stoic face as I lazily say, "Yeah, Forrest. He likes the way I sound when I eat it."

"Emery Granger," my mother says.

Connor coughs and changes the subject to the hotel his team is staying in ahead of tomorrow's game. Not the same place we're staying at, and he's wondering how the amenities compare. Mindless bullshit I couldn't care less about.

Alexei watches me lick a bit of asparagus foam off my

spoon, something flickering deep in his otherwise serious gaze, and I smile.

———

"Emery! Wait!"

I turn around just short of the entrance to the hotel I'm staying at with my parents.

Alexei jogs across the street, an unexpected grin on his face. "You are alone."

It sounds like a statement, rather than a question, and he has no idea just how accurate that observation is.

Baby Granger has always, will always, be alone. Even when I fly to a whole other country to see my family.

"Where are your family?" His breath puffs out between us, reminding me just how effing cold it is here in Calgary tonight.

"My parents went to Forrest's apartment." I rock back on my heels as recognition glints in Alexei's eyes. "But you knew that."

His nod is bold and unashamed. "I knew that." He gestures at the hotel. "I could…buy you a coffee?"

"We just had coffee after dinner."

His smile broadens. "Black espresso, one sugar cube. Yes."

The fact that he noticed how I took my coffee does funny things to me, leaving me speechless. And judging by the way his expression shifts, it's no secret. I'm pretty sure my pleasure at being seen is written all over my face.

He steps closer, and suddenly he's all I can see. Thick

black hair falling forward over slashing eyebrows. His skin is paler than my hearty Midwest pink-cheeked aesthetic, and his jawline is impeccable. If his hockey career ends too soon, he could pivot to playing an elegant vampire on the big screen no problemo. "Then I wish I could walk you home. But I am too late."

"Too late for what?" My question is breathless and silly. He's already said it, but I don't want this conversation to end. I like the way he's curved over me way too much for my own good. I lick my lips. "I'm not home yet. You could walk me to my room?"

His mouth curves into a beautiful smile. "Yes. I will."

His hand ghosts in the small of my back as he guides me through the lobby to the elevator.

We have to wait a minute, watching the floor indicator count down, and neither of us say anything.

My heart is pounding. I know what I'm doing here. I'm inviting my brother's teammate to my room. Not just to walk me to the door, but inside.

And once he's in my room, we'll do things that I haven't done with anyone else yet, and tomorrow when I see him play hockey in the net behind my brother, I'll pretend this never happened.

I've been around hockey players my entire life, and for the last four years, I've shared an arena with an entire team of college-aged boys.

I know what this is and what it isn't. I've just never wanted *this* before tonight.

The elevator dings, and the doors slide open.

We have the lift to ourselves, and as the doors begin to close, we turn to face each other.

"My brother can't find out about this," I start to say.

Alexei's already looking at my mouth. "You will be my secret."

"Yeah, I get it—" The rest of that thought dies on my tongue as he takes my face in his hands and tips my head up to meet his confident mouth.

I will be his secret.

My brain goes fuzzy at the first lush, experienced press of his lips. It's a take charge, confident kind of kiss, which is exactly what I need.

For all the surface similarities Alexei might have with the annoying, immature hockey players that surround me, this kiss promises he's a different type of man. Cosmopolitan and mature.

A guaranteed good time, worth pausing my preferences on for a single night. Fantasy material for the foreseeable future.

And maybe, just maybe, reason to visit Calgary again.

"Kiss me back, solnishko." He chuckles as he strokes his thumb along my jaw, guiding my mouth to open wider for him.

I blink in surprise, then lunge up at him just as the elevator dings, arriving at my floor. He's laughing, too, as he lets me kiss him for a hot second before slickly putting distance between us in time for the doors to open.

When my tummy does a nervous free fall, though, he catches my hand and squeezes. "It's okay?"

The way he says it is different than in English, more of a question that I interpret as *Are you okay?*

I nod. I'm fine. Breathless and on the precipice of something I haven't done before, but very eager.

Too eager?

Screw it. If he doesn't like my too eager energy, then that's for him to sort out.

I drag him off the elevator and around the corner, down the hall to my hotel room. My parents are on the same floor, but in the other direction, and they aren't here right now. That's a problem for later, when I'm going to have to sneak the hot Russian goalie out. But there's a stairwell right next to my door.

This is happening.

My fingers shake as I pull out my room key. He takes it from me and turns me around, pressing my back to the door, leaning over me, fisting the key just above my head. A slick, smooth move he's done a hundred times before, I'm sure. He takes my cheek in his other hand, his fingertips leaving electric pathways on my skin as he angles us together for another, deeper kiss.

This time, there's no ding to interrupt us.

His fingers sink into my hair, burrowing under my wool beanie, and I wind my arms around his neck, closing the gap between our bodies.

"I want you," I whisper between kisses.

"Yes," he pants back.

And then he's opening the door and we stumble into my room, winter clothes unzipping and falling here and there.

By the time we get to the bed, he's pulled my shirt out of my jeans and is squeezing my bare waist in his hand, a hot, electric touch that puts the kisses to shame.

I unbutton his shirt as fast as possible, wanting to see the hard, muscled body I can already feel through his clothes. His shoulders are ridiculously wide, the rest of him narrowing down in an exaggerated vee to tight hips that feel as if they were built for wrapping thighs around.

My legs move restlessly against his, already thinking about doing just that.

He settles his weight beside me and tucks me in against him, cocooning me into a warm, delicious kiss-filled space. Up close, he smells faintly tropical, like coconut and something else. It's unexpected, and I breathe him in as I work at his shirt. When I get his last button free, my fingers brush the erection straining beneath his fly, and my breath hitches.

His, too.

"Touch me again," he grinds out.

I turn my hand and cover the bulge pressing against his dress pants. Even through fabric, I know his cock is long, proportionate to the rest of his oversized body, and thick enough around that the thought of him being inside me makes my head spin.

"Fuck." His breath catches, and that's so unexpectedly beautiful I have to take a second.

I made Alexei Artyomov make that sound. I did that. Tomboy, little sister, virgin-at-twenty-two-not-that-there's-anything-wrong-with-that Emery Granger.

I grin and squeeze him.

"Oh," he says, a less flattering sound for sure.

"Is that too hard? I'm not sure…"

He searches my face, his expression confused at first, then softening. "It's perfect."

It isn't, but when I ease up, he rocks his hips forward. His eyes burn, and *that* feels perfect. We find a stroking rhythm quickly, and his hands work their way up under my turtleneck.

I haven't been this aware of my breasts since puberty. Each inch of lazy progress he makes adds another throb of heaviness to my smaller-than-average-and-kind-of-pointy tits.

By the time his thumbs stroke the underside of my sports bra, I'm arching my back and practically preening for his touch.

"This is okay?" There's a rich, cocky edge to the question, though. He knows it is. He's teasing me, making me wait and want more than I ever knew I could.

"Yes," I whimper. "Very okay."

"*Very okay*," he parrots. "I like that. Can you say, touch me, Alexei?"

I laugh weakly. "Touch my breasts, Alexei."

"Good girl." He sweeps his thumbs up, just barely glancing my nipples with the fleshy part of his palms.

I want so much more.

"Touch my nipples, Alexei."

He catches my mouth with his as he strokes me again, this time more firmly. He drags his thumbs across my nipples, back and forth, back and forth, and then his fingers hook into the top of my bra and tug it down.

I sob into his mouth.

"My sexy secret," he rumbles against my lips. "I need to taste."

The surreal sight of his dark hair disappearing under my turtleneck—and then the feel of his mouth latching on to my bare breast—is a new core memory.

This is what it feels like to be intimate with someone. Literally like being licked by fire.

He sucks at both breasts until I'm panting, then grazes my nipple with his teeth before he rears up and hitches my hips up in his hands. "Get naked. I taste you now."

I stare up at him.

He grins. "Please?"

I laugh. "Are you for real? You don't have to beg for that, I promise."

"You promise what?" He looks confused.

I wonder just how much English he speaks. He's got the dirty talk cornered.

As I'm trying to figure out the simplest way to tell him he's way sexier than anyone at college, he misreads my pause as nervousness. "Don't be shy, solnishko."

I repeat the endearment. "What does that mean?"

"Little sun." He leans forward and twirls his fingers through my short blonde bob. "Are you like the sun everywhere?"

"What…" Then understanding dawns, and my face turns hot. "Yes. I'm blonde everywhere."

He mutters something in Russian as he unzips my jeans. The urgency is a universal language that I understand, though.

I may not be experienced, but I'm not exactly shy about my body. I know what it can do, and I know I'm physically fit. Cute, even. A solid eight, maybe a nine to the average guy. A seven to jerks, but Alexei doesn't feel like a jerk. I would wear a bikini in front of him and feel pretty confident.

But he's going to get me *naked* naked.

Satisfying his curiosity about my pubes kind of naked.

That's…so naked.

My belly quivers as he peels me down to my panties, my jeans scraping down my thighs, then his hands skimming back up them. His gaze drags all over my body on its way to my face, and when his attention settles there again, it's magnetic.

I can't break the connection.

There's a distant vibration of a phone, and that doesn't break the connection.

Don't read more into this than simple sex, Emery Granger.

I'm really trying not to, but he's staring at me like I'm a wonder. How is a girl not supposed to fall head over heels in love with this kind of attention? I've never in my life had this much attention.

He finally ducks his head and kisses me right below my belly button, his lips just as sure and confident here as they were everywhere else. As he inhales deeply—*try not to think too hard about what that means*—he shifts his whole body, levering down a bit. His hips unmistakably grind into the mattress—*focus on that, that's fucking hot*—and then his mouth is on the cotton covering my mound, kissing me through my panties.

"Solnishko," he murmurs. "Smells like summer."

I cover my mouth to keep from screaming something silly like *I love you* or *marry me,* and it's good because the next thing he does is tug my panties to the side and lick up the seam of my pussy, and that makes me actually scream.

"Fuck yeah," he growls. "Be loud, Emery."

Can't. This room is booked in my parents' name. Oh god, oh god…

His tongue goes everywhere. Deep and up and down again, then up, all the way up, licking between my pussy lips until he finds my clit, and there he stays, tongue kissing my virgin pussy in a way that makes me plant my heels on the bed and press my hips up into his face. Shamelessly. Needfully. Desperately.

"Alexei," I groan around my fingers.

He mumbles something back. I close my legs around his head, and he pushes them wide open. My panties get in the way and he rips them off, sending them flying through the air.

I forget about muffling the sounds I'm making and I reach for him, my hands grabbing his head and holding him… *there.*

His long, capable fingers wrap around my hips and lift me to his mouth.

Thighs shaking, I try not to wrap myself around his head again, but he's turning me inside out, his suction on my clit is so perfect. My thighs curl in, my legs sliding over his broad, strong shoulders, and then I'm coming so hard I see stars.

Deep, incredible pulses start at my clit and rocket through my belly, out to my limbs, leaving nothing tingling pleasure in their wake. I drift in the thick wonder of it, my breath hitching and my ears buzzing, until Alexei peels my thighs off his ears and presses his mouth to the inside of one leg.

"Good, yes?"

I laugh and nod. "Um…yes. Incredible. I didn't know mouths could do all of that, but now that I do know, I feel very, very special."

"Yes, incredible. Special." He laughs with me, kissing my mound and then my bare belly, before crawling up beside me. He's still wearing clothes, his dress shirt merely undone.

He looks elegantly debauched.

I am…

I glance down.

My turtleneck is shoved up into my armpits. My sports bra is yanked down below my breasts. And beneath that…I'm totally naked.

We need some balance here.

"Your turn," I whisper.

He leans in and kisses me, tasting like me, his mouth still wet. "In a minute. First you enjoy."

"I'm enjoying." I tug at his belt. "I want—"

From somewhere near the door, a phone vibrates again.

I sigh. "I should get that. If it's my parents, and they come here next."

He groans and rolls onto his back, waving me off. "Yes. Okay."

I peel off my turtleneck and bra first. If I'm going to roll off the bed naked, it might as well be all the way naked.

He watches me, his attention wolfish.

I twirl at the end of the bed, then point to his erection. "Unzip, mister. I want to taste you next."

As I search my coat for phone, I hear the unmistakable sound of his zipper, then a sexy string of Russian words. My phone's not there, so I turn back to see if it's in my jeans, when I feel the vibration again next to my foot.

Not *my* phone.

His.

I hold up his coat. "Your phone, Alexei."

"Don't care," he says, his eyelids hooding his gaze, his attention locked on my face. "I want you. Need your mouth."

I set the coat down again, and his phone tumbles out of the pocket, screen up.

Tatyana calling

It's none of my business, of course. We're just… Whatever we're doing.

But then the call ends, and on the Lock Screen there's a notification that he's missed three calls and a bunch of messages, too.

"Who's Tatyana?" I ask lightly. Picking up the phone, I lob it in his direction. "She keeps calling. It might be important."

He swears under his breath in Russian. I mean, I don't know that it's a swear word, but it sounds like one. "I turn it off. Come here."

Against my better judgment, I crawl onto the bed as he fiddles with his phone, and wind my arms around his neck.

But as I kiss his jaw, his body goes from hot and needy to rigid and cold.

Definitely don't fall in love with this one, Emery Granger.

Hockey players are all the same.

"Is it, umm…?"

He peels me off his body with a heavy sigh. Closes his eyes for a beat, then opens them again, and the expression there…it's not the man who was just between my legs.

Without saying a word, he disappears into the bathroom. There's running water, and I use that as cover to race to my suitcase to find something that's easier to pull on than a turtleneck and jeans.

When he returns, holding a glass of water, I'm in an oversized t-shirt and underwear. The flimsiest of armour, but it'll have to do.

"Drink," he says, pressing the glass into my hand. "I have to go."

I stare as he heads for the hotel room door.

Then I find my voice. "No goodbye?"

He turns around and shoves his fingers through his hair, making it stand on end. "I am trouble for you."

"Why, was that your drug dealer?" It's a joke, and a bad one. I hope it's a joke, anyway.

"It is my ex-girlfriend." His mouth pinches. "She is having a baby."

Is that worse than a drug dealer? It feels like it is. I barely hear my voice over the ringing in my ears. "What do you mean?"

"In labour, yes? You know the thing? She is having a baby."

"Right now?"

"Yes. Now."

I huff a shocked breath. "How ex are we talking here?"

He doesn't answer that, which makes me feel *great.* "You will find better than me, Emery. And then you will forget me. It is for the best."

CHAPTER 4
EMERY

present day

I can't believe I let my parents talk me into another Granger Road Trip that, for the first time in two years, has brought me into the same arena as Alexei Artyomov.

And we'll be sitting with his dad!

His mom said she would give up her seat so the three of us could watch together—despite my vocal defence that I could buy a last-minute nosebleed ticket on the Ticketmaster app.

Or, you know, just loiter at a nearby coffee shop until the game was over.

Both fine options for me.

But every time I suggest we don't need to sit together, I get guilty eyes from my mom. That look that says, *you're moving to Europe and we might never do this again.*

It's not like I'm going forever.

I am going to be gone for a while, though. Long

enough that I've put my fledgling personal chef business in Minneapolis on hold. There's no point in trying to hustle to get customers and build a reputation only to leave the city for three or six or more months. But once I had the acceptance letter from the Swiss culinary institute, I started packing and immediately put my social media marketing on pause.

And being honest about *that* is what locked me into this collision course with my past mistakes. No sooner had the words *My calendar is suddenly very empty* left my mouth than my mother got a gleam in her eye.

I couldn't come up with a good excuse, and here we are.

Trepidation mounts as we move through the crowd looking for Alexei's father.

"Mom, can you send my ticket to my phone?" I point at the team store just before the security gates. "I want to check out the jerseys."

She laughs. "You always need to be defiant, don't you? Are you going to wear Rusty's number for his game against Camden?"

"Yes!" My eyes light up. "Exactly. I'll meet you at the seats."

Rusty is Russ Armstrong, one of the veteran players on this new Hamilton team. Years ago, he played in Minnesota with my oldest brother, Camden. Tonight, they're playing against each other.

The NHL is a very small world in some ways. Too small.

As soon as she AirDrops the ticket to me, I zip away,

losing myself in the surge of people who want the silly, plaid-wearing, bagpipe-playing mascot gear that you can only buy here. I've been in almost every arena in the league, and this is among the busiest stores.

Good for Hamilton, and good for my delaying tactic.

I make my way to the jersey section, but to my dismay, the Armstrong jerseys are all sold out.

Last summer Rusty was in a sports energy drink commercial that went super viral for how awkward he was in it, and the fact that he's Scottish and the team aesthetics have a Scottish vibe…it's a marketer's dream.

And then the company, BioPunk, followed that up with a new product called SPUNK, and tapped him again to awkwardly endorse the sweet and tangy complete meal drink.

He's now enjoying a fandom most bottom six forwards never see.

I love it for him, but it does mean I'm out of luck on the jersey plan.

Turning around, I run smack into Alexei. A cardboard cutout version of him, anyway. He's staring solemnly at the camera, which means he's making intense eye contact with me, too.

Getting eye fucked by cardboard is a new and unsettling experience.

"Hate you," I whisper, even though it's not really true.

I just hate what I would have given him that night if we weren't interrupted. Even though we didn't do everything I'd planned, I picked *him* to pluck my cherry, proverbially and literally.

What a near miss that was.

Shuddering, I jerk back and bump into the person next to me, who clearly ignored the *no food or beverage* sign at the front of the store, because he's holding an iced coffee. Or he was, until I knocked into him, and now that coffee is quickly seeping into my long-sleeved cotton shirt.

"What the fuck, lady?"

He gestures wildly, and coffee droplets spray onto the display jersey in front of us.

I snatch the cup from his hand. "This isn't allowed in here."

He disappears into the crowd, leaving me looking responsible for a stained jersey.

One of the shop staff narrows their eyes at me and pulls a mobile card payment device out of a holster on their hip. "Would you like me to ring that up for you, miss?"

Me? I didn't bring a coffee in here!

But I can just see the hockey gossip spreading if I make a scene. *Jeff Granger's daughter…* Or insert any of my brothers. Connor, maybe. He's the most conventionally good-looking of them. Or Forrest. People write fan fiction about him. Wouldn't take much to twist the idea that his sister is a spoiled brat into A Whole Thing.

Heart in my throat, I accept my fate. Apparently, I'm going to pay…

He scans the tag.

Three hundred and fifty dollars?

Mother of God.

That's a serious punishment.

"What do I have to do to make this better?" I mutter under my breath.

The clerk is clearly not listening. "Enjoy the game!"

I most certainly will not.

I drag myself to the line for the nearest bathroom. By the time I get inside, my Minnesota t-shirt is pretty ugly looking. It actually looks like a fan deliberately threw something at me for daring to wear the visitor's colours.

I take it off and set it on the counter and focus on the brand-new jersey I just bought instead, since that has fewer coffee spots on it. I rinse the arm under the sink, rubbing at the marks until they fade. Then I grab some paper towels and turn it over to dry it from all angles.

That's when I see the name on the back.

You've got to be kidding me.

Heart sinking, I pull Alexei's jersey over my head. It's way too big for me. I try to style it in the mirror, but quickly give up.

Whatever.

My mother will be amused, at the very least.

I toss the ruined shirt in the garbage, then make my way through the concourse. It's my first time visiting the Hamilton arena, and I like it. I know a bunch of the players on the team from spending a week with them last summer—before Alexei was traded here—so if circumstances were different, I would be happy to cheer for them.

Right now, some of the friends I made on that trip are probably gathering in a suite upstairs for the WAGs and other family members.

I haven't told them I'm here, for complicated reasons I don't really want to think about.

Reason, singular. Six feet, four inches tall. Two hundred and ten pounds before a game, one ninety-nine after a hard match, apparently, according to Forrest, who doesn't know that I never want to know interesting facts about his best friend.

And now I'm thinking about him *again.*

On the ice, and over the loudspeaker that pipes out to the concourse, the national anthems are played.

I slip into my seat just before the puck drops.

As expected, Mom is deeply entertained by my outfit change.

"Look, Sergei," she says, patting Mr. Artyomov's arm. "My daughter has switched allegiances."

He looks confused until he looks at my jersey, and then he gives me a big thumbs up.

I smile weakly and nod. "Yep."

"Nice to meet you," he says in accented English.

"Same."

We're saved from the rest of that conversation as the game gets underway. We're right down at rink level, just three rows back from the ice, and the play swirls in front of us, fast and furious right from the whistle.

The first goal comes forty-five seconds into the game, from Hamilton's side, much to the delight of the over-sized boar mascot dancing a few sections over—and the rest of the crowd.

Sergei and I cheer, too, as my parents groan, because Camden was on the ice for that.

This part will be fun.

Hamilton is an exciting team with fast forwards and brutish defencemen. Their systems are a bit of a mess, but that also makes them hard to read, and the chaos is their advantage.

My dad mutters something about Camden's plus/minus stat. He's dash five over the last two weeks, and it's stressing my dad out, even though being on the ice for a goal against is a reductive way to determine value.

I'm tempted to push that bruise and start a debate about the utility of the plus/minus stat, but then Hamilton scores *again*—thankfully not when Cam is on the ice this time—and I'm too busy cheering.

The Highlanders have complete control of the game now, keeping the puck in Minnesota's end consistently until we reach the middle of the period, and the long TV commercial break that sends the teams back to their benches.

As the ice clean-up crew skates out with their shovels, I sink lower into my seat, even though the team bench is all the way on the other side of the ice.

Alexei skates in slow circles as his coach talks to him. He's too far away for me to be sure, but I don't think he says anything back. He seems really locked in, just keeping warm and hydrating through the break. Then as soon as the crew is done cleaning up his crease, he beelines it back to his net.

He's a guardian, a warrior with a mission, and he doesn't like being pulled away from his post.

When the game starts again, I find it harder to follow the play. Now that I've gotten sucked into watching him, I can't stop.

I'm pretty sure Alexei can't see our seats through the curve of the plexiglass—and given his hyper focus, I think that might be intentional.

When I'm on the ice, I actually love to see people I know in the stands, but I'm extroverted and feed off that energy. Like a lot of forwards, I'm all about the hype.

Goalies are different.

Alexei is—

Looking right in our direction.

I fold myself in half and pretend to fix something with my shoe.

When I finally peek again, he's focused on the game play.

From my lifetime of experience watching NHL games, I know I'm being paranoid.

But I really wish I'd bought a hat in the team shop, too. Maybe I'll go there at the first intermission between periods, because I'm deeply uncomfortable, both with the situation and my complete lack of a backbone when it comes to my mother.

This trip is giving me anxiety-induced heartburn and it's just begun. I knew this was a bad idea.

As the teams have an epic puck battle in front of the Minnesota net, I dig in my pocket for a pack of antacids I bought at the airport.

"Get it up the ice," my dad snaps. "Come on, now!"

Camden's team does not get it up the ice.

Instead, the puck bounces loose, Hiro Watanabe snaps it to Hayden Calhoun, who beelined it to the net, and Hooner scores.

The arena goes crazy.

My dad mutters something about goalie interference. Sure enough, the coaches think the same thing, and they issue a coach's challenge on the goal, and the play is paused while they go to the video review.

The Jumbotron starts showing people in the crowd while we wait for the decision.

I slump in my seat again, covering my face.

My mother pokes me. "Stop fidgeting."

I roll my eyes. "I'm not—"

"You are, and it's distracting."

Distracting from what, I have no idea. The refs are going to take their time on this review. It's already two nothing for the home team, and this goal would make it three zip before the end of the first period.

It's not looking good for Team Granger, that's for sure. I think Alexei's only faced three shots on net so far, and he's handily dealt with all of them.

Besides, she was just deep in conversation with Alexei's father. *Now* she suddenly can't ignore that I'm restless?

My fingers itch to pull out my phone and text some friends I've ignored for far too long. To beg for an excuse to get up out of this seat and not come back until the end of the game.

The refs finally make a call on the goalie interference

—yes, it was, so the score remains 2-0 for the High-landers.

My dad is elated, and I manage to keep still until the end of the period, but it's a real challenge.

Especially now that the conversation right beside me has turned to Alexei's *baby*.

Toddler.

Not a baby anymore.

"Emery, look!" My mom shoves Sergei's phone in my face. "Isn't she precious?"

The worst part is that she *is* precious. Of course she is. She has Alexei's dark hair, dark eyes, and porcelain skin.

I snap my gaze up to the Jumbotron. The crowd cam happens to flash a shot of the WAGs, up in a suite today, and that's enough of a sign for me.

"Mom, I'm going to go find Rusty's girlfriend," I say in a rush.

When I was a teenager, Russ Armstrong was one of the few players who recognized my hockey ability, and he earned my lifelong friendship. Last summer, after reconnecting at Camden's third wedding, I spent a week with him and some of his teammates at his cottage, filling in as a plus-one of sorts that morphed into being a fake girlfriend. Despite that questionable decision, because he's never been anything other than a brother figure, I managed to strike up a real friendship with the woman he was secretly in love with at the time, and Shannon has been poking me to come to a game ever since.

I have politely refused every invite, because Alexei

was traded to the Highlanders a month later—and I have preferred to keep an international border or at least a few Canadian provinces between me and my greatest mistake for the last two years.

But here I am anyway, so…

Before my mom can reply, I'm out of my seat and heading for the concourse, my phone out.

EMERY

Hey pals. Surprise. I'm at the game tonight! Do you have room for a friend in the suite with you?

The group chat I'm messaging includes all the WAGs who were at Russ's cottage last summer. And one by one, they all react to my text with exclamation marks and hearts.

SHANNON

Absolutely! Kiley's already out the door, looking for you.

HARPER

This is such a fun surprise!

BECCA

Get up here, I need an Emery hug!

ANI

Ahhhh! You sneaky girl!

Their affection makes me feel extra silly. They have no reason to bring up Alexei or his daughter to me.

And if I'm upstairs in a box with them, I don't need to

keep slouching down out of paranoia. I might actually be able to enjoy the rest of the game...if I can stop hyper-fixating on the Highlanders goalie.

CHAPTER 5
ALEXEI

As we head to the locker room, I block out the excited chatter.

Yeah, we're up two. It's not a runaway lead, though, and there are still two more periods.

Our trainers are waiting for us with fresh sports drinks and snacks for the guys who eat during breaks. We have two docs in house tonight, too, and Rusty's getting his shoulder looked at by Grant Forge, an orthopaedic surgeon and sports medicine specialist.

Everyone has a different ritual.

Hooner strips out of his gear lightning fast and races for the showers. He does that every time he has a bad play. He claims it resets him, so his brain thinks the next period is a clean slate.

Whatever works.

There's no way I could get my feet back into skates if I took them off mid-game. I strip down my top half, though, leaving my shorts and socks on. A fresh base layer top is hanging behind me in my stall, ready for me to put on before the next period.

And I jam headphones on, so I don't have to listen to Malik Zondi and Roan "Smash" Dodaj go back and forth like excited puppies next to me.

I drain the water bottle handed to me, then I get up to go take a leak.

As I hang up my headphones on the hook inside my stall, I swear I hear Zondi say Emery's name.

"What?" I snap.

Malik shrugs, unbothered by my bark. "Just saying I saw Rusty's ex-girlfriend in the stands."

I nod. I must have misheard. "Not Shannon?"

He shakes his head. "Someone else. Doesn't matter."

Smash laughs as Malik's brown cheeks darken in embarrassment. "Doesn't matter because she doesn't return Zondi's DMs."

"She did." He pauses. "Once."

Smash dissolves into laughter, and I leave them to go relieve myself.

As I'm flushing the toilet, we get the five-minute warning, and everyone starts re-dressing.

I put on my new base layer, adjusting the built-in custom protection padding over my collarbone before quickly adding everything else.

I haven't been challenged much in this game, which is a challenge in itself—staying focused, ready, for the moment when the momentum shifts and the shots start piling up.

I can't have a certain blonde on my mind.

I certainly can't be imagining her name in every over-heard conversation, or dream up glimpses of her in the stands, wearing my jersey.

That's never going to happen.

CHAPTER 6
EMERY

I'm inundated with questions as soon as I step inside the family suite, which isn't fair, because I have questions, too, but it's five against one.

"I've found her, and look, she's wearing an Arty jersey. Refuses to tell me why," Kiley says. The WAGs' resident theatre nerd, Kiley Forge has a flare for the dramatic and never passes up an opportunity to be a matchmaker.

"I told you I was forced to buy it," I protest, but my explanation about the coffee is lost under her best friend Harper's question, which comes next.

Harper Roberts is a paediatric nurse who loves her hockey-playing husband a *lot*, but hates the limelight. She and Kiley are total opposites, but they've been besties since elementary school. "How long are you in town?"

"Just overnight, but I'll be back next week..." I trail off as Shannon Barker, Rusty's girlfriend, elegantly moves our friends out of the way and wraps her arms around me, giving me the world's nicest, least earned hug ever.

Because next week's game will be between my brother's team, Alexei's old team, and the Highlanders, who traded Max "Shannon's Ex-Husband" Tilman away after Rusty smashed his face into the dressing room floor.

That game will be the return of the former captain to the building.

Really puts a pale on my own personal drama that nobody knows about.

I squeeze her back.

"Hi," I whisper.

"We've missed you," she whispers back.

I was never meant to be a part of this friend group. My whole introduction to them was a ruse I pushed on Rusty because he clearly needed a shove—I just didn't realize that shove should be into Shannon's arms.

If I had, I would never have pretended to be his girlfriend.

A lot of other people might hold a grudge or be wary of me for that choice, but not Shannon. She is a stunningly beautiful person, inside and out, and even though I've kept my distance for other reasons, we've forged an unlikely friendship over text messages and video calls.

She now works for the team as part of their marketing and public relations department. And she's quietly, deeply in love with a man who would hang stars in the sky for her if she asked.

The last time we talked, she was at Rusty's apartment,

and he was talking about finding a house or a bigger apartment.

I pull back and look at her. There's a brightness in her eyes that is unmistakeable happiness. "How goes the house hunting?"

She laughs. "Did Russell ask you to say that?"

"He doesn't even know I'm here."

Her eyebrow curves up in surprise. "Really?"

Guilt guilt stabby guilt.

"Share the hugs," Ani Hale says. She has to lean in to make room around a baby bump. When I last saw her, her and her husband were just talking about having kids, and now one is on the way.

It underlines how many months have zoomed by.

"Hey, friend," I say softly.

And then Becca Kincaid joins us, her son shadowing his mom. She asks me what I've been up to, how cooking is going.

I take a deep breath. "Well, I'm actually going back to school! I've been accepted at a culinary institute in Switzerland for a program that starts in July."

Shannon squeezes my hand. "That's amazing!"

"I honestly didn't think I'd get accepted, so it was a bit of a shock. And then I immediately went into preparation mode and stopped taking on new personal chef clients, which has left me a little at odd ends for the next few months."

"You could come visit."

"Thanks. But I'm—"

The door to the suite opens behind me, and something

about it, like an energy I can't ignore, has me pivoting to see who it is, even though everyone I know is right in front of me.

There's a faint warning at the back of my mind that it could be Alexei's girlfriend, but no, it's worse.

It's his mother, Maria Artyomov, and she has his daughter in her arms. I recognize them both from photographs very recently shoved in front of my face.

"So sorry," Maria says, out of breath. "Inessa is hungry."

"That's okay," Becca exclaims. "Hey, sweetie. Come on in."

I try to hold my breath as if that might make me invisible, but no such luck. I can't escape Artyomovs today, apparently.

Becca reaches for Inessa. "Do you want to sit with Charlie?"

The little girl gives her a shy nod, but still hesitates before releasing her tight hold on her grandmother.

Heart in my throat, my gaze follows them as Becca circles around the buffet spread and effortlessly picks up a few things a toddler might want to eat, then carries the little girl and the plate down the steps to where her son is watching what's happening on the ice with rapt attention.

"Say hi to Inessa, Charlie."

"Hi Inessa," the little boy says, his gaze darting to her briefly.

The little girl doesn't say anything back. Becca nudges an apple wedge into her hand, and she carefully takes a tiny bite.

Maria touches my hand. "Emery?"

I jump. "Yes. Hi. I am Emery, yep."

She smiles. Up close she looks pale and there's perspiration on her brow. "Your mother is very kind."

I nod, heart racing. "Yes, she is."

"She shows photos of you." She pats my cheek. "Beautiful girl."

I'm as much a sucker for a compliment as the next beautiful girl, so I smile back. "Thanks."

She leans on the table, still catching her breath.

I fill the silence. "Hey, so I met your husband already. He's sitting next to my parents."

She frowns, like I've said too much, too fast.

I pull out my phone and quickly tap it all out in the translation app.

She nods. Then she pushes the microphone button and says something in Russian, which my phone translates on the screen as she talks.

The little one doesn't like watching hockey. It's too noisy, so we explore the building while her dad plays.

"Do you want something to eat?" I gesture to the buffet.

She shakes her head and makes a face, tapping her chest, then my phone.

Heartburn.

Do you need medicine?

I pull the Tums from my pocket and hold it out.

Medicine doesn't help.

She grimaces and waves her hand. I look at her more closely. Her colour really isn't great.

Maybe we could get you something stronger?

I glance at Shannon, who senses my attention and lifts her head. "What is it?"

"Mrs. Artyomov doesn't feel well. She says it's heartburn, but…"

That gets Harper's attention. She comes over, too. "What usually helps?"

I type the question into my phone.

The older woman shrugs. Her hand shakes as she reaches for my phone.

I don't usually have this.

"It's been a couple years since I did first aid training," I say softly to Harper. "But isn't heartburn and sweating two signs of a heart attack in women?"

"Heart attacks aren't a thing I usually see in my patients," she says. "But we could go down to the medical room and get checked out. it can't hurt to have a doctor look at her."

Doctor is a word the Russian grandma recognizes. Her eyes go wide. "No, I am okay," she says, laughing. But there's a wince at the end of it, and reluctantly, she rubs her chest.

Harper immediately pulls out her phone and texts a quick message. "You know Kiley?" She gestures to her best friend. "You're in luck. Her twin brother is working today. He's a bone doctor. Also not really a heartburn expert. But he's…" She glances at her screen. "He's on his way."

"Twin brother?" That distracts Maria. "Is he pretty, too?"

Kiley laughs. "Very. Please tell him that."

Less than a minute later, the suite door opens and someone who really does look like Kiley's twin brother strides in. Behind him is a woman in a team track suit who introduces them in quick, fluent Russian.

Maria immediately gets flustered, protesting that she's fine. But as the conversation goes back and forth, they quickly decide not to take her down to be checked out, but rather to call for the paramedics stationed downstairs to come up and just directly transport her to the hospital.

At every NHL game, there's an ambulance in the Zamboni bay, just in case there is an emergency on or off the ice.

Tonight, it's happening right in front of me. Someone from team services gets on the radio, and down at rink level, a whistle blows, and the play is stopped.

"Ladies and gentlemen, we ask everyone to remain seated. One of our guests tonight is having a medical event and requires assistance. The game will resume shortly."

CHAPTER 7
ALEXEI

One of the linesmen skates over to me and I flip up my visor. "What's going on?"

"They need to use the ambulance on standby for someone in attendance, so we can't resume the game until a replacement team of paramedics arrives. They're on their way."

I nod and grab my water bottle from its pocket on the back of the net.

Both teams are invited off the bench to skate on the ice, basically a repeat of warm up, just to keep muscles loose while we wait.

"Arty!" The head coach waves me over to the bench.

As I approach, Makie steps past me onto the ice, and my head swivels in confusion as he starts to go through a quick warm up routine.

"What is happening?"

"Son, there's been a medical emergency…"

The rest is a blur.

The equipment guys meet me in the dressing room and help me get out of my gear in record time. Dr. Forge meets me in the hallway between the dressing room and our street lockers.

"Your mother is stable, alert, and talking. You need to get to the hospital, but we don't need to break traffic laws to do it."

I nod. For all that my English is so much better than it was two years ago, at the moment words are beyond me.

"She has symptoms consistent with a cardiac event, possibly a heart attack. But it could be something else." He lists panic attacks and a few other options.

I'm sure it's not any of those.

She's been complaining about heartburn and rubbing her chest for two days now.

I feel sick.

"Do you want to have a quick shower?" he asks.

I stop and sniff myself. "Fuck."

"You've got time." He leans back against the wall. "I promise."

After the world's fastest shower, I dress in team clothes, sweatpants and a t-shirt, and shove my feet into socks and slides. "Where is my daughter?"

"She's upstairs with Shannon Barker and some of the other team family members, including my sister. Your mother was with them when they called for a doctor."

I relax slightly. Shannon's very kind. She and Ani Hale both helped me a lot when I bought my house. "Tell them—"

"They know. It's okay. They'll take good care of her. Harper's there, too."

I exhale. Harper Roberts is a nurse at the children's hospital. She works with little kids every day.

Grant drives me to the hospital, where he slides into a priority physician parking spot and takes me directly to Emergency through the back entrance.

All of it is much appreciated, but I still don't breathe properly until I hear my parents talking to each other in Russian as we approach a curtained off hospital bed.

"I need to go home," my mother says.

"You need to stay here," my father retorts.

"He has to leave tomorrow. He has two games—"

I swear under my breath. It's my fault that she worries about that right now, even when she's in the hospital.

"The team will take other goalies on the road trip," I say, sweeping the curtain aside.

"Alexei!" My mother reaches for me, but as soon as she lifts her arms, she winces.

"Don't tax yourself," I mutter. And then I let out a sound that's suspiciously like a sob.

My father grabs me in a tight hug. "She's going to be okay."

She has to be. My parents are my rocks.

But I lean on them too much. Since Inessa's arrival, I've sponsored them to emigrate and they've completely transformed my life from a young bachelor pro athlete to that of a family man. When I was traded, they flew across the country with my toddler. They live with us full-time, sharing in the parenting work, and fully carrying that burden when I'm playing at home and on the road.

In return for that, I make sure they want for nothing. In the off season, I send them on incredible cruises and land trips with Russian speaking guides. I pay for them to take English classes.

But I didn't fucking notice my mother having the warning signs of a heart attack.

"I'm sorry," I manage to get out.

Someone behind me quietly clears their throat. I turn and find Dr. Forge standing with a hospital doctor in scrubs. She introduces herself as an ER doc and gives me a quick update on the tests they're going to run. "I expect your mother to be admitted soon, I'm just waiting to hear where we have a bed for her. Depending on what we see, we might initially put her in the ICU..."

My mother looks...tired. Pale. But the ICU?

"She'll be able to come home in a few days, maybe a week at the outside. But there will be rest and recovery—"

"I have a toddler. My parents take care of her."

The two doctors exchange a look.

Yeah, they won't be able to do that for a while. Or maybe ever again.

CHAPTER 8
EMERY

When the game resumes on the ice, without Alexei, it's hard to focus. My parents text, letting me know they've gone to the hospital just in case they can be helpful there.

Which leaves me with the WAGs, feeling strangely unmoored.

"Should we go somewhere quieter?"

"That's a good idea. Shannon, can we—"

"Of course."

"Emery?"

I jerk my head towards Ani, blinking. "Pardon?"

She rubs my arm. "It's okay. Come on."

With a start, I realize Becca and Harper are already gone, and Kiley is at the door, holding it open for the rest of us.

As if from a distance, I see myself put one foot in front of the other and follow them to the team offices. A security guard lets us in a locked door, and the noise of the arena fades away.

Shannon appears out of a supply room carrying a stack of printer paper and a variety of white board markers. "Improvised babysitting materials," she says. "I'm not sure two-year-olds draw, though. These might be more for Charlie. Emery, can you grab that stuffed piper?"

I pick up the oversized plush bagpipe-holding boar she points at and follow her down the hall.

Becca and Harper are in a conference room with the two kids, watching carefully as Charlie helps Inessa climb onto a couch—and then immediately jumps off.

She stands on the soft cushion, as if to follow, and my heart leaps into my throat.

"Be careful." The words rip out of me, and I'm crossing to her before I know what my feet are doing. "Here, want a friend?"

She drops back onto her bum, safely sitting on the couch.

I crouch in front of her and hold out the stuffed mascot. Big, dark eyes blink back at me.

"Hi, baby girl," I say with a sigh, my heart squeezing. She's so little. "I'm Emery."

She stares.

"I know, I'm a stranger. But Shannon thought you might like this guy." I wiggle his bagpipe, and the corner of her mouth twitches. "Do you know him?"

That gets a reluctant nod.

"Do you think he might want to jump off the couch, too?"

Her eyes light up, and she grabs at the toy. I shift back,

and she walks him to the edge of the cushion, then sends him flying and laughs.

Charlie climbs up beside her again and jumps.

Behind me, Becca groans. "You are a terrible influence, Charlie."

Inessa laughs and covers her face with her hands.

I tickle her fingers with the retrieved toy, and she clutches it against her chest for a second before shoving it at Charlie and babbling something I don't understand.

Keeping one eye on her, I turn to Becca. "Does she mostly speak Russian?"

She nods. "She seems to understand English as much as I'd expect a toddler to, though. But she's pretty shy."

"That's okay," I murmur, my gaze dragging back to the little girl.

Inessa studies me right back, both of us unsure of what to make of the other.

I give her a small smile. "I think we're going to hang out together tonight, okay?"

Before she can answer, I get a text message from my mom.

MOM

They're going to admit her, but it'll take a few hours. Alexei and his dad are in with her. Dad and I are going to a diner across the street from the hospital, do you want us to pick you up?

EMERY

I'm with Alexei's daughter...is there a plan for her?

> Not yet. Do you want us to come back?

> Some of the WAGs are here, too. I'm okay.

> Sorry, honey. Your dad is hangry. You know how he gets.

> Really, it's okay. We'll hang out here for a bit.

"Is there an update?" Shannon asks, dropping to the floor beside me.

I tell her the little that I know, then shrug. "How long can we stay in your conference room?"

"All night, if need be."

Harper joins us, holding up a keyring. "I have Mrs. Artyomov's car keys. If Alexei can't come back to pick Inessa up, one of us could take her home and put her to bed."

Shannon glances at her watch. "We have some time before we need to make that decision."

On the couch, Inessa rubs her eyes with her little fist.

Harper winces. "Think she might nap here?"

"I might need to take Charlie home for that to happen," Becca says.

"What!?" Charlie exclaims. "I don't wanna go home!"

"Which probably means we should have left half an hour ago," his mother retorts. "Ten more minutes of playing, and then we'll go find Daddy."

Inessa watches this exchange, and when Becca says *Daddy*, her lower lip just out. "Papa?"

"Your grandpa is busy right now," Becca says.

Inessa shakes her head. "No Deda. Papa." Her face crumples. "Papa."

Ah. Papa is Daddy. Deda must be Grampa.

"She wants Alexei," I say.

And then I get an idea. I pull out my phone and type his name into the search engine.

Thank God the internet is chock-a-block full of photos of Alexei Artyomov—something I never thought I'd say.

Inessa grabs my phone, her eyes wide and her voice watery. "My Papa."

"Yep." I show her how to scroll. "That's your Papa."

She jams her thumb down on a photo and giggles when it goes blurry.

That gives me an idea. "Can I see that for a second?"

She warily hands me back the phone, but crowds closer so she can see what I'm doing. I quickly save a couple of photos, promising myself that I will not keep them. This is just about entertaining a little girl who doesn't have anything to do with the grown up, complicated feelings I have for her dad.

Then I open a photo editing app I sometimes use. I select the first download, then apply a clown filter to it.

Inessa shrieks in surprise. "Papa!"

I gesture to the different filters. "Do you want to play?"

She reaches for the phone tentatively, and when I don't pull it away, she locks on and smashes her little thumbs down on the different filters.

When Becca finally scoops Charlie up and makes him

say goodnight, Inessa barely notices that her friend is leaving.

Shannon flicks on a lamp, turns off the overhead light, and closes the conference room door. People start to filter into the outer office now that the game is over—and Hamilton won.

Harper, Kiley, and Ani slip out.

Shannon gets her laptop and sets up at the far end of the table.

I curl up on the couch, and Inessa slides right up against me. We spend the better part of an hour morphing the photos I saved, and searching for more. Sometimes it seems like she's on the verge of tears again, but she's pretty easily distracted.

And then her head drifts to the side, leaning heavier and heavier against my arm, until my phone falls into her lap.

Harper steps back into the room, carrying a child-sized bright pink winter coat, and I lift my finger to my lips.

"She's asleep," I whisper.

She nods. "Do you think you could lift her up so we can get this on her?"

Slowly, I ease Inessa up against my torso. In her sleep, she winds her arms around my neck, and my chest squeezes tight. "It's okay," I murmur. "Harper's going to take you home."

CHAPTER 9
ALEXEI

By the time my mom is admitted to the ICU, it's almost one in the morning. I'm exhausted, wrung out physically from the game and mentally from the hours spent at the hospital translating for my parents.

But my father—who also reacts to stress by turning into a stubborn bull—is refusing to come home with me.

When I tell him it's time to go, he gets a mulish set to his mouth. "What if she needs me, Alexei? You go home and sleep. I'll wait until morning. When you come back, I'll sleep for a bit."

"You'll have to use English."

"I can use English."

I'm going to hold him to that later, I think darkly.

To prove his point, he switches languages and asks a passing porter, "Where is the waiting room?"

It turns out it's just around the corner. There are two of them, a quiet room for families only, and across the hall a bigger space with more chairs, a play area for children, and some vending machines.

I steer him into the quiet room, where I hope he can maybe stretch out on a couch or something, and I'm so tired I don't immediately register why my body comes to a sudden stop.

Recognition on a cellular level happens first. The brain takes a second to catch up.

In front of me, leaning back on a recliner, is Emery Granger.

She's wearing a Highlanders jersey, and my daughter is sleeping on top of her, clutching one of the team's plush mascot toys.

"Emery?" Her name tears out of me, my brain still short-circuiting from seeing Inessa sleeping in her arms.

She lifts her head with a jolt. Blonde waves, like silk, brush her shoulders.

"Alexei."

My name on her lips, soft and worried, is so fucking wrong.

"What are you doing here?" My voice sounds hoarse as I rake my gaze down her arms to the number on the jersey.

My number.

Emery's gaze widens for a painful, confusing beat, then she glances down at Inessa. "She woke up on the way home and wouldn't stop crying, so we came here."

We?

Who the fuck is *we* in that sentence?

She pulls a lever on the side of the seat and sits up.

Inessa protests, but Emery shifts her to the side and slides out from under her and the plush toy.

Somehow, my daughter stays asleep.

My dad folds himself into the recliner beside Inessa's seat and closes his eyes.

Time slows as Forrest's sister rises to stand in front of me.

Two years has made her…brighter.

I search for words, fatigue making everything harder, more prickly. "Why are you in Hamilton?"

And why is she wearing my jersey?

Emery takes a deep breath and shrugs. "Oh, you know. The Grangers never miss an opportunity to do a hockey family road trip." Her words are meant to sound light, but her voice is just as rough as my own.

As I stare at her, she shifts back and forth on her feet. "How is your mom?"

"She's…" I trail off. I don't know how to answer the question.

From a few chairs away, her parents rise and I'm vaguely aware of them joining us, but Emery is all I can really see.

"Emery was with your mom when they decided to call for the doctor," her father says.

She ducks her head, visibly uncomfortable.

I feel rocked on my axis, as if my entire world has been moved by a cascading sequence of earthquakes.

She was *there*. In the arena.

I didn't know.

I should have known.

I should have been on guard for that.

I always thought that if she was this close to me, I would know. Has she been at other games?

"We were hoping that there might be news tonight," her mother says.

I shake my head.

I remember this intense Granger caretaking instinct from when Inessa was born. It's very kind, but it's also overwhelming at the best of times, and this is not that. Right now, I don't have any answers. "She's sleeping now. She's being closely monitored."

Each sentence is hard to get out, and as I find the words, Emery's brows pinch together.

"Thank you for staying," I add thickly. "And for bringing Inessa to me. I can take her home now. My father is going to stay here tonight. But you can go back to your hotel."

Her parents nod and go back to their chairs, where they left their coats.

As they get dressed for outside, Emery tilts her head to the side, her blonde waves brushing her shoulder.

That fucking hair has haunted me for two years.

I want to wrap it around my fist and hold her still. Hold her down. Just…fucking hold her.

And that cannot happen.

That cannot happen under any circumstances.

An unexpected smile crooks at her mouth. "Your English has improved a lot."

She sounds genuinely shocked, as if she hasn't heard

me in as long as I haven't heard her. Maybe she really has stayed away.

"Surprised?"

"Maybe," she says in a breathy rush that sends a jolt of inconvenient heat through me.

Arousal doesn't mix well with frustration, fatigue, or panic, and I'm maxed out on all three. Irritation rises again.

Fucking hell, I need to leave. I need to sleep, if only for a few hours.

And it doesn't matter if Emery is surprised that my English is better. That's a trap, one I could fall into so fucking easily.

I know that—and yet I hear myself making fucking small talk.

"I got my parents lessons. Have to set a good example for them." I shove my hands in my pockets to keep myself from reaching for her. "How have you been?"

"Fine." Emery swallows hard. "Great."

"She's going to Switzerland this summer," her mother says, as if that's on the same level as English lessons. Small talk. "Can you imagine?"

"Switzerland." I frown. I opened the door to this sledgehammer, swung so casually, as if it's good news for everyone. And it is. It should be. "For hockey?"

Emery lifts her chin. "Culinary school."

"You're a chef now." I knew that. Forrest had said she'd done some training, but I thought...

Her eyes now. "I've been accepted by a very prestigious institute there."

Of course she has. There's nothing Emery can't do if she sets her mind to it. That's Granger Lore.

I learned that firsthand, just what a fast learner she is—

No.

Fuck.

I rock back on my heels and just look at her.

Somehow, she looks exactly the same and completely different simultaneously. Her unwavering gaze heats me from the inside out, and I can't believe I went two years without seeing her. Now that she's in front of me, I never want to let her go again.

Stay, I want to say. *Tell me everything you've done since that night.*

Even the hard parts. Even the life experiences that matured her, because that's the part that's different. Two years ago, Emery was young and innocent. Now she glows with a confidence that takes my breath away.

I'm not that girl, her body language screams. *Don't underestimate me.*

Something in my chest goes hard, and my voice takes on an edge that immediately fucks up the conversation. "Good for you. That sounds exciting. Are you leaving behind a job, or a boyfriend?"

She tips her head up and exhales audibly at the ceiling. "Oh, my God."

"Emery!" Her mother nudges her. "It's been a long night for us all, but most of all for you and your dad, Alexei. What do you need?"

"Right now? Just some sleep." I stare at Emery, who is

now staring at a poster on the wall. I bet I could wrap myself around her tight, uncooperative little body and sleep for a week.

"Can you drive? Emery drove your mother's car here. And tomorrow, do you want help with Inessa? We can stay, it's really not an inconvenience."

It's hard to know what tomorrow with bring. Or the next day.

"I need to find a Russian-speaking nanny." I scrub my hand over my face. "Not sure how—"

"There are agencies," Emery says.

I frown. "I know."

"You said you weren't sure." She shrugs, as if she's indifferent to my plight.

There's a sensible part of my brain that knows that's not the case. She was holding my sleeping daughter. She's not *indifferent*.

But she's something.

Hurt, you asshole. She's hurt.

"Thank you," I manage to say. I should say *I'm sorry*, but we have an audience. I'm trying to think of the best way to ask to speak to her alone for a minute when her mother says something about helping with agency contacts in the morning.

I stiffen.

I should accept their help, but I don't want to look weak.

"I'll find a nanny," I interrupt. "But I need something else."

The air in the waiting room suddenly feels heavy.

But I've said it.

"Of course, honey. Anything. Whatever you need."

I don't think her daughter is going to agree. My pulse pounds in my neck. That's not going to stop me. "I need to borrow Emery."

Her head jerks up, her eyes going wide. "What?"

"My mother does all of our cooking. So now I need a chef."

"I'm not available," Emery says just as quickly.

Her mother nudges her arm. "Of course you are. This is Forrest's best friend."

"What about our family road trip?"

"Emery," her mother scolds. "A crisis is more important than that. And you didn't want to spend the next few days driving to Toronto and Buffalo, anyway."

"But it won't be just a few days," she says desperately. "And I have to pack up my entire life."

She's never coming back. The threat is like a pounding drum in my head.

I can't hold on to her.

I can't *have* her.

But I can bring her close, for a while. I can employ her, and maybe after some sleep, I can find the words I need to say. The privacy, too.

Her mother tsks. "Every day we don't help is a day Alexei can't be with the team, Emery. He needs to get back on the ice sooner than later."

It's true. I'm going to need to hire a lot of help over the next few weeks. A personal aide worker for my mother. And a nanny for Inessa. But those people will be strangers. If I had a professional cook in the house, too, a family friend, it would be easier to leave.

She doesn't say anything, but I can see it. *That's* the angle I can use to leverage her here. I can't hold her, but I can have her at arm's length, and that's better than half a world away.

And if you are her boss, will you keep your hands to yourself any more than you did when she was your best friend's little sister?

Yes. Because I'm not that selfish young man anymore.

And maybe I need to prove that to the both of us. If it takes begging her for a favour to get that chance, so be it.

"From one hockey player to another," I say softly. "Can you do me a solid?"

"I liked you better when you didn't speak English," she mutters.

But I exhale in relief, because it's an admission of how much she liked me two years ago. A reminder of the path we could have been on if I hadn't fucked everything up.

It's a first step in the right direction—of restoring Emery to her rightful place in my life, as a family friend. An off-limits girl I must respect.

"Sounds like a plan," her father says as Emery stares at me in disbelief. "We'll drop her off tomorrow as we're heading out of town. Do you have room for her to stay with you?"

CHAPTER 10
EMERY

I cannot believe this is happening.

My parents are excited to see Inessa when she isn't asleep, and I…

We've just pulled into Alexei's driveway, behind a G-Wagon and beside a little red sedan, and I haven't screamed at the top of my lungs that I *cannot* do this, they *cannot* leave me with him, because as much as I know he's *Forrest's best friend* and he does desperately need help over the next few weeks, it cannot be me who does it.

Except now I'm getting out of the car and following my mother up the walk.

Emery Granger, I thought you had more of a backbone than this.

But each time I open my mouth, I feel Inessa's arms tighten around my neck. She's so little, and a lot of strangers are about to storm into her life. I know I'm a stranger, too, but at the very least I know what it's like to have a hockey player for a dad, to have that constant coming and going chaos.

And when Alexei answers the door, he looks terrible.

I'm reminded like a gut punch that on top of the hockey lifestyle chaos, there's also the family emergency chaos.

Tired and tense, his hair is standing on end and he has dark circles under his normally seductive eyes.

"Come in," he says, his voice tight. He gestures for my parents to step inside as he locks his intense, bullish gaze on my face. "I'm sorry, I have a nanny here for an interview."

My eyebrows jolt up. Already? That was fast. Eleven hours ago, he seemed flummoxed at where to even start with that. I would have thought it would take a few days to find a qualified, experienced childcare provider, even if money is no object.

"We won't stay long," my mom says. "But how's your mom?"

He nods. "She's better. They will do a procedure soon. We went to the hospital this morning. I got to her for a minute while Inessa had a second breakfast with my father in the cafeteria." He exhales in visible frustration. "He refuses to leave the hospital."

My mom makes sympathetic noises. "You know what? I bet there is someone who lives really close to the hospital who is a fan of the team. And someone from the team's foundation would know who to ask. No, don't say that you couldn't accept that kind of charity. It would make a fan very happy, so I'm not going to let you deny them that joy. Do you want help asking for that?"

Surprise ripples across Alexei's face, and I stifle a smile. It's fun to see him at a loss for words, and it's very fun when it's someone other than me being bullied in a loving way by my mom. Finally, he nods. "I didn't think of that."

"It's okay, sweetie. You have a lot on your mind now. I'll make some calls for you." She glances past him. "And where's our sweet little girl?"

Inessa comes running, only to turn shy and hide behind her dad's leg. Her hair is wild, only barely contained in a single, sideways ponytail, and her t-shirt is big enough it could be a little dress. Totally different than the neat outfit Maria had her in last night.

It makes me think that her grandma is the one who usually dresses her and brushes her hair.

I wave as I set my backpack down just inside the front door.

"Hello, princess," my father says, crouching down. "Do you remember us?"

Inessa peeks out from behind Alexei's leg but doesn't move.

"We're your Uncle Forrest's parents," Mom adds. "We saw you last night, but you were pretty sleepy."

"Not sleepy," Inessa says crossly.

Alexei runs a hand through his hair, and the stress lines around his mouth deepen. "It's been a long morning. I make terrible pancakes. Not like Baba." he exhales. "Come in."

He leads us to the living room.

A stern-looking woman sits stiffly on the couch. She looks straight out of central casting for nannies who leave children with lasting nightmares. I worked with some early childhood education students for two summers at a hockey day camp and they didn't resemble this woman at all.

"This is Ms. Petrova," Alexei introduces her. "And these are the Grangers. Emery is my new chef."

I'd like to think there's a hitch in his voice as he explains my presence in his house, that it's hard for him to describe me as *staff*, but the truth is that it sounds just fine.

He's the same elegant European prince he always has been, an elite athletic star, and I'm the Midwest hayseed who will cook for him. Literally the hired help, and if I hear anything, it's probably relief. Anything else that happened, once, was clearly a mistake to be swept under the rug.

I should just be lucky he doesn't ask me to do that for him, too.

The nanny candidate ignores us and focuses on Inessa's behaviour. "Does the child always run after you like that?" Her brows snap together, and while I like to frown at Alexei as much as the next girl, I don't like it at all when this woman does it. "She needs structure. I can provide this."

Something in her tone makes me uneasy. Inessa must feel it too because she's clinging to Alexei's leg like it's a life raft.

"Inessa," Ms. Petrova says sharply, followed by something in Russian. I don't understand the words, but her tone is clear: get out from behind your father's legs.

Inessa's bottom lip trembles.

The next Russian instruction is clearer. *Nyet placha* must mean no crying, and boy does that get my back up, because frankly, sometimes a girl just has to cry.

"She needs to learn proper behaviour," Ms. Petrova continues. "No hiding behind legs. Stand straight, speak when spoken to."

My parents exchange a look. I can't help myself.

"She's two," I say in disbelief.

Ms. Petrova's eyes narrow at me. "Discipline begins early. The child needs routine now more than ever, when her grandmother is unexpectedly out of the picture."

Alexei coughs, interrupting us before I can turn this into a stand-off.

My parents pick up on that, loudly changing the subject to the hockey game tonight in Toronto that they're going to see.

"How about you, son?" my dad asks. "The team giving you a few days off here?"

Alexei looks uneasy. "Yes."

"Back in my day, we didn't take time off in the season. Wasn't even there for two of my kids' births."

I wince, and the way Alexei's attention leaps to my face, I know I haven't done a good job of keeping that reaction to myself.

His gaze is so hard to read.

And as my mother quickly smooths over what my dad said, Alexei's eyes stay on me.

"Times have changed," my mom says. "And the team has other goalies."

Since he's still looking at me, I can't miss the brief flinch.

At this point in the season, every game he sits out—and someone else plays—is a chance for someone else to scoop the starting position in the first round of the playoffs.

Last year, the Highlanders only had one round.

Even though I did my best to ignore Alexei's season this year, I know how much he wants to be a difference maker in changing that outcome.

"I'm just saying," my dad protests.

"Shush," my mom says.

"He's right," Alexei says at the same time as I say, "It's complicated, Mom."

I flush and look down.

Alexei clears his throat. "I do need to get back to the team. Right now, they are in St. Louis, and I understand I cannot be there with them. That is okay. But by the time they return, I want to be back on the roster, and so it is important that I figure out the right care for Inessa and the house. It's why I am so grateful for Emery coming to stay with us."

The reminder that I'm going to stay here, *here*, alone with him and his daughter, and maybe this horrible Russian nanny, too, is just too much.

"Mom, I—"

"Well, keep us posted," my mom says brightly, her peak midwestern cheer effectively cutting me off, and then transitioning them out the door before I can protest.

Alexei sees them out, which puts me alone with Inessa and Nanny Nyet.

As Ms. Petrova stares at me with undisguised curiosity, I can hear Alexei getting caught up in another conversation with my dad at the door.

"You are a chef?" the nanny finally asks bluntly.

"Yep." I pop the p on purpose, which makes Inessa giggle. She might not speak a lot of English, but my girl clearly appreciates a good dose of attitude.

Smiling shy, she comes over and tugs on my hand.

We might not speak the same language, but in this moment, I can read her mind. I sit down so we're at the same level. "Do you want to see the photos of your dad?"

She takes my phone with glee, whining a little as I whisper for her to wait for me to open the app.

"I would have to insist on a no screen policy," Nanny Nyet says. "For everyone in the house while the child is awake."

My head snaps up. I give her a *what the fuck* glare. "I use my phone while I'm cooking."

There isn't a chance in hell I'm going to cook all of Alexei's meals without suitably distracting entertainment.

Nanny Nyet sniffs. "If she sees your phone, she wants to play with it."

Yeah, because she knows I've got cool Papa Makeover apps on my phone. "Phones are fun."

"Fun?" Her eyebrows arch. "Well. That's a simplistic way of thinking about it."

I glance back to Inessa, but she's already figured out the app and doesn't need my help.

Since Ms. Petrova asked me about being a chef, I figure that's a safe question to pop back at her. "How long have you been in childcare?"

"Twenty years."

I wonder how many times in those twenty years she's been fired for having a stick up her butt. "That's great. A lot of experience. Do you find that people really like rigid rules?"

She sucks in a disapproving breath.

Awkward.

"I'll just go say goodbye to my parents," I say, pushing to my feet.

The front door is ajar, and as I walk down the hall I can see them still talking on the steps.

But as I reach the door, I hear my name, and I go still.

"Emery is still very strong willed," Alexei says.

I gasp. Excuse me? Pretty sure the last time we were together, I was pathetically weak-willed and he enjoyed it very much.

"I think the word you're looking for is stubborn as hell," my dad says.

Alexei laughs. "You can call it like that, yeah."

"But you know, she's also a bit lost," my mother says. "Her chef business never really got off the ground in Minneapolis."

White hot embarrassment courses through me. That's not true. Not exactly.

"I'm not surprised," Alexei says in his accented, confident way, his words hollowing me out.

He's not?

"She's inexperienced, right? And naive. She has a lot to learn about the world."

"Of course you understand." My mom sounds relieved. "This is going to be good for her, Alexei. Maybe you can help her figure out what she really wants to do with her life."

Inexperienced?

Naive?

I already know what I want to do with my life.

July can't get here fast enough. The sooner I put an ocean between me and my family, the better. And Alexei, too, for that matter.

CHAPTER 11
ALEXEI

I'm on edge after I manage to extricate myself from that conversation.

My parents taught me to always see guests out, to make small talk. That did not prepare me to navigate Emery's parents blindsiding me with their doubts about her life choices.

I return to the living room. Emery is sitting on the floor now, and Inessa is in the chair beside her, clutching what I assume is Emery's phone.

Phones are Inessa's most prized possessions when she can get her hands on one, and they're giggling together.

I frown, trying to process what the Grangers said about their daughter.

She doesn't seem lost to me, but I don't actually know her.

"Mr. Artyomov—" The nanny rises to her feet, her gaze cutting sharply to the phone in Inessa's hand.

"Thank you for coming," I say in Russian. "I will contact you soon."

There's the briefest hesitation, as if she's considering saying something else, but she thinks better of it and nods.

Unlike with the Grangers, I don't step outside with Ms. Petrova. I see her to the door, then close it firmly.

I don't remember the last time I felt this tired. Maybe in the first few months of Inessa's life. That summer, after Tatyana left.

I quickly fire off a text message to dad, asking how he's doing, and then pick up Emery's backpack from where she left it by the door.

I get back to the living room just in time to see Inessa give Emery back her phone and point to the kitchen.

"Are you hungry?" Emery asks. She sounds delighted to be able to solve that problem.

"We haven't had lunch yet," I explain. "But maybe I should give you a tour of the house first. There is a fully furnished suite in the basement that you can use. It has its own entrance. I thought my parents would want to use it, but they prefer to live upstairs with me and Inessa full-time."

She doesn't look at me when she responds. "That's all right. I don't mind getting right to work."

My daughter's head swivels back and forth between me and her new personal chef. "Ya khochu bliny."

I groan at the specificity of the request. "Inessa."

She crosses her arms over her chest and pouts.

I count backwards from five and decide at three that

it's not worth trying to be firm. I give Emery a strained look. "Can you make fluffy pancakes? I tried this morning but…"

Emery smiles down at my daughter. "I can make you the best pancakes you've ever had."

"Boo berries?" Inessa adds in a whisper.

"You bet, baby girl. Absolutely with blueberries."

They go ahead of me, flowing past me like I'm an ornamental statute, irrelevant to the moment.

Which I am.

The only reason Emery is here is that she's doing a favour for my family, for my daughter and my mother, because they are innocent of the mess I made two years ago when I left her hotel room so quickly.

And then I made it so much worse by not reaching out soon enough to explain what happened…

Because by the time I did, it was too late. She'd blocked me and moved on with my life.

I had to spend the next year listening to her brother update me on her new adventures and her new dating life.

"Hard to see your baby sister grow up suddenly, man. I don't know what's gotten into her, but she's got a new boyfriend or girlfriend every single week it seems. Definitely testing my parents' limits."

It made me burn with jealousy. And if she hadn't blocked me, I would have thought that hurting me was the point.

But she went out of her way to make sure I couldn't see it.

I couldn't forget the taste of her, and she wanted nothing to do with me at all.

And now here she is. In my house, in my kitchen. About to make my daughter pancakes, because Papa doesn't know how to do that, and it's a lot to process. Really fucking hard.

For two years, I wondered what it would be like to see Emery again.

I knew it would be hard. Complicated, messy. I expected old wounds to re-open in one way or another.

Never in a million imaginings did I imagine being instantly passed over for my daughter. This makes it all easier, I suppose.

And it's nice to see Inessa happy.

But there's something about seeing their heads bent together conspiratorially that feels as if I've been hit in the chest with a cleaver.

Inessa's mother will never make her pancakes. I'm not sure if she'll ever want to *buy* her daughter pancakes.

Over the last two years, I've made my peace about Tatyana's choice to give me a child, but not participate in the raising of her. We were young, and family life in Calgary was never going to be right for her. Hamilton even less so.

I can't imagine what she would have done when I was traded if we still lived together. Had a tantrum, probably.

As it was, when I informed her that we were moving closer to the east coast, and would be a short flight from New York City, she told me that she looked forward to taking Inessa shopping there "when the girl is old enough." Like it was just a given that, after eight or ten or fifteen years of abandonment, any girl would want to have a big city shopping spree with her absentee jet-setting birth mother.

"Is this your pantry?" Emery's question pulls me out of my thoughts.

I put her backpack by the door that goes down to the basement and nod. "My mother keeps everything very organized."

"I can see that." She puts a container of flour on the counter, then opens the fridge, revealing my mother's effort. It's always neatly organized and well-stocked, through no work on my part, but I like seeing the impressed look on Emery's face all the same.

She adds blueberries, eggs, and milk to supplies she's going to use, then holds up a container of cottage cheese. "Do you want protein pancakes?"

I want you to look at me.

Because she hasn't yet.

Inessa tries to pull the bag of flour off the counter, so I scoop her up and put her on my hip. "Do you like them?"

Emery rolls her eyes. "I wouldn't make them if I didn't like them."

"Then yeah, I'd like to try them." I shift closer so I can grab the blueberries, planning to distract Inessa.

Emery's gaze follows my hand.

"Toddler distraction device," I explain.

"Ah."

"What did you think of Ms. Petrova?"

Instead of answering me, Emery gestures at the cabinets. "Where are your mixing bowls?"

"I'm…" I frown. "I'm not sure." I ask Inessa in Russian if she knows where Baba keeps the big silver bowls.

"Down," she says in English, looking at Emery.

"Are you a kitchen expert?" Our new chef gestures at the lower cabinets. "Then show me where it is, baby girl."

Inessa wriggles her legs until I set her down, and then she pulls open every door, giggling, until she finds the right bowls. "This," she says, shoving it at Emery.

"Gentle," I caution my daughter, then turn my attention back to our guest. "You didn't answer my question."

"Because it's not my place. I'm here to help for a few days, and then—"

My phone rings, cutting Emery off. We both look at the screen, and my heart leaps into my throat when I see it is the hospital.

I grab it. "Hello?"

"Is this Mr. Artyomov?"

"Yes."

"I'm a cardiology resident on your mother's team and…" I listen numbly as the doctor explains about a procedure they're going to do this afternoon.

"I can be there in twenty minutes," I manage to say. There's a click, the call disconnects, and then I drag my attention back to Emery, who is staring at me with wide eyes. "I'm sorry. I need to go."

"God, no, don't be sorry, of course. It's okay." She gestures to Inessa. "Do you want her to be close by at the hospital? I can come with you and take her for a walk."

I bury my face in my hands. It's so hard to think right now.

"I don't know," I mumble.

"Papa?" Inessa bumps into my leg. "Papa up."

Hot tears spring to my eyes—*fuck*—and Inessa repeats my name again, this time with a warble in her voice. "Papa?"

"Okay. Here's what we're going to do." Emery takes a deep, audible breath, and even with my eyes closed, I can see her picking Inessa up, calmly covering my daughter's hands as she reaches for me.

Waiting.

Soothing.

I haven't even given her a tour of the fucking house yet. Haven't said I'm sorry yet. Haven't addressed the elephant in the room, and now that's just not...I can't...

I feel like a piece of shit, falling apart in front of her.

"We're going to stay here and make pancakes," she says softly. Talking to Inessa, but also to me. "Your dad has to go to the hospital for the afternoon. Can you show me your bedroom after lunch, and maybe teach me how you have a nap?"

"No nap."

"But what if *I* need a nap?"

"Can-cakes."

"You're right. That's good prioritization. Can-cakes first, then Emery needs a nap."

I wipe my eyes and look sideways.

She's wrapped her arms around my daughter, holding her safe and secure, and carrying on a patient, amused one-sided conversation. She shines so fucking bright, like high noon on the warmest summer day.

I don't deserve her kindness.

But Inessa does, and Emery clearly gets that distinction.

"Thank you," I say roughly. "I'll make this up to you."

She doesn't look at me as she shrugs.

But her smile slips just a little, and I'm sharply reminded that the time to make anything up to her was two years ago.

And now it's too late.

CHAPTER 12
EMERY

As soon as Alexei is out the door, my phone is out of my pocket.

"What are the chances you want to learn how to make a toddler take a nap?" I ask Inessa.

She solemnly shakes her head. "Can-cakes."

"We're going to multitask."

I pull a chair up to the counter and give her a whisk so she can mix the dry ingredients together while I scroll TikTok for some babysitting tips.

Crowdsourcing life tips is my superpower. I love learning new things, and I'm pretty sure I can tackle spending the afternoon with a tiny, bossy little girl the same way I do everything else in my life.

"What's dat?" Inessa asks, flicking the flour-covered whisk in the direction of my phone.

"I'm learning how to be an emergency back up babysitter," I murmur. "Oh, let's try to keep the flour in the bowl. Gentle stirs. That's good."

I melt some butter, then convince her to switch tools to a spatula as I add in the wet ingredients.

"Do you want the blueberries in the pancakes, or on top of the pancakes?" I mime adding the fruit to the batter.

Inessa's response is immediate distress.

"No?"

"No," she repeats.

"Okay, cool beans. We've got this. Blueberries on top." I look at the stove. "The next part, I need to do myself. How do you feel about sitting in your highchair, for safety's sake?"

She blinks up at me.

"No context? Okay, baby girl. Surprise attack it is." I scoop her into my arms and march her to the highchair.

She protests, but I remember Alexei reaching for the berries when he wanted to distract her. I scatter a couple of blueberries on her tray, and that buys enough time for me to start the frying pan.

And when I slide a tall, fluffy pancake onto her tray a few minutes later, all is forgiven.

"Yummy?"

She nods.

I let out a sigh of relief. "Excellent."

Pancakes, check.

Next up…nap time.

CHAPTER 13
ALEXEI

When I get to the hospital, my mother's procedure has been pushed because of an emergency. Since I don't have Emery's phone number, I have to text Forrest.

He drops her contact card in a reply and doesn't ask any further questions.

I add her to my address book, then send her a quick update.

ALEXEI

This is Alexei

EMERY

How's your mom?

Procedure is delayed

Okay

Might happen at 6 pm, they say

How is Inessa?

Managed to trick her into having a nap
by pretending to sleep on her floor

I have done that

Now I'm cleaning up the mess we made
in your kitchen

She attaches a photo. Flour is everywhere.

I stare at the picture. Someone else might see mess, but I see Inessa having a really good time flinging flour this way and that way. In the background, her highchair is covered in smooshed blueberries and pancake crumbs, too.

ALEXEI

I'm sorry I missed pancakes

EMERY

Batter is in the fridge and lasts for a
few days

Might not be back for bedtime

I'll do my best

I flip back to my messages with her brother. I start to type out a few things. *Your sister is amazing. How do I thank her for stepping in to help? What does she like?*

But they all feel too revealing.

And they are things I either need to say to her directly, or figure out for myself.

———

It's midnight by the time I finally get home. I let myself in quietly. The text updates from Emery stopped around nine, and just in case she's passed out on Inessa's bedroom floor, I don't risk messaging her again.

The house is pretty dark, but the light in the stairwell leading upstairs is on—so that's where I expect them to be.

But when I go into the kitchen to grab something to eat, a low voice from the family room says, "Don't turn on the light, okay?"

I turn around and dimly make out Emery's face peeking over the back of the couch. Bright sunshine in the darkest hours of the night.

She stretches, looking rumbled and warm and so fucking sexy it makes my throat close tight.

"Bedtime wasn't as easy as nap time," she admits softly when she joins me in the kitchen. "Inessa is passed out on the couch, and she took me down with her."

"That's okay," I manage to say. "Thank you for spending all day with her. I know it's a lot."

"I just did what any EBUB would do. Slapped on a jersey I've never worn before and tried my best."

It takes my brain a minute to catch up. EBUG. Emergency backup goalie.

"Back up babysitter," she mutters when I don't respond.

"I get it."

"It was funnier in my head earlier, when I was Googling how to put a toddler down for a nap."

"It's funny."

"Then you should laugh," she says lightly.

I sigh and lift my hand, reaching out to touch her. It's instinctive. Instinctively stupid.

She takes a big step back, just before I wrap my fingers around her arm.

"Sorry," I mutter before I shove my hand back in my pocket.

"We made turkey meatballs and spaghetti for dinner, if you want some leftovers? They're in the fridge." She covers her mouth, but the big yawn that escapes is unmistakable.

"You're tired," I say. "There's a bedroom in the basement you can use."

"You said that earlier."

Oh, right. I scrub my hand over my face. "And, if it matters to you, the door between it and the rest of the house locks."

Her lips part in surprise, then she nods. "Got it."

I tip my head toward the living room. "Today... I know my daughter..."

My voice catches on the words.

The last time we were alone together in the dark, I didn't have a child.

Emery holds my gaze for a moment, and I'm not the only one who has profoundly changed in the last two years. The last time we were alone, she didn't have this sizzling confidence.

It's unnerving.

It's also very, very attractive.

Lock it down, Artyomov.

"My daughter can be exhausting," I finish. "I know how much work it is to watch her. Thank you."

Emery's eyebrows lift, as if to say, *that is an understatement.*

"She's fun." She pauses, trying and failing to school a comical expression on her face. "More fun when we're cooking. Less fun when I'm trying to convince her to do something she doesn't want to do."

I nod. Accurate.

"But we survived the night." She takes a deep breath. "Do you want me to heat up the meatballs for you?"

"That sounds good."

Silence stretches between us as the microwave counts down.

"Is your mom still okay?" she finally asks. "And how's your dad doing?"

I'd already texted her that the procedure went well.

But the rest of the night...waiting with my father,

trying to convince him to leave the hospital for at least a few hours…

That didn't feel within the scope of what we could text about.

"One of the nurses found him an extendable chair to sleep on. I might drag him back here tomorrow. He needs a shower."

She laughs easily, the corners of her eyes crinkling.

My mouth turns up, and the brightness in her gaze intensifies.

"Oh, you can laugh at your own jokes," she teases.

"It's not a joke. He really stinks."

She tips her head back, her throat working on a silent cackle, and my smile falls away as I stare at the long, creamy expanse of her neck.

Intense, visceral need claws at the inside of my chest.

The microwave beeps.

"I'm going to move Inessa to her bed," I say quickly, before striding into the living room, leaving my off-limits temptation behind me.

My daughter is curled up in the corner of the sectional, a favourite blanket tucked in all around her.

Her hair smells like shampoo, and she's in clean PJs. The living room might look like a bomb went off in it, and they might not have made it back upstairs, but Emery did better than I would have on my own tonight.

"To bed we go," I murmur in Russian.

Inessa rolls into my chest with ease and doesn't wake up as I carry her upstairs, not even when I put her down in her little princess bed.

I leave her door open and close the baby gate at the top of the stairs before returning to the kitchen. I tell myself I don't need the baby monitor. I'm just going to eat really quickly, maybe find out where Emery got that newfound confidence, and then crash in my own bed.

And perhaps leaving the monitor upstairs is a little insurance that I don't do something stupid, like crowd her against the counter and kiss her neck until she laughs for me again.

But it's not necessary.

When I get back to the kitchen, the meatballs are on the counter, my emergency back up babysitter is gone, and the basement door is firmly closed.

My pulse hammers thick and heavy in my neck.

I need to be careful here. Emery is the best childcare option I have, and step one here has to be convincing her to stay for the next few weeks. But if she says yes, then the last thing I can do is let any latent chemistry spark between us.

The way she split is almost definitely a sign that chemistry is one-sided, anyway.

Fuck.

I grab a fork.

The meatballs are fucking delicious.

She survived a day with my tiny hurricane of a child, and she cooks like a goddess. Nothing else matter. The more boundaries I build around my worst instincts the better.

CHAPTER 14
EMERY

I expect to have a rough night of sleep, but to my surprise, I fall asleep quickly. Maybe having two locked doors between me and Alexei is enough to maintain the crucial distance I need to keep this relationship professional.

When I go upstairs in the morning, the house is still quiet.

I decide to make muffins for breakfast, because yesterday it was one of the pictures on Pinterest Inessa got excited about, and Maria has frozen bananas.

I set the oven to pre-heat, then dig out Alexei's binder from the team with his nutrition plan. While I can't read the Cyrillic writing on the Post-it notes Maria has added, I understand the basics of his needs. I have a lifetime of experience eating and cooking around and towards pro hockey players. This part, I can do with my eyes closed.

I pull the protein pancake batter I made out of the fridge and get a cast iron griddle heating up, too.

The muffins have just gone into the oven when I hear footsteps upstairs. Water runs. It stays on long enough that I picture Alexei in the shower—*unhelpful*.

After ten minutes, footsteps move from one end of the house to the other, and there's low murmurs, off and on.

I hate how my heart rate picks up, anticipating seeing Alexei this early in the morning. I try not to imagine what his hair might look like fresh out of the shower, glinting like obsidian under the kitchen's pot lights.

I have my professional private chef smile on when he finally shows up. He's carrying a sleepy-looking Inessa, but he looks wide awake—and yes, freshly showered.

A white t-shirt clings to his shoulders as if he just saved its life, and he's wearing black slim-fit team sweatpants that show off every inch of his long, powerful legs.

"Hi," he says, his gaze raking over me.

That won't do. He can't look at me like that.

"Good morning," I say briskly. "I've got breakfast under way."

He murmurs something to Inessa.

"Morning," she says, looking at me shyly.

I beam at her. "Remember the muffins we looked at on my phone?"

She shakes her head and buries her face in her dad's neck.

"She's better after some milk," Alexei says, pulling open the fridge. With one hand, he manages to fill a cup for her.

For all the stress and chaos of yesterday, I think he's a more capable solo parent than he gives himself credit for.

I return my focus to cooking the pancakes. These aren't as fluffy as the ones I'll make for Inessa, but they are macro compliant and pretty tasty.

He fires up the espresso machine, then asks, "Would you like a coffee?"

"I can get one for myself while you two are eating," I say politely.

He doesn't answer. He just makes a black espresso, puts a sugar cube in it, and sets it on the counter next to the griddle.

I'm so distracted by watching him that I forget about the pancakes, and the first four are a little dark on the bottom.

Those can be mine.

Taking a deep breath, I force myself not to look back at him again until I have a plate of perfect looking pancakes for my new boss.

I slide them onto the counter in front of his bar stool. "Here you go. Can I get you anything for on top of them?"

He shakes his head. "I'll get raspberries."

"Basberries!" Inessa gasped, her eyes going wide.

Alexei frowns. "Really?"

"Papa!"

He switches to Russian, and she pouts. You can practically see the storm cloud gather above her as she shakes her head.

He closes his eyes for a moment, then counts, out loud, backwards from five.

I try to hide a laugh behind my tiny espresso cup, but he notices anyway after he blinks his eyes open again.

"She had a tantrum because the raspberries were too soft two days ago. These are the same berries. They will only be softer today."

"Bas. Berries! Papa!"

"Why is it when Baba tells you no, you listen to her? But if I say no, you just yell Papa louder? Hmm?" He crouches a little so he's eye to eye with her in her high-chair. "Why do you test Papa so much? You are making Emery laugh at me. That is not nice."

Inessa swivels her head to me, her face suddenly soft and sad. Waterworks are on their way. "Basberries?" she asks me in the most plaintive voice I've ever heard. "Pwease?"

"That's *very* polite," I say, heaping praise into my tone of voice. "Can I show you all of the fruit options in the fridge?"

That seems to avoid the imminent crisis to both of their satisfaction. After considering the raspberries, the now very familiar blueberries, and a package of blackber-ries, she goes with the trusted blueberries after all.

Alexei takes a few enthusiastic bites of his own food, then puts his fork down. "Tell me about Switzerland."

I move the mixing bowls to the sink and grab a cloth. "It's a country in Europe. Lots of mountains."

"Emery."

I shrug. "It's not Minneapolis."

"You moved home after college?" He asks it like a question, but I think he knows the answer.

I shouldn't be surprised. He did work with my brother for a year after our hook-up, and Forrest is a talker.

"I missed it," I hear myself admitting. "Boston was great, but it never felt like home, so I didn't really want to stay there. And my closest friends on the team and in my program all scattered on the wind."

"And you went to culinary school."

"Yep."

"And now…"

I laugh as he leads me right back to Switzerland, in between bites of pancakes. "And now I want to do more culinary school. The first program was really about the basics. Learning to work on a line, get the foundational knowledge. Skills, techniques, etc."

"What will you learn in Switzerland?" He pushes his plate away and leans forward.

I go to grab the dish and he waves me off, standing.

"I mean, I'll learn a lot—plating, recipe development, refinement of skills—but going to Europe is more about the access to a different level of on-the-job training, too."

He brings his plate around to the dishwasher, then leans his hip against the counter right next to me.

A subtle, warm note of coconut and something else tropical meets my nose, and a memory of unbuttoning his shirt washes over me. How eager I was to get at his bare skin, how out-of-this-world hot he was that night.

Still is, even in basic athletic wear.

"On the job training?"

I jerk my head up.

He's looking at me, really intently. His hair has mostly dried now, just a few strands still damp. Less obsidian and more like a warm, deep ebony. Very, very touchable.

"Pardon?"

"What kind of on-the-job training can you get there that you can't get here?"

"It's…" I swallow hard. "Staging," I manage to say.

"Stah-zhing?" he repeats, stretching out the unfamiliar word.

"It's French for like, apprenticing. Short internships or observationships in high-end restaurants. Harder to get as an American without some European training."

"That's a new word for me." Inessa bangs on her tray and he glances over his shoulder, holding up his finger to her. *One minute.* "Is that what you want to do, work in high-end restaurants?"

"Not forever." Not exactly, but I've never said exactly what I want out loud to anyone. First steps first.

"But it's the next step."

I nod.

"And you start that program in July?"

Another nod.

"Good." He searches my face. "That's exciting."

I inhale slowly, pretending it's simply to steady myself, and not at all to catch another whiff of that coconut scent. "Thank you."

"So can you stay with us until then?"

"Pardon?" Surely I misheard him because I was sniffing him. Until when?

"I'd love it if you could help us out until the summer."

"I can definitely stay for a few days. But…"

"A few days?" he frowns. "I need you longer than that."

Oh, the way he says that is dangerous. I could misconstrue that so easily. "A week, then. I have a flight back to Minneapolis the day after Forrest's team comes to town."

"Flights can be rebooked. I will pay you an advance for two weeks up front. Or whatever you need."

"It's not about money." I try not to sound desperate, but I just thought—

"Do you have a job? I can speak to your boss."

"It's not— I'm saying, I can only give you a few days. A week at the absolute most. Just until you hire the right people."

Alexei's eyes glitter darkly. "I agree that I need to hire the right people. I think you are the right people."

"I'm not—"

"I know you say you are only an EBUG. But you are very good with Inessa."

"Well, I know how to distract—"

"Do you think I should hire Ms. Petrova instead?"

I shrug. "If you think she is the best option for watching your daughter, I can't argue with you."

His brows slam together. "You can argue."

"Not my place. But I know she doesn't approve of me, so that's a good reason for me not to stay very long. I can cook some meals in advance and stock your freezer, though."

"How could she not approve of you? You spent what, ten minutes together?"

I shrug again, casually, as if I couldn't care less what she thinks of me. As if I haven't been annoyed since yesterday. "Maybe she could sense that I will be a terrible influence on your daughter."

The storm cloud reaction is genetic. Alexei glowers about this exactly the way his daughter did about the raspberry standoff. "Nonsense."

"You don't want to know how I bribe her to stop crying. Your nanny would never approve."

"That person is not my nanny. Unless you abandon me in a few days. Then I will need to hire her."

He says that silkily, like a threat. As if he knows I don't want him to do that, and I *hate* that he can see me that clearly.

"You should hire someone," I say as neutrally as I can manage. "Maybe I could help you find some better nanny options."

His eyes light up. "I would be so grateful."

I don't want him to be grateful. I want…

I want to be able to help him, and Inessa, without it getting too complicated. Except it already feels complicated.

You have choices, I remind myself.

I could have gone to Toronto with my parents. A few days of being told I'm a bad friend would have been the worst of my punishment, and then I wouldn't have two or three months of *this*.

I could call up Shannon or Kiley, and they would come rescue me in a heartbeat, no questions asked.

So why I am considering staying for two weeks, or however long he needs me for?

The truth is, I know it'll be six weeks, at least, and maybe eight or ten depending how deep they go in the playoffs.

You're leaving for good in the summer. What does it matter if you stay here through to the end of the playoffs? There are two locking doors between you and the man you once begged to suck his cock.

Maybe I didn't beg. Maybe that's just a distortion of time and fucked-up nostalgia. Because I think about that night way more than I should. I twist it into all sorts of fantasy outcomes, including when I take him deep in my mouth and he finishes so fast I feel like a triumphant conqueror.

It would be good for me to let Alexei hire me for as long as he needs a family chef. I can help him find proper childcare, too. This could be a form of exposure therapy to drum that nostalgia out of my heart and my mind and my memories.

He's a father now.

He's staring down the possibility of being a starting goalie in the NHL playoffs.

He needs childcare, and Nanny Nyet is *not* an option.

I hold up my phone. "What is your email address? I have a standard contract and a website you can pay me on."

His eyes light up. "You will help us?"

Heart pounding in my chest, I nod. "If you already

have a grocery service, I can do an hourly rate for my labour. I prefer to bill two weeks ahead, and there's a standard retainer which I itemize the receipts against and carry forward—"

"Emery. I don't care about the details."

"But I do. They matter." I take a deep breath. "This will be easier for me if we make this as formal as possible. You are my boss. I am in your employ. The nanny search I'll do for free, because I want the best for Inessa."

His brows furrow and a new tension tightens between us. Understanding. Recognition.

If this is going to work, he can't misread my kindness as anything other than human decency.

In the two years since we met, I've grown. A lot, no matter what my parents might think. And in this moment, all that matters is that Alexei knows what I'm offering—and what I'm not.

I am now very clear on who I am and what I want. What I will do, and what I won't do. *Who* I won't do.

Finally, he nods and holds out his hand. "May I?"

I let him put in his email address and ignore the little jolt of heat that races up my arm when our fingers brush as he hands my phone back.

There will be more of that. More nostalgic reactions to incidental contact, more fleeting moments of basic physical chemistry. They can be ignored. Or at least, I can learn to ignore how they make me feel.

I change the subject. "What is your plan today?"

"I need to skate. They have a training plan for while

the team is away. But first, I want to take Inessa to the hospital. My mom would like to see her." He shoves his hand in his hair. "She might be a little bear if I bring her back and then leave again. I'm sorry."

"It's okay. I get it. Of course she doesn't like it when you leave. You leave a lot."

He blinks at me, clearly surprised.

I shrug. "I was her, remember? My dad was in the NHL when I was a toddler. My earliest memories were of him always leaving for road trips."

"Yes, it's exactly like that." He growls in frustration, and I have to laugh.

He meets my gaze.

Oh.

Ignore those feelings, Emery.

"Would you come with us to the arena?" he asks. "You can skate, too. If you want to? Might be fun."

"I don't have my gear."

He shrugs. "What size skates do you wear?"

———

They go to the hospital without me, which gives me some quiet time to further familiarize myself with the kitchen and start to make a shopping list for groceries for the next week.

And then I get changed for skating. I have limited clothing options since I packed light for the Granger Road Trip—a situation I will need to rectify, but can't fix in this moment—so I go for my thickest black leggings and my

Buffalo hoodie that I was going to wear to that game. I snap a picture of me in it and send it to the Granger sibling group chat and tag Logan so he can see that I was thinking of him.

EMERY

Wearing this to skate at the Hamilton barn today.

LOGAN

That's my baby sister! Yes! Represent. Get Ty Connor to sign it. He's from Buffalo.

The team isn't there, sorry.

Wait, so who are you wearing it for, then?

I frown.

You, you dummy! For this photo! And I have limited clothes here.

What's going on?

OMG, doesn't anyone in this family talk about anything other than hockey? Alexei Artyomov's mom had a heart attack. I stayed in Hamilton to help their family.

Oh shit. That's nice of you. Maybe don't rile him up with a division rival sweatshirt, though.

He can handle some riling, don't worry

FORREST

Catching up... be nice to Alexei, he's not
a brother stand-in

Oh, if Forrest only knew just how true that is.

I take another picture, this one flipping them both off, just before I hear the front door open upstairs.

"Emery?" Alexei calls out. "We're back."

"Coming!"

He's waiting at the door when I emerge from the basement. His quick sweeping gaze takes in my sweatshirt, but he doesn't say anything about it.

Inessa is excited when I get in the passenger seat. She waves at me in the lightweight mirror attached to the headrest in front of her rear facing car seat and babbles at me in Russian at first, until Alexei reminds her to use English.

"Baba sleeping," she says.

He backs the car out of the driveway before expanding on that. "Yeah, my mom is pretty tired. She did wake up briefly, which was nice to see. The nurse said she's responding well to medicine."

"That's great."

He nods. "And more great news—your mom was right. There's a season ticket holder who lives half a block from the hospital and has a short-term rental suite in their basement. So, my dad has a place to go to have a shower and sleep that is walkable to the hospital. I booked it for him for a week. Hopefully, by that point she'll be able to come home."

His voice cracks on the last few words.

My fingers ache to reach across the centre console and squeeze his arm.

"We'll make it easy for her once she does come home," I promise.

"Thank you." He exhales and taps his head back against the head rest. "It's hard to see her in a hospital bed."

"I bet."

We come to a red light at the exit from the subdivision, and as he checks traffic on the busier road we're about to turn onto, I twist in my seat to wave at Inessa in the mirror.

She laughs and covers her face with her hands.

"Do you want to listen to music, malyshok?" Alexei lifts his voice, but he doesn't look back at the mirror. He carefully keeps his eyes on the road, which means I can slide my gaze back and forth between them as he drives.

She claps her hands and asks for something I don't catch, but he understands clearly. He taps his phone screen to find a playlist called Inessa's Tracks, and then drops his hand to the console between us.

His long fingers curl around the edge, invading the space where my knees are. His knuckles press against the outside of my thigh as his thumb presses on the volume control button on the console.

Why would Mercedes put that button *there*? Do they not understand how weird it feels for Alexei to casually rub his hand against the outside of my knee?

If he is affected by nudging me, he doesn't show it.

His hand returns to the steering wheel and I pour all my attention into watching Inessa dance in the mirror.

Neither of us say anything else for the drive to the arena.

By the time we get there, the equipment team have skates set out for me. They're brand new, right out of the box, and I suspect someone was sent out to buy them.

"What do you think, Inessa? Should we skate some laps while your dad practices?"

"No," she says very clearly. "Jump?"

Alexei responds in Russian, and again she shakes her head.

He looks at me. "Do you understand jumping couch?"

I throw my head back and laugh. "Yep," I say. "That's upstairs in the front office area. I'll take her up to see Shannon."

"I'm sorry. I thought she would like skating with you. I know I would have." He finds me a keycard that will get me upstairs, and hands it over.

"Another time, maybe." I offer my hand to Inessa, and she slides her fingers into my grip. "Let's go, baby girl."

But we've barely made it to the elevator before we run into Kiley. She has her dog with her on a lead, and when she sees Inessa, she tells Puck to sit—and Puck does, immediately.

"Doggie," Inessa whispers, her grip tightening on me.

"Do you want to pet her gently?" Kiley asks.

We move closer, and Inessa tentatively reaches out.

"We're heading up to find Shannon," I explain. "What are you doing here?"

"There's an indoor dog park upstairs. And it's wet outside, so…we're here to burn off some energy. Becca and Charlie are coming, too. They just got a puppy who needs some lessons in how to play from Puck."

"Charlie?" Inessa yells the name. "Charlie!"

Puck, to her credit, doesn't even flinch.

As if summoned by the full force of a demanding toddler, there's yapping in the distance, and thundering footsteps. Charlie runs into view with Becca and an excited puppy right behind.

"Hi Nessa," Charlie says.

"Jump," she says.

He gives her a wicked little look, immediately knowing what she means.

Becca greets me and I tell her about our mission.

"Maybe Inessa wants to come with us to the dog park instead," Becca offers. "So we're not jumping on the furniture while people are trying to work."

From down the hall that Inessa and I just came, I hear Alexei call my name. "Emery? Are you still there?"

He comes jogging around the corner holding Inessa's diaper bag. "Oh!" He takes in the other people who've joined me. "You found friends."

"We're all going up to the dog park," Becca says. "Today it is going to double as a preschool playground because it's raining outside."

"Great." Alexei goes to hand me the backpack but then stops. He looks at me, he looks at Becca, he looks at Inessa, and then he says, "Can you take Inessa with you? I promised Emery she could skate today."

"It's okay," I protest.

"It's not," he says firmly. "You are helping me. I owe you some fun."

Kiley reaches for the diaper bag. "I'm happy to be on Inessa duty."

"I don't mind—" I start to say, but Alexei has already grabbed my hand.

CHAPTER 15
ALEXEI

Taking Emery's hand was a mistake, because holding Emery's hand feels fucking good.

I like the way she squeaks in surprise and then wraps her fingers around mine, holding on tight when I lead her back into the empty equipment room.

Dragging her around at my pleasure is definitely not within the very tenuous terms of her employment.

"I don't need…" She trails off as I yank a helmet off the shelf. "I was just going to skate a bit with Inessa. You don't need…"

I grab shoulder pads next. "I don't think anyone else is skating today. It's you and me and one of the trainers. You can't tell me that you haven't fantasized about taking a few shots at me in net."

She laughs out loud. "Excuse me?"

I raise my eyebrow at her.

"Okay, fine. It might be fun."

"Yes, good." I put the pads over her head.

"I've got it," she murmurs, her gaze catching mine. Sharp. Warning.

I find her elbow pads next.

"You can go get dressed."

I glance down at her little legs, clad only in black yoga pants. "Shin guards…"

She grabs them from me. "If you try to dress me, I'm taking these very expensive skates and going to the nearest public arena."

A knock at the door saves us both from testing that boundary.

"Arty, are you in—" One of our rookies, Malik Zondi, steps inside. His dark brown face lights up with a bright white smile. "Emery?"

"Hey, buddy!" She steps past me and almost throws herself at him—*What the fuck?*—ready to give him an enthusiastic hug, when she stops at the last second when she realizes he's in a red no-contact jersey. "What happened?"

He laughs and pulls her into his arms.

My jealous reaction is immediate, visceral and intense.

I've never so clearly understood the English idiom for seeing red before. It's not only the jersey, but the air shimmering around them as they embrace as well.

I clap Zondi on his shoulder that I know is still tender—hence the no-contact jersey and him staying home from the road trip to work with the trainers—and I push them apart.

"How do you two know each other?" I ask as I bodily

move Emery back to the counter where I was getting her ready for the ice.

Zondi ignores the distance I put between them and leans in, giving Emery a look I recognize.

It's a look I gave her two years ago.

There's no fucking way.

"We spent a week together at Rusty's cottage last summer," he says, and the pit of my stomach burns.

"With like, half your team," Emery adds, rolling her eyes at him. "And I was *Rusty's* guest."

Zondi winks. "Yeah, but that wasn't serious. How do *you* know our Emery?"

Now there's blood rushing through my ears so loud I can't think, let alone find the words in English to convey that it doesn't fucking matter what happened *last* summer.

Emery is Rusty's ex-girlfriend that Zondi saw in the stands two nights ago. The one he has exchanged messages with.

Emery.

My Emery.

"We go way back," I snap at the same time as she cheerily tells him, "I'm his temporary babysitter."

I give him my back and grab the jersey off the counter that I'd set aside for her. It's one of our practice jerseys. Not one of mine, it's a regular jersey cut, but the equipment guys put my name on it anyway. And Emery notices that just before I put it over her head, muffling her protest.

Once her head pops free, she glares at me.

"This is the second Alexei Artyomov jersey I've put on against my better judgement this week," she mutters, her chin extra pointy.

The urge to take her face in my hands and kiss her so hard she bites me is nearly overwhelming.

"I'm going to start getting them tailored into chef coats," she adds. "Maybe Inessa wants to paint in them, too?"

And that's the dump of ice water my possessive instincts needed.

"Be my guest," I snap. "I'll be on the ice in ten minutes."

And then I shove Zondi out the door, and keep pushing him until I deliver him to the medical team myself.

Our injured new D-man, Luca Carter, is there, too, getting a treatment on his knee. He looks back and forth between us.

Zondi shrugs. "Don't hit on his babysitter."

"Wasn't planning on it," Luca says.

Good. That's good—for him. For his tenuous health.

Everyone needs to keep their fucking hands off Emery.

Including me.

CHAPTER 16
EMERY

I stare at Alexei's back, and then the empty doorway, as my pulse races and my head spins. Who in the possessive heck was *that* man?

Grumpy.

Growly.

He even *grunted* when Malik implied more than is accurate about our friendship, if one can stretch it even that far. Acquaintanceship.

And now I'm wearing Alexei's jersey for the second time in three days!

Unreal.

I grab the skates.

I need to find a bucket of pucks, a really expensive hockey stick, and get on the ice.

My goalie boss and former mistake of a hook up had better get ready, because I feel like smashing some pucks into the net. Preferably off his blocker and his shoulders and his face mask, and most definitely five-hole, right between the legs.

CHAPTER 17
ALEXEI

I'm calmer by the time I step on the ice, fully dressed in my goalie gear.

Emery is skating a looping warm up pattern on one half of the rink, her skates leaving a carved path in the fresh ice.

I skate right to the middle of her path and start to do my own warm up, getting a bit of cardio in while finding my edges. She's faster than me, and picks up extra speed as she rushes past.

I grin.

She narrows her eyes at me on the next pass. "What are you smiling at?"

"You," I say, but it's quiet and I don't think she hears it under the slice of her blades against the crisp surface.

The cure for being jealous of my teammate wasn't stalking away from her and getting dressed on my own—it's being alone with Emery on the ice and giving her a chance to be mad at me.

She hasn't had that chance yet, because we had other things to worry about. But my mother is recovering, and in good hands. Seeing her this morning, knowing my dad has a place to stay…it lifted some of the panic that had consumed all of my thoughts.

And in the quiet that replaced it, I felt Emery's thigh flex against my knuckles. I felt the loss of her when Inessa wasn't agreeable to skating. And I saw another man want her the way I have always wanted her.

The way I can't have her.

And all of that made her justifiably mad.

I think of how my mother sometimes yells at my father when he frustrates her.

I would give anything for everything to be different, for us to be in a place where Emery could lose her shit at me, to trust that our relationship was rock solid enough for her to snap and know it'll be okay.

Like a toddler having a tantrum.

Another unexpected lesson I've learned as a parent—we are at our best, and our worst, with those we trust the most.

Nobody else gets Inessa's sweetest side. Her hugs and kisses, her sweet little worry when I'm in an ice bath, the way she curls up against me when I get home from a road trip, as if my heartbeat against her cheek is all she needs for the world to be right again.

Nobody else gets the worst of her tantrums, either, because she tries to be so good for everyone else. But me? She knows I will always love her, no matter what, and so it's with me she can truly fall apart.

Toddlers need to fall apart more often than one might think. They're little powder kegs of learning new things, getting frustrated, not understanding why they can't say what they need yet...

And they aren't alone in that. Grown-ups have powder keg emotions sometimes, too.

I'm reminded of how I started to cry in the kitchen yesterday—and the grace Emery gave me.

"Speed up, old man," she yells as she zooms by.

I swing my stick out and tap her ass. "I was just thinking about how nice you are," I holler back.

She laughs and tightens up her circle, spiralling around me now.

I stop skating and switch into some side-to-side drills, opening up my hips as I drive to a hard stop to the left, then to the right.

Emery matches my shift in pace and finds a puck to do some tricks with. "When was I nice to you?"

"You taught me to appreciate asparagus."

She trips over her feet as she reacts—"Alexei!"—but catches herself and keeps skating.

I'm undeterred. "Does Zondi like asparagus?"

"Stop."

"I don't think I will."

She flicks a puck at me, thumping it hard off my left pad. "He's just a friend."

"And Rusty?"

"*He's* in love with Shannon. You know that. Has been since forever."

"I know you have dated a lot of people, Emery. I accept that. But—"

She comes to a sharp, ice-spraying stop in front of me. "But *what*? You *accept* it? My dating life is none of your business."

"I *know*." I'm a foot taller than she is, and I use every inch of it to glare down at her. "I know. I'm sorry. I shouldn't have said that about asparagus."

"Nobody knows about that night," she says quietly. "If you're going to act like a jealous asshole, people will ask questions."

Fuck. "I wasn't thinking."

"I could tell."

"It's just that…You were not experienced when we were together. I cherished—"

"*You* were hella experienced," she snaps, cutting me off. "And you forgot to tell me about a *pregnant girlfriend*."

"Ex," I bite out. "Very much ex. I told you that."

"I asked for clarification and you decided to dip instead."

"I had to leave."

She tips her head back, staring up at the ceiling of the arena high above us for a long, angst-filled beat. "I know."

"Do you know?" My voice is tight and tense, and this isn't the place for this conversation, but somehow, the door to it has swung open, and I'm taking the opportunity to set the record straight. "I swear, Emery, I didn't know Tatyana was pregnant. Everything changed in that moment. I wanted to stay, but I couldn't."

She makes a face.

I take a deep breath. "I had to leave quickly that night because I didn't know how long she would stay at the hospital."

Emery sucks in a breath, her gaze jumping to meet mine. "What do you mean?"

I choose my words carefully. "I never speak badly of Inessa's mother. Never. To anyone. This is another secret, yes? Between us?"

Her head bobs carefully. Yes.

"Tatyana thought she was an expert at getting my attention. And there is the most attention when one is being chased, you know? But I was tired of that game. I had to make it clear that I would be a father, but nothing else to her. And there were legal steps that had to be taken because she was a visitor here in Canada."

"Was there a difficult custody fight?"

"No. She realized she didn't want to be full-time parent. She stayed in Calgary for the first two months, but by the end of that period she wanted my parents to watch Inessa all the time. She signed over full custody without argument."

Emery's eyes soften beneath tight brows. "Does she ever see her daughter?"

"Last summer in the off-season, we went to France. I rented a villa where everyone had their own spaces. She brought her new boyfriend, and they didn't stay very long. She made noises about coming here for Christmas, but their lives are in Europe. Calgary doesn't really compare well to Monaco. And then I was traded and the plans fell apart, because Hamilton… Even less so, apparently. I hope that when Inessa is older…"

I trail off.

It's hard to say out loud what I hope for, when I'm not sure it'll ever happen.

"Of course." She takes a deep breath and whacks her stick against my pads. "We should practice. What kind of shots do you want?"

"Up high first? Then down low."

"You got it."

She twists, my jersey riding up on her hips as her strong little thighs power her away from me.

My name and number plastered above that tight, round ass…I wish we had a photographer on the ice right now, because I'd take a banner of that view for my bedroom.

Mine. All fucking mine.

I shake my head, testing my helmet and refocusing myself on the task at hand.

I settle into my stance in front of the net, and Emery starts skating a predictable pattern, warming me up with easy shots to my glove on one side, then my blocker on the other.

She skates so much like her brothers that I find myself anticipating her moves, coming out of the crease a bit more. But she's not exactly like her brothers—and she makes that crystal clear when she snaps her next shot high, bar down, and the puck tumbles into the net behind me.

"Look alive," she taunts.

"So we're done with the soft warm up shots?" I smack my glove against my blocker. "Bring it on, Buzz."

She gasps. "Is that how it is, *Arty*?"

I grin. "What are you fucking waiting for, solnishko?"

She drills a slapshot right to the centre of my chest.

I'm laughing as she circles around to pick up another puck, but the laughter dies as she shoots low, forcing me to butterfly.

There's a thread of respect in how she works me over, sticking to the low shots for a bit as my legs get warm. But there's a competitive edge, too, and I'm not surprised when she's decided I've had enough kindness and starts disrupting the pattern. Really making me work for the saves.

And then, just as one of our trainers steps onto the ice, she shifts her speed to another gear—and now she's flying.

This isn't anything like watching her brothers barrel down the ice towards me.

This is something different.

Her edge work is incredible. She shifts directions like a video game player, as if gravity means nothing when stacked against her determination to evade invisible defenders, to get to the net and beat me at my own game.

This is my house.

My barn.

And she's owning it as she becomes a blur, her shoulder dropping, her knee bending, taking a shot I can barely track—except *no*, she didn't shoot, because she's paused and flipped the puck to the back of her stick.

Time stops as I realize what she's doing.

I feel every one of my two-hundred-and-ten pounds as I try to fight the momentum in my body and reverse direction to protect my blocker side.

She stares me down, then flicks the puck just below my glove anyway. The original target, after all.

Fuck me.

Our trainer is clapping as she skates over and introduces herself. "Nice shot."

"Thanks." Emery shrugs. "I'm just his babysitter."

I swear in Russian.

She winks at me. "I'm going to go find Inessa now. Can I keep the skates?"

"We're not done here," I growl.

"But I'm done," she says sweetly. "Come find us when you finish."

Fuck me.

Fuck fuck fuck me.

I need more time with her. I knew she was a good athlete—she's been on the national team since she was seventeen, I think, and has been to the Olympics twice—but I've never seen her skate.

Why is she not playing professional hockey right now?

Why, instead of doing that against the best women goalies in the world, is she my emergency back up babysitter?

There's something there that doesn't line up.

I watch her skate off the ice, then reluctantly give my

trainer my full attention, because that's my job and I'm a professional.

Also, I truly do appreciate the Hamilton program.

After coming up slowly through the Calgary system as a prospect who didn't get a ton of NHL ice time, and more often than not sat on the bench as a backup goalie when I did get rostered, this season in Hamilton has been a revelation—in so many ways.

Calgary has a good program with a lot of history, but they're in a weird holding pattern right now, waiting for their new arena to get built.

Hamilton, on the other hand, is a brand-new expansion team, and the billionaire owner has thrown money at the team in every way possible. The facilities are extra impressive, the support staff is extensive, and nothing is off the table.

The only downside of getting traded to this region is that the Ontario hockey press is unlike anywhere else. Even in Alberta, where the Calgary-Edmonton rivalry is fierce, there's only a fraction of the coverage that the Toronto team alone has.

Add in Hamilton's newness, just an hour around the curve of Lake Ontario from Toronto, aka the epicentre of the hockey universe, and the spotlight is bright. The start of the season was really rough. I was coming into a dressing room that had been rocked by team division—and my trade was supposed to fix that, but the wounds lingered.

As a relative newcomer in every way, I quickly realized all I could do was keep my head down, work with the goalie coaches, and wait for the lines in front of me to sort themselves out.

It was a strategy that paid off.

Hamilton has three goalies on the roster right now. The other starting goalie is a Finnish player named Tuomo Makinen, and we also have a young American named Ryan Monaghan who is waiver-exempt—so he goes back and forth between the Highlanders and their AHL affiliate team in Niagara Falls, as the roster and salary cap require. Right now, he's travelling with the team for the games in St. Louis and Detroit, but Makinen will probably play both of them.

Makie is four years older than me, and a steady, career goalie, but he's emotional, and when the team isn't playing well in front of him, he gets frustrated.

The more frustrated he got as the first half of the season rolled out in rocky chaos, the cooler and calmer I got—which resulted in me getting more games under my belt.

And then the team got their shit together and started winning again.

Now we have less than a month until the playoffs, and I'm in a head-to-head battle with my teammate for who will get the starting net in the first round.

I want it so fucking much.

I spent eight years being reined in, being cautioned that I needed more time, more experience, to finish fully growing into my six-and-a-half-foot frame. On the one hand, I knew I was good and getting better with each year. On the other hand, it felt so fucking far in the future.

But now, suddenly, I'm on a team that doesn't have a clear number one starting goalie.

And while it's actually good for us to alternate games in the regular season—we need to rest and save our bodies for the playoffs—once we switch to best of seven series, the coaches will want to stick with a winner in net.

I have carefully constructed my entire career to peak at this moment. Being blindsided by parenthood didn't knock me off course. Getting traded was a rollercoaster, too, but I hung on.

Now there are fifteen games left in the season. Every single start matters.

I can't let myself be distracted by my *babysitter* for God's sake.

So, I put Emery to the back of my mind and run through a complete workout.

"Good job," my trainer says when we're finally done. "Let's take tomorrow as an active rest day, to mimic the team's travel day to St. Louis, and then we'll repeat the same workout day after that. You can bring your babysitter again. She's a lot of fun to watch on the ice."

"She played college hockey in Boston for five years," I say. "Has two Olympic medals. The babysitter thing is a favour."

"That makes more sense."

"She is a very good babysitter, though." *Shut up, Alexei.*

My trainer also looks surprised that I'm still talking.

I never talk about non-hockey stuff.

But apparently, Emery being thought of as *just* a

babysitter is a dam buster. "She didn't even want to be my babysitter."

"Hence it being a favour."

"Because she's very kind. When she is not taking shots at me, I mean."

That makes my trainer laugh. "I know what you mean."

"I think I should—" Luckily my random train of out loud thinking is cut off by one of our assistant general managers and our travel coordinator appearing out of the tunnel.

They both look worried.

"Alexei, can I have a minute?"

"We're done here," my trainer says. She pats my arm. "This guy was a beast today."

The AGM nods. "First of all, I need to ask how your mother is doing?"

"Very good, thank you." I tell him briefly about the procedure she had yesterday. "She will be in the hospital for a week, but then will come home."

"And have you organized childcare?"

"His babysitter is *amazing*," the trainer says.

Which is true, but I'm concerned about where this is going. I frown. "Yes, I have some childcare in place, but I haven't found a professional yet. Why?"

The AGM and the travel coordinator look at each other. "We know this is a lot to ask, but we got a call from the team on the road. Makie is sick. We can't dress him tonight, and it's not looking good for the Detroit game, either. Monaghan can play if you're still not available, but we're going to have to call up someone on an emergency basis to be the second goalie dressed."

I hear Emery's father's voice in my head. *That's a no brainer, son. You step up now, and you cement your spot as the starting goalie in the playoffs.*

But then I picture Emery, who right now is searching this building for my daughter. Who has only been my babysitter for a few hours.

And my mother and father—fuck, my father still hasn't slept in his own bed yet.

"I need to talk to my family," I hear myself saying.

"Of course."

"How much time do I have?"

"Jack Benton can send a plane to pick you up in ninety minutes."

I'm already moving past them, heading for the dressing room.

CHAPTER 18
EMERY

"Look at you, Miss Sweaty," Kiley says when I finally join them in the very cool little indoor dog run that's up in the rafters of the arena. It took me a while to find the space, because it's not marked anywhere.

Kiley eventually had to drop me a pin and I followed it on my phone.

Thank God for technology.

She's closer to the door, keeping an eye on the two dogs at one end of the space, and Becca is at the other, carefully supervising Charlie and Inessa on a raised platform. "Did you have a good skate?"

I pat the skate bag that was helpfully left next to my tennis shoes by the equipment team, and which is now slung over my shoulder. My second Alexei Artyomov jersey is folded up inside it, too. "Come to Hamilton for a hockey game, stay for some accidental childcare work and sweet new blades, I guess."

"Is that how he's paying you? In gear? Because you deserve—"

"No, that was a joke." Although we haven't actually signed a contract yet, I have no doubt Alexei will agree to whatever I ask.

What I'm going to ask for, I haven't yet decided.

She frowns. "Don't let him take advantage of your helpful nature."

I laugh out loud before I can stop myself. "Trust me, I'm not naturally inclined to help *him* out."

"I know he can seem cold and standoffish, but that's just a goalie thing."

I open my mouth to correct her, because I don't think Alexei is either of those things. If anything, he's the opposite. Too intense, too hot, too relentlessly personal.

But I haven't actually seen him interact with anyone on this new team.

"Our families were pretty intertwined in Calgary," I say, which is true. I wasn't a part of that, save for an hour and a half where Alexei and I were literally intertwined, and I was naked. "My parents think of Inessa as an honorary grandchild, and she needs someone to make her pancakes right now. I'd probably do that for free, but I'm no dummy. I'll get her dad to pay me well."

Inessa catches sight of me and waves excitedly, teetering on the edge. Becca's hand immediately floats right in front of her, but I still panic a little.

I leave Kiley to watch the dogs and cross to her at a jog.

"Hey baby girl," I barely manage to get out before she flings herself off the platform and into my arms, laughing.

"Oof," I say. "You're a fearless monkey, aren't you?"

"Again!"

"Charlie taught her that word," Becca says apologetically.

Inessa wiggles out of my arms and climbs up the little ramp. I dump the skate bag so both of my arms are free, and she flies through the air.

She's chaos wrapped in pink and glitter, but I'm learning her rhythm. When she's about to jump, when she's testing a boundary, when she just needs to feel someone catch her and hold her tight.

It doesn't take long to start to pick up on those little imperceptible tells in a person.

Maybe that's why I feel Alexei before I hear him.

That pressure shift in the air. The feeling in my chest, like a gravity-free plunge.

"What are you teaching my daughter?"

I jolt, but I still catch her before I whirl around.

Inessa clings to my neck.

Alexei plants his hands on his hips. Unlike me, he's managed to shower, and he looks sleek and sexy in a military green Highlanders hoodie, black jeans, and expensive looking black boots.

I'm pretty sure my hair is curling in chaotic and weird directions, fuzzy from having been in a helmet, and my face is red from both exertion on the ice and the misplaced shame at being caught encouraging his toddler to do something dangerous.

Except it wasn't dangerous.

"I've got her," I manage to get out.

His mouth tightens. "Can I talk to you privately?"

Becca looks like she's going to try to intervene, but I give her an *it's okay* look. Because it is.

"No more jumping," I tell Inessa as I put her down.

She starts twirling in wobbly circles on the floor, making Charlie laugh.

I follow Alexei out the door.

"It wasn't dangerous," I point out as soon as we're alone. I leave off the part where I did think it was scary the first time.

His brows pull together. "Of course it was. She's a terror. Everything she does is dangerous."

"I was watching her closely, though!"

He just stares at me like that's not the point.

Irritation rises, fast and furious. "Am I too naive to take care of your child?"

"What?"

"Definitely inexperienced, am I right?" I prop my hands on my hips. And I put enough emphasis on the middle word that he doesn't miss it's deliberate.

He rocks back on his heels. "You overheard me yesterday."

"Yes." I refuse to let him see how much those words hurt. I lift my chin and don't look away.

He sighs. "Your parents want the best for you."

"Sure. But we don't agree on what *the best* is. And you can't know that, because you don't know me at all."

"It was a conversation I should have gotten myself out of sooner. I'm sorry."

"That's it? You're sorry?"

He shrugs. "I can't undo that it happened. I won't get sucked into another conversation like that, is that better?"

I frown. Yes, it is better. And I didn't expect him to be so…reasonable. "Thank you. So…what's with the concerned dad *'what are you teaching my daughter?'* routine?"

He looks up and to the side, as if replaying his words in his head. "Dry humour," he finally adds. "With an edge of anxiety because I need to ask you for a favour."

My eyebrows lift in a wordless question. *What now?*

"The team wants me to rejoin them. Makie's injured. I talked to my parents and they understand. It's up to you."

"Me?"

"I'll be gone for three days."

He doesn't have to explain the rest of his concern. He doesn't think I can handle Inessa for that long. Which is fair. I'm not a trained professional.

My mouth goes dry. Are there enough Tiktoks in the world?

"It'll be fine," I hear myself say. "I understand that you need to go. If it's okay with your mom, then it's okay with me."

It will have to be.

He studies me for a long moment, like he's trying to figure out if I mean it.

Maybe I do.

Maybe I don't.

But I'm saying it anyway.

He finally nods, but doesn't move. Doesn't turn or speak. His jaw flexes, and he drags a hand through his hair, fingers catching for a second like he's surprised at how tightly he's wound.

"I didn't want to ask," he says finally. "I don't want to leave her right now, with everything going on," he says, and he gives me a look so raw and vulnerable, it's like an entirely different man standing in front of me. What would it be like to have him be that torn over missing *me*, too? Once upon a time, I dreamed about that. Now, I'm just his hired help. "But I also want—"

He stops himself.

"It's okay to want to win. To be indispensable to the team. I get that." I try for lightness. "I'll make sure she eats something other than blueberries. Maybe I'll even try to brush her hair. And by the time you get back, I'll have some real nanny options lined up, too."

"You don't need to—"

"I do." I take a deep breath. "Nanny Nyet wouldn't let her climb, I'm sure."

"Nanny—" He stares at me incredulously, then barks a sharp laugh. "Okay. That's not—"

"I'm not nanny material, Alexei. Do you know how I've distracted her every single time we've been alone so far?"

He crosses his arms over his chest and sighs warily. "How?"

"We draw moustaches on you." When he doesn't

react, I double down. "I found an app where we can turn you into a clown. Where she can scribble on your photo and make you look ridiculous."

His eyes flare. "You have photos of me on your phone?"

Of course he would pick up on that piece.

So I make it clear that he's wrong. "I very much did *not* until two days ago. Then your daughter gave me a wobbly lower lip, big watery eye look, and suddenly I was downloading every terrible picture of you that I could find for her to decorate."

"With moustaches."

"And clown wigs. Also, duck lips and fake eyelashes."

"You're joking."

I pull out my phone and fire them off to him in text messages, one at a time. *Ding. Ding. Ding. Ding ding ding ding ding.*

"Okay, you weren't joking."

"A little girl was sad and I did what any thoughtful person would do—I distracted her. But you have to know that I'm never going to enforce your screen policy. I'm never going to tell her not to jump off of things, even if it makes my heart leap into my throat when she wobbles on the edge. We all have to learn to jump, Alexei. And it's fun."

"Fun."

"Yes, *fun.*"

He rubs his jaw, then looks down at his phone again. "I don't have a… screen policy. I let her play with my phone, too." He taps on the screen. "I don't need you to be Ms. Petrova. I don't need you to tell Inessa *no*. I just need you to keep her safe, and you've already proven that you can do that."

Ding.

It's a text message from his surveillance camera app to join his home network.

"I sometimes use that app instead of a baby monitor. There are cameras in the kitchen and in the family room, as well as front door and back yard."

Ding.

Rapid fire, he sends me links to everything I need to be in charge of his house.

Ding. Ding.

"I trust you with my daughter, Emery. More than I would trust anyone else."

———

Alexei takes us home. I finally get the full tour of the place, now out of urgent necessity. I can't sleep in the basement while he's gone, so we start upstairs.

The second floor is divided into two distinct spaces, separated by a long hallway that Inessa likes to sprint up and down. At one end is the bathroom, surrounded by bedrooms—Inessa's princess nursery, her grandparents' room, and a small library with a daybed in it.

"It's small," Alexei says doubtfully.

"It's fine."

"She stays in bed when she wakes up. She'll just call out for someone to come and get her. This is close."

"For sure."

At the other end of the hall is Alexei's room, and a doorway that has a child lock on it.

"My gym," he says. "In the attic."

"Got it."

He gets me a baby monitor and plugs it into the wall in the library, aka Emery's Temporary Room. "You can take this upstairs with you if you want to use the gym after she's asleep."

"Thanks."

"I gotta pack now." He looks conflicted.

I give him a big, bright smile. "We'll be fine."

And after he leaves for the airport a short drive away, we are fine—for the afternoon.

I manage to keep Inessa entertained and distracted from the fact that it's just the two of us in the house until bedtime. But as soon as she starts rubbing her eyes and I herd her upstairs, everything falls apart.

While I'm running her bath, she's racing up and down the long hallway, and keeps coming back to tell me that her Baba isn't home, her Papa isn't home, her Deda isn't home.

"I know, baby girl," I tell her. "We're having a sleepover tonight. Maybe we can go see Baba tomorrow, okay?"

"Papa not home."

"He's playing hockey. Do you want to watch him play?"

She nods reluctantly, but when I open the app on my phone to show her the game, it's a commercial break instead, and she starts crying all over again, asking where he is.

She sobs through her bath, which breaks my heart, and then refuses to read any stories once I get her into her jammies.

I take her back downstairs to watch the game on the big TV in the living room. I turn the volume down, because she doesn't care about the hockey, she only wants to see her dad when the camera cuts to him in the net.

By the time we tune in, it's the top of the third, and Hamilton is leading St. Lous 3-0, so the camera cuts to Alexei a lot. Every time she sees him on TV, Inessa gets happy, but it's right on the edge of panic.

The last two minutes of the game are wild, non-stop onslaught on Alexei, and he blocks every shot attempt like a superhero with a dozen limbs.

I turn up the volume a bit to listen to the commentary.

"They try to thread that through, but the Hamilton D are on it. Artyomov looks sharp. The extra attacker isn't a problem for him. He's been on fire all night, hasn't he?"

"He sure has. And that's another shot stopped, glove down, and he'll get the whistle. Finally a chance to breathe."

"St. Louis will probably call a timeout here. And indeed they do. While they discuss a strategy to break through the strong Russian in this final minute, let's look at some of the saves he's made tonight."

Inessa stands in the middle of the room, rapt attention pointed at the TV, as they show save after gymnastic save.

When the camera flips to the St. Louis bench, she runs over to the couch and does a flying, all limbs splayed imitation of her dad diving to block a puck.

And then she snuggles into my side.

I wish I could pause this moment for three days, because this? Right now?

This is perfect.

She's so small and soft, warm and cuddly.

But the game has to end.

We get another few minutes of stop and start play, with the puck getting chipped out into the stands, and an icing call, but the seconds tick away.

And when the buzzer goes, Alexei has a shutout— incredible—and we get a long shot of his teammates lining up to hug him and tap his helmet.

But then they cut back to the studio talking heads, and Inessa's brief happiness bubble bursts.

"Papa?"

"He won his game," I say softly.

She doesn't care. She climbs off the couch and wobbles to the front door. "Papa?"

I follow her, offering every distraction I can think of. When I run out of ideas, I pick her up and carry her upstairs, clicking the gate shut at the top of the stairs. One way or another, we're doing bedtime again.

Time slows to a crawl. An hour passes, and I'm lying on the floor of Inessa's room, pretending to sleep, while she hiccups in her bed and tells me in broken English that she's never going to be tired and I need to wake up.

On the floor between us, my phone lights up. One of

Alexei's stupid cartoon modified faces flashes on the screen. I didn't even realize we'd added that to his profile. Maybe my phone picked it automatically. Technology is too smart these days.

"Papa," Inessa says between hiccupping tears.

I answer the call and try to put on a brave face, but there's no hiding the fact that we're both crying.

"What's wrong?" Alexei asks.

My voice cracks. "Bedtime broke us a little."

"Oh no," he says. His gaze goes from me to Inessa, and he murmurs something in Russian.

Her lower lip gets fatter, jutting out more.

"What a long day for you," he says, and it takes me a second to realize he's looking at me again.

"I'm sorry." Wet tears track down my cheeks.

"What are you sorry for? We have difficult bedtime sometimes. It happens." He says something in Russian next, then nods along with Inessa. "Take her to my bedroom. I think she will fall asleep while we talk if you lay down with her there."

"Your room?" My eyes go wide.

He shrugs. "It won't bite, Emery. And it is late."

Inessa climbs off my lap and tugs at my hand.

Sighing, I follow her, willing to try anything right now.

His bedroom is dark, so Inessa stops in the doorway—which means I stop in the doorway, and am immediately hit by the subtle but unmistakable scent of two years ago.

A vicious ache sears through my chest. The ache of what ifs, of what could have been.

"Light switch is to the left," Alexei says through the phone, misreading the reason for my extended pause. "It's on a dimmer."

I give my phone to Inessa, grateful for the excuse to not be holding Alexei in my hand right now, and turn on the overhead light. As promised, it's set to a very low level, but it's enough for Inessa to see her way to her dad's bed.

She throws my phone up onto it, then climbs up like a monkey, wedging her sleeper-clad foot in between the frame and the mattress for leverage and hauling herself up with two determined fists on the fitted sheet.

A duvet is shoved to the foot of the bed, and the pillows are in disarray, but Inessa doesn't care. She grabs the phone and climbs right up to the pillows, making herself at home.

"Sorry I didn't make the bed this morning," he says.

I'm guessing that's to me.

I sit gingerly on the side of the bed.

It's a *nice* mattress. Extra thick, and the sheets feel clean and still smell like the laundry.

But they also smell like him. Like coconut shower gel and warm skin.

"Where did Emery go?" Alexei asks Inessa.

She giggles and rubs her eyes.

"I'm here," I say softly.

No matter what my complicated feelings are in this moment, I'm grateful he got her to stop crying.

"Rub her back," he says, just as softly. Like we're

conspirators. Like he's helping me diffuse a bomb or something.

To do that, I need to crawl onto the bed, too.

I take a deep breath and join her.

I stroke my hand down her back, and her eyelids flutter shut. She fights it, trying to talk to her dad in Russian, but with each gentle stroke up and down her spine, her eyelids stay shut a little longer, and pretty soon they stay closed.

"Keep rubbing," he whispers. "Another minute or two and she'll probably be out for the night."

I hold my breath, and he stays quiet, and my entire focus is on the slow rise and fall of her back beneath my fingertips.

When I lift my hand, she stays asleep.

I silently make an excited face at Alexei, and he gives me a thumbs up.

"Can I leave her here? She's in the middle of the bed."

"Yeah, she's okay there."

I move some pillows to the side of the bed, giving her little bumper guards in case she rolls. But the bed is massive, and she's a tiny slumbering loaf in the middle of it.

As quietly as possible, I tiptoe out, turning the light off and leaving the door open.

"Thank you," I say, still whispering as I head down the hall to the library. "I didn't know what to do. She just kept getting more and more upset. It wasn't like last night at all."

"It's because she is getting more familiar with you."

He shrugs. "I know it's difficult. But you didn't do anything wrong."

"That's more faith than I probably deserve." I flop on the day bed and hold my phone above my tear-splotched face.

And that's when I realize that Alexei is reclining in a hotel room, also on a bed—and he's not wearing a shirt.

CHAPTER 19
ALEXEI

As Emery relaxes, probably for the first time in hours, she gathers herself and finally focuses in on me—and immediately gets flustered.

Does she know how revealing her wide, startled gaze is?

I should end the call. Inessa is asleep. There's no reason for us to keep talking.

Except the way her cheeks go pink and her eyes dart left and right before finally settling on looking just above the camera…that feels like a reason to stay on the line.

That feels like a reason to do a lot of things I shouldn't.

"Good game tonight," she says. "Really good."

Maybe she thinks that's a safer subject than my bare chest, but she's wrong. The fact that she tuned in means more to me than it should. "You watched?"

There's a flash of vulnerability in her eyes. Not the same kind of fluster. This is something else. "The last few minutes."

"That was the best part." I grin. And it was—I can still feel the adrenaline coursing through me. "You didn't miss much before that."

She laughs. "Nobody scored on you! I must have missed some good saves."

"I practically had a nap in the second period."

She giggles. Replacing whatever doubt or worry was in her expression with that pure glee... that feels good.

Too good.

"Inessa loves watching you. When they were replaying your saves during the timeout, she was mimicking your splits and your glove saves. Which were very impressive."

My pulse does a weird thing in my throat. "Thanks."

She nods once, then shifts the phone. Her loose t-shirt slides off her shoulder, exposing the thin strap of something soft underneath. I swallow.

"In between the tears, we had a lot of fun tonight. She's very cuddly."

Her voice is softer now, and the blotchiness has faded from her face. She's so fucking gorgeous, I want to reach though the phone and bury my face in her neck.

But she's asking me about my *daughter*, because that's the whole reason she's in my house.

I nod and pull myself together. "Nothing can prepare you for the unconditional love of a toddler. It's the best part of being a parent. I had no idea." I scrub my hand over my face. "I didn't have any idea about any of it, to be honest. I knew I wanted kids, but I didn't think about any of the specifics."

"I don't think I appreciated enough how hard that must have been for you. To just become a father with no warning."

"It was hard. It still is hard. But I loved her immediately, so that made it…" I mutter in Russian, trying to remember the English word.

"Doable?"

"Of course. Yes. I knew as soon as I held her in my hands that I would do anything for her. I will always feel that way. It's what gets me through terrible bedtimes." I find her gaze again and hold it through the hundreds of kilometres that separate us. "It's what makes me so appreciative of you taking this one."

"Anything for the team," she murmurs.

"You haven't sent me your contract yet. Maybe we should negotiate your pay higher, hmm?"

She makes a face. "I know. It's weird to charge you for this, though."

"I'm inconveniencing you."

"I wasn't doing anything anyways."

"At the very least, you are missing out on watching your brothers play hockey."

She blows a raspberry.

"And maybe you are missing some hot dates at home?"

Another raspberry, then she laughs. "No."

I shouldn't be relieved.

But I am.

She swallows hard. "Can I confess something?"

"Anything."

She takes a deep breath. "When your mom and Inessa came into the WAG suite the other night, I…I think I felt her presence. I knew, even as the door was opening, that it was someone connected to you. I can't explain how. But I was convinced it was your girlfriend."

I frown. "I don't have a girlfriend. I haven't dated anyone since Inessa was born. I don't know if I ever will again. That's just not my life."

"I didn't know that. I thought maybe Inessa's mother was still in your life." She blushes. "I did a really good job blocking out anything and everything to do with you."

Guilt sears through me. "I don't blame you for that. That was a horrible night. I never should have—"

"Was it horrible?" She cuts me off, really looking at me now. Challenging me. "Do you regret it?"

The directness catches me off guard, and I respond honestly before I can think better of it. "Never."

Confusion twists her expression, just for a moment, before she sucks in a quick inhale. "Right up until the end, it was the best night of *my* life. Really eye opening."

"Jesus." I laugh in surprise, and relief. "Okay. Good. But I hate how it ended."

"Also eye opening," she says dryly.

"I walked right into that." I roll my shoulders. Tightness is starting to settle in. I'm going to need a massage tomorrow. Should have asked for one tonight, but I had media availability and then I wanted to get to the hotel.

I wanted to get to privacy, so I could call Emery, so she could flay me alive for hurting her two years ago.

I'm not running away from this conversation.

"Since we're confessing things, can I tell you something?" I ask.

She nods.

"It wasn't horrible. That's just a thing I tell myself now so I don't get consumed by *what ifs*."

"Oh, Alexei."

"Fucking hell, don't give me *pity*. I'm the asshole who ruined it, all right? That's all me."

She nods, sagely agreeing with me, which makes me laugh with her—and at myself.

"I wanted you from the moment I saw you, Emery. In that bar, I was already thinking about how to approach you. And then your brothers came in and that barely deterred me. That night, all night, I was obsessed with you. I need you to know that, just…for yourself. Don't ever doubt how much you consumed my thoughts then. When I got those text messages, I was genuinely shocked. I hadn't seen her in seven months."

And if there wasn't a hitch in her breath, I'd leave it at that.

But we went two years with her only understanding part of what I was going through that night. I don't want there to be any doubt in her mind that if everything was different, she would've been mine from that night. I never would have let her go, and she would still be mine today.

"That night was the hottest experience of my life. If I'm lonely forever, I won't be completely alone. I have my memories, and they are…incredible. The only thing hotter would be if you'd been wearing this jersey."

Silence hums between us like feedback.

She shifts on the couch, one leg curling under her, and the sweatshirt dips a little further. I drag my gaze back to her face. Her cheeks are pink now, but she doesn't break the stare.

Her lips part, but no sound comes out. Then she smiles—small, secret, like we just agreed to something without saying it out loud.

"It's good to have some closure on all of that," she says. "I should go to bed."

And before I can respond, the screen goes black.

CHAPTER 20
EMERY

Inessa's soft little snore is the first thing I hear when I wake up, because despite Alexei's assertion that she will stay in his bed, apparently that's not true.

At some point in the night, she woke up and came to find me, and now she's sleeping on the carpeted floor, a plush pink baby blanket clutched in her little fist.

"Oh, baby girl," I say softly as I swing my feet to the floor. "Aren't you a quiet little bit of mischief? We have to sort out this sleep thing, don't we?"

She keeps sleeping, unaware of my angst.

I reach for my phone, so I can send Alexei a picture of just how much his daughter does *not* stay in her bed, *actually*, but then our conversation from last night starts rocketing around in my head.

God, why did I say all of that?

Why did I tell him I worried he was in a relationship?

Why did I force him to tell me that he didn't regret our hook-up?

The room is still dim, early morning light just starting to seep through the curtains. I slide out of bed slowly, carefully, but I needn't worry—she doesn't wake up even after I step over her and head down the stairs to the kitchen.

I need coffee.

I need a reset button.

I need to forget the way Alexei looked at me last night, as if I was something breakable and beautiful at the same time.

I press the start button on the espresso machine and lean both palms on the counter, bracing myself.

You're the babysitter, I remind myself.

Not his girlfriend. Not his confidante. Not *his* anything.

Last night was too much. I need to avoid soft, whispered late-night conversations with him. This was the second time we'd been alone in the dark, the air thick with emotions best left unexamined—and the second time we've immediately gone straight down that path.

It felt like I could tell him anything.

And worse—like he *wanted* me to.

But it's morning now, and I know better.

As soon as I have my first bracing sip of espresso, I find the mantra I need to keep reminding myself—he's my boss now.

This is just a job.

This is temporary and some professional distance is my best strategy.

It doesn't matter how easy it is to talk to him late at night.

Or how good it feels when his knuckles press against my thigh.

Or how his eyes get all hooded and intense when he says—

Nope.

I take a long sip of coffee and force *that* thought out of my head.

If I want to survive until the end of the playoffs, and then get out of town with my heart in one piece, I have to be careful.

No more vulnerable confessions.

No more soft, sleepy conversations.

Because I know how awful it feels to get my hopes up and then have them dashed.

Alexei may be the only man who ever made me feel seen. But at what cost? And what would I have to give up to call that attention *mine* in a real way?

He's also the only man who has ever broken my heart, and I'm not going to let him do it again.

Distance.

I need to maintain some friendly but professional distance.

———

After breakfast, we meet up with Becca and Charlie at the playground at the end of Alexei's street. Becca brings coffee for us and apple slices for the kids, and we stay there for two glorious hours.

Inessa is so tuckered out, she wants to be carried all the way home, which definitely feels like my workout for the day.

She is very agreeable to her nap, which delights me, so while she's asleep, I search TikTok for other ideas to tire out toddlers, and any other babysitting tricks the internet wants to give me.

By the time she wakes up, I have a plan.

First tactic I test out is a single location outing. According to multiple TikToks I saw, trying to run more than one errand at a time is the danger zone. But a single outing can be fun, especially if it includes a chance to run around.

My target is the grocery store, so I make sure that I put a few snacks in the diaper bag and Inessa has a cup of milk and some toast before we leave the house. The specific tip I like the most is to scout out a spot in the parking lot where your toddler can play for a bit after you finish shopping. I park in a spot at the edge of the lot, next to a couple of carefully placed landscaping boulders, and I take Inessa out of the car on the far side of them, so she doesn't see them yet.

I buckle her into the shopping cart, and power shop like a pro.

It's not until we get to the checkout that she starts to whine, because the cart is no longer moving—so that's when I bust out the snacks.

Apple sauce.

Animal crackers.

A sippy cup of water.

And when we survive, and the groceries are in the back of the car, I show Inessa the giant rocks and she climbs on them until her little cheeks are bright red.

It's the high point of the day, though. By the time we get home, she's over tired and hungry, the apple sauce and crackers not quite enough, but she also can't tell me what she wants for dinner. I make her some toast, since that seems safe, and she eats that and watches videos of Alexei on my phone while I quickly prep some basic stuff to cook in the oven—chicken, roast veggies, meatloaf.

Then I wipe her hands and face, and we collapse on the couch.

"That was a good day, right?"

She snuggles in against me, pressing her ear to my chest, and I take that as a yes.

I text a photo of her to her dad, and he calls back immediately.

"Hi," he says as soon as we answer. He's wearing a suit, no tie, and his dress shirt is unbuttoned at the neck. It doesn't look like he's shaved since he left yesterday, and the pop of dark stubble against the pale skin on his jaw is…distracting.

Inessa grabs the phone and babbles a question in Russian.

"Where am I?" he repeats in English. "I'm at a restaurant." His gaze flicks my way, and I ignore the jolt of awareness that slices through me. "Team dinner."

"Nice," I murmur.

"What are you two having for dinner?"

"Toast," Inessa says solemnly.

Alexei laughs. "Good listening, little one."

"Toast was our first dinner, yeah." I yawn. "I'm batch cooking some other stuff now, but it may all go in the fridge and freezer."

We tell him about the park, and grocery shopping, and then he says goodnight, because he'll still be with the team when Inessa goes to bed.

Right before he signs off, he looks at me and says, "How are you doing?"

"Fine," I say brightly.

From his expression, I think he knows that it's an exaggeration. Crap.

"I really am fine." I smooth my fingers over Inessa's dark curls as she presses the side of her head against my chest again. Her hair is like silk, and the next smile I give him isn't as forced. "It's been a long day but a really good one. I promise today was better." And then I get over my own doubt and give myself a compliment. "I'm taking good care of her."

His grin says that was what he wanted to hear. "I can tell you are."

From behind him, someone yells his name. *Arty!*

He winces. "They're getting rowdy."

"Go. Have a good dinner. We're going to…" I crane my neck back so I can look at Inessa. "What should we do tonight? Do you have mini sticks?"

Alexei laughs. "In the workout room. She doesn't like hockey yet, though."

I squeeze his daughter tight. "Oh, I'm going to change that. She'll be your training partner soon enough."

Alexei's workout space is not the kind of high intensity gym I was expecting. He does have a bike and a rowing machine, but there's no heavy duty treadmill, no weight rack. Just some free weights, a set of tethered TRX straps, and a big floor area with foam mats for stretching and body work.

Inessa makes a beeline for a big exercise ball. It keeps her busy while I find the mini sticks and a rubber ball.

Then we go back down to the second floor, and I close all the doors, creating a long "rink" for us to play in.

It's not until after we've finished playing and I go to send her dad a sweaty selfie of the two of us that I see he's sent a warning.

ALEXEI

Don't wreck up the pace.

EMERY

Sorry, your walls already have marks on them.

But my daughter is smiling!

She sure is

And her hair looks brushed

Even braided, in fact

You think you can teach me how to do that?

Of course

But be warned, she doesn't like to sit for very long

I know

I'll have to practice my braiding on you

Fuuuuck.

I stare at the message until Inessa knocks my phone out of my hand.

I think about it as I corral her downstairs for a second dinner, and then back upstairs for a bath, and the whole time I'm rubbing her back as she falls asleep.

And when I ignore a video call from Alexei an hour later, my pulse pounding, all I can imagine is his hands in my hair, his fingertips sliding against my scalp, and I fear that distance might just be impossible.

Holding him at a professional distance until the play-offs are over?

At this pace, I'm not sure I'm going to keep him at arm's length until the week is over.

CHAPTER 21
ALEXEI

After my big win against St. Louis, the coaches decide to give Monaghan some ice time in his home town, so I don't play in Detroit. They still need me to dress as the backup, although they did offer to call someone up on an emergency basis so I could go home.

My parents both loudly dressed me down for that.

"This is what we have dreamed of, Alexei," my father said. "I went home today and saw Emery and Inessa. They are fine."

I knew they were. I have a growing collection of photos Emery has sent me, selfies of two happy, busy girls, that prove they were fine on their own for a few days.

But I still let out a sigh of relief when I finally get home at two in the morning, after being gone for almost four days.

Too long.

And yet I'll have to do it twice next week, and again

the week after that. Three more road trips until we get to the playoffs.

Thirteen more games.

Emery thinks I didn't see the tear marks on her cheeks again after that first call, but I've noticed every hesitant note in her face, every blotchy red mark. I know she's doing the best she can, but she didn't ask to be thrown into the deep end caring for my two-year-old.

I leave my suitcase in the foyer, toe off my dress shoes so I don't make any sound, then take the stairs two at a time.

The baby gate at the top of the stairs squeaks a little as I swing it open. There's a light on in the shared bathroom beside Inessa's nursery. I peek my head into her room, but she's not in her bed.

The door to the library on the other side of the bathroom is open as well, so I don't feel like I'm invading Emery's temporary space when I glance in there. Nobody's there, either.

My mouth tugs up at the corners as I quietly stride to the other end of the house, noticing now that there's a dim glow from my room.

Sure enough, they are curled up in my bed, Inessa in the middle, holding on to Emery's shirt with a tiny but fierce hold.

I go into my closet, pushing the door closed before turning on the light so I can change out of my suit.

Once I have sweats and a t-shirt on, I try to wake up Emery, but she's dead to the world.

Inessa, though, wakes up at the slight jostle.

"Papa?"

She sleepily reaches for me, and I scoop her up. "Let's give Emery the bed to herself, okay?"

She whines and shakes her head.

And I almost give in and let her lie down again. The temptation to stretch out on the other side of her myself is strong.

It's a massive bed.

It wouldn't even be the first time I've been in a bed with Emery, not that she'd appreciate that reminder.

But I've pushed against her boundaries enough over the last few days. It would be wrong to crawl into bed and fall asleep next to her.

The problem is it also feels wrong to carry my daughter away from the big, warm bed where her babysitter sleeps.

In an alternate universe, I should have every right to slide into bed next to them in the middle of the night, and hold them both tight.

CHAPTER 22
EMERY

I wake up before Inessa, and there's a bit of victory in starting the day with a minute to myself.

I slowly blink the sleep away, the ceiling coming into focus, as I listen for the usual rustling from her room. Nothing yet. No babbling. No footsteps.

Then I remember that we've been sleeping in Alexei's bed and she should be right beside me, but when I look sideways, she's not.

I jerk upright, then dash to the hallway, where I skid to a halt.

Alexei's at the top of the stairs—barefoot, shirtless, and staring at me with an intensity that takes my breath away.

"You're home," I say inanely, because of course he is. I even knew that he would be, but I'd been so tired last night that I forgot. And it's embarrassing how excited I sound, how relieved I am to see him.

His gaze flares. Too hot for this early in the morning.

Warning. Danger.

I break the invisible connection between us and look down, but that just lands my attention on where his sweatpants ride low on his hips, where shadows tease at the edge of hard, lean muscles I've never seen before, because when we—

He never—

I take a step back.

"You were dead to the world when I got in," he says softly. "I moved Inessa, then crashed in my parents' room."

Because I was in his bed.

Heat swarms through me, and he notices.

His gaze drops to my chest, where I'm sure I'm turning red, then slides up my neck, lingering on my mouth, before finally meeting my eyes again. "She's still sleeping. I was going to start coffee."

"Good idea," I whisper.

Neither of us moves.

And my fucking nipples tighten.

No, nipples. Don't betray me now.

"I'll just..." I cross my arms over my chest. "I need a sweater. I'll, um..."

He watches as I slide past him.

The space between us feels charged with electricity. Like something could spark if either of us breathes too hard.

It's so intense, so immediate, that I don't know how I thought I could ever maintain an arms-length professional relationship with him.

What have I gotten myself into? And how many days until he leaves on the next road trip?

In my temporary room, I cross to the reading chair in the corner that has turned into my temporary clothes storage device and grab a Minnesota hoodie, one of my faves. Oversized, well-worn, and most importantly, not *his*.

I don't look at the carefully folded stack of two Artyomov jerseys I've tucked onto a shelf.

All of this is temporary.

My hands are shaking.

I pull it over my head and try to ignore how my body reacted to the heat of his eyes on my skin. How quickly I can unravel, it turns out.

This is your job. This is not your fantasy. This is not your forever.

I drag in a tight breath.

In.

Out.

"Fuck," I whisper.

Then I turn around and Alexei is there, in the doorway, watching me.

Fuuuuuck.

"Better?" His voice dips low, a little rough now.

I narrow my eyes at him. "Yep."

He doesn't move as I close the gap between us, not until the last second, when he steps into the room to let me past.

Except I don't move past him.

I slow down, and my gaze rakes over his bare chest again, his chest and his abs and all that skin.

"Do you see something you like, solnishko?"

I suck in a breath.

Maybe I didn't expect him to call me on my reaction. Maybe I thought he would let me hold on to the pretence of not being affected, when of course I'm affected by him.

He's the only man who has ever undone me completely. The only man who I ever wanted to get under my skin and do some damage.

Doesn't mean I'm going to let him do it again.

I step abreast of him, and I'd like to think I would have made it into the hallway, except he shudders. I'm weak, I guess, but knowing that he's as affected as I am by whatever this moment is—*an inevitable culmination of all the moments over the last week*—is enough to make me turn. My back bumps up against one of the bookcases lining the wall.

There's no retreat now. No way to hide from the burning need in his eyes.

I don't know who moves first.

One second I'm standing still, and the next his hand is on my waist, pulling me in against him, and my arms are curling around his neck, holding on to him as if he's a lifeline and not the churning storm.

And his mouth—

God, his mouth is *right there*.

He searches my face as he cups the back of my neck with his other hand. There's no space left between us now, only breathless need and pounding pulses.

His mouth finds mine, sure and soft.

If it was anything other than soft…*maybe maybe maybe.* So many maybes, but they're all irrelevant, because the truth is I was never going to avoid this.

It's still extra-devastating when he kisses me with a tenderness I didn't know was possible. This definitely isn't the kind of embrace that haunted me as I tried to move on. The feeling nobody could match, for two long years.

Of course Alexei Artyomov is the only person who kisses me better than Alexei Artyomov.

He tastes faintly of toothpaste but mostly of desire, sweet and warm and perfect, and when I lick at his lips, he growls and deepens the kiss.

I open for him and his tongue spears against mine. So, so good. I make a sound I don't mean to. Something desperate and wanting.

He answers it with a groan so low it vibrates through my bones and makes my toes curl. Then he wraps his arm around my hips, a solid band holding me tight, and he *feasts.*

His hunger makes me whimper, a sound he devours. And he works me against his body, hitching me up, up, up, until one of my legs is wrapped around his thigh and the thick, hard press of his erection is slotted right against the soft, thin cotton of my sleep pants through which I can feel everything.

As we explore each other's mouths, he slowly starts to rock against me.

This is so much more than a kiss.

I moan again, louder this time, as his fingertips work their way under the hem of my sweatshirt, searing my bare skin. A secret, forbidden touch that sets my already heated flesh on fire.

I'm trembling against him, rubbing my needy sex on his cock like I've completely given up on the whole off-limits pretence, when there's a tiny two-year-old cry from the next room.

He immediately goes still, but he doesn't let me go.

"She's awake," I whisper against his mouth, my voice catching.

He rests his forehead against mine. He's breathing hard, and his gaze is possessive.

As my pulse pounds, I wriggle out of his tight grasp. He lets me down, but doesn't let me go.

I lean back against the bookcase, trying to create some space between us within the caged confines of his body. "We shouldn't have done that."

He pretends to agree with me, nodding, but the look on his face says otherwise.

"Alexei!"

"What? No, it was so bad. Especially when you moaned into my mouth. That was the worst."

Oh my God.

"No, you can't say that," I protest weakly. "I work for you."

He smiles slowly, confusion still tugging his brow a little. He looks confounded. "Do you? I don't think you've sent me a contract yet, solnishko."

A startled sob bursts out of me, and I turn it into a laugh because I have no other choice.

His gaze feels like a caress as he searches my face. "Do you need a minute?"

"I need more than a minute." I close my eyes and press my head back against the bookcase behind me. "This *really* is a bad idea. We can't do that again."

He kisses my throat. "Okay."

"I mean it." I don't sound like I do, though. I sound weak and needy and very persuadable.

He groans and steps back. "Coffee, then?"

My pulse hammers in my ears. "Yeah."

"I'll—"

He's interrupted by a now indignant call from the next room. "Papa?"

He groans and squeezes my hips one last time before stepping back.

"I'll make the coffee," I whisper before darting past him and down the stairs, as if I'm being chased. By him. By the kiss. By the stupid sounds I made while he kissed me.

I fire up the espresso machine and pretend that my lips aren't still swollen and my panties aren't probably soaked.

If he'd wanted to have sex, I'd have gone along with it, I'm sure.

I will *not* think about how his bare skin felt under my fingers.

Nope.

As I finish making the second cup of espresso, Alexei

strides in holding Inessa. I slide it to him, then grab her a sippy cup of milk and a muffin.

She sits in her highchair without argument, and if I hadn't made out with her father to start the day, I'd think that was another win.

"Do you like eggs?" he asks, as if this we're having a normal post-road trip morning.

"I can make them," I mumble, not looking at him.

"I'm offering." And there's an edge to his voice now, that says maybe it's not a completely normal morning for him.

He leans against the counter beside me, arms folded over that broad, bare chest. He makes the kitchen feel way too cozy, makes it feel as small and intimate as the library upstairs.

"Actually," I say, my voice pitching a little high, "since it's your day off, I thought I'd go out for a bit."

"This early?"

"Yeah." I force a shrug. "Becca said something about a Pilates class. And I need to do some shopping."

Although instead of going to buy more clothes, I should be buying a plane ticket straight back to Minneapolis.

No, I don't need to run away. I simply need to get away from his bare chest for a few hours.

His brow lifts, but he just nods slowly. "Okay."

"Cool," I say, not sounding *cool* at all. "Great. What time do you need me back?"

"Take all the time you want. We'll be fine all day. We'll

go to the hospital, won't we, little one? Shall we visit Baba?"

"Emmy too," Inessa said solemnly.

I shake my head. "I gotta run some errands, baby girl. You know how you don't like to go to six different places? That's what I'm going to do this morning. Go to *all the places* in one morning so I don't have to do that with you tomorrow and the next day!"

She laughs, like I'm being silly, but five days into knowing her, I'm completely serious. Our days just go better when we have one thing to do in the morning, one thing to do after a nap, and that's it.

I shoot back my own espresso and then hightail it back upstairs, to the scene of the kissing crime.

The first thing I do is text the WAG chat to see if Becca really is going to a Pilates class this morning. The next thing I do is search for a walk-in clinic that is open this morning, because the way that Alexei looks at me isn't safe, and I'm not the innocent girl from two years ago.

I don't think that accepting this job was a mistake. He needs my help right now, and *Inessa* needs me right now.

But it's getting harder and harder to separate the professional from the personal.

Maybe there's another reason that I'm here right now, something private and intimate. Maybe we have unfinished business to deal with, Alexei and me.

I know that he's not the person for me.

He's too worldly and I'm too much of a Midwest college girl. Deep down, I will always be that person when it comes to him. My heart is too soft, too innocent despite my effort to change, for me to enter into what I'm sure would be an incredibly hot fling with my boss.

So I'm going to resist the pull between us.

But I'm not stupid. I can feel myself reacting to him, and so I need to take some precautions just in case I make a terrible mistake and let Alexei act on the promise in his eyes.

If we kiss like that again, it might go further than we expect, and I'm not going to be showing up on his doorstep nine months later with another baby surprise.

Your girl needs birth control pills, and she needs them *stat*.

CHAPTER 23
ALEXEI

The kiss consumes all of my thoughts until we get to the hospital mid-morning—and I find out the window on quality alone time with my temporary nanny has just slammed shut.

"What do you mean, they're discharging you?"

My mother shrugs, as if she didn't just have a heart attack less than a week ago. "They say I can go home."

"But you're sick!"

"I can be sick at home." She rattles a pill bottle. "They say I'll recover better in my own bed."

But her bed is two doors down from where I dry humped Emery against a bookcase this morning.

"Great," I say weakly.

And it is great, of course.

I don't want my mother to spend a minute longer in the hospital than she needs to, I just thought she needed to for a few more days.

I thought I had more time.

ALEXEI

My parents are coming home today

EMERY

I just got back, I'll move my stuff back to
the basement

The basement. Two floors away is too far. *What are you going to do when she's on a whole other continent, asshole?* Fuck.

No, you can't

Why not?

My parents need it

...

She literally spells out the ellipses. I laugh out loud, drawing my dad's attention.

"What is it?"

I shake my head. "Nothing. Just Emery being funny."

"Emmy funny," Inessa repeats solemnly, nodding her head.

We'll talk about it when I get home

Nothing to talk about

That's where she's wrong. We still have *everything* to talk about.

———

It takes two hours to get the formal discharge. After my mom shows the physiotherapist that she can manage a flight of stairs, we're given the all clear, and I push her wheelchair out to the car while my dad carries Inessa.

At home, Emery meets us at the front door. She's showered and done her hair in soft beachy waves, and she's wearing a new outfit, black high-waisted pants with a belt and a soft, flowy white t-shirt.

She smiles politely to me, then more broadly at my mom. "Mrs. Artyomov, you look great."

"Not true," my mom says with a laugh. "Thank you."

Emery takes her coat. "Let me get you settled on the couch. Do you want tea?"

I translate into Russian, even though it's probably not necessary, since she's already nodding.

By the time I get Inessa's coat and shoes off, Emery's already in the kitchen, pulling mugs down with her back to me.

Inessa runs into the living room, clambering up onto the couch next to her Baba.

"Let's be gentle," I caution.

My mom whispers something to Inessa and she immediately sits down quietly, leaning against her grandmother.

Which means I have ten seconds to go talk to her babysitter, maybe.

"Deda?" I say, and my dad waves his hand.

Yes, go, we're fine.

Painfully aware that we aren't alone, I walk into the kitchen.

Emery passes me one of the mugs without looking at me, her hand steady, her expression perfectly blank.

I take it. Our fingers don't touch.

I hate that they don't touch.

"Can I speak to you for a minute?"

"I'm making tea."

"After that."

"They like it strong." I put the mug down and catch her wrist. Her pulse leaps against my fingertips. "Please."

She pulls her arm free, but then nods.

I thought this house was huge when I bought it, but I'm suddenly very aware of how open the main floor is.

And if we disappear upstairs, that will draw attention.

Emery rolls her eyes and grabs my hand, pulling me into the walk-in pantry just off the kitchen.

I close the door behind me. "Okay. This will do."

"I apologize for reacting the way I did when you told me. Obviously, I understand that your parents can't be upstairs. Downstairs is quieter, and there's a kitchenette down there. I'll arrange to stay somewhere else while you are home and—"

"Somewhere else?" I back her up, until she's against the shelves for the second time today, and I'm bracketing her between my arms. "Oh no, Emery. I need you to stay here."

"I— I *can't.*"

"Why not?"

Her mouth falls open. "Are you really going to make me say it?"

"Because we kissed?"

"Because of our history, Alexei. Because of all the reasons the kiss was a mistake."

"Didn't taste like a mistake to me." I drop my gaze to her mouth. "I want to do it again."

"Not going to happen."

"You enjoyed it."

"That's irrelevant."

Actually, it's very relevant.

She repeats her protest. "I cannot live down the hall from you. And now that your parents have returned, we need to find you better childcare."

"You are the best."

"I am *not*."

"So you think I should hire a nanny, hmm? You want someone else to sleep just down the hall from me? Meet me in the hallway in the early morning, wearing almost nothing?"

"I was *not* wearing *nothing*."

"You didn't want me to see how tight your pretty nipples got when I looked at you."

"It was cold."

"But I could see feel how hot your pussy got for me, Emery. You couldn't hide that. And you didn't want to hide it, did you? You rubbed yourself on me like a happy little kitten."

She growls under her breath and I duck my head, covering her mouth with mine.

Instantly, her hands come up to clutch at my head, to hold us together as I sip at her, as I taste her lower lip and then tease my way deeper.

It's only been a few hours, and it feels like it's been too long already.

This time, though, I won't take too much.

This time, I'll leave my sweet sunshine girl wanting more.

I rear back, hating the way she gasps in confusion—but loving the way she clings to me for a second before she finds herself.

Her hands drop to her sides.

"I know," I grind out. "We can't do that again."

She gapes at me for a minute, then finds her voice, even if it's a bit faint. "You need to hire a nanny."

"With a no-kissing policy firmly in place?"

Her gaze flares possessively. "You can't kiss—"

I cup her face in my hand. "Careful, solnishko. You wouldn't want me to think you might be jealous."

"I'm not your..." She make a frustrated little growl in the back of her throat.

I lean in and brush my lips against hers ever so lightly. "You are, sunshine." I whisper. "And you always have been."

CHAPTER 24
EMERY

Alexei doesn't try to corner me—or kiss me—again for the rest of the day.

He and his father spend the afternoon moving everything of his parents' downstairs to the basement apartment, which I have to admit is better for them—it has a walk-out side door, which is easier for Maria to go to her follow-up appointments. She has a calendar full of them. Next week she will start an outpatient rehab program that will last for months.

Alexei's parents need quiet, and stability, and I need to get over myself.

I move into their old bedroom upstairs, which has a bigger bed than the daybed in the library, and a proper dresser and closet, both of which were emptied for me to use.

It will be easier to be this close to Inessa, I can see that.

I make dinner for everyone, then Alexei tells me he has bedtime covered, and the rest of the night is my own.

I take the opportunity to escape up to the third floor and get a long workout in, exhausting my body in an effort to ignore my racing mind.

Just as I'm making some notes in my fitness app, a text message from my brother flashes at the top of the screen.

Then again.

And again.

I swipe out of the app and groan, because Forrest has started a new group chat with me and Alexei, and he's named it *My Hamilton Fam.*

> **FORREST**
>
> Dinner tomorrow, yeah?
>
> I guess we need to include Mom and Dad, too
>
> Em Bear, can you cook? Is that imposing too much? We can order in, but I'm guessing you guys don't want to take Inessa to a restaurant.
>
> Full disclosure, I arrived at that conclusion because I'm banging this single mom
>
> TMI

Oh no.

I can't decide if I want to scream or laugh.

Another buzz.

> I'm starting to think I'm the only one in this conversation
>
> Bueller? Bueller?

I push to my feet and check the time—it's almost ten. Inessa is probably asleep, but Alexei might be trapped next to her.

EMERY

> Hey, lay off the mass texting, some people are putting toddlers to sleep

> Did the hot single mom not teach you about bedtime?

FORREST

> Her kids are almost my age

> Wow

> It's amazing

> Save it for the brothers only group chat, you weirdo (compliment)

> Fine fine but what about dinner?

> Alexei's putting Inessa to bed, so try to be patient

> Not my strong suit

I wince as I imagine Alexei watching all of this, trying to keep his phone silent while lying next to Inessa.

Or maybe he knows better and he's got Forrest on auto-mute.

I tidy up the workout space, then turn the light off and quietly head back down to the second floor.

As soon as I step into the hallway, I hear my name called, low and soft, from Alexei's bedroom.

I turn and look through the open door. He's changed into sweatpants and a t-shirt that clings to his thick shoulders, and he's standing at the foot of his bed, folding clothes from one laundry basket and putting them in another.

Was it only this morning that our positions were reversed? That I came out of his room and saw him standing at the top of the stairs?

Now it's him who stares at me, who drags *his* gaze down my body as he finishes pairing up two socks.

I'm barefoot, because I left my shoes upstairs, and my cropped tank top and tiny shorts are soaked with sweat, but Alexei's gaze suggests he sees something different.

He slowly strides to the doorway.

I back up a little.

His searching gaze follows me, lingering on my bare legs again, sending a bolt of heat through me. When he finally finds my face once more, he's wrapped his hand around the doorframe, his knuckles turning white as he grips the wood.

"I saw the texts," he says, his voice low and unreadable.

"I'm sorry that my family is so much."

He shrugs. "How do you feel about dinner?"

That's not the question I expected. "What do you mean?"

"Will you be comfortable having them here?" There's an unexpected hesitancy in his expression.

I don't know how to read that. "That's your decision to make."

His brows snap together, fast. "I don't like that."

I cross my arms, suddenly cold despite the heat lingering on my skin from the workout. "Like what?"

"You sacrificing your comfort for your family's preferences."

I laugh. "That's my entire life."

The words come out sharper than I mean them to.

"It's your house," I add quietly. "You're allowed to decide who's in it."

He doesn't flinch, but his jaw tightens like I've said something wrong. "You live here, too."

"Temporarily."

Alexei shifts, stepping into the hallway's dim light, his gaze dipping—again—to the hem of my shorts. His throat bobs as he swallows. "You think that's all this is?"

I freeze. "What else would it be?"

He doesn't answer.

He just looks at me, eyes dark and steady, and it feels like my heart is sprinting in place. I want to look away. I don't.

Inside, everything is tight. Twisting. My body wants to lean into him, wants to feel that heat again.

I can't let that happen.

I clear my throat. "It's just dinner. We can do dinner."

He snorts, and the tension breaks just enough to breathe. "If it gets awkward, we'll just ask Forrest about his new friend."

A smile tugs at my mouth. "Do you know anything about her?"

He shakes his head. "We don't talk about women."

My eyebrows shoot up in surprise.

He shrugs. "*I* don't talk about women. He says stuff sometimes, but those messages tonight were for you. To get a rise out of you."

I groan. "I walked right into it, too."

"But he gave you a good tool to use against him tomorrow." Alexei's gaze slides again, like he can't stop looking at me.

I shift my weight, suddenly aware of just how little I'm wearing. His gaze flicks back up to my face, trying to be respectful—but it's too late. I see it. And deep in my belly, I *feel* it.

I need out of this moment before I do something stupid. "I should shower."

"Okay." A smile tugs at the corner of his mouth.

I make it halfway down the hallway before I glance back.

His eyes are locked on my ass. Slowly, unashamedly, he drags them up to meet my gaze. "Goodnight, Emery."

He steps back into his bedroom.

I race into my own room, and close the door before I lean back against it and close my eyes.

This thin door is all that between us now. I'm no longer two floors away from him in a suite that is separate from the rest of the house.

There's a lot to be said for me living up here, close to Inessa. That will be easier.

But now he's going to hear me go into the bathroom

for my shower. Hear the water turn on, and know that I'm peeling off my workout clothes and standing under the hot spray, rinsing off the day and trying hard not to think about how good his gaze feels on my skin.

That part… That's going to be so much harder.

CHAPTER 25
ALEXEI

The next morning I have a practice and team meeting at the arena.

When I get there, I pass two local reporters in the hall. They give me friendly nods but don't try to talk. That's been the routine since I arrived.

The first time I spoke to the Hamilton press, I was shellshocked—fresh off the plane, just traded, translating every thought and emotion into a second language. I stumbled over my words, and they decided I didn't speak English well. I've done nothing to correct that impression in six months.

Some assumptions are useful.

I do my turns pre- and post-game as the team asks me to, but the questions are always pretty simple and I give canned answers.

Every win I can get the team is a good one.

Is six wins in a row a good streak? Nice. Is it the season record? Not yet? Not good enough.

And if they ask me about something I don't want to talk about, which isn't often, I fall back on the language barrier. *What do you mean? Sorry, can you say again?*

This is my first time playing on a team without any other Russian players, which means that behind the scenes, I can't rely on a buddy to translate. So my teammates know the truth. I speak English just fine. I contribute in meetings, on the bench, on the ice. But even with them, sometimes it's easier to pretend I don't catch every joke, every barb, every invitation to open up.

Sometimes I need the space that silence gives me.

Today, I'm grateful for it, because I didn't get even a second alone with Emery this morning, and it's put me on edge.

She's very good at putting distance between us, especially after an unexpected bit of closeness.

Yeah, you dummy. She doesn't want to get in deep with the guy who hurt her. Not breaking news.

I don't know how to reconcile that with the way she clings to me when we kiss. But that's a problem best solved later. After dinner with her family. After I play her brother on the ice tomorrow. After the Grangers all leave town again, and we can have some breathing space to get back to figuring out who we are to each other now, instead of rehashing what we were two years ago.

I stride into the locker room, change quickly, and head to the lounge room where we eat our team meals. Hayden "Hooner" Calhoun spots me from across the buffet. "Arty! How's your mom?"

"Yeah, good. She came home yesterday." I duck my head as a cheer goes up around the room.

Roan "Smash" Dodaj comes out of nowhere to wrap a big, heavy arm around my shoulders. "Buddy, that's amazing."

"Thanks, man."

Hayden gets a text message on his phone that makes him put his plate down and head around the corner for privacy, leaving Smash to guide me to the food. "You ready for tomorrow night? What can we get you to fuel you? Gotta keep that winning streak alive."

I shove him away and grab a plate.

Undeterred, he narrates what I select. "Veggie hash, turkey sausage, and oatmeal. Good choices."

Kieran Marsh, one of the players I look up to the most on the team, joins us and grabs a plate. "Arty, good to see you. How's your morning going?"

I can hardly tell him the truth, which is that I woke up early to jerk off thinking about Emery's hot, wet mouth. And now I'm annoyed by my teammates.

What I say instead is, "It's going."

It's one of those English phrases I picked up early, one that always sounds casual and natural, but doesn't invite further discussion.

Dodaj looks back and forth between us, but Marsh isn't a huge talker—one of the reasons I like him so much —and that's the end of the conversation.

Sighing, I give the oversized puppy D-man my full attention. "Do you need something, Smash?"

"Just a win tomorrow night against your former team."

"Yep." As I hear myself say it, popping the p the way Emery does, I grin.

His eyebrows go up. "Is that a smile?"

"Fuck off." I carry my plate to a table as Calhoun rejoins us.

"I smile," I say to both of them.

They exchange a doubtful look.

"I smile," I repeat with more of a growl. "I literally just smiled."

"And it was noteworthy," Dodaj says.

I roll my eyes and start eating. Then I stop and lift my chin towards Calhoun, wanting to be thoughtful. "Everything okay with you?"

He looks startled. "Yeah?"

"You got a text message and had to leave."

He rapid blinks a few times as his cheeks turn red. "Becca sent me a private photo," he finally stammers.

We both laugh.

"See? I'm fucking smiling," I point out.

Then I stab a piece of hash with my fork. End of conversation.

He doesn't mind. Just turns to Dodaj and starts debating last night's games from around the league. I listen with half an ear, letting the rhythm of their voices wash over me.

Our captain, Jenson Hale, joins the table with a nod and a calm presence. He's young for the captaincy, but he's going to be a franchise stable for a decade, and he has the right personality. Our teammates call Haler "Mom" sometimes, and after the last captain got pushed out—both from the team and his marriage—some loving parenting is what the team needs.

Especially today and tomorrow, because that former captain? I was traded for him, and he's now on Forrest's team in Calgary. He had a broken jaw at the start of the season, so when the two teams faced off in Calgary, he wasn't on the ice.

Tomorrow night, though, Max Tilman will be in the building where he once wore the C, and it's going to be ugly.

The room fills slowly. Malik Zondi slides into the seat next to me, apparently unaffected by my show of jealousy over Emery. "Good news, boys. I'm out of the no contact jersey for practice today. Might be on the ice tomorrow for the dragon slaying."

Dodaj and Calhoun drum on the table in unison, making our plates jump.

"Fuck yeah," Haler says, pumping his fist.

Marsh stops on his way to the next table, where he'll sit with the other veterans on the team, and gives Zondi a fist bump. Where Haler is our "Mom", Marshie is "Dad". Part emotional support veteran, part mentor, part myth.

"Best vengeance is a dub," Marshie says dryly.

And that's all the reframing our table needs.

The conversation shifts to the practice and team meeting ahead. One of the coaches comes in and writes the schedule on the whiteboard, because we need to be kept on track.

I finish eating, clear my dishes to be nice to the kitchen staff, and then head to the dressing room.

I can hear some of my other teammates down the hall, having treatments done first. According to the schedule posted, some other guys are in pre-practice meetings with the coaching staff, too.

For right now, I have the dressing room to myself, and I like it that way.

I think about how surprised Dodaj was by me smiling.

I smile, don't I?

I laugh with Inessa all the time.

Emery sure as fuck makes me smile, even when she shouldn't. Even when she's mad at me.

If it wasn't incriminating as fuck, I'd find the trainer who saw us together on the ice and drag her out to testify to how recently I've smiled in this building.

But I don't need my teammates to start thinking about something being different about me. Not right now. We're on the cusp of making the playoffs. Tomorrow is an important game in that regard, too, to get us two important points and move us even further into safety.

My teammates want a win to beat Max Tilman.

I want a win to extend my streak, because seven wins in a row…surely that will secure my starting spot in the playoffs.

And if not, then I'll turn my attention to the next game after that. Eight. Nine would put me in the lead across the league for the season. Ten would break me away not only from Makie's recent seasons, but most of the pack, and put me in Vezina territory.

Not the point.

The point is always the play-offs. Team first, personal accomplishments second.

But for the young man who just two years ago was eager to get a single start, and then fucking missed it because he was at the fucking hospital becoming a dad, it's hard to pretend this run of wins doesn't matter.

It fucking matters to me.

———

The house smells like apples and cinnamon when I return from practice, and it sounds…exactly like the arena I just left.

"That's it, pass it to me, put it on my tape!"

There's a little whacking sound, hard plastic hitting rubber. No actual tape on those mini sticks, but Emery is right into it, and from Inessa's giggles, so is my daughter.

Beneath it all is the upbeat bounce of a pop song, and even before I take my shoes off, I can picture the scene in the kitchen. Emery's phone propped against something, a custom playlist for Inessa on the screen. The two of them on the floor as something amazing cools on the stove. Apple pie? A cobbler?

It's wild how quickly Emery's presence has changed my home.

Quietly, I pad down the hall. The hockey game has stopped and they're whispering to each other.

I stop in the doorway.

Emery's sitting cross-legged on the floor with Inessa in front of her.

Inessa is patiently, miraculously sitting still while Emery weaves a braid down one side of my daughter's head.

I fucking stop breathing.

It makes no sense, because it's nice to see.

There's no reason for my chest to feel caved in.

She picks up a tiny pink brush that usually lives beside the couch, and causes non-stop protests when I try to use it. But Inessa has no complaints as Emery smooths out the other side of her hair, then repeats the quick but neat-looking braid.

"Papa!" Inessa calls when she spots me. She scrambles to her feet and grabs a mini stick, hacking at the rubber ball, sending into a cardboard box pinned between two kitchen chairs. "Goal!"

"Nice," I praise. "Very good goal."

I cross to Emery and offer her a hand up. She takes it, a flicker of guarded carefulness on her face when the predictable warm current of energy flows between us.

I pull her to her feet, letting her bump into me a little. A good excuse to wrap my arm around her hips and see that she's standing just fine before letting go.

"You've turned her into a proper hockey girl," I murmur. "Didn't take long."

"She's a natural." Emery's voice is steady, but her eyes keep moving—like she doesn't quite trust herself to look at me too long, but she can't help but glance back every few seconds.

Fuck, I like that way too much.

"Her braids look good," I say, moving closer again, my hand finding its way to the small of Emery's back, just barely touching her—but it's enough to feel her warmth radiating against my palm. "She sat still for you."

"I told her if she won our game, I would braid her hair in victory." She twists to the side, showing me that her own hair is braided the same way, matching French braids on either side of her head. She taps the end of the braid. "It's the glitter clips. They're only for champions."

"Champion," Inessa parrots, sailing into my leg with a proud and victorious hug.

I crouch down, resting my elbows on my knees. "You want to play with me next?"

"No goalie," Inessa says solemnly.

And fair point—I could block the little cardboard box too easily. "No goalie," I agree. "Just one-on-one."

She finds Emery's stick and shoves it at me. "Papa stick."

Emery drops the ball for us at the face off point, and we have a fierce battle. Inessa gets the first goal, I get the second, and as soon as she scores again, she declares victory, tackling me to the ground.

"Papa juggle," she says, waving the ball above my face.

I hold my hands up. "Okay, go."

She drops it and I snatch it out of the air.

Giggle, she goes to find another one as I start to toss that one in a loop.

While she hunts for another ball, I look over at Emery

and find her watching me out of the corner of her eye as she tidies around the stove.

I grin, and she blushes.

Remember when we first met, I want to ask her. *Remember how we knew before we'd even said something that it would always be like this?*

But then it wasn't always like this.

This has only ever been a temporary gift the universe then takes away from me.

I'm going to appreciate the fuck out of it while she's here, though.

"Papa, catch…"

I snap my attention back just in time to catch a second ball sailing through the air.

"Good reflexes," Emery says.

I wink.

Inessa finds me a third ball, and then returns to sitting on me as I juggle for her.

"What did you make for dessert, by the way?" I ask Emery.

"Apple crisp. Two versions, one classic and one high protein, low sugar for hockey players two weeks away from playoffs."

I snort. "Your brother isn't making the playoffs."

She laughs out loud. "Okay, fair. Then you have an entire tray of healthy crisp all to yourself. Don't worry, it will freeze. Although your mom might like it. I need to see how it fits into her recommended nutrition plan."

"Have you seen them yet today?"

"Briefly. Your dad came up to get Inessa for a Baba

visit, and I got a shopping list from them for the fridge downstairs. I thought I'd run errands during nap time."

Inessa gives me a horrified look and slides away, grabbing her mini stick and beelining it to the living room.

No longer her personal jester, I catch the balls in one hand and set them aside.

Emery laughs and comes over to offer me a hand up.

I take it, letting her pull me to my feet with surprising strength.

"And here I was hoping for braiding lessons during nap time," I murmur once I'm towering above her.

The basement door is closed.

My daughter is out of sight, playing in her toy nook in the TV room.

We're all alone.

It might be my only chance all day to steal a kiss.

"You made me laugh today," I tell her as I tuck an errant strand of sunshine behind her ear. "In front of my teammates. They accused me of smiling."

"I've heard you have a grumpy reputation on the team," she whispers back.

"You're a threat to that."

"How so?"

I can't tell her that she's always on my mind. That the littlest things make me think of her, and every time I do, another crack forms in the protective shell I've built around myself for the last two years.

"Because you're distracting," I growl before reaching for one of the sparkly clips holding the end of her braids.

Her gaze doesn't leave my face as I pause.

"I like your hair in braids." My voice is husky. "But I like it wild and free even better."

Her lips part, her eyes darken, and she lets out a shuddering little exhale that I feel all the way to the base of my spine.

I pinch the clip free and toss it to the counter.

Do the same on the other side.

And then I loosen her blonde waves from their braids, spilling the silky strands over my fingers before I cup her head in my hands and tip her face up so I can kiss her.

CHAPTER 26
EMERY

For a kiss that Alexei telegraphed was coming with clear, careful, and slow intent, it still takes me by surprise when his mouth slots over mine and his hunger takes over.

It's not a long kiss, but it's deep and powerful, and it leaves my lips tingling in a way that I can still feel hours later.

After he takes Inessa upstairs for a nap.

While I go grocery shopping.

And even after my family arrives and I've had to school my kiss-dazed expression into a neutral mask.

My parents head downstairs to catch up with Alexei's parents, and Forrest and Alexei follow me into the kitchen.

"Fucking hell, did you make crisp?" Forrest feigns his knees buckling beneath him and grabs the counter for support. "I'm not strong enough to resist that."

"I made a healthy version, too."

He scoffs. "Fuck that, we're not making the playoffs."

Alexei's gaze meets mine, as if to say *I told you so*, and I smother a laugh.

Forrest glances between us. "What?"

"Nothing."

Alexei opens the fridge. "Do you want a beer?"

Forrest shakes his head. "I'm not that checked out yet. Gimme a seltzer water." He grins after Alexei hands one over. "Thanks. Looking forward to scoring on you tomorrow."

Alexei gives him a deadpan glare. "Not going to happen. I've been studying the Granger weaknesses."

Forrest laughs.

Alexei doesn't, and a weird little sizzle skates down my spine.

My brother narrows his eyes. "What do you mean?"

"Nothing," I say at the same time as Alexei says, "Your sister is a better skater than you. Did you know that?"

I sigh.

Forrest frowns. "Fuck off."

"The truth hurts," I say lightly, pushing past Alexei and giving him a *leave it alone* look that he immediately ignores.

I'm never going to worry about my brothers' feelings being hurt—hurting their feelings is a fun sport, after all. But I don't like conversations that bring up why I quit hockey.

Unfortunately, Alexei doesn't know that.

He claps Forrest on the shoulder. "*She* can score on me. She came to practice last week and smoked me. You, though…You are slow in comparison and you project your target too clearly. You have no hope."

My brother swings around to stare at me. "You skated with him?"

"I skate," I say like it's no big deal.

"Not with us."

"You live in Calgary," I point out. "A city I haven't visited in…"

Thankfully, Forrest doesn't notice the hitch in my voice.

Two years.

Alexei notices, though. Of course he does.

From somewhere that's not right in the kitchen, my phone chimes. I've had to turn on sound notifications because Inessa has a habit of running away with my phone now.

"Excuse me," I say, grateful for the interruption.

"What are you smiling at?" I hear my brother say behind me.

"Your sister," Alexei says, and I trip over my own feet.

Pivoting, I glare at him.

He shrugs before leaning back against the counter. "So tell me about this woman you're seeing…"

As he predicted, Forrest is happy to talk about himself.

I find my phone—wedged in the couch. It's a group chat message from Kiley, to the WAGs (and me), but excluding Shannon.

KILEY

Hi friends! I know that tomorrow's game against Calgary is going to be emotional for Shannon. She wants to go to the game, though, so I think we should surround her with as much love and community as we can. You're all invited to our place first, and then we're going to walk over to the arena as a group.

ANI

I'm making her a bedazzled Armstrong jersey to wear! Jerseys optional, of course, but it would be cute.

BECCA

Charlie and I will be there! #HighlandersStrong #TeamShannon

I wasn't going to go to the game. I was going to use Inessa as an excuse to stay home and avoid my parents, my brother, and the goalie I keep kissing.

But I can't ignore my friend in her time of need.

Heart pounding, I watch myself type back a response I would never have sent only a week ago.

EMERY

Count me in (I'll have Inessa with me)

"Everything okay?" Alexei asks, coming up behind me.

I glance up at him. "Yeah."

"Okay." He glances over me. "I'm going to see if Mama is feeling up to coming upstairs for dinner. And maybe rescue her from Inessa."

"And my parents," I say dryly.

He winks and heads to the basement.

I take a deep breath and join my brother in the kitchen again.

He salutes me with his can of water. "You're a real gem for helping Arty out through all this."

"He's paying me," I say as I open the fridge, even though that's not completely true.

He will, once I send him a contract.

"Sure, but this can't be what you want to do with your life," Forrest says.

I shove a veggie tray I made earlier at his chest. "Put this on the island."

He does that without complaint, so I give him a little truth.

"Sure, veggie trays, grilled chicken, and apple crisp isn't really where I see my career going, but I didn't love the personal chef stuff back home, either. The program that I'm going to do in Switzerland has a great reputation with fine dining chefs in Europe, so I can leverage that into some stage placements."

"In Europe."

I shrug. "Yes! Why not?"

"Because…" He frowns.

"Because we live in Minneapolis? Except you live in Calgary and Logan lives in Buffalo and Wyatt lives in Utah, and if any of you couldn't make it in the NHL, you'd one hundred percent be playing on pro contracts in…" I draw my hand out between us, asking him to fill in the blank.

"But you're the baby." He makes a face. "I'm still struggling with you being old enough to drink."

"Fuck right off," I mutter.

He dips his head in acknowledgement. "Fair."

I pull the three dips that I've made out of the fridge and take them to the veggie tray, making a bit of room for them. And once they're nestled in, I add a few herbs in around the bowl to give the tray a bit of complexity.

"Is that a rainbow?" Forrest asks, his head tipping to the side.

I grin. "Yep. Saw the Duchess of Sussex do it on her TV show and borrowed the idea. I've been making little food rainbows for Inessa all week and she gobbles everything up."

"And what are the dips?" He deftly swipes a purple carrot spear.

I point to them one by one. "Whipped feta ranch, known simply as *ranch* if Dad asks. A sweet beet dip because Inessa likes all things pink and Alexei's mom loves beets. And the last one is caramelized onion hummus with a spiced olive oil drizzle."

"Damn." He scoops some of the hummus, pops the carrot in his mouth, and groans low and long. "All right," he mumbles. "Go to Europe and get even more amazing."

I blush. "Thanks."

He washes the bite down, then leans in close. "Hey, so… is Arty dating someone?"

My hand slips and a celery stick falls into the ranch.

He sees it.

"Emery."

"I don't know."

"Liar."

"I'm not lying." My voice shakes. "I, uh, haven't asked."

I cross the kitchen and grab my notebook, pretending to make a recipe note just so I'm doing *something* other than being completely, pathetically transparent.

Forrest follows me. "So you *have* noticed something's up."

"Why are you like this?"

He grins, all older-brother smugness. "Because I'm good at reading people. And Arty has that look. You know the one."

Maybe I'm not as transparent as I feared if the only person he thinks he can read here is Alexei. "I really don't."

"He's quieter. Looser in the shoulders. That's a man who's gotten laid recently."

Blood rushes to my cheeks so fast it feels like my ears are ringing.

"I'm serious," he goes on. "He looks like he's not carrying the whole world on his back for once. Like maybe he's got someone who makes it a little easier to breathe."

I swallow. "Like your older woman?"

"Oh yeah." Forrest whistles and gets a dreamy look in his eye. "She makes it a *lot* easier to breathe, let me tell you."

Alexei was right. Forrest is easily diverted into talking about himself, and that saves me—for about seven minutes, as he waxes eloquently about his situationship.

"It turns out, the longest and best relationship in my life is one where it's someone else who puts all the boundaries up, because it's just sex—"

He cuts himself off as the basement door opens and Inessa twirls into the living room with her dad right behind her.

Forrest coughs into his fist. "Anyway, I'm just saying."

I meet his gaze as steadily as I can manage. Since he's not going to let this go, I need to shut it down. "He's not sleeping with anyone."

"You sure?"

"Yep."

Because I don't know if I make him more relaxed, exactly, but three kisses in to whatever is swirling between us, I do know that we're both changed by it.

So yeah, there might be *a woman*. But technically, Alexei hasn't slept with her…yet.

CHAPTER 27
ALEXEI

Emery's family doesn't do quiet, ever, and it escalates when her mom decides to get her other three brothers on a group video chat.

"Mom, we're about to have dinner," Emery protests.

"Just for a minute, I want to see all my babies together."

Emery huffs and turns around, turning a little pink when she sees that I'm watching her. I like the way her gaze holds mine and everything else fades away.

She re-braided her hair after I took it down earlier to kiss her, and I'm already thinking about scattering those glitter clips once everyone is gone.

Which isn't helpful when we're surrounded by her family. I clear my throat. "What do you need help with?"

"There's a salad…" She steps around my dad, who has crowded in to wave at her brothers on camera. Then she picks up Inessa, meeting me in front of the fridge.

"I don't like salad," Inessa tells me in Russian.

Emery tickles her. "No Russian secrets, baby girl."

"Sorry," Inessa says in English, burying her face in Emery's shoulder.

"She wants extra lettuce," I say.

"Papa!"

"What?" I switch to Russian.

"We don't like salad," Inessa protests.

"But we will like Emery's salads because she is an amazing chef."

"I heard my name." Emery narrows her eyes at me.

"Only good things, I promise." I gesture for Inessa. "Give me the troublemaker. I'll be the prison guard who traps her in her highchair."

Inessa protests, but Emery needs both hands to take the chicken she's prepped over to the grill pan on the stove.

I distract my daughter with the rainbow veggie tray.

"Look at that plating," I say loudly, for the chef's benefit. Emery rewards me with a secret smile. "Isn't it beautiful?"

"Uh huh." Inessa nods enthusiastically.

Once we're all settled around the table, Emery turns to my dad. "How do you say bon appetit in Russian?"

"Priyatnogo appetita," he says quickly, then slows it down.

She repeats the syllables, then speeds it up. Her accent is unmistakably American, but the effort is A+.

I want to know what else she'd like to learn in Russian.

Beside me, Inessa picks up a purple carrot and dabs it

in her special pink dip and then tries feeding it to Forrest. He plays along. Emery watches them, one elbow on the table, eyes bright.

For a second, it feels like the last two years didn't happen, that we're on an alternate timeline where this is *our* table. Our family, combined, instead of two families connected primarily by hockey and crisis.

And then Emery's mother turns to me with a big, wide smile and says, "And how is Tatyana, Alexei?"

Emery's fork pauses halfway to her mouth.

As if I needed a clearer reminder from the universe about *why* our two families will never be one. Regret churns in my chest as I force a polite smile. "She's fine, I believe. We haven't spoken recently."

"Because she is infantile," my mother adds in Russian. "She only cares about her jet-setting yacht life."

"Mama."

"What? I almost died. I can say what I think now and you can't stop me."

My father laughs. "She has a point."

"Excuse us for speaking in Russian," I say to the Grangers.

"I'm sure it's very complicated," Emery says under her breath, and if nobody else notices the jealousy-tinged sarcasm, that's a miracle.

I narrow my eyes at her. She knows exactly how complicated it is, because I bloody well told her.

My mother keeps going in Russian. "You don't need to be polite about her to these people. They are like family."

I wish they were.

But the way a simple dinner has so quickly gone off the rails, I don't have much hope of that happening. My chance for that was two years ago and I blew it.

"Rice?" Emery asks brightly, picking up the bowl and passing it along.

I wish I'd sat next to her, so I could take it from her and make sure our fingers brush in the contact.

I crave connection with her and am irritated that tomorrow's game has brought everyone here, when we could otherwise have a quiet night together.

How many of those will we have before she leaves us behind?

Not enough.

I grab the salad, following her lead. I take some, then pass it along, and everyone follows suit. Our plates fill with the delicious dinner, and the conversation turns to the game tomorrow, and the rest of the season.

I'm on edge until everyone is gone. My parents have retired for the night. Emery's family has left for the hotel.

Now it's just the three of us.

Inessa has brought her favourite blanket to the edge of the living room, where the carpet stops before the kitchen tile, and she's spread it out for some of her toys to have a rest. Tucking them in for the night as she hums to herself.

Emery moves around the kitchen, barefoot and quiet,

scraping plates and loading the dishwasher. A few wavy strands of hair have tumbled free from her braids.

"I should apologize," I start to say, then stop.

She goes still, her head tipping to the side. Not quite looking at me, but listening.

I laugh a little, under my breath. "Fuck, I have so much to apologize for, Emery. But also, dinner was..." I trail off, searching for the right word. "Really fucking good."

Her expression softens just a touch.

And yes, I need to apologize again and again and again, but I probably need to praise her even more. I lean into that, liking the way it lifts her chin. "You're a spectacular cook. As good a chef as you are a hockey player."

Her laugh comes quiet and unexpected, like I caught her off guard. And now we're both smiling, at least a little.

"It wasn't fancy," she says.

"That's not what I said. I know you like fancy food. I wish we had more time for you to introduce me to more of it. But you make regular food special. With the little flower garnishes and the sauces and secret techniques and devices and—" I drag in a breath because my chest is tight. "I see how fucking good at it you are. I want you to know that."

She finally looks at me.

"You didn't have to do that," I say. "You don't have to do any of this. So it means a lot that you do."

Her mouth opens, then closes again. Her eyes flick

toward the living room, where Inessa is now lying flat on her back.

"I'm going to get her to bed," I say after a moment, pushing away from the counter. "But when I get back down here, I want to see you sitting in the living room, scrolling your phone. Leave the rest of the clean-up for me."

"It's fine."

"Emery. Go sit. You've done more than enough. I'll clean."

She holds my gaze, and I think she's going to argue again, but then she shrugs. "Okay. That's fair."

I exhale and nod. "Inessa, say good night to Emery."

"Night night," my daughter says, waving as I pick her up. Her gaze stays locked on our favourite person as I carry her out of the room, and she whines a bit when we start to climb the stairs.

"I know, little one," I say in Russian. I'd like Emery to come upstairs with us, too, but that would be asking even more labour from someone who has given us enough already.

Despite the whining, Inessa brushes her teeth almost entirely by herself, then picks out her own pyjamas. She's rubbing her eyes by the time I get her tucked in, and as soon as I start to read her a story in English, she rolls onto her side and falls asleep.

I turn her lamp down and put the book away, my pulse picking up.

There are no clattering kitchen noises from downstairs, so Emery has followed my stern instructions and taken a break. Good. A muscle in my jaw ticks at the thought of finding her cozy on the couch, her legs tucked underneath her.

I'd be lying to myself if I pretended that she isn't the reason I'm grabbing the baby monitor and heading for the stairs.

Yes, I want to carry some of the load tonight. She cooked. I can clean.

But I want to spend time with her, too.

I want— I need to heal some of the wounds that keep getting picked at.

In the living room, I see that Emery has turned on the TV and found a game that one of her brothers is playing in—Utah is at Montreal.

"What's the score?"

"Tied at one, top of the second."

I set the baby monitor on the counter and tackle the remaining dishes. I get everything clean and put away, then wipe down the counters.

By the time I join her on the couch, the second period is over and she's muted the talking heads on the panel in the intermission.

"I'm not sure I put the pots away in the right spot," I confess as I lean back against the cushions. Her toes are a half foot away from me, and when I stretch my arm out across the back of the sofa, I almost reach her shoulder.

Almost, but not quite.

She slides a glance my way. "How do you not know where your own pots go?"

"I'm spoiled?"

Her eyes spark with undisguised amusement. "You think?"

I inch my fingers closer to her. "Come here."

"Why, so you can undo my braids and kiss me again?" She catches her lower lip between her teeth, and fuck, yes, I want to do that. I think she wants me to as well.

But I need to do something else, first.

I snag one of her hair clips and flip it to the coffee table. "Nope."

"You're literally—" She gasps as I wrap my long arms around her and haul her up, pulling her onto my lap for a second, just a glorious fucking second where I feel the warm press of her ass against my thighs, and then I slide her to the floor in front of me.

She spins around and gapes at me. "What are you doing?"

I pluck the other clip and toss it to join its friend. "I want to learn how to braid hair. I know it's asking you to help me again, but if you teach me now, then you won't need to do Inessa's hair when I'm here."

Her expression softens. "You don't need to do this. Your mom is going to be able to take that over soon enough."

"I should be able to braid my daughter's hair," I say stubbornly. "And maybe learn where my own pots go, too."

"Maybe," she says dryly. "But I'll warn you, it's not as easy as it looks."

That might be true, but actions speak louder than words, and apologies sound hollow when I try to just *say* them. I want to show her I can be better than she expects.

"I can stop a slap shot traveling a hundred miles an hour with two guys screening me. I can learn to braid."

She smiles. This time it's real. "Fair point." She straightens out her head and shakes her hair with her fingers. "Okay, I'll show you how I do it on myself, first. Your hands will be in different positions, but this is the basic pattern. Split the hair into three sections—like this—and then cross one of the outside pieces over the middle chunk, then under the opposite side. Always keep the tension even. And as you reset your hands, you draw a little more hair into the section that just did the braiding motion. Over, under, keep it tight. Add a bit. Over, under…"

I watch as she plaits a neat braid over the crown of her head and down, until there's no more hair to add, and then she's just twisting the three strands a few more times to complete the braid.

"Got it?"

"Umm…"

She laughs and shakes her hair loose again. "Let's start with a simple braid, with just three sections, no adding hair."

She shows me how she braids three pieces of hair together, then gets me to try with her hair.

My braid doesn't look anything like hers. It's loose in places, and lopsided as well.

"Tension is the game changer," she says as she runs her fingers over my effort. "It's…" She twists and looks up at me, then plants her hand on my thigh—*whoa*—and pushes herself up, climbing onto the couch. "Sit in front of me."

"What are you…"

"I'm going to braid your hair so you can feel what I mean," she says, shoving at my shoulder.

I slide to the floor and she scoots around behind me.

Her fingertips brush the back of my neck, and I go completely still.

"Relax," she murmurs. "It doesn't hurt."

That's where she's wrong. *Hurt* might not be the right word, but it's in the right territory. *Sladkaya bol*. Sweet pain.

Her hands are warm and steady as she gathers a chunk of my hair, then divides it in three, her thumb gliding against my scalp.

"Like this," she says, tugging on the strands. "Keep it taut."

Oh, I'm fucking taut all right.

I nod like I'm absorbing it, but mostly I'm just trying not to moan out loud.

She leans closer, breath brushing my ear. "You okay?"

"Fine."

"Can you feel that? How I pull on it, keeping the pressure—"

I twist and catch her face in my hands, kissing her hard before pushing up to my knees.

I like how glassy-eyed she is, and speechless, and when I pat her hip, it takes all of my control to not keep my hands on her and haul her against me. But I've asked her to teach me a thing and I'm going to learn it. "Let me try again."

This time when she's sitting between my legs, I'm painfully aware of how soft and warm her body is. I take my time gathering her hair into three chunks, and I tug firmly, making her gasp—and then sigh.

"Tension all right?" I ask innocently.

"Mmm," she manages to get out.

I lead with my thumb, the same way she did, stroking against her scalp as I weave her hair together. Always holding taut, trying to be good even as my mind is half-distracted by being very, very bad.

The little noises she makes aren't helping.

"Ahh..."

I twist the strand in my right hand up and over and under, moving it to my left hand. Grazing my pinky finger along her neck, too, because I can multitask.

"How does it feel?" she manages to ask.

Incredible. Like silk. Like trembling, needy, horny silk. I clear my throat. "Good."

She reaches back, her fingers blindly tracing my work. "Oh, yeah, you've got it!"

I tug on the end of the braid. "Excellent."

She tries to lean forward to grab a clip, but I don't give her any slack.

She squeaks.

"Come here," I say roughly, low. I'm needy, too.

The braid starts to fall apart as she twists, as I let go and grab hold of her body instead, lifting her up to straddle my lap.

"Alexei," she breathes.

"Just a kiss," I promise.

It's not, of course.

She sinks down, her warm little centre finding my cock immediately, and I buck my hips at the perfection of the contact. Jesus Christ, she feels good.

My kisses trail over her jaw, and down her neck. I lick at her collarbone, tasting the day on her. All her hard work. She smells warm and sweet, all turned on, her private musk rising between us as she works her clit against the ridge in my pants.

I cup her ass, squeezing her cheeks in my palms, and I'm about to mouth my way down to her pointy little tits when the baby monitor in the kitchen goes off, a staticky cry breaking the mood with painful success.

"Fuck," Emery breathes, panting against my temple.

Not tonight, no.

"*Papa…*"

"Go," Emery whispers. "It's okay."

It's not, though.

She climbs off my lap and pats me on the head.

Pats me on the fucking head.

The worst part is I know I'll be jerking off to this in the morning, head pat and all.

CHAPTER 28
EMERY

I don't sleep well at all, so when I wake up for the third time and it's almost six in the morning, I roll out of bed and put workout clothes on. Might as well make the most of the pre-Inessa hours of the day.

The house is completely still. I use a bottle of water I filled last night to brush my teeth, lest the running water through the pipes wakes up my tiny and adorable-but-dictatorial charge, then I pad down the hall barefoot, grateful for the thick carpeting that allows me to glide silently past her bedroom.

At the other end of the hall, I've just turned the door-knob to go upstairs when I hear Alexei murmur my name from his room.

Surprised that he's awake already, I turn, thinking he's seen me, but his door is pulled to—not shut, but not ajar, either.

Frowning, I lift my hand to knock, wondering how he knew I was in the hallway, and then I freeze.

Because he says my name again, but it's not…

It's not like he's calling out for my attention.

It's low, it's growly, and it's private.

"That's it," he breathes. "Ride me."

What the fuck?

If the house wasn't so completely still, I wouldn't hear him at all. He probably thinks everyone is still asleep.

My ears turn hot as the next thing I pick up is the unmistakable sound of skin slapping.

He's…

I need to move, but my feet are made of lead. I sway forward, straining to hear what he says next. My hand comes up to brace myself, because all the blood rushing to my head means I can't think straight, and I don't remember that the door isn't latched.

My palm connects with the panel and the hinges squeak.

It's the loudest sound in the world, worse than a shotgun going off, and in the crack that forms between the door and the frame, I see Alexei's body arch off the bed, his horrified gaze meeting my prying eyes.

He's almost naked, a pair of black boxer briefs pushed down around his hips.

His hand is wrapped around his straining erection, which stands out like a spotlight is on it, shining wet at the tip.

"Emery," he chokes out, and his whole body convulses, his cock erupting in his hand. My eyes go wide as his release sprays up his torso.

My head spins, feeling faint now, and suddenly my

feet can move. They move so fast, spinning on the spot and darting for the stairs, yanking the door shut behind me as I flee to the third floor and stumble to my knees.

My thighs are shaking, my hands too. Everything. Shaking. Panicking.

I can't hear anything over the pounding of my pulse in my ears.

And then it fades, slowly, and my cheeks are so, so hot, but the house is…quiet.

Maybe it's okay. Maybe Alexei is cooler about sex than I am, and it's no big deal that I stumbled across a private moment and invaded his space and watched him—

Watched him—

It replays through my mind like black and white art prints. The long stretch of his body spread out on his bed, legs flexed, cock in his hand. The taut contractions of his muscles as he sat up, his hand still…there. The shape of his cock, how hard it was in his hand, straining and *big*.

And the way he said my name again…

That's not a photo. That's a moving video clip, seared into my mind. It makes me short of breath and achy even thinking about it for a second.

The choking sound. The uncontrollable spurts.

There was so much—

Downstairs, a door opens. Closes. Another door opens, and then there are footsteps on the stairs. Coming up.

I turn, still kneeling, bracing myself for the world's most awkward conversation.

Alexei turns the corner. He's pulled on a t-shirt, something softly worn, a logo faded beyond recognition, and a pair of jeans that are pulled on but not zipped up. His hair is sleep-tossed and standing on end, but his face is a careful, blank mask.

His chest rises and falls, and we just stare at each other for a long beat.

"Why did you run?" he finally asks, his voice tight.

I open my mouth, but nothing comes out. There's a fierce buzzing in my ears.

He takes two slow steps towards me, then stops again. "I didn't know you were awake."

"Same," I whisper.

"Are you okay?" His brow pulls together and his mouth draws into a firm line.

"What?" I practically gasp the word.

"I—" His frown deepens. "Are you upset with me?"

I laugh in disbelief. "Could have been my question to you."

His chest rises in a deep inhale. He's so tall, always, but especially when I'm kneeling.

And from this angle, it's hard to miss the bulge of his underwear in the open fly of his jeans. His cock is still pretty big, even after a climax that tore the roof off.

"I'm not upset with you, Emery." His frown deepens. "I like you watching me. You didn't need to run away if you wanted to see what I was doing."

"I didn't..." But I did. I stood there and wondered what he was doing, what it would look like. I was deeply curious and I tried to hear more, see something...and then I ran as soon as I was detected. "I thought it was private."

A slight smile tugs at the corners of his mouth, even as his eyes darken and grow more intense. "We can share private things."

It's a flash back to two years ago.

And he thinks I'm so much more experienced now.

"Do you want that, Emery?" His voice is silky now.

I swallow hard.

His hand comes to rest over his thick, straining erection, his fingers curling into his open fly. "Do you want to see how hard I get when I think about you?"

"You already came," I say inanely.

His eyes flash. "But you're on your knees in front of me, sunshine. So I'm aching all over again. And if you keep looking at me with that hungry gaze, I'll probably embarrass myself again, too."

It was shocking, yes. Intimate...oh yeah.

But embarrassing?

I lick my lips. "It was actually hot, and I'm sorry I interrupted you. Did I...ruin it?"

He groans and squeezes himself. "No. You just surprised me. And then I couldn't help myself."

Because of me.

"Can you do it again?" That lightheaded feeling is back again. "You said you'd show me. I want to see you, Alexei. I want to see how hard your cock is."

And if my voice wavers on *cock*, I pretend it doesn't.

"Fuck." He goes to push his underwear down, then stops. "Can you touch yourself, too?"

He steps closer again, until his toes bump against my bare knee.

That's it. That's all the contact he makes with me, but it's enough to light me on fire.

I was already hot inside, but now I feel burning desire licking all over my skin.

"Slide your fingers into those tight little shorts. Touch your pussy for me." He exhales hard. "That would make me come again. Just seeing your hand moving inside your clothes. Knowing you are touching yourself. Seeing that secret pleasure."

His words are hypnotic.

This hardly feels real, and maybe that's what makes it possible for me to ease my fingers into my shorts, then into my panties.

The fabric tents over my knuckles as I push my middle two fingers down over my cleft. I gasp as I feel how warm and swollen and wet I am already.

Above me, Alexei groans. "Fuck, Emery, I can hear how wet you are."

Oh, God.

He pushes his own hand into his underwear, obscenely straining the limits of the fabric.

"You promised to show me," I pant. My fingertips find my clit, and I shudder at how sensitive it already is.

Maybe if I wasn't such a scaredy cat, I could have crawled onto his bed and he would have fucked me.

My breath picks up.

But I'm not scared now. By following me upstairs,

Alexi has unlocked a deep desire inside me, to see and be seen.

He growls as my hand moves faster, my fingers swirling now.

With my other hand, I tug at my sports bra, wanting my breasts to be free, needing to pluck at my nipples.

His gaze darkens. His pupils dilate, and he pushes his underwear down.

His cock is right in front of me now, and if I thought it looked big through the crack of his bedroom door, that's nothing compared to how beautifully, terrifyingly large it is right in front of my face.

I don't think I would be able to wrap my fingers all the way around him, and I seriously doubt that thing could fit inside me. But at the same time, his scent swirls through my senses, imprinting in my memory in a special way. I'll never forget this.

My mouth from falls open, my tongue slicking against my bottom lip.

Alexei moans and his stroking hand speeds up. His voice, when he speaks, is heavy with lust. "Do you know how much I want you?"

I blink up at him.

"You're so fucking beautiful." He pumps his cock. "I don't think I can stop."

"Don't stop," I beg.

"You have to keep touching that pussy," he growls. His gaze slides from my face back to between my legs. "We don't need to have any secrets between us, Emery. You can show me how pretty you are when you come."

My knees shift wider, my hips tilting up. My clit is so hard now. I wish I was naked. I wish he could see—

We don't have any secrets between us.

"Nothing is off limits," I breathe.

He nods. "That's right. No secrets. No limits. If you want something, all you have to do is ask. Or show me."

Show me.

Those two words are so powerful.

I slide my legs out from under me and lie down, shoving my shorts down my hips as fast as I can, before I lose my nerve.

I want him to see me like this, aching and on fire for him.

Alexei makes a desperate sound low in his throat as I spread my legs for him, and he drops to his knees, yanking off his t-shirt.

If he tried to take me like this, right now, I would let him.

Bare cock, nothing between us. It would be stupid, and I would still let him.

But he doesn't.

He just bites his lip and strokes harder and faster, his eyes locked between my legs.

"Never seen anything more beautiful than you," he says. His free hand ghosts over my thigh, and that's all that it takes for the tight coil in my belly to snap.

As my clit starts pulsing against my fingertips, I press my lips together, my back arching, and I swallow a scream.

I come hard against my fingers, my whole body shaking, wetness slicking my fingers and the tops of my thighs.

I recognize the next sound he makes, a choke low in his throat, the same sound he made when I opened the door,.

This time, his seed splatters all over me. My bare thighs, my hand between my legs, and up onto my belly.

"Oh, fuck. I'm sorry," he groans. "I'm so sorry."

"No…" I catch his hand and interlace our fingers as he tries to wipe it off me with his t-shirt, even as he's still coming.

"Nothing is off-limits between us," I repeat breathlessly.

He curves over me, his cock wet against my belly, and he presses his mouth against mine, so close it's almost a kiss, and I can feel his next words more than hear them.

"Moya polovinka," he murmurs. The unfamiliar Russian words roll right through me, followed by the deepest kiss he's ever given me.

And in this moment, it feels like it might actually be true that there's nothing I couldn't ask of him, and nothing I wouldn't give him.

CHAPTER 29
ALEXEI

The only thing as beautiful as Emery coming apart for me is Emery trying hard, hours later, to not to look like she remembers coming apart for me.

I get that gift over and over again.

Over breakfast.

When I make her sit next to me on the couch so I can practice braiding Inessa's hair.

As I kiss Inessa goodbye before heading to the rink for morning skate, and Emery is *right there*, so I buss a quick kiss on her cheek, too.

When I get back and catch them playing mini sticks again, and her wide-eyed gaze flies to my face, and I know she's thinking about how breathless and sweaty she got for me upstairs in the gym.

It's the strangest, most wonderful feeling, all bubbly and powerful. I want to bottle it just in case it's a difference maker in tonight's game.

Emery and Inessa leave right after naptime, heading

downtown to a WAG gathering with a big duffel bag of supplies Emery tells me I don't need to worry about.

"Are you going to wear one of my jerseys tonight?"

She rolls her eyes at me. "You'd like that."

"Very much. And if you don't, I'm climbing over the plexiglass and giving you the jersey off my back."

She snickers. "You saw that on TikTok."

"Someone shared it to the group chat. Said it was romantic."

Her cheeks slash with heat. "I don't want romance."

"I know." I lower my voice, even though we're basically alone and Inessa is happily playing. "You want dirty talk and secrets."

Her eyes flare wide in warning. *Don't.*

I don't really understand why not, when the chemistry between us is so undeniable, but I accept that she needs a pause after we burn that bright.

"I see you," I murmur. "And fine. I won't pretend I can scale twelve feet of boards and glass. But if you don't wear my jersey tonight, I'm bringing another one home for your collection, moya polovinka."

"The horror," she whispers before winking at me and whisking my daughter out the door.

After they leave, I go downstairs to have coffee with my parents in the basement.

My mother pats the couch seat beside her. "How is my son?"

"I've got a big game tonight."

"We'll be watching." She wraps her arm through mine and leans against me. "And Emery will be there."

I've been waiting for her to bring up Emery. It was probably wishful thinking to hope they wouldn't notice how I look at her. How I feel about her.

"Mama, she's leaving after the season is over. Don't hope for another happy ending."

"I'm sorry to hear that. She makes you happy."

"And she always will, even when she's in Switzerland."

"Switzerland!"

"It's a long story. She's following her dreams."

"Silly girl. She should dream of marrying a handsome goalie."

I laugh out loud. "Oh, Mama. That's nobody's dream, I hate to tell you."

My father brings a mug to my mother, with extra milk just the way she likes it. "Are you waiting for someone to dream of you?"

I frown. "No."

"Whatever her dream is, you make that happen. And then you will be her dream, too."

"I didn't come down here for relationship advice, because I do not have a relationship. I also don't have time for a relationship."

Literally the only uninterrupted time I've managed to find with Emery was pre-dawn. The thrill of that is going to wear off sooner than later for her.

We don't have a relationship. We have a secret connection. It's intense and profound, and while I will never forget her, I know the part of our story where we are actually *together* is temporary.

———

It doesn't stop me from looking for her as soon as we skate onto the ice for the warmup that night, and my chest gets warm and puffs up as soon as I catch sight of her at the glass.

And my heart beats faster.

Moya polovinka.

She's in the VIP area, holding Inessa up, helping her stand on the narrow ledge of the boards.

They're both wearing my number, and I'm glad my parents aren't here to see that, because how do I explain this isn't a relationship?

It's just not.

It can't be.

But I'm not lying to myself about how good it feels that, for the time that I do have her, she's giving me this—no scaling of the glass required.

Even bruised, Emery Granger's big heart is a thing of wonder.

After stopping to high-five Inessa through the glass and give Emery a blush-inducing wink, I join my teammates in the looping warm up flow.

Calgary is doing the same thing on the other half of the ice, and the tension is already crackling.

I break away from the group, slide into the crease, and drop into my rhythm—glide, stretch, butterfly, pop back up. Talk to the net, praise the posts. The usual routine.

But at the same time, I'm clocking the energy in front of me.

On our side of the ice, Armstrong looks like a lion who has been just let out of his pen. More than once, he looks towards the VIP area. His girlfriend, Shannon, is standing at the back of the WAGs, and they don't stay at the glass for very long.

Once they leave, he starts prowling back and forth at the centre red line. It doesn't take long for Max Tilman to start mirroring him on the Calgary side. He's a sharp-looking player, sleek like a panther, and while Armstrong outweighs him by a good twenty pounds or more, Tilman has speed on his side, and the sharp snap of his skates on the ice as he picks up his pace sounds…violent. There's no way around that.

I'm too far away to hear if they say anything to each other, but it doesn't take long for Marsh to cut his warm-up short, grab Rusty, and push him to the exit.

Tilman stays on the ice.

The warm-up clock ticks down, and the number of people still stretching and skating starts to dwindle.

Haler is often the last one on the ice, but when he comes over to start rounding up pucks at the net, I tell him I'll stay out and be the last man off if he wants to go check on Rusty.

"You sure?"

"It's my barn too, Captain."

He grins at me. "Sure fucking is."

Which leaves me as the final Highlander on the ice, a sentinel waiting for Calgary to clear out. Two of my former teammates are still circling, shooting pucks in their net, and the third player with them is the man who I was traded for.

They're talking to each other, and I think they're trying to get him off the ice, but he won't leave.

The time runs out, and I stop circling my net and go to stand in front of it.

Waiting.

Fans start booing, and then someone jeers at him. *"Get off our ice, Tilman."*

I stand taller again.

"Off our ice, off our ice, off our ice."

He twists and slaps a puck in my direction.

I don't move.

It goes wide, utterly harmless.

He stares at me, then turns and heads down the visitor tunnel.

I'm sure that won't be the last time tonight he shoots a puck my way. The rest of his shots will be closer, faster, and actually count if they get through me.

But I'm not worried, because after that pathetic display, I don't think Max Tilman returned to play hockey.

He came to pour poison on this ice—but I'm not letting it anywhere near my net.

I raise my stick in a salute to the crowd, then head back to the dressing room.

It's fucking quiet.

Not silent, exactly—there's tape being ripped, skates being re-laced, and someone is tapping on their shin guards with the butt end of their stick—but there's no chatter.

There's something to prove tonight, and it's probably going to get rough.

I've heard all about the day that fractured this team. Hooner and Dodaj both need to process everything out loud—even if I'm just a silent sounding board. So while I wasn't here for the brawl, I can clearly picture it. The shoving match on the ice during practice, and the escalation in the middle of this very dressing room that led to a fractured jaw. The details that spilled out about Tilman's marriage falling apart, and Armstrong being in the midst of that.

Front office had no choice but to do *something*.

I was the something.

So I didn't see the big break up of the original expansion team, but I've had a front row seat for the fallout.

And tonight I'll be in net. A different kind of front row seat.

Across from me, Armstrong is rolling his shoulders. Definitely ready for a rematch. Hale has one eye on the big Scotsman. Watanabe's bouncing his leg like a live wire. Beside me, Zondi hasn't blinked in two minutes.

Even Marshie looks tense, and nothing ruffles him.

I wonder what was said before I came back from warm-up.

The door swings open and our coach walks in. He's tense, too. "All right. Let's keep it clean and focused. We don't need a circus."

A few of the guys nod. Rusty cracks his neck with a sound like thunder.

Coach looks at each of us in turn. "Play our game. Be smart. We're on a roll. Home ice advantage in the playoffs is within reach, fellas, so eyes on that prize. We're not trying to make a point tonight—we *are* the point."

That lands. I can feel the ripple it causes.

Then a low rumble of agreement rolls through the room.

That's all we need to prove tonight. That we are one.

Hale stands. "Let's do this, then. Tonight we're starting with the beasts. We've got Marshie at centre with Rusty and Gusty on the wings. Mo and Smash behind them on D. And in the net, our stoic Russian, Arty's going for win number seven. Let's fucking go."

"Let's fucking go," the whole team says as one.

I stand, shake out my legs, then give Hale a fist pump as I lead the team into the hallway. Toward the thunderous noise building in the stands.

At the mouth of the tunnel, just before the ice comes into view, the team always has a few kids waiting to cheer us on.

Tonight, Charlie and Inessa are waiting there, wearing tiny Highlanders hoodies. Becca kneels behind them, holding on tight to both kids as they jockey for space with some bigger kids.

Inessa spots me and breaks into a grin so wide her cheeks puff out. "Papa!"

I crouch down, ignoring the tight pull of my pads. "My good luck charm."

She holds up her hand. I offer my blocker and she slaps it, then switches and goes for the glove. Double tap. Serious face.

"Win the game," she says with firm, toddler authority.

"Yes, coach," I murmur, and she giggles.

I glance up and catch Emery watching me from the back of the crowd, her eyes soft.

I don't let myself look too long, just long enough that she knows I see her.

And then I turn, tug my mask down, and leave everything but the battle behind.

CHAPTER 30
EMERY

It's not enough for this high-stakes game to be close.

It's not enough for it to go to overtime.

It goes all the way to a shootout, and the first skater up for Calgary is Max Fucking Tilman, who I bet will be facing some disciplinary action from the league for his unsportsmanlike conduct in the warm-up.

Ironically, I think his most unsportsmanlike conduct was fighting Russ in the second period, since that was purely personal. But fighting is a part of the game, like it or not—and I do like it—and karma made sure he didn't win that fight. Not that there was much of a chance of it going well for him.

Russ pounded him into the ice and then stood over him like a gladiator.

The crowd loved it.

And they love this shoot-out match-up, too.

Alexei squares up as Tilman starts to build speed, then he tracks back, waiting...waiting... and just as the forward snaps the puck, *my* goalie drops his right leg and blocks it perfectly.

The final rejection of the former captain in this building, and the crowd goes wild.

Beside me, Shannon lets out an audible exhale.

Hale is up next for us, and he snipes it top left, bar down, and that's one.

Next for Calgary is my brother, and I recognize his approach. It's what I would do, too, because we learned how to shoot from the same man.

Somewhere below us in the arena, my dad is muttering coaching notes I can hear in my head. *Don't slow down too much, no fucking showboating, and don't fucking project your shot.*

Unfortunately, Forrest projects his shot, and Alexei blocks it easily.

They exchange a few words before he returns to the Calgary bench, defeated.

Ty Connor is next for Hamilton, and Kiley rises to her feet.

His shot is a beauty, the puck starting low and rising slower than the Calgary goalie expects. But the blocker catches enough that it bounces up and out.

Close, but not enough.

Calgary's third shooter is one of their rookies—fast hands, good edges, cocky as hell.

He cuts hard right, then left, trying to catch Alexei off-balance. But Alexei doesn't bite. He follows every move, mirroring and waiting.

The rookie flinches. Shoots.

And Alexei gets right in front of it, absorbing the puck right in the middle of his chest for a save.

The arena explodes.

That's a win, with Haler's goal meaning Hamilton doesn't need a third shooter.

On the bench just behind me in the suite, Inessa is fast asleep, completely unaware that her dad is a victorious gladiator.

And like Shannon, I can finally exhale.

I shouldn't be feeling this much.

Not when I'm trying to keep things professional. Not when I've dismantled every part of my life because I'm moving overseas this summer. I have *goals*, and they have nothing to do with being Alexei's emergency nanny or secret…whatever I was to him this morning.

But watching him be absolutely unshakeable tonight did something to me. I don't just feel pride or admiration, it's deeper than that. Something has cracked open that I've been trying really hard to pretend wasn't growing inside me.

Tonight he felt like he was *mine*.

Not officially. Not something I would say out loud. And definitely not forever.

But right now, he's mine, and I was happy to be wearing his number as he chalked up another win.

"Long night," Shannon murmurs as she stretches her legs out in front of her.

She won't be in a rush to leave tonight, not until the cheers have long faded from the rafters of the arena.

"I'm going to wait until it's quieter to leave," I say

after the other WAGs say goodbye and head out. "Increases the chances of Inessa staying asleep."

"You don't need to keep me company."

"Who says I'm doing that?"

She smiles at me. "Hey, how would you feel about helping me plan a baby shower for Ani?"

"I would be honoured."

"Harper has volunteered to host it at her house. I've got the decorations organized, but I could use some help on the menu planning."

"I'm in. Do you want to come over for dinner one night while the team is away this coming week?"

"One night?" Shannon teases. "You might find yourself feeding me every night."

I laugh. "Dinner isn't Inessa's favourite time of day. You might find it exhausting."

She gives me a scrutinizing look. "Will I?"

I shrug. "Some do."

"But you don't?"

"No," I say, surprising myself. "Maybe it's because I've been spending all day with her? So I get the good stuff, too? But I can see how she's tired, I get the *why* of tantrums. She doesn't have the vocabulary yet to explain her big feelings, and even if she could, a lot of what she wants just isn't possible."

"The world doesn't cater to the whims of two-year-olds," Shannon says dryly.

"Deeply unfair." I look at my sleeping charge. "She's really very sweet. Especially at lunch time, if you can swing that instead of dinner."

Shannon giggles and nods. "Noted. But I don't mind a glimpse into a challenging dinner hour, either." A lovely glow blooms from deep inside her, softening her expression. "We talk about kids, you know. Or at least one kid. I'm not in a rush, obviously." She waves down at the ice. "I need Max to be fully out of my life first. There's some family court legal stuff that is going to take longer than I'd like. And Russ is thinking he might retire next year or the year after, so...if we wait until then, he'll be more hands-on. But I look forward to learning about things like tantrums."

My mouth has fallen open. "Shannon!"

She laughs and nods. "I know. I know I know I know."

"I'm so happy for you both."

"One thing at a time." But her expression is now so blissful, after what was a really hard day.

I press my hand to my chest and sigh.

She smiles. "What about you?"

"What about me?" My voice shakes a little, worried that I've revealed too much of my feelings for Alexei.

"What comes after Switzerland?"

I exhale in relief. "Oh."

Her eyebrows arch up. "What did you think I meant?"

"Nothing. Um..." I shrug. "I'm not sure. It depends how long I can work in Europe for, which depends on how well my placements go. Switzerland is just the first step down a path that hasn't fully revealed itself yet."

"That's exciting."

"It really is. I like tackling short term projects. It's what I thought being a personal chef would be."

"But it wasn't?"

I shook my head. "I mean, I did get hired for some one-off events, but the bulk of the market in Minneapolis was more about regular customers, and…" I shrug. "It stopped being exciting. People wanted the same things over and over again, and I'm not the right chef for that."

"Cooking for a hockey player must be hard, then."

"Not at all. Alexei isn't a client."

I hear myself say it at the same time she does.

She doesn't react to that, just waits.

"I know how that sounds." I can't look sideways at her again. I'm afraid she's already figured out too much as it is.

Still, I can feel her studying me. After a long beat, she makes a little humming sound in her throat. "Do you know why I haven't moved in with Russ yet?"

I blink, refocusing on her, and think about the conversations we've had over the last eight months. And the confession she just shared, that they're already thinking about kids. They're obviously a forever couple, deeply in love. "It's not because you haven't found a bigger place, is it?"

She shakes her head. "I needed to find myself. I needed to fully *be* myself, and that's not an overnight process. And a little bit, I need to know that he'll love me even when I push back. Even when I need time and space to figure out who I am, what I want. I won't live a life someone else has picked for me, and provides for me, ever again." Her eyes are a little glassy, but her voice stays calm. "I need to build a life of my own before I merge it with someone else's. Because if I don't know what I want, I'll just get lost again."

She pauses. "Russ gets it. Even if he isn't the biggest fan of my apartment. He still chooses me, and meets me on my own terms. And it feels so, so special, because I was in a lopsided, unhappy relationship for so long. But *Russ* would be the first to say that's the minimum standard. That's how it should be. I'm still learning to trust that, and to trust him."

That's how it should be.

My entire life has been wrapped around other people. I've compromised and gotten out of the way and picked up the slack around *their* accomplishments. And then plastered on a jersey and cheered my heart out because of course I love them, and I'm proud of them.

But after that night with Alexei two years ago, when he had me naked on a hotel bed, halfway in love with him, and something else came up... Even though that *something* was really fucking important, I realized that I always bend too far. Give too much.

I can't do that again.

"You don't have to erase yourself to stay," she says gently. "But you can stay if you want. That's a perfectly good choice to make, since you're clearly smitten."

I squeak and bury my face in my hands. But I'm not going to deny it. I am smitten, for better or for worse. "Is it that obvious? Does everyone know?"

"I don't think so." She leans her shoulder against

mine. "But they weren't all studying you for a week last year, trying to figure out who you were to Russell."

I laugh and groan. "Oh my God."

"I became an Emery expert, maybe. And there's a new light to you. You...glow."

That's the same word I used to describe how ridiculously in love she is. Crap. Craaaaapppp.

"It's...we're not..." I swallow hard. "It's just a thing. Like we haven't talked about what we're doing, we just do it."

And not even *it*, not yet.

"It's mostly kissing," I say, which sounds so juvenile I have to cover my face all over again.

"Kissing is pretty amazing," she whispers. "But you should talk to him, too. With the right person, talking is also amazing."

CHAPTER 31
ALEXEI

There's always things to do after a game, but tonight it stretches on and on. I just can't get out of the arena quickly.

First, I have media, because of the shoot-out and the fact that it's my former team. As I'm waiting for my turn at the podium, I hear the journalists talking about the fact that we didn't do a video tribute to Tilman and pretend not to understand.

Then I notice a tender spot on my side when I'm getting dressed, so I have to get that looked at by our medical team. They're pretty sure it's just soft tissue bruising, so there's some therapy for that before they tape an ice pack to my side.

By the time I get to my phone, there's a text message from Emery that they're home and everyone is in bed.

EMERY

You were really great tonight, btw

ALEXEI

Thank you

I'm heading home now

I wanted to stay up for you but my eyes
are pretty scratchy

That's okay, sleep tight, sunshine

I'll see you in the morning

You can wake me up if you want

She doesn't reply to that, and when I get home, the entire house is still. Fast asleep, tucked in their beds.

I get rid of the ice pack, then head back downstairs to the kitchen in search of something to eat.

In the fridge, I find a variety of meal options. Emery has taped macro counts to them, too. I grab two servings of meatloaf, suddenly starving, and heat those up as I catch up on the scores of the other games from around the league.

The west coast games are still going, so I sit at the table and quietly watch the Vancouver-Colorado game on my phone as I eat. I like watching other goalies work. Then I rinse my plate, put it in the dishwasher, grab a fresh ice pack from the freezer, and head upstairs.

It feels like one minute I'm brushing my teeth, and the next I'm drifting back to wakefulness because I'm surrounded by dozens of Emerys, big and small, whispering and teasing and…dancing on my bruises?

"Easy," I mumble, catching her hands as her hair

brushes my belly. Okay, that's fine. More than fine. That feels good.

"It's early," she whispers, her voice like silk, wrapping around my still-sleeping brain. "But you said I could…"

"Yeah. I wanted you to wake me up."

"Like this?" Her breath teases against my hardened flesh. And then she takes my cock in her mouth.

My toes curl and my ass clenches tight as she sucks my soul straight out of my body.

At some point, I'm going to stop coming real fucking fast for her, but it's not this moment in time.

"Good morning," I growl when she's finished, licking her lips like a very satisfied wildcat. "Come up here and sit on my face."

She blushes and presses her forehead to my chest. "That was just for you," she mumbled. "I got my period overnight. But I worried we might not get another chance before you left for the next road trip, so…"

I pull her up my body, nestling her against my side. "Wait, what? Moya polovinka, why would you not tell me? Do you need anything?"

She rolls her eyes at me. Rolls her eyes! "I'm fine."

"Do you have bad cramps?"

"We can stop talking about my period immediately."

"No need for secrets between us, but of course, I want you to be comfortable. Would an orgasm feel good? Maybe I could touch you a little if you don't want me to lick you?"

She squirms. "I didn't do it so you would feel like you need to…" She presses her face against my shoulder this time, and I can feel how hot her cheeks are.

My sweet, innocent girl.

It's fucking hot to watch her discover how intimate we can be together, even just talking.

"The only *need* I feel is the one that makes me rock hard simply by holding you," I say roughly. "My offer to eat your sweet pussy is entirely about *want*, not need. Not a tradeoff. You are delicious." I inhale deeply as I gather her deeper into my arms, one hand cupping her ass as I roll her on top of me. "I want to feel your clit pulse in my mouth. I want to push my tongue deep into your pussy to feel your clamp down on it. I—"

She kisses me, cutting me off. She tastes faintly like my seed, earthy and real.

"Please, Emery. Do you need me to beg?"

"Yes," she whispers.

I roll us to the edge of the bed, then scoop her up and carry her into my bathroom, grateful that it's private.

I have two plug-in nightlights in here, which provide just enough visibility that I don't turn the lights on. Maybe the shadows will be freeing for her.

After I get the shower started, I back her up against the vanity and drop to my knees in front of her.

She buries her hands in my hair as I press my face to her belly.

"Let me make you feel good," I say, my voice low and private under the hiss of the steam building. "Please let me."

"We need to be careful." Her voice catches.

"I know." Trust me, I fucking know. "Just my hands. Just my mouth."

"Alexei…" Even uncertain and conflicted, my name on her lips is the best sound in the world.

I squeeze her hips in my hands and look up at her. "I just want to be close to you. I'm on my knees for a reason."

"Will you regret this when I'm gone?" The way her voice cracks destroys me.

"Never," I swear. "I'll never regret anything that we do. I'm begging for your sunshine. Can you let me have a taste in the shower?"

She nods, biting her lower lip, and I tug her sleep shorts down her legs. Slide off her panties, too.

Even in the dim light, I can see her eyes go wide as I nudge her legs apart, but she lets me stroke her inner thighs and the soft pout of her pussy lips.

Her grip on the counter tightens when I duck my head again, breathing in her scent.

"Please," I whisper.

She trembles, then spreads her legs for me, giving me more access.

Fuck, the trust that takes. "Thank you," I groan against her belly, pressing my face in against her skin as my fingers find the string of her tampon.

I ease it out of her body and get rid of it, then wrap my arms tight around her hips, squeezing her against me before I strip us both of the rest of our clothes and pull her into the shower.

Will you regret this when I'm gone?

When it comes to Emery, regret is a complicated word. The first time I touched her, it was a mistake. The second time, it was a secret. The third time… it'll be forever.

We're past the point of just fooling around. I want her in my bed, in my shower, on my face, on my mind…

I trace my fingers over her shoulder, onto her chest, and down to where her little breasts strain away from her body in eager points.

"I'm obsessed with you," I whisper. "Moya polovinka."

She shudders.

"There hasn't been anyone else for me. Not in my thoughts, not in my bed, and not in my shower. You have consumed me even when you weren't here, even when I thought you would never be here. Now that I have you again, I never want to let you go."

"I can't…"

"I know." I swallow hard. "I won't say it again."

She flattens my hand against her chest, pressing her fingers against mine, urging me to squeeze her tit. "I'm not the same girl, Alexei."

"I am not the same man. It's okay."

"But—"

"We are different people, yes? But the fire between us, it is the same. It needs to burn, Emery. Let yourself burn, if only for right now. Then we can forget again."

She twists in my arms.

"I never forgot," she whispers, her breath warm and sweet. Her lips brush against mine. Almost a kiss. Agonizing. "I tried. You told me to. Do you remember?"

"I remember everything." I kiss her forehead, my heart pounding in my chest. "But I meant it. I wanted you to find better."

"I didn't." She sucks in a quick, sharp breath and turns her face to the spray.

I wrap my arms around her from behind, and she leans back against me.

"Tell me."

"Nobody has ever made me feel what you make me feel."

I shouldn't take such vicious pride in that, but I do. I've wondered, ever since she hugged Malik. No, before that. From the first time Forrest told me she was suddenly dating everyone under the sun, I wondered if they were treating her well enough, if she came like a firecracker for them, too.

"I haven't even tried." I skim my hands down her torso. "I don't want to feel this with anyone else. I'd rather be alone with the memory of you trying to be quiet."

She shivers.

"Yes? You liked that?"

Her pupils dilate. "Mmm…"

"Maybe you need the thrill, hmm? The risk of being overheard?"

A shudder wracks her body.

I push my hand between her thighs, cupping her pussy. "I should have done this when your family was here. Pulled you upstairs and made you come on my fingers. It wouldn't take long, would it? If you had to be quiet for me?"

She convulses in my arms, and against my fingers, her soft cunt slicks even more.

"That's it, sunshine. Let me feel how much you like it." I kiss the side of her head and skate my other hand up to play with her tits again. Her nipples are so hard, little pebbles that beg to be pinched.

When I do that, she whimpers and her hips rock, pushing her clit into my fingers.

"I haven't even begged yet, and you're already going to come, aren't you?"

"Alexei…"

"Don't come yet," I growl, but I don't mean it, because I want that more than anything. I want her to come and come and come.

She shatters on my hand, and it feels fucking amazing. Fluttering flesh and a silky pour of arousal that coats my fingers and makes my mouth water.

I turn her, pressing her back against the tiles, and kneel. I touch her reverently, tracing the shape of her hips and the curve at the top of her thighs. The incredible softness where her legs meet her slick, swollen pussy.

"Put a leg over my shoulder."

She laughs weakly. "I don't know if I can stand on one leg."

"I'll hold you up."

She tips her head back and lifts her left leg. I help her hook it over, tipping her hips out and lifting her up onto her toes.

"Alexei!"

I chuckle as I kiss her inner thigh. "Hold on tight."

The groan she makes as she sinks her fingers into my hair—and digs her heel into my back—is almost as delicious as the sharp sweetness between her pussy lips.

And then when I push my tongue into her tight, clutching hole, the faint tang of copper alongside her honeyed arousal is everything I didn't know I needed.

Nobody else has ever tasted her like this, I'm sure of it.

This is mine.

She is mine.

And when she comes for me, again, it feels like I'm hers, too.

CHAPTER 32
EMERY

In hindsight, waking Alexei with a blowjob and then letting him take me into his shower was not the smartest use of our early morning kid-free time when I want to try to find time to talk about what we're doing (beyond the obvious and incredible).

But Inessa wakes up before I get a chance to bring that up, and then we discover a new problem—overnight, she's developed a cold.

And possibly the only thing worse than a Granger Family Man Cold might be an Artyomov Toddler Cold.

She wakes up crying and distressed, and even after Alexei calms her down, she remains clingy and sad, because she can't breathe properly. All she wants is her dad, but her dad needs to stay healthy, so he wants to wash her hands and wash his own hands and open all the windows.

And all she wants is to cling to him and wipe her snot all over him.

It's...stressful.

"I'll take her to my room," Alexei says in between hiccupping cries. "Can you bring up some... not milk, that will just make her more congested. Water, I guess, and some berries? And do we have any yogurt?"

I wince. "It was on my grocery list to buy today. I'll do a quick grocery and pharmacy run. What kind of medicine can she have?"

Together, we make a shopping list.

Then I bring him a coffee and her a sippy cup of water, and they snuggle down in his bed to watch cartoons.

At the nearby shopping centre, I stock up on paediatric electrolytes, as well as popsicles, more berries, yogurt, and a few loaves of bread because when in doubt, toast works for every meal.

I also ask the pharmacist for tips on de-snotting a toddler, and then put all the options in my cart—as well as air purifiers and a few immune booster packs for all the adults.

"Tissues," I mutter to myself as I approach the checkout. I turn back.

I know it's just a cold, but it feels like more than that at this point in the season. It's a test of Alexei's trust in me, in my ability to hold his family together.

By the time I return, Inessa has fallen asleep again. Her cheeks are bright red and her dark waves are damp with sweat.

Even though Alexei has opened the windows, I don't think he should hang out with her all day.

"I can't ask you to take over," he protests.

"You can't risk getting sick, either." I wave it off. "I know what this point of the season means to you and the team. You've got a road trip ahead of you. If you get sick, the whole team could get sick. I brought home some immune boosters. Check with the team to make sure you can take them."

He scrubs his hands over his face, then gives me a long, sober look. "What would I do without you?"

"You would have other help, I'm sure, but luckily I'm not doing anything else." I smile to lighten the moment. "And it's hardly a difficulty to lie around in your big bed all day scrolling social media and cuddling your daughter."

"I feel badly."

"It's fine. Honestly. I grew up with this end of season pressure, didn't I? Go. I've got Inessa."

"I'll wait on you hand and foot."

And he does. He brings up food trays and beverages on demand, which is often once Inessa gets a bit more rest.

I try to convince her to mimic me in lying with our heads hanging off the bed, and doing some sinus clearing massages, among other ideas I see on TikTok. She doesn't care.

The day drags on.

Alexei brings dinner up and we have a picnic in bed, and then he takes over for bedtime while I go to have a long shower.

When I come back, he's fallen asleep with Inessa.

Gently, I scoop her up and carry her back to her room, so she isn't breathing on him all night.

And then I go to sleep in my own bed, because hockey comes first, and hockey requires that I keep any potential germs I might have picked up today to myself.

CHAPTER 33
ALEXEI

"Did you see that Tilman got fined for firing that puck at you in warm-ups?" Dodaj cackles as he strips off his suit jacket and drapes it over the empty seat in front of us.

We're both early to get on the plane every road trip. Me, because I'm early for everything. Him, because he likes to strip down to his undershirt because he only has three nice shirts and needs some room to get sorted before everyone else piles on.

I shrug.

The asshole missed, so what do I care?

He stows his garment bag in the overhead bin, the slides in next to me and glances at my phone. "Whatcha doin'?"

"Looking at summer vacation rentals."

"Ooh, nice." He grabs my phone and starts scrolling. "God, you goalies are so fucking weird. There isn't a beach in sight. What are you going to do, some marathon mountain hiking?"

I snatch it back. "Yeah. Me and your mom."

He stares at me for a long, confused second, then dissolves into uncontrollable laughter. "Arty, no. Just… no."

I shrug again.

"It's not…that's not how a *your mom* joke works, bud."

"You're laughing."

"Because that makes no sense. If you want to make a *your mom* joke, it's gotta be about sex. Not marathon hiking."

"I didn't say anything about hiking. You did. Why do you want me to make a sex joke about your mom?"

Ty Connor stops at the row beside us and takes his earbud out. "Smash wants you to fuck his mom?"

Dodaj flips him the bird, then looks back at me. "That's how you do the *your mom* joke, though."

"I'll tell your mom when I call her tonight about our hiking trip."

He groans. "She's never going to Switzerland with you."

Marsh slows down on his way to the back of the plane. "Who's going to Switzerland?"

Up the aisle, Armstrong hears that, and his big Scottish head does a sideways tilt that tells me I'm fucked, secret-wise.

"Let's sit here," Rusty says to Marsh, indicating the row right behind us.

Out of the corner of my eye, I see Kieran stop, swivel is attention between us, then shrug.

Yeah, I'm so fucked.

"Smash, you stupid puppy," I mutter under my breath.

That sends him into another giggling fit. "What?"

I show him the latest Highlanders Instagram post, where one of Mabel's interns has posted player comps to different dogs.

"Everyone knows you are a puppy," I say. "I am a fierce guard dog, and you—"

"I'm a fucking golden retriever, bud." He grins at me. "It's a meme."

"You're a meme."

"You're a German shepherd."

"Shut up." Since he's looking at my phone, I switch to my text messages and start a new one, typing in *smashsmom* in the recipient line. It doesn't matter that it won't actually send.

ALEXEI

Your puppy son says you want to go on a hiking love trip with me, please confirm

"I hate you," he says, closing his eyes with a giggling huff.

I grin, because he can't see me with his eyes closed. "Don't look at people's phones."

Then I switch text screens.

ALEXEI

Taking off soon, will call when I get to the hotel

EMERY

Have a safe flight

The last few people file on, then our general manager says a few things before settling into the front row. The flight attendants come through and offer us drinks before takeoff, and then we're taxiing down the runway.

As soon as the wheels are up, Armstrong leans forward, his big fist squeezing the top of my seat, compressing the cushion there. "How long are you going to Switzerland for, Arty?"

I sure hope counting backwards from five works to buy me some time and calm with overprotective teammates as well as with toddlers. Three, two, one… "I go to Europe every summer. This year, I'll pick the country Emery is going to."

"Did she invite you?" His big hand gestures over my head, to some of the single guys in front of us. "You might not be alone in wanting to follow her everywhere she goes. Half the team has a crush on her."

I resist the frustrated frown pulling at my brow. More than just Malik?

Armstrong grabs Dodaj's head. "Even Smash was all over her last summer."

"Whoa," Roan says, throwing his hands in the air. "What the fuck? Don't throw me under the Arty bus. I'm not into your girl, bud. I swear. Stop fucking growling."

I turn the frustrated rumble into a sharp grunt, instead.

The seat belt light turns off with a quiet ding, and I

give Smash a quality elbow in the side as I unbuckle so I can turn around.

I look Armstrong straight in the eye. "Emery is important to me. But it would be very bad if her brothers heard something taken out of context by a *dumb puppy*."

"That's me," Dodaj says, sticking his hand in the air, unbothered.

Rusty's eyes narrow. "Emery's a grown-up. As long as she's happy, I'm not going to say anything to anyone. You treating her right?"

I think about the way her pussy clenches around my tongue when she comes. "Of course."

"You taking care of her while you're away?"

I hesitate a beat too long. I don't think he means phone sex.

Marsh groans and shakes his head. "Bud, you gotta send her stuff."

Dodaj unbuckles and stands up, too, fully invested in this conversation. "What do you mean?"

From across the aisle, Jenson says, "I like to send Ani a new book every week."

Ty gives him a high-five. "That's a good one. Do you pick them or does she have a wish list?"

"Little bit of both."

"Flowers are good, too," Marsh says.

"Chocolate. You can't go wrong with chocolate," Russ says.

That's actually a great idea. I'll find some amazing, weird, foodie chocolates for Emery. "Yeah, okay."

"Whatever she's into. And like, make her life easy."

Jenson shrugs. "Ani's getting pretty uncomfortable in her pregnancy, so I increased the number of times a week our house cleaner comes."

Fuck.

Right.

I could hire more people to do the things that Emery is helping with.

And then Ty gives us all a sly wink. "And of course, you can take care of her from afar. Make sure you get quality phone time, you know? Don't short change that connection."

Well, I'm relieved to find out that my phone sex instincts weren't completely off. And I can totally do that.

To his credit, Russ doesn't even wince. He doesn't change the subject, either. He keeps his eyes on me, like he's tracking whether or not I'm taking notes.

Be mindful of what she needs. Check.

Give her attention. Check.

And firm up what the fuck we are doing before her brothers find out. Triple. Check.

CHAPTER 34
EMERY

The day after Alexei leaves, Inessa has bounced back to health, so I invite Becca and Shannon over for dinner.

I'm in the middle of making a yuzu shaved ice for dessert that I think might be nice for Ani's baby shower, but need to practice a few times, when the doorbell rings.

Sergei comes up the stairs from the basement to answer it, and from what I can hear, it sounds like a delivery.

"It's for you," he says when he comes back to the kitchen.

I raise my eyebrows and accept the rectangular package. Sure enough, it has my name on it.

Inside, I find a food memoir, *Koshersoul* by Michael W. Twitty. A piece of paper flutters out with it, a printed gift receipt. There's a typed message in the note space:

I would love to hear if you like this book - Alexei

Unexpected heat races through me. I take a picture of it and text it to him.

EMERY

Thank you for this...it looks super interesting

Hopefully you find time to read today

I'm actually throwing a dinner party tonight, but I will read it at bedtime

A party?

A wild, rambunctious party...I invited a boy over to wreck up the place

Emery, no, say it isn't true

I giggle and drop a thumbs up reaction on that message.

The boy in question—Charlie—shows up a half-hour later with his mom in tow, and it doesn't take long before he and Inessa are jumping on the couch, cushions flying everywhere.

see?

Don't let that little monster steal your heart, you're mine

okay

This time, he's the one to drop a reaction character, and it's a little heart on my text.

Another blast of heat ripples through me.

The doorbell rings again.

"Keep your eyes on them," I warn Becca before I go to answer it, expecting it to be Shannon.

Instead, it's another delivery, this one from a local chocolate company—although I can see my friend has just pulled into the driveway.

I take the box from the courier driver, then hold the door open for Shannon.

"What's that?" She asks as she gives me a hug.

I haven't read the tag yet, but I'm guessing it's another Alexei gift.

"Chocolates." I close the door behind her. "Alexei sent me a book earlier, too."

"Really?" Shannon laughs. "Russell sent me a book, too. A spicy romance novel."

Becca's head pops into the hallway. "Did you get sent some reading material, too? They must have been comparing notes! Hayden loaded a whole bunch to my e-reader account and then texted me a screenshot."

"For the record, the book I got was a food memoir," I say to Shannon under my breath.

She winks at me. "He's still being polite, that's so sweet."

I'm blushing like mad. "Okay, let's eat and talk about the baby shower."

As Shannon tells me her vision for the party, I open the gift-wrapped chocolates from Alexei. There's a card on this one, too.

I would love to hear if you like these chocolates - Alexei

I would love to hear…

Those words keep echoing through my mind as I get the girls to help me assemble another rainbow veggie tray, and then we make grilled cheese sandwiches—gourmet for the grown-ups, and classic for Inessa and Charlie—for dinner.

"Do you two ever send the guys anything on the road?" I ask abruptly, just as we're settling onto the couches to watch the game. "Does the gift giving go in both directions?"

"Not really," Shannon says. "But I do like to have surprises waiting for him when he returns."

Becca taps her chin thoughtfully. "I send Hayden tittie pics right before a team meeting, does that count?"

"That definitely counts," Shannon and I say at the same time.

CHAPTER 35
ALEXEI

I get a weird cramp in the warm-ups for our first game on this road trip, so I'm pulled and the net is given to the back-up goalie. We lose, although he does a good job and holds it to a one-goal difference.

Once we get back to the hotel, Dr. Forge checks on me and decides I need an IV infusion. I'm sitting in the conference room the team is using, my left arm hooked up, chatting with him about my mom's recovery, when I get a text message from Emery.

I tap into it immediately out of habit—and immediately flip my hand down, because there's a photo.

"Sorry, could you give me a moment," I say to Grant. "Message from home."

"Yeah, sure." He checks the hanging IV bag. "I'll be back in five minutes."

I wait until he's out of the room, then look again—and I groan.

Emery is in the pantry, reading the book I ordered for

her, eating a chocolate I sent her…and she's not wearing a top.

Her chest is flushed, pink stain spilling onto her pointy, perfect tits. I want to devour her whole.

I stroke the screen for a moment, wishing I was more alone than I am right now, and then I tap the screen.

"You naughty girl," I growl when she answers.

She giggles in my ear.

"I am not alone for very long." I drag in a frustrated breath. "I'm hooked up to an IV, and I have a hard-on. Are you happy?"

"Alexei!" Her tone shifts abruptly. Concern floods her voice. "Why do you have an IV?"

"It's just a precaution. Why aren't you wearing a shirt?"

"I'm literally putting my shirt back on."

"No, no, that's not what I need right now." I'm laughing. "Please, sunshine. I loved the photo. Send me more, but give me twenty minutes. All right?"

"You're okay?"

"I'm okay."

"Good." And there's so much sweetness in that one word, I'm going to have to send her books and chocolates every day for the rest of time.

———

I rebound, health-wise, but my winning streak ends in the next game. Two sniping goals get past me and we just can't respond.

I get mad in the third period and draw a penalty that someone else has to serve for me. We kill that off, and I keep the goals against just to the two, but it's…not great.

"Are the vibes off?" Dodaj asks as we undress.

I don't respond.

One of the assistant coaches sticks his head into the visitors dressing room. "Arty, there will be media questions for you."

Again? Fuck my life.

The team is pretty good about spreading out who gets tapped for media availability, but given my streak, I guess I can't get out of this.

I grunt and nod.

And so it goes.

We win the third game, thank fuck. I get into another scuffle, but this time I don't draw a penalty, because it's a bit of a melee and the refs call it a draw. Someone rips my jersey, which is a great excuse to pop them in the helmet with my blocker.

"I think you liked that," Smash says as we're separated from our opponents.

I laugh. "Of course."

"Good."

And that feels like playoff hockey. We need to hold on to that.

After that win, which we wore our retro jerseys for, I ask the equipment team if I can have my jersey to take home. I need the reminder that even rocky stretches can have some bright moments.

But overarching the entire trip is an unusual weight.

I miss my girls.

While we've talked a few times every day, I don't feel like Emery and I have *talked* in a solid week.

Maybe that's why the vibes are off.

After a team dinner at our final hotel the night before our final game on the road, where the food isn't half as good as what Emery makes, I head back to my room, with my laundered jersey in a bag from the equipment guys.

There's a card game going on down the hall, but I said I needed to call home, and I meant it. There's only one person whose company I want tonight.

This close to the playoffs, I know the right answer is to spend time with the team. But we'll reset and try again in a few days. Right now, I need to focus on the home vibes.

I prop a pillow against the headboard and stretch my legs out. My pulse kicks up as the screen rings, which is fucking stupid. I know she'll answer. She always does.

She picks up on the second ring.

"Hey." Her voice is low. Soft. *Home.*

She's sitting on the couch, and as she shifts to get more comfortable, I see there's a pile of toys beside her. She's wearing one of my sweatshirts, the sight of which gives me a nice possessive punch in the chest, and her hair is up in two messy little pigtails on top of her head.

"You're awake," I say, because the other things I want to say aren't allowed if anyone else is in the room with her. *You're gorgeous. I miss you. I need to kiss every inch of you again.*

She gives me a lopsided smile. "I am."

"I got you a present."

Her eyebrows curve up in curiosity. "You did?"

I grin. "Yeah. Okay, might also be a present for me, too."

She winks. God damn, I miss her.

"How was bedtime?"

"Easy peasy. She's happy she can play with your parents again. We all walked to the park today, and she really tired herself out. Your mom did, too, but in a good way."

"Anyone else still up?" My voice dips low. I'm pretty sure she's all alone, but I want her to say it.

"Nope. Everyone here is tucked in for the night."

I exhale, relief coursing through me. "Everyone except you. Who's going to tuck in Emery?"

Heat pops in her cheeks, and her lips darken, too. She's turned on, and I know it, and I can't push those buttons too hard, but pushing her buttons is all I can think about.

Silence stretches as she looks at me through the phone. My pulse grows heavy.

And then she licks her lips. "I was hoping you would."

Fuck yeah. "Take me to bed with you, sunshine."

She gestures as the mess around her. "I was just tidying up."

"Okay. Tell me about your day while you do that."

She sets her phone down and disappears, but she keeps talking. "I've been researching childcare options, actually."

"What?"

She reappears and gives me a nervous smile. "The EBUB program doesn't last forever."

I try not to scowl. "I know."

"Umm, so today's research was for like, next year maybe. Did you know that preschool registration is actually kind of competitive?"

"I did not."

"Same." She finishes moving the toys to their bins, and picks up the phone again. "So yeah, Charlie just got off a waiting list for a program, and Becca was mentioning how it took her a while. And I was thinking about your dad..."

She goes quiet as she climbs the stairs.

She checks on Inessa, quietly showing me that my daughter is fast asleep, then steps back into the hallway.

"Go to my room," I say quietly.

She crooks an eyebrow at the camera. "Yeah?"

I want her on my bed.

I want her underneath me, but that's going to have to wait one more night.

As she walks down the hall, I'm struck again by that profound sense of rightness that she's in my space.

Once she clicks my door shut, I drag my mind out of where it wants to go—her tits, her mouth, her soft, soft pussy—and back to the conversation she started.

"You were saying something about my dad..."

"Right. Um, I think another option, rather than a nanny, might be enrolling Inessa in daycare."

"Daycare?" I'm confused where this is coming from. "She's too young, don't you think?"

Emery settles on my bed, her blonde waves spilling over my pillow, exactly as I've dreamed of. Her eyes are bright, and her words spill out fast and furious. "I don't, actually. She loves spending time with Charlie, who is older than her. I bet socializing with other kids more often would be good for her, too. And your dad could manage the daycare drop-off and pick-up on the days that you aren't home."

It's a lot to think about. "What brought this up? Why did you do this research?"

"Because it needs to be done. And you're focused on the season."

"I am still her father."

"I know. I'm not making any decisions for you." She gets a funny look on her face. "Are you mad about this?"

"No." I scrub my hand over my jaw, trying to get my thoughts clear. *I don't know why you care about next year*, is my first thought, but I can't say that.

If I'm going to ask her what she sees in the future, I'm going to do it in person.

"Moya polovinka, tell me. It's okay, I'm sorry. I just wasn't expecting this conversation. Tell me what you think. I want to hear all about it."

She rolls onto her side, her phone coming closer to her face. "She sleeps so much better when she's spent the day playing with another kid."

Oh. Fuck me. "Okay. Thank you for telling me that."

"I know I can go kind of all in on an idea, but I just get curious about things."

"I like your curiosity." I slide down and roll onto my side, too. Now it's like we're lying side by side in bed, heads on pillows next to each other. "Did you read more of that book today?"

"Yeah, a bit. It's really interesting."

"Do you want me to send you another one tomorrow? I think there's still time to order tonight."

She laughs and shakes her head.

"How's your chocolate supply?"

She reaches for the screen, her expression softening. "I'm savouring them. They're so good. Well, some are weird. But I like weird stuff."

"I know. I love that."

Silence stretches. A funny smile plays at her mouth.

"So…"

She nods. "So…"

"I need to tuck you in." There's a strange lump in my throat. I wanted her in my bed so I could talk her through making herself come, but now I want something else. "Crawl under the blankets."

That smile quirks as she does what I tell her.

"I want to find you just like that when I get home," I say. "I want to come home and wrap myself around you. When I saw you in the hospital that night, and you were so…"

Her eyebrows curve up. "Yes?"

"You were fiery. You were perfect. And I was so tired.

I knew I needed to sleep, and I knew it would be hard to rest, but I also knew that if I could just drag you in against me, I would sleep better than I had in two long years."

Her lips part.

Her eyes flash.

Fiery, but soft.

Mine.

"You don't have to say anything like that to me, ever. But I want you to know." My voice catches. "I want you to always know, no matter what, that you have that effect on me. Even when you're mad at me."

She relaxes into her pillow and nods. "That's the nicest thing you've given me this week. And that's a very high bar given the weird chocolates."

I tip my head back and laugh.

When I look back at the camera, Emery is gazing at me with a completely bare, vulnerable stare. And I can't tell her what I see there, but it's an incredible gift, too.

"Good night, moya polovinka."

"What does that mean?" She smiles sleepily. "You've stopped calling me solnishko."

"No, never. I think I just call you sunshine in English now."

"I need to learn Russian."

"When I get home, I'll teach you."

I'll whisper it against her skin until she knows it by heart.

CHAPTER 36
EMERY

Shannon comes over for lunch the last day of the road trip. We've narrowed in on a tea party menu for the baby shower, but we both want there to be some surprises that really blow people away.

I'm in the middle of enthusiastically explaining how silken tofu makes an amazing dessert base for lime and yuzu when my phone lights up with an unexpected email notification—from Montrose Atelier Culinare, the school I'm going to in Switzerland.

Or… the school I *was* going to go to, I realize, when I tap into it.

My voice trails off as I start to read the message.

It is with sincere regret that we write to inform you that the upcoming July cohort of the Montrose Atelier Culinare program has been postponed due to unforeseen environmental damage to our facilities. A recent mudslide caused significant structural impact to our kitchens and lodging quarters, and for the safety of our students and faculty, we will be unable to proceed with the summer session as planned.

We understand this is unexpected news, and we want to acknowledge the time and dedication you've already invested in preparing for this program.

Our team has been working diligently to protect your opportunity for advanced culinary training. We have secured an alternate placement through our partner institution in New York City, but the enrolment dates would be...

"Sorry," I say, my voice distant. "I just need to read the rest of this email."

We understand that this disruption may cause disappointment or uncertainty. If you'd prefer to defer your Montrose placement, we will reserve your spot without penalty.

My heart immediately knows it wants to do that. Just... defer. Put it off until next year. I can go to Switzerland next year, and...

And what?

Spend a year playing house and secret orgasms?

"You look like you've seen a ghost," Shannon says.

I have. It's the Ghost of Emery Past, who was ready to fall in love with Alexei at the first hot press of his mouth between my legs.

"My culinary institute emailed," I say numbly.

I explain the gist of the email. And I get choked up when I repeat the option they've given me. "I'm sorry. I don't know why I'm so upset."

She shifts sideways in her chair and rubs my back. "You had a plan, and it's been derailed. I would be upset, too."

I wipe my eye, furious that tears are trying to get involved here. There's no reason to *cry*. That's ridiculous. "Look at me. This is nothing. It's fine. I just need to make a decision."

"Do you need to make it today?"

My thumb twitches as I scroll through the email. "No. I've got a few days."

"Take that time, then."

I nod. "Yeah."

"Do you want to talk it out?"

How do I explain that since Switzerland was a done deal, and on the other side of the playoffs, I'd pushed it out of my mind?

But now this email has thrown me for a loop.

You have a choice, Emery Granger.

I don't want a new choice. I want the old choice that I already made. I want the strength of that conviction.

"I don't know what the right thing to do is here." My voice sounds raw. I *feel* raw. "I can't go to New York. It's too soon."

"Why is it too soon?"

I lift my head in surprise.

Shannon is looking at me so carefully, like she's afraid I might break.

I won't break. I'm fine.

"Alexei needs me until the end of playoffs."

"What do you need?"

"I—" I drag in a breath. "No, I know, but Inessa…"

The thought of abruptly disappearing from her life steals my breath.

"If I were in your shoes, what would you tell me?" Her words sound carefully chosen. "And I don't mean the advice you'd give if you were trying to be polite or keep the peace. I mean the thing you would tell me because you really love me and want me to be happy."

That lands harder than I expect. I swallow against a sob that wants to leak out around the lump in my throat. "Oh, Shannon. I do love you."

"Then give me good advice. I have a plan, and conditions have changed. What would you tell someone who has a big, beautiful dream, and a heart that is trying to hold all the space for someone else's life at the same time?"

CHAPTER 37
ALEXEI

I drag myself in the front door of my house at two in the morning, really over this whole *vibes-aren't-vibing* week, and I find Emery asleep in my bed.

Everything immediately feels better.

I quickly change into a t-shirt and sweats, and climb in with her, wrapping myself around her soft little body.

As I correctly thought two weeks ago, I sleep spectacularly with her in my arms.

———

"Shhh, don't wake him up."

"I'm up," I mumble, right before Inessa burrows herself in between me and Emery little a warm little bowling ball of joy.

"Papa," she whispers happily.

"I'm home," I say, rubbing her back as I blink my eyes open. "What time is it?"

Emery has slid over in the bed, but she didn't bolt, so that's a good sign. "Just after six."

I groan. "I got in at two."

"She must have sensed your presence. Think she might go back to sleep with you?"

I nod sleepily.

"Okay. Send her out to me if she doesn't let you rest. And I'll come check on her after my workout."

Wait, I want to say. *Come back and cuddle with us.* But my eyes are already sliding shut again, fatigue and exhaustion pulling me back under.

———

When I wake up again, it's half-past nine.

Inessa is no longer asleep next to me. I find her downstairs in the kitchen. My mom and Inessa are working at the table, and Emery has an assembly line of food on the island.

"What's all this?"

Emery looks up from where she's piping something white onto what looks like a rectangular piece of Russian black bread. "We're recipe testing sandwiches for Ani Hale's baby shower."

"Delicious breakfast," my mother says, then giggles.

"Hi, Mama," I say, crossing to drop a kiss on the top of her head. She looks so much better than when I left last week. Her cheeks have more colour in them, and her eyes are brighter. "You look like you have lots of energy today."

"I do. It's all of Emery's excellent cooking," she says in Russian. "Oh, exciting news. I taught her to make borscht. And it's even better than mine."

"Did you?" I groan and pat my stomach, then switch back to English. "Tell me there's leftover borscht, Emery."

She laughs. "In the fridge."

While the soup heats up, I ask about everything laid out on the island.

"Fresh pickles for sandwich toppers." Emery points one by one. "Shallots, radishes, tiny cauliflower florets. Do you want to try some?"

"If you're making it, I'm eating it."

"The black bread is an unexpected base for fresh cream cheese with chives and garlic." She grabs a long pair of tweezers and carefully layers on three pickled radishes on top of the cheese before finishing it with a garnish of pea sprouts.

I open my mouth as she lifts the sandwich and holds it for me to take a first bite. Flavours explode in my mouth, fresh and tangy and sweet all together.

I groan and lunge forward, taking the rest of the finger sandwich before kissing the tip of her finger.

She laughs, a delighted peal that goes straight to my chest.

I swallow and gesture for more. "Yes. Make me another one."

The next one is ham and mustard.

I'm already in love and I haven't tried it yet. I lean in as she prepares it. "And how did you make ham and mustard fancy?"

"Well, the mustard has some honey in it. Just a little sweetness. And underneath that is a smoked butter."

"Smoked…" I blink. "Did you make your own butter?"

Her smile is a thousand kilowatts bright. "Yep."

"Feed it to me."

"Alexei, let the poor girl finish her work," my mother says.

And that's when I remember we aren't alone.

Emery's cheeks turn pink as I pick up the delicate finger sandwich, topped with a few pickled onions.

It's. Fucking. Amazing.

"Stop moaning," she whispers. Then she lifts her voice. "Your borscht is ready."

"Good. I'm starving."

And then, because my mother has turned her attention back to her task at the table, I slap Emery on the ass.

She jumps and whirls around, and the bright eyes and pink cheeks are everything I've ever wanted in a response. "What was that for?"

"For making everything better. Just like sunshine."

—————

After sandwiches, they move on to decorating sugar cookies. I'm given the task of moving decorated cookies to drying racks—and also keeping Inessa's icing-covered fingers away from the official cookies for the party.

She's got her own little batch that she has free range to

decorate as she wants, which is…lots of icing. All the colours.

But there are limits for little girls, and she tires of the project long before Emery and my mom are done.

"Is this a sign we need to go to the park?" I try to wipe her hands and face, but she has icing in her hair, and she needs a change of clothes, too. "Come on, little one. You're a mess. We'll get cleaned up, and *then* we'll go to the park."

Upstairs, I strip her down to her diaper, then go into the bathroom she now shares with Emery to get a damp washcloth.

Emery has made the space her own. Makeup, perfume, face cream, hair clips. So many hair clips.

A bright pink hair iron, probably the tool that makes those perfectly smooth waves, catches my eye on a high-up shelf.

And then my gaze slides to a small foil packet next to the iron. It's something that I haven't seen in this washroom before, and I pick it up before my brain can stop my inappropriate curiosity.

Birth control pills.

I turn the packet over, blood pounding in my ears. Two pills are gone. Her period must have ended the day before yesterday.

I picture Emery standing at the sink, popping one in her mouth, swallowing it down with water before she brushes her teeth in the morning, taking care so that she doesn't accidentally end up a single parent like I have.

Something wild curls in my chest, a sharp, complicated feeling that I have no right to allow to foster.

She isn't *mine*, exactly. Not yet. Every time we're intimate, she makes it clear that she's leaving. And we haven't done *this* yet. We haven't needed *these* yet.

Her personal life is her own, I know that, but my fist clenches around the pack, crumpling it in an irrational reaction.

Fuck.

She's taking these pills to avoid getting pregnant. She's taking these so she can have a cock inside her and—

I smooth it as much as I can and put it back on the shelf.

I didn't miss her all fucking week to lose my mind to irrational jealousy.

Of course I know that when the playoffs are over, she's leaving us. She needs to follow her dreams, and I'm not an asshole. I won't stop her from going to Switzerland —wouldn't even if I could, but I know I can't.

But I can give her all the reasons in the world to come back to me when she's done.

And I can set a standard so fucking high, no Swiss dick will ever compare.

CHAPTER 38
EMERY

It's so, so hard to pretend I'm not affected by Alexei as much as I am. There might be a language barrier between his mother and me, but her gaze is knowing.

I feel utterly transparent.

When we're together, everything fades away, replaced by this wild, fizzy wonder. Like champagne bubbling up inside me. Joyful. Light. Dangerous in its own way. Like celebration trapped under skin, aching to be released.

The sandwiches and cookies were a distraction device. I have filled my week with them: childcare research, big cooking projects, extra-hard workouts, and so many trips to the park.

Anything to pretend that I'm just a temporary nanny. A helping friend.

Not...*more.*

But then he came home and wrapped himself around me, literally and figuratively, and it turns out, even sandwiches and cookies don't lie about what we are to each other.

I need to talk to him as soon as they get back from the park.

Right on cue, the front door opens.

Unfortunately, the first thing I hear is the screaming protest of an unhappy two-year-old.

"Emmy," Inessa sobs in the foyer.

Alexei's sigh is so audible, it carries all the way into the kitchen.

I exchange a nervous look with Maria.

"Go," she says, smiling, her eyes twinkling like she's happy it's no longer a plaintive *Baba* cry all the time. "I'm going downstairs now. Time to rest."

My heart squeezes as I pop my head into the hallway. "What's up, baby girl?"

She wrenches out of her little pink coat and falls down.

Alexei tips his face up to the ceiling and counts backwards.

"Frustrating walk back from the park?" I whisper, touching his arm for a second before I crouch down next to Inessa.

"You could say that," he growls. "She wanted to take big steps all on her own. But her legs literally aren't as long as mine."

I swallow a laugh.

Then I touch Inessa's hand and whisper, "Was it hard to take big steps?"

She climbs to her feet and throws herself at me, nodding.

I pat her back. "Did you try shrinking the world?"

Both father and daughter look at me in confusion.

I keep a straight face, and keep whispering. "You're a giant girl."

Inessa giggles. "No."

"So big."

"Emmy silly." But now she's laughing, not crying.

"And your Papa is *tiny*."

She twists away from me and stomps over to him, growling exactly the same way he does. "Tiny," she repeats.

He stares down at her.

She stares back.

And then she twirls away and runs to the kitchen, cackling.

Alexei's unreadable gaze shifts to me, and I squirm inside, remembering our heated conversation about daycare.

But then, as I stand, Alexei pulls me up and into his arms and plants a fast, hard kiss on my mouth.

Fizzy fizzy joy.

Damn it.

"How did you do that?" he asks when he lets me go.

"Oh, um…" I shrug. "TikTok. Whispers cut through the big feelings. And then like, echo the problem and try to provide a play solution."

He frowns. "You whispered to me, too."

I give him an innocent look. "Did I?"

"You did."

"Huh."

His gaze flares hot. "Are you going to suggest a play solution for me, too?"

Heat swirls low in my belly. "Maybe."

"I think it's nap time for Inessa." His gaze rakes over me. "And for us, too."

"Okay," I say, my heart suddenly pounding. "Good. Um, because I wanted to talk to you about something."

His gaze sharpens—intense, focused entirely on me.

"I love talking to you," he murmurs. "But we've got limited nap time, and I've missed you."

My stomach flips.

"I've missed you too," I admit.

His mouth is on mine before I can say more—soft, addictive. My mind goes hazy and all I can feel is—

"Emmy!"

Alexei drops me like a hot potato.

Cheeks on fire, I scoop Inessa up from where she's tugging at my pants. "How about some lunch real quick?"

She rubs her eyes as she eats, and it doesn't take long for me to get her upstairs, her little arms wrapped tight around my neck, her soft breath puffing against my skin.

Alexei meets me at the top of the stairs and takes her from me.

"There's a present for you on my bed," he murmurs. "I'll put her down and then come find you."

I see it as soon as I step into his room. The retro jersey he wore a few games ago. Not one of the clean, crisp replicas. This one is *his*. Game-worn. Goalie-cut. Enormous.

I pick it up, soft and heavy in my hands. It's been washed, but the battle of the game is obvious. There's a significant tear at the neck, and there's still a puck mark in the middle of the chest, just above the stylized boar logo.

It wasn't that long ago that I longed to fire shots in that exact same spot. To make him take all of my frustration, all of my longing, to absorb it because I didn't think there was any point of talking about what had happened between us.

Water under the bridge.

All in the past.

A mistake we once made together.

In such a short period of time, all of that has faded away. It's so bittersweet to realize just how much he means to me now, when I'm the one who is faced with the decision to walk out a door at the wrong moment, for a good reason.

"Put it on," he says from the doorway, voice low.

I glance back.

He's gripping the doorframe, his gaze hot and focused. "Inessa went straight to sleep. I'm all yours."

And the way he says it…he means it on more than one level. I know that in my soul.

So I give him a show.

I set the jersey down and unbutton my jeans. Slowly unzip the fly and slide them down my legs.

I turn around, giving him my back before I peel off my

shirt. Then I reach behind me, unclasp my bra, and hold it out to the side until I hear his groan.

Slowly, the bra slips off my fingertips and tumbles to the floor.

Before I take off my underwear, I tug the jersey over my head. The fabric rubs against my hard nipples and makes me shiver.

Alexei doesn't miss that I'm still wearing something other than his jersey, and that won't do. "Your panties belong on my floor, too."

I glance over my shoulder and hold his eye contact, my breath shallow in my chest as I shimmy them down slowly.

Flick, they go flying off my toe.

Then I crawl onto his bed and kneel for him—bare except for his number.

He makes the most satisfying growl low in his throat.

"See something you like?" I ask, a little breathless.

He steps inside and closes the door behind him, cocooning us in his bedroom.

"You look good enough to eat," he says. He wipes his mouth, his fingers pulling at his lower lip as he prowls closer. Then, softer, "Can you be a quiet girl for me?"

I bite my lip and nod as he closes the gap between us, tumbling me onto my back, climbing over me fully clothed while I burn beneath him.

"I found your birth control pills earlier," he murmurs. "Do we need anything else? I haven't been with anyone since you."

A tremor of desire flutters inside me, low and deep

and absolutely certain. We have to close the loop we started two years ago.

It matters.

I shake my head. "We don't need anything else."

He kisses me then, long and slow, and his hands roam over my body—first over the jersey, then beneath it. Insistent, but never rushed. He cups and squeezes, gropes and caresses. Exploring for his own hungry reasons and stoking my need at the same time.

"I would have waited forever for you," he says, reverent.

My throat tightens.

And in that moment, I know there was never going to be anybody else.

"Me too," I whisper. "I want you inside me, Alexei."

CHAPTER 39
ALEXEI

How many times over the last two years have I imagined her saying that? And it sounds better than I ever imagined.

"Soon, baby," I promise, my head spinning.

She feels so fucking good. And looks so fucking good, too, in my jersey. My number on her sleeves, her naked body hidden like a treasure.

I tug at the ripped collar, dropping my head to kiss at her collarbone. The fabric gives way a bit more.

"Easy, tiger," she laughs.

I lift my head and she bites her lip, pulling my attention to her mouth.

"I mean, don't go too easy on me," she breathes. "But don't wreck my present, either."

"Not wrecking it," I growl. "Making it ours."

She pulls me down for another kiss as the side seam pulls loose under my fist, and the heavy fabric gives way to warm, firm flesh.

With a gasp, she arches beneath me as I fill my hand with her breast.

She's so responsive. I love the little sounds that she makes.

I brace myself and push my other hand between her legs. Her pussy is so soft against my fingertips as her thighs fall open for me.

Watching her pleasure build does something profound to me, deep inside.

As I stroke her entrance, her gaze widens, her pupils dilating.

"I'm ready for you," she says, her voice aching as much as my cock is.

And I can feel how wet she is, but she's also so tight, barely taking one finger. Her soft, silky walls are going to feel incredible around my cock.

Her hips lift, meeting my hand as I drag my hand out, then thrust my finger back into her.

"You like that?"

"Yes." She moans, her gaze losing focus.

"I know you do. I love your greedy little pussy. It can't lie to me. It clamps down on everything I give it. Did the same thing to my tongue."

She whimpers and bucks her hips harder against my hand, and I know she's eager, I am too. But her little body isn't as ready on the inside as I can feel she is on the outside.

"Slow down, baby. I don't want to rush. I've missed you so much. Let me play with you."

I give her a second finger. Her breath hitches.

"Okay?"

She nods quickly. "Yes. More, Alexei. Please…" She grabs at my t-shirt. "I want to feel you on top of me."

I ease my fingers out of her, licking them clean before I help her get me naked.

It's our first time like this, so I know I should make her come a few times. But nap time doesn't last forever, and I need to be inside her as much as she clearly craves that connection, too.

As soon as my cock is freed from the confines of my clothes, he arches away from my body, the tip curving straight to the core of her body. Her hand slides between us, circling my shaft, squeezing me as she pulls us together.

As soon as my cock meets the slick wetness between her pussy lips, I'm a fucking goner. I swear under my breath in Russian and in English at how perfect she feels.

I look down between us.

I need to see what I can feel.

Her pussy is dark pink, puffy and split open around my erection. As I stare at where she's rubbing me against her entrance, pre-come pulses to the tip of my cock, adding to the slick, shiny mess.

"Look at you," I groan. "You're so fucking gorgeous."

"You feel bigger than I thought," she says, her voice trembling.

"Just move yourself against me." I cover her hand with mine, both of us working my fat crown against her hole now, trying to fit inside. "Do what feels good. It all feels incredible to me."

"Oh God," she breathes, her thighs flexing against my hips. "Oh God…"

The more she rubs, the bigger, thicker, and harder I get, stretching until my foreskin is pulled all the way down and my sensitive head is fully exposed to her lush little cunt.

Her sweet, bright musk rises between us from where she glistens against my cock. Nothing has ever smelled so good, fucking delicious.

I need a taste.

I push her thighs up, propping them on my shoulders as I lick between her lips and suck on her clit, but it doesn't take long for her to drag me back on top of her. She's clear about what she wants, what we both need.

She's a horny, beautiful creature writhing in my jersey, begging to be fucked.

I kiss her mouth, then drag my mouth down to her bare tit, sucking on her tight peaked nipple for a long moment as she fucks herself on just the very tip of me.

And then, just as I brace my arms on either side of her head and shift my knees up to gain more leverage, she figures out the right angle. She hitches one of her legs up around my waist and pulls me inside her.

Shock flares across her face, her eyes widening as she stares up at me. Her lips part in a wordless *oh* and there's the tiniest, hitching gasp as her slickness gives way.

The urge to drive into her quivering belly is nearly overwhelming, needing to be inside her, to feel her clenching down around me and but there's no thrusting all the way into her, Not in one push.

She's too tight for that.

As my tip works into her an inch, then two, her hands come up between us.

I ease my hips back, then roll forward again, claiming a bit more of her. This time, there's more give, and her tightness feels more welcoming, squeezing as I pump deep and work her open.

"Alexei, slow down," she pants. "It's…um…"

Her fingers curl into my bare chest and I go still.

The profound surprise on her face is unmistakable. I should have clued in sooner.

I stare down at her, my pulse pounding, pleasure licking up my shaft and deep into my core as I finally, finally get to be inside her—only to realize that I'm probably the first one to say that.

All this time, Emery was a virgin?

I breathe her name, my voice breaking.

She shakes her head and winds her arms around my neck.

"It's okay," she promises, lying to me, because I can see on her face that it's not.

How can this feel so fucking good for me, so perfect and hot and incredible, when I've just stolen something precious from her.

"You haven't done this before."

"Only wanted it with you." Her eyelids flutter shut, and she takes a deep breath.

"Why didn't you tell me?" I grind out, planting my hand against the mattress as I wrestle my baser instincts for control.

She blinks her eyes open again and wraps both legs tighter around my hips, not letting me retreat. "Because I wanted this. I wanted all of you."

"Let me make it feel better." I kiss her mouth, sinking more of my weight down onto her. Promising her I'm not really going anywhere, not for long.

She trembles around me, but as we slowly make out, she softens and calms.

"I want to make you come first," I finally whisper against her lips. "I should do that every time, moya polovinka. But especially this time. And once you come, I will be back inside you, I promise."

She unwinds her limbs, trusting me. I rear up, taking a deep breath as I look down at her in my jersey.

"You look perfect." I squeeze her in my hands. "Let me see the number on your back."

She smiles as I roll her over, until I can't see her smile anymore because she's face down and I've pulled her hips in the air.

"My number always looks better on you," I groan, spreading my fingers wide on her hips, her ass. Holding on tight. Fuck yes, my number on her back looks incredible. Like I've claimed her inside and out. The soft curve of her bare ass and the slick secrets peeking out between her legs look even better.

I remember how responsive she was in the shower when the lights were off.

There's something freeing about getting to hide her face in the mattress as she humps back and against my face, and I want that for her—and selfishly, for me. I want everything she gives me, nothing held back.

I drop to my belly and eat her out from behind. She tastes so fucking good, and feels so warm, as her sweet pussy softens against my tongue. It doesn't take long until we're both making desperate whining sounds.

My cock throbs to get back inside her, and I have to take myself in hand. As I lick and suck at her, I squeeze myself hard, needing to be patient. Fuck. *Fuck.*

Then her hips start shaking. That's all I need to keep going, to get even more of her all over my face, because once she comes, then I'm allowed to sink back into her tight, virgin pussy.

I shouldn't like that as much as I do. Shouldn't take a sharp, savage pride in being the only person she trusts this much. I sure as fuck haven't earned that loyalty from her, and I'm not sure she'd even call it that.

If she could have given her virginity to anyone else, she probably would have, and I want to repair what is broken between us so she never considers this a mistake.

We are not a mistake.

We are forever.

We are perfection.

With a cry, her whole body flexes, and then she's pulsing against my tongue, and I push into her, tasting her tightness as she rides out her wild release.

I let go of my cock and stroke her thighs, swallowing her arousal until she goes limp. Until she's softer than she's ever been for me before.

Now, finally, I can roll her over again.

This time, when I work myself into her, I do it with the profound awareness that this is new for her. That her startled expression is a precious, fleeting gift.

Somehow, her body takes me like she was made for me.

Nobody else is ever going to have her.

I scoop one arm beneath her, anchoring her to me as I bring my thighs under hers, lifting her hips up. Then I brace one hand on the mattress and stroke the other over her belly and her mound, where her pussy is stretched tight around my shaft—and her clit is standing up, desperately in need of some loving attention.

I'll make it perfect for her. She deserves her first time, her every time, to be perfect.

As I give her clit slow little circles, Emery stares up at where my cock disappears into her body. "How do you fit? You feel too, um...."

I fucking hope that it feels good for her. "Is it too much?"

"No, it's too incredible to be real. Why didn't we do this two years ago? God, Alexei, please start moving."

That's all I need to hear.

I roll my hips tentatively at first, making sure she can take it.

"Fuck," I breathe.

"Yeah?" The look of wonder on her face is everything.

I'm trying desperately to ignore how fucking good it feels to drag my cock against her inner walls, and keep focused on making this good for *her*, but... "Yeah," I groan. "You feel so fucking good around me."

"Go faster," she whispers.

"Don't want to hurt you."

"I'm okay." And deep inside, she squeezes her body around me. I jerk against her, and her eyes go wide. "Oh!"

I laugh desperately. "Yeah, you've got some power over me, sunshine."

She exhales and does it again.

I thrust into the tight internal squeeze.

When there's no hints of pain in her expression, I push my jersey up so I can see her tits bounce, and I pick up the speed.

She meets me hip roll for hip roll, a little uncoordinated at first, which has its own thrill, but then she starts to trust her own pleasure, and *Goddamn,* but getting fucked back by Emery is the best thing I've ever felt.

This isn't just sex.

She holds my gaze, eye-fucking me with a raw intensity that makes me want to crawl inside her and never leave.

How many times did I fantasize about being inside her? And for all the times I came so fucking fast to that image, now I feel like I could go all afternoon. Take her to the brink, over and over again.

And maybe I would, except when she starts to come apart, and she realizes that she's going to have another orgasm, she looks…genuinely surprised. Like *I've* given *her* something, instead of the other way around.

"Alexei, I'm going to…"

"I know, I can feel it. You're close, yes?"

"Mm-hmm." She sucks in a breath and holds it, her

back arching and her thighs straining. She goes still, and then her pussy clamps down and her clit jumps against my fingers.

I tumble forward, wrapping both arms around her now, cradling her in my arms.

"That's it, pretty girl. Come for me. Be a good girl and come hard, so I can fill you up."

She cries out, and I thrust my hips deep, holding myself there as she quivers around me, her body trembling from the inside out as I kiss my way down her jaw, her neck, to the flutter point at the base of her throat.

Against my lips, her pulse races as she rides the aftershocks of her orgasm.

"Alexei, I..." She sobs and laughs, and then she tilts her hips up, and I find a new depth to her that is my undoing.

The soft, clutching squeeze of her pussy around my cock is suddenly more than I can bear.

She sees it, too.

"Are you going to..." She wraps her legs around me, squeezing me tight, leaving no doubt about where she wants my release.

I moan her name, probably too loud, but I can't stop myself as my hips snap hard. "Coming inside you, fuck, going to fill you up. Take it all."

My vision blurs, and then goes dark. I fall heavier on top of her, pressing my face into her neck. My cock burrows deep, pulsing as my balls release so much pent-up need.

And I stay there, inside her, *moya polovinka*, until she's milked every last drop.

Even when I roll onto my back, I plaster her against me. I can't get enough of our skin to skin contact.

Her face is pink, and she's flushed everywhere, down onto her chest under the ripped jersey.

As if she can tell I'm cataloguing all the ways I've messed her up, she presses her hand to her cheek, then tries to smooth her hair.

"You've never been more beautiful," I say, and I mean it.

The beaming smile she gives me only adds to that beauty.

As her breathing settles, I trail my fingers under the jersey, up and down her spine, and nuzzle against her cheek.

"You feel so good," I whisper against her damp skin. God, I just want to hold her tight. Hold her close. Hold her endlessly. "Never want to forget this moment. I love you."

She goes very still.

"You don't have to say it back." My heart speeds up, pounding against my ribcage. "It just slipped out. But it's true. And…you deserve to know that you are loved."

"Alexei…" She twists onto her side and pushes the jersey down, covering her body. "I need to leave next week."

CHAPTER 40
EMERY

As soon as I've said it, I know it's the wrong moment to break the news to him.

He slides away from me and wraps himself in the bedsheet. "What do you mean?"

I explain about the email, my voice wavering as he stays silent the whole time, his expression unreadable.

"Why didn't you tell me?"

"I am telling you."

He nods sharply. "And what we just did? What was that? A parting gift?"

My spine snaps straight and I scramble off the bed, his jersey falling to my knees. I ignore the slide of his seed down the inside of my thighs. "You think I gave you my virginity as a *present*? Like, *see you later*?"

His throat works for a long silent pause before he finally grinds out, "It's hard not to think that, yes."

All the air whooshes out of me in a shocked gasp.

And then right on cue, Inessa wakes up. Because that's

life with a toddler. The universe really thought I needed a reminder of what it would mean to love Alexei—no honeymoon period, just a lot of real life. Arguments and misunderstandings and constant interruptions.

It would be real from day one, it already *is* real, and all the incredible intimacy we just shared now needs to be packed away with this disagreement on top of it.

We both stare at the baby monitor.

"I have to get dressed," he mutters.

"Wait," I say. "Please let me—"

He gives me a disbelieving look that shuts me right up.

I sit down on his bed, heavily, and watch in disbelief as he stalks into the bathroom first, then to his closet. He avoids eye contact with me as he quickly and efficiently transforms back into Inessa's Dad, and then leaves me alone to wonder if the man who I'd just seen, and held, and loved, was nothing but a mirage.

CHAPTER 41
ALEXEI

By the time I get Inessa changed, Emery has disappeared into the bathroom and the shower is running.

"Let's go downstairs," I say, my heart sinking.

"I do it," Inessa insists, not wanting me to carry her.

"Hold on to the railing."

"Yep," she says, and she sounds so much like Emery it physically hurts.

She's leaving.

Inessa is oblivious, chattering away to me in Russian.

"Let's go to the park, Papa."

"Can we play mini sticks, Papa?"

"It's okay, I'll get it, Papa."

"Wait, what?" I realize I've followed Inessa into the kitchen, and she's trying to open the fridge. "I'll get it."

I open the door, then look down at her. "I'm sorry. I wasn't listening. What do you want?"

"Papa!"

"What?"

"I want milk." She gives me an exaggerated pout.

"Try using your manners."

She takes a deep, exaggerated breath, then gives me a very sweet smile. "Please have milk?"

"Of course."

I fill a sippy cup for her, then mix up a supplement shake for myself, too, while I'm at it. The routine of it is like a lifetime.

She's leaving.

It's a drum beat in my head for the next few hours. Emery escapes for an hour, going grocery shopping and dropping off the baby shower supplies at Kieran and Harper's house.

By the time she gets back, she has busy work in the kitchen that occupies her until my parents appear for dinner.

She puts on a good mask with them, asking them to teach her phrases in Russian, and practicing the vocabulary she's already learned. And I can't pretend that I don't need the space she's created, too.

I'm still reeling.

But when bedtime for Inessa rolls around, and my parents head downstairs for the night, I'm also glad for the chance to be alone again, and try to repair what I broke earlier.

I lift Inessa into my right arm and press a kiss to her temple. She's already half asleep, soft and heavy against my shoulder.

"Say goodnight to Emery," I murmur.

"Night-night, Emmy," she mumbles, lifting her head just enough to offer a sleepy kiss.

Emery leans in and kisses her back. "Goodnight, baby girl," she whispers, brushing her fingers down Inessa's curls.

For just a second, I wrap my free arm around Emery, and I press a kiss to the top of her head.

"I'm sorry," I say, low.

She nods, but doesn't look at me.

"I'll come back to clean up."

I carry Inessa upstairs, settle her in bed, trying to pretend the night is normal. It isn't, though. Everything feels unmoored and my thoughts are spinning fast and furious, the panicky drumbeat growing louder again.

She's leaving.

She was always leaving, but… in the summer. When I could follow her like a lovesick puppy.

Now she has to disappear before the playoffs even begin.

She promised me the playoffs.

But did she?

I browbeat her into agreeing to work for me. And then I seduced her. I didn't take no for an answer, ever, because it's unfathomable to me that we aren't meant to be together again.

She didn't argue because I wouldn't hear it.

But behind the scenes, she made a decision to leave.

She's leaving, she's leaving, she's leaving.

It's been hours, and I'm still not able to think about it without my body wanting to fight, and fight hard.

And downstairs, the steady clatter from the kitchen tells me she's ignored my instruction that I would clean up.

By the time I make it back downstairs, Emery's even tidied the living room. The toys are stacked. The dishwasher's humming. The couch looks untouched except for her—sitting there like she's bracing for impact.

"I would have…" I trail off, then gesture to the spot beside her. "Can I sit?"

She nods.

I lower myself to couch, wanting desperately to stretch my arm out across the back of the cushions, to wrap my hand around her far shoulder and tug her into my side.

She's leaving.

I don't pull her into me.

We don't speak for a long time.

"I'm not handling this well," I finally admit. "I am sorry."

"I know."

"I was looking at vacation rentals in Switzerland last week." My voice is rough.

She doesn't say anything, but her shoulders go tight. I press on.

"I never want you to think I don't support your dreams. I do. I would do anything I can to help you get there." I swallow hard. "So if you need to go to New York, you go. I'm not going to stop you." My pulse is so loud in my ear, I can barely hear my own voice. "But I don't like being blindsided by it."

Her voice is small. "I just found out yesterday."

I look over at her.

"And then you came home, and…it felt really good. I missed you a lot." She exhales shakily. "I knew I needed to talk to you, and I meant to, but then I just… I just wanted to be with you. It wasn't like a parting gift."

"That was a shitty thing for me to say. I'm sorry." I reach for her hand.

But she pulls her fingers into the sleeves of her sweatshirt and shakes her head.

"Emery…"

"No, I just…" She makes a face that looks like she's trying hard not to cry. "I can't."

Fuck.

Fuck.

I close my eyes and nod. She needs some space.

She goes to stand up.

"Wait," I say, knowing there's something else I need to tell her, so *she's* not the one blindsided. "When I was looking at those rentals… It was on the plane. It turned into a group discussion. I swore them to secrecy, but…at some point, your brothers are probably going to find out that I'm in love with you."

She laughs weakly. "Great. Cool. All right. I'm going to bed."

Let me…

But she's heading for the stairs.

This really isn't how I thought a day where I told her that I loved her twice would end.

———

Her door stays firmly shut for the rest of the night.

In the morning, I listen for any movement at the other end of the hall. My bedroom door is open, but she doesn't appear. That would be asking too much.

When I finally hear her door open, I leap out of bed, and make it to the doorway just in time to see her step into the bathroom, her hair sleep-tousled and her clothes rumpled.

So fucking squeezable.

Did she sleep like shit, too?

She doesn't glance my way.

She doesn't close the door, either, so I have a direct view of her from the side as she runs the sink, fills a glass with water, takes her pills off the shelf, and pops one into her mouth.

I take a step forward, but then there's a creak from Inessa's room, followed by a thump.

I wait for the inevitable *Papa?* but it doesn't come.

Instead, Inessa comes into the hallway and immediately turns into the bathroom door.

"Emmy," she says happily, throwing herself around Emery's leg.

"Morning," Emery says softly, her voice tight with a bittersweet sadness. "Do you want to see Charlie today, hmm?"

"Yep." Inessa moves around her, climbing up onto the closed toilet.

Emery instinctively hovers her hands behind my daughter, but lets her be fearless.

Quietly, I fade back into the shadows of my bedroom.

They aren't going to have much more time together, and Emery has made it clear she doesn't want to spend any time with me right now. The least I can do is give them their space.

But I want…

Fuck, I really want to keep watching them.

She's leaving.

Yeah, she's going.

But she's leaving her heart here, too. I have to get out of my own way and find a way to show her that we'll protect it. That we'll miss her, and we'll wait forever for her to come back.

CHAPTER 42
EMERY

I'm a zombie this morning. I barely slept a wink, tossing and turning all night. It didn't help that I could still *feel* Alexei inside me. Even this morning, I feel so changed by what we did yesterday—and the fight after—that I wonder if I will always have this cell-level awareness of what it was like to be that close to another person.

That person.

My person.

My frustrating, emotional jerk of a person.

He's not even a jerk, that's the worst part. I know he thought we would have a couple of months together before I left, and I've yanked that out from under him.

But it's not like New York is on the other side of the moon. It's a short flight. Probably an eight-hour drive.

And on top of our crappy communication and my terrible timing, I now have the stress of my family on top of all this.

He's thinking about my brothers finding out about us.

I'm not.

Whatever, they are idiots. If they try to pull any macho "don't touch our little sister" bullshit, I know how to handle them.

But once they know, then my parents will know.

And the only thing worse than my parents expecting me to drop everything to celebrate my brothers' job performances would be my mother expecting me to drop everything to become a WAG.

Even if it feels in my heart of hearts that I love Alexei as much as he loves me, that's *ours*. That's *private*.

I have spent my entire adult life coming to terms with the fact that I don't want the life my family crafted for me, and now I'm a few gossipy text messages away from that being the only life they will ever see for me.

It would be one thing for Alexei and me to announce that we're together in a few months, once I'm well into my training.

But right now?

I can already hear my mother suggesting that I shouldn't go, because Alexei can just take care of me. And it's so hard on the players when their wives are gone.

"Arghhh," I say out loud.

Inessa looks up from where she's taking snapshots on a stuffed hippopotamus. "Argh?"

"I will never expect you to follow in anyone's footsteps, or be anyone else's cheerleader," I promise her. "You get to be your very own person, always."

And then I burst into tears, because for the next six months, I won't actually be here to keep that vow.

"Emmy?" She drops her stick and runs over.

I slide down the side of the kitchen island and fold my knees up, accepting her concerned tackle.

She wraps her arms around my neck and I take a deep breath.

"I'm okay, baby girl."

She pats my cheek. "My Emmy."

"I am. I always will be, I promise." I stroke her curls off her cherubic face. "I'm going away for work. It's going to be really hard. But then I'll come back."

"No work," she says. "Play hockey."

I laugh weakly. "I'm going to tell you a secret I've never told anyone else. There was a time when all I wanted to do was play hockey. When I was a bit bigger than you, I thought I was going to play in the NHL. And I was good. I was amazing, actually.

"But one day my mom told me that I couldn't play in the NHL, and I don't think she meant to hurt me. She was just telling me the truth, as she saw it. She knew there was pressure from other parents on my team, and league official, to get me off the boys' team I was play- ing on.

"It wounded me that *she* was the one who told me, and I've never gotten over the way she told me, like I should just accept that I would never be in the NHL. That didn't seem fair, and it didn't make sense.

"I was a Granger. Of course I could play in the NHL. My dad did. By then, my oldest brother was already there, and my other brothers were being scouted and in development. And the very next tournament I was in, my parents couldn't come to watch because my brother was in the playoffs in his first year."

I swallow hard.

You understand, don't you, Emery?

Except I hadn't.

And they never again prioritized any of my non-Olympics games over my brothers' games.

"To this day, I think the only reason they came to the Olympics was because it wasn't at the same time as the playoffs," I mutter.

Inessa has stopped listening. I mean, she wasn't listening to any of it, really.

I kiss her head. "Anyway, I don't want to play hockey anymore. I want to be able to walk away from something I'm good at, because that's not all I am, and it causes me this weird, quiet stress. Except when I'm playing you, of course. And playing your dad was fun too, I—"

"Noooooo." She sighs dramatically, done with my monologue. "Nessa play hockey."

"Ooooh. Of course. If you want to play hockey, I love that."

She runs back to her game, and I pick myself up off the floor.

If there was ever a sign I should call my parents before they hear about this from anyone else, that confession to myself was it.

I pop downstairs and ask Sergei if he could take Inessa to the park. Maria is feeling well enough to go with them, and I promise to catch up as soon as I've finished the phone call I need to make.

Then I go upstairs.

Alexei isn't back from practice yet, but the house is quiet for now.

I know it's going to be a challenging conversation, where no matter how calm and mature and certain I sound, they're going to second-guess me.

Rip off the Band-Aid, Emery Granger.

I stab the screen and close my eyes.

My mom answers. "Hey, sweetie."

"I have some news," I say. "Can you put Dad on, too?"

She finds him, and once they're both on speaker, I launch into it.

"There's been a change of plans. I can't go to Montrose this summer. It's a whole saga. But they went to a lot of trouble to find me an alternate placement in New York, and I've accepted. It starts next week, so I probably won't have time to come home before moving there."

I can hear their surprise through the glaring silence.

Then…

"Oh," Dad says.

And then Mom sighs. *Sighs.* "Next week?"

Not, *That's so exciting* or *We're proud of you for rolling with a new plan* or even *Do you need help?*

Instead—

"Well… what's Alexei going to do?" my mom asks. "If you leave that soon, will he be able to find another nanny in time?"

I blink.

Seriously?

"He's a grown man," I say sharply. "And I was never his *nanny*."

I mean, I'm going to help him, but seriously??? Why do they put that on me?

"But Inessa—" my dad starts.

"Inessa has a healthy grandfather, a roster of WAGs willing to help, and a father who is more than capable of hiring professionals," I snap. "She's not going to be abandoned."

There's a long pause.

"But you have to understand it's quite sudden, at this time of year."

Because it always comes down to hockey.

"You know, that's funny," I hear myself say distantly. "Because Alexei didn't bring up the playoffs when I told him. But glad to know that's where your priorities lie."

And then I end the call before I say anything I might regret.

I sit there on the edge of the bed, fists clenched, jaw tight.

I don't know why I'm surprised. I could have told myself this is how it would go.

But I was hoping for a different response.

I was hoping for offers of help. For once, I wanted them to worry about *me*.

Fingers shaking, I text Alexei.

> Told my parents. They reminded me that I can't leave you high and dry without a nanny, so I'm going to make some calls today.

Immediately, dots start to appear on the screen.

Then they disappear.

I wait a minute, but when he doesn't actually send whatever he typed, I get up and try to busy myself by doing a load of laundry. I only get as far as taking the basket of clean clothes to Alexei's bed—and then I promptly crawl onto his side and bury my face in his pillow.

"You're ridiculous," I tell myself.

I blow a big raspberry, then check my phone again.

Still no message.

I push myself off his bed and get back to the laundry. I'm not sure where any of his stuff goes, but the door to his closet is open, so I carry a folded stack of clothes in there—and whistle.

"Okay, well, your closet is bigger than my bedroom," I mutter under my breath.

He only uses part of it, too. There's a whole empty side to the room, so I put his stack of clean clothes on one of those shelves. There's no way he'll miss them.

Then I step back and take a look at myself in the floor to ceiling mirror on the wall.

"Nice lighting, too," I murmur.

I step closer to the mirror to check on just how splotchy my face is—not bad—then check my phone *again*.

Still no message.

Whatever Alexei was going to say, he put it on delete instead of send.

I twist a few strands of hair back into place with my fingers, then put my hand on my hip and cock a leg out.

"It's good to stand up for yourself," I tell myself in the mirror.

And then I take a picture for posterity.

Maybe it's the self-talk, maybe it's the click of the shutter, maybe it's the emotional overload, but for whatever reason, I don't hear Alexei until he appears in the doorway to his closet and leans against the jam.

"There you are," he says.

I shriek and jump two feet in the air, spinning around.

"Oh my God," I mutter, pulse racing. "You scared me."

His eyebrows lift. "You didn't see me come in on the front door cam?"

I wave my phone in the air. "I have notifications turned off because Inessa has a habit of taking off with my phone and she clicks on all the banners on the screen. Wouldn't want her to accidentally start talking to a delivery driver."

He muffles a laugh as he nods. Then he gestures to the mirror. "Don't let me interrupt the selfie."

I flush. "It's not a vanity thing."

"You can be vain. You're fucking gorgeous."

I scrunch my nose.

He frowns, making my pulse race.

"No, I mean I know I'm cute." I exhale. "But I was—"

"Cute?" He scowls and prowls right up behind me. "Take your selfie, Emery."

"I'm—"

"Take a video of us." His voice is taut with tension. "Something for you to watch over and over again while you're in New York."

My breath catches in my throat.

His gaze holds mine in the mirror. A challenge. A command.

I lift the phone and turn the camera around so instead of a mirror selfie, it's a video of the two of us.

We don't look like we match. I'm Midwest adorable, he's European sophistication. I'm blonde-haired and pink-cheeked, and there's a little pimple on my chin that I didn't notice before. His dark hair slashes forward over his forehead in a way that money simply cannot buy, and his jaw line is impeccable.

I shift my face this way and that, looking for the right angle to make the zit disappear, and he tugs on his lower lip as he watches me.

"Say cheese," I whisper.

His gaze darkens as I tap the record button, and as the video starts to roll, he wraps his hand around my throat from behind, nudging my jaw up and my head back as his head comes around and his mouth slides over mine in a hot, searing kiss.

I gasp against his lips and he takes the opening, giving me his tongue.

My phone tumbles from my hand as he turns me around and backs me up against the mirror at the same time.

He plants one hand on the mirror above me and slides

the other one down my body, possessively, before he settles it tightly at my hip. "Fucking. Gorgeous."

I stare up at him.

His face is tight with so much tension as we glare at each other. "And you're fucking brave, too."

"What do you…?"

"I didn't understand why your parents would say that about our childcare." His gaze drops to my mouth, hot and needy. "So I checked the kitchen camera."

"The…" Oh *shit*. "Alexei…"

"I'm sorry. I know that was private. But I wish you had told me how hard it was for you." He skates his hand up my body again to cup my face, his thumb tracing my lower lip. "But I'm not sorry that I saw how much you love my daughter, moya polovinka."

"*Moya polovinka*. What does that mean?"

He shakes his head. "Later."

"Not later. Tell me." I lick my lips, the tip of my tongue grazing his thumb.

His gaze darkens.

"Alexei, what does that mean?"

"My soul." His voice cracks. "It means you are my soul, and I will hold you in my heart forever, even if we can never be together again. It means I will not forget you, but I hope that if you can find better, you do, because I want you to be happy. I want my soulmate to have everything she's ever dreamed of."

CHAPTER 43
ALEXEI

"Don't say things like that," Emery whispers, shock and confusion rippling across her face.

But I have to. If I let Emery go without her knowing how I feel, she's gone forever. She moves to New York, she meets someone who loves asparagus sorbet more than any human being possibly should, and they have a herd of foodie children with pointy little chins and flashing eyes.

I shake my head. "I need to. I didn't get to say them for two years—"

"I'm never finding better than you." She grabs the front of my shirt and tries to shake me. And she's strong, but she's not that strong, so she just pulls herself right up against me as I brace my hands on either side of her again. "And *never be together*? Shut your face, Alexei Artyomov. We're going to be so together. I'll show you. Because *you* make me happy."

Her words ring through me like someone has rung a massive bell. "I make you happy?"

"So happy," she breathes.

"I thought you were mad at me."

"I—" She stops and really thinks about that, her eyebrows tugging together. "Well, I'm not— I mean, if I am mad at you, it's only because I'm in love with you."

I exhale in relief and laugh a little as I lean in and rub my nose against hers. "In that case, be as mad as you want."

"We never have enough time to talk." She tugs and shoves at my chest. "Even right now. Inessa is at the park with your parents and I told them I'd meet them there."

"We'll go together in a minute. I want to enjoy you being mad at me first." I step back and catch her hands, then scoop her up by the hips and toss her over my shoulder.

She pummels her little fists against my back. "Alexei, put me down!"

It's a few strides to my bed, where I do exactly as she asks.

She glares up at me. "My phone is still recording, you know."

I grin and jog back to the closet to pick it up.

"I love you, sunshine," I say, winking at the camera before I end the video.

When I hand it over, she takes it, but the storm clouds don't fade from her face.

Immediately, I turn serious again as well. I settle on

the bed, sitting up against the headboard. "You're still unhappy."

"I'm *not* happy, but I'm…" She blows a raspberry. "I guess it's what I said. We never have time to talk. You're gone half the time, and when you are here, it's very regimented. As my parents love to point out, it's an important time in the season."

I take a deep breath. "Yes. Right. We need to deal with your parents at some point. And of course, I cannot change my job. I don't want to change my job. But I am a grown-up, Emery. I can handle many things at once. We will make time to talk. You said my parents are at the park?"

She nods.

I pull out my phone and call my dad.

He answers on the third ring. "Yes, Alexei?"

"Papa, I'm at home with Emery, and I need some privacy to speak to her," I say in Russian. "Are you all right with Inessa? When you come home, can you keep her in your apartment for a bit?"

"Yes, of course."

"Thank you. I love you."

He laughs. "I know, son. I love you, too."

I hang up and gesture to Emery. "Go on. We have all the time we need right now."

"What did you say?"

"I told my dad that I love him."

Her expression softens. "That's sweet."

"And before that, I told him I needed time and privacy to talk to you."

"Oh." Her eyes go wide. "So they…"

"They live with us. Of course they can see how I feel about you."

She presses her lips together, her cheeks turning pink. "They're going to be so disappointed when I leave."

"No." I drag in a rough breath. "Fucking hell, come here. Let me hold you, please."

She crawls towards me, tentatively, and we both exhale in relief when I pull her into my lap and hug her, an embrace that starts out tight and gets even tighter. I wrap my arms all the way around her, my face burrowing into her neck.

"They could never be disappointed in you for following your dreams," I mumble. "And neither could I."

"But…" She takes a deep breath. "I know your mom doesn't like Tatyana."

Ah, fuck.

I squeeze even tighter. "That's more complicated than her dreams simply being elsewhere. You are your own person, and our relationship is completely different." I grunt, hating what I'm about to admit, but Emery deserves to know everything. "This isn't about her. But Tatyana never got mad at me. She would pout and beg and plead, but if I put up a limit about anything, she would just…how do you say it, take her ball and go home? And when she was gone, she didn't miss me. Our lives were never entwined, until we had a child together. And I'm grateful for the gift she gave me, but I will never understand it, because even after that, she somehow managed to disentangle herself from us with ease. That's why my mother doesn't like her. She is not objective when it comes to her only child and grandchild."

"No, of course she isn't." Emery kisses the side of my head softly.

I spread my hands wide across her back, wanting to anchor as much of myself to her as I can. "And that fierce energy? That protective mama bear vibe? The only other time I have ever seen it, Emery, is when I watched that video of you talking to Inessa this morning."

"I can't believe you watched that," she says, then groans. "I fell apart."

"I have done that, too. It's okay."

She takes a deep breath, then wriggles backwards. I give her just enough space for her to take my face in her hands, so she can look at me. "She never got mad at you?"

I laugh. "That's the part you picked up on?"

"I don't know. I just...I feel like I could get mad at you a lot."

I grin. "Because you care."

She exhales carefully, her lips pursed in an oh, and she nods. "So much." Her voice hitches. "I know this isn't about Tatyana, but I'm glad you told me. I...I don't have any experience with serious relationships."

"I need to be very clear. In hindsight, neither do I. You're right. This isn't about her. But also, I didn't want *this* with her. I only want this with you."

"And what is *this*?"

"It's everything. But don't worry. I know that your

everything includes an adventure in New York. And I'll miss you, but I miss you when I have to travel for work, too. And I do that half of the season, don't I? So it's hardly fair for me to begrudge you the same thing."

"I'll miss you, too. And Inessa…" She makes a face, clearly trying not to cry. "Fuck, I'm going to miss her so much."

"We'll come to New York as soon as the season is over."

"Don't rush through playoffs for my sake," she says, laughing through her watery words.

"I won't. Maybe we'll luck out and New York will meet us in the conference finals."

"Can you imagine?" She gets a bright, hopeful look on her face.

And for all the bruised feelings she has about hockey, I can imagine it very clearly. Her in the stands, and then on the ice after we win. Her pure joy, because that's what we are always going to have for each other—love, and respect, and celebrating each other in every way.

Which starts with putting her first.

I thread our fingers together.

She looks down at our hands. "I don't know how summer vacation in New York sounds to you…"

"It sounds great," I say immediately. "We'll make it work. We would anyway, because it's where you need to be. But there are some really solid off-season goalie coaches in Jersey. We can spend the entire summer with you if that's what you want."

The little hesitation even as she nods makes me feel

like shit. I pull her back against me with my free arm, our hands still clasped. My heartbeat slows as soon as I'm wrapped around her again.

"I'll even get Inessa into a preschool there," I murmur into her hair.

"Pretty sure New York preschools are more competitive than Hamilton's," she mumbles.

"I've heard money can make things happen. For us to be with you? I would happily spend it."

"Or we could find you a proper nanny this week, and they could come with you."

"I don't—" I cut my protest off. Because she's right. I do need to find a nanny, at least for the playoffs and the summer.

And they won't be a replacement for Emery.

Because Emery was never my nanny. She was my chef, and my EBUB, and a friend, and then my lover.

And unlike her parents, I don't think it's her job to fix this gap in childcare for me.

Which brings us full circle back to the text message she sent me that brought us to this moment.

I stroke her thumb with mine. "Tell me about your phone call with your parents."

CHAPTER 44
EMERY

"Ugh." I roll my head, my neck suddenly tense. "I don't want to."

"But I want to know. And you heard my struggles."

I lean my cheek against his. "I love being this close to you."

"Same." His free hand drags up and down my spine. And then he lowers his voice and whispers, "Did your parents make my problem your problem?"

"Yeah." I take a deep breath.

He keeps rubbing my back.

"What else?" Again, he whispers the question. Low, slow, soft.

"Wait, are you…" I gasp. "Are you doing the TikTok hack for *toddler tantrums* on me?"

"I…forgot it was for tantrums," he continues to whisper. And his rubbing hand slides up to the base of my neck. "Would a neck rub help?"

I'm never going to say no to a neck rub.

"Maybe," I admit, letting my head fall forward, until my forehead is resting on his shoulder.

He releases my hand and gives it his full attention, his thumbs finding all the points where I'm holding tension and working me into a puddle of goo in his lap.

As I relax, I start to tell him about the phone call. The whole story just slides out of me, no hesitation, no distress.

"I don't want this to sound like *I* don't care about the bind this puts you in, because I do, but I also know we'll figure it out," I mumble. "But that was literally all they cared about. I had to hang up on them."

"You wanted them to be excited for you."

"Yeah."

"And maybe they could have asked if *you* needed any help with a last-minute move."

"Mm-hmm."

"Anything else?"

"They could have asked how I felt about leaving you guys..." I squirm against him, feeling loose and warm now, from the inside out. "If they had, I might have told them how I really feel."

He clears his throat and his hands sink to my ass, palming both cheeks. "And how do you really feel?"

"I'm going to miss you all so much..." I moan under my breath as his cock grows against my core.

"Fuck." He clamps his hands tight and pulls me to a stop.

I hadn't even realized I was rocking my hips back and forth.

"Emery." His voice is strangled. "Tell me you don't want this right now."

"I can't."

"Then tell me what you need."

"I don't know!"

"Are you sore?"

"Mmm, a bit. It's like…" I breathe through the pulsing between my legs. "I can still feel you inside me."

He repeats my name, saying it like a prayer, and then one of his hands is in my hair, making a fist, and tugging my mouth to his.

We kiss like it's the first time again, desperate and disbelieving, and so, so hungry. He pushes his tongue into my mouth and his hips up between my thighs at the same time, grinding hard now.

"Make yourself feel good," he pants in between deep kisses. "Another orgasm will take the edge off the ache."

Will it? Will anything?

I've felt empty since yesterday.

"Like this?" I kiss the corner of his mouth. "Just rubbing on you?"

"Fuck, yeah." He tugs my head back so he can look at me, his lust-filled gaze heavily hooded. "Do whatever feels right for your sore little pussy."

"What about you?"

"Moya polovinka." He gives me a slow, filthy smile that makes something deep in my belly tug hard. "If you come from dry humping me, I will follow you immediately. Or maybe before, but don't let that stop you."

"Before?" I tremble at the thought of making him come in his pants. "Really?"

His pupils dilate. "Try. Try to make me come, sunshine."

I roll my hips and moan. The ridge of his erection feels better on my clit than my fingers ever have.

His hand on my hip pulls me against him as I rock forward, telling me it feels good for him too, that I could go harder.

"I've thought about you on top of me so many different ways. Every morning, I wake up hard for you," he says, voice cracking. "Right here. Just like this."

I gasp when he snaps his presses up into me, perfectly aligned, the friction all I need. I'm trembling already, my breath hitching, my thighs shaking.

"You've ruined me so many times in this bed," he whispers. "But it's never been this good."

"Alexei—"

"You hear me?" He flexes his fist in my hair, his fingers soft against my scalp. Making me shiver. And then tightening his hold again. Claiming me. "You do this to me. Just you. The real you."

Before I can reply to that, he kisses me so roughly— just right—I forget how to think. When he pulls back, his eyes are wild.

"Come like this," he growls. "Cream in your panties for me. Let me feel it." His mouth is on mine again, but he keeps talking, barely pulling away. "This is all I need. You are all I ever want."

The tension in my belly coils tight, heat building and

firing down my thighs, licking between my legs where I'm riding his cock. I start shaking, but he holds me tight through it, whispering everything I need to hear, taking my desire and turning it into something focused, hot, and forever.

"Yes," he breathes as my body starts to shudder. "Good girl. Come for me. God, you feel incredible. Fuck, you're going to make me come, too."

I fall apart for him, my body pulsing like I'm made of the entire universe, and he might not me inside me again, but he's *inside* me on a whole different level.

I can barely breathe, but I don't stop moving.

I can't.

Not when I can feel the thick, hard throb of him, even through his pants. And I can feel how close he is, how he's barely holding on.

"Moya," I breathe.

His head tips back, jaw clenched. His hands are shaking.

"Teach me, Alexei."

"Polovinka," he rasps, his lips dragging along my neck. Breathing it against my skin.

"Moya polovinka," I repeat, and I mean it. "My soul."

"Fuck—don't stop," he groans. "Can you feel what you're doing to me?"

"I feel it," I whisper. "I want to make you come, Alexei."

"Say you're mine."

"I'm yours."

He groans—and then breaks.

The hand on my ass tightens, and his hips jerk, his thighs going hard beneath me. He convulses, pulling me into him. Breathing hard against my throat, and then as he slumps, into my chest.

He turns his head to the side and presses his ear to my heart.

"I'm yours," I repeat.

And we exhale together.

CHAPTER 45
ALEXEI

In the next fifty hours, a lot of things happen. Emery finds an apartment to sublet in Manhattan. We clinch our spot in the playoffs with a mid-week win at home. Who we are playing is still up in the air, but mathematically, we're past the point of being eliminated.

And on a Thursday morning in early April that feels suspiciously like spring might be here to stay, like a real turning of the seasons, finally… Emery finds a nanny for Inessa.

I did tell her that I could handle it myself, but she cheekily replied that she was already fully packed for New York—since she only has a backpack, and she's leaving her jerseys in my closet to keep me company in her absence.

I kissed her silly and told her how grateful I was for her help.

So when I come home from practice on that Thursday,

with presents for my girls in the back of my G-Wagon, I'm not surprised I have to park on the street because there's an unfamiliar car in the driveway.

I know who is probably inside, and I know this is all for the best.

I take a deep breath before opening the front door.

"Papa!" Inessa comes running, grabbing my hand and dragging me inside.

In the kitchen, Emery is leaning on the kitchen island, chatting with a woman who looks a bit older than both of us.

She's great, Emery's eyes say as she finds me and holds my eyes. *The exact opposite of Nanny Nyet.*

"Hello," I say, holding out my hand.

Our guest takes it enthusiastically. "Georgiana."

"Alexei."

"Time got away from us," Emery says. "We were talking about TikTok."

That makes Georgiana laugh, which makes Inessa laugh.

Emery rubs my arm. "Do you want a coffee?"

"Sure. Thanks."

As the espresso machine hisses to life, I ask Georgiana about herself, in Russian.

She's Romanian by birth, but she speaks Russian and English pretty fluently, and she has a ton of experience with toddlers and pre-schoolers. When her own children were young, she worked in daycares, but they are in high school and college now.

And while she has her own family and would prefer a

live-out situation, she is willing to work evenings and overnights as needed.

Most importantly, she seems curious and supportive of Inessa, getting down to her level and asking all sorts of questions about her toys.

"I don't know how to play hockey," she says to me after a third pull-away by my daughter. She adds an endearing little giggle that reminds me of my mother. "But the tiny sticks seem to keep Inessa occupied, so I will learn."

It's the right answer, of course. Still, my chest feels like it might cave in at the thought of coming home and hearing the slap of mini sticks, but it not being Emery playing with my daughter. "Great," I hear myself say from a distance. "And you don't mind the late nights?"

"Oh, no." Another laugh. "I'm not a morning person. Do you know how hard it is to find childcare that doesn't start so early in the morning?"

"None of us are morning people," Emery and I say at the same time.

We share a bittersweet smile, because it's a lie.

I am a morning person now. Morning is when I get Emery all to myself.

The basement door creaks open, and my father pops his head out. "Oh, Georgiana! You're still here," he says in Russian. "Would you like to meet my wife? She's awake now."

Our new nanny claps her hands together. "Of course, of course. Bring me to meet Baba."

Inessa runs over, happy to lead the way downstairs.

"We'll meet you down there," I say, my voice hoarse, but they don't seem to notice.

Emery does, though.

As soon as they disappear, she crosses the kitchen again and wraps her arms around me.

I make a wounded sound, and she laughs.

"You're *laughing*?" I mutter.

She tips her head up and I crush my mouth to hers. It's bittersweet and aching, and every time I try to deepen it, she pulls away just enough to keep it soft.

But she doesn't cut it short.

She kisses me and kisses me and kisses me, until I can taste her tears. Because we're both this emotional, we will be all week. Saying goodbye is hard, even if it's not forever.

And then I wrap her in my arms again, tight, tighter, and press my face into her hair because then she won't know that I'm crying, too.

"I got you a present," I finally say when I don't sound choked up.

"Is it another jersey?"

"In a manner of speaking. Come outside with me." I weave our fingers together and lead her out to my car.

In the trunk there are two boxes. One very, very large and the other a flat rectangle, just like a jersey box. I hand that one to Emery. "Carry this."

I manhandle the massive box into the foyer, then indicate for her to open the gift she's holding.

Inside, it does *look* like yet another of my jerseys.

But I think Emery figures out what it is pretty quickly,

because her fingertips go to the collar, and the new buttons that have been added, before lifting it in the air.

"Oh, Alexei." She looks pleased, really pleased.

"I know you can't wear it in a real kitchen, but—"

"I'm never wearing it to *cook*, in any kitchen, but I'm definitely going to wear it to a game, and I'll have pictures taken in it!" She pulls off her sweatshirt, then slides her arms into the custom chef's jacket I had made for her out of my jersey.

I button it up for her, then hold on tight as I brush a soft kiss on her mouth. "I'm proud of everything you do. I want to celebrate it as much as you celebrate me."

Her eyes shine up at me. "I love you."

"I love you, too."

She looks at the big cardboard box. "And what is that?"

"A play kitchen."

Again, she gives me a pleased look, and the feeling I get when I surprise her like this is as good as any other high I've chased in my life. Being drafted. Winning a hard fought game. Getting the nod as a starter in the NHL.

Loving Emery Granger with my entire being is such a fucking rush.

I hook my arm around her, holding her close, because I can. Because I love fucking touching her, and in a few days, I won't be able to. "Since you taught Inessa to play hockey while I was away, I thought I should play chef with her while you're in New York."

"She's turning that thing into a net, you know."

"We're a multi-tasking family. It's fine." I drop another

kiss on her, and it gets a little wild, because that, too, is going to stop being a thing in a few days.

I'm going to miss you, my heart pounds.

But she clings to me in a way that promises, *I'm coming back.*

CHAPTER 46
EMERY

Friday morning

EMERY

> I'm texting you idiots first, so you need to keep this secret

FORREST

Who are you calling idiots?

WYATT

You and Logan, clearly

> No, I mean all of you

CAMDEN

Not me

> You most of all, Mr. Twice Divorced

CAMDEN

But I'm also Mr. Finally Married Forever
This Time, I've matured

You don't get flowers for finally maturing at the ripe old age of thirty-nine, idiot number one

CAMDEN

Did you call this family meeting just to be mean to us? That's fine, but I need to make my wife coffee, so I'm multi-tasking

No, I have news

FORREST

Mom told us about New York

And what did she say?

WYATT

Never mind that, what's your news?

FORREST

That is her news, dummy

WYATT

No, DUMMY, she said she was telling us first, so whatever it is, it's not about going to New York for fancy ass chef training

LOGAN

Are you going to the national team training camp?

No, I'm done with hockey

CAMDEN

What?

WYATT

Why?

FORREST

How?

LOGAN

Seriously?

EMERY

I mean, I actually quit hockey two years
ago and none of you noticed, but
anyway, that is also not my news

CAMDEN

Sorry, okay, what's up?

You can't freak out

FORREST

Shit, you're pregnant

Oh fuck right off

LOGAN

She's totally pregnant

Unlike you MORONS, I know how to use
birth control

LOGAN

Ew, that means she's having sex, tho,
don't like that mental picture

Stop talking about me like I didn't initiate
this lovely chat

CAMDEN

Hang on, who doesn't know how to use
birth control?

WYATT

We all do, she's distracting us

FORREST

What are you distracting us from?

LOGAN

Emery?

WYATT

I think she's dipped out of the chat

CAMDEN

Logan, you asshole

LOGAN

It wasn't me

WYATT

I'll talk to her

———

Friday afternoon

EMERY

What are you wearing tonight?

SHANNON

That sounds suspiciously like a WAG
question

Shhhh

What does this mean for your training?

Oh, I'm going to New York…with Alexei's
full support

Ahhhh I love it!

So I'm going to soak up tonight as the last home game I'll see for a while... I'll try to come back for playoff games that fall on my days off, though

How low-key shhhh is this WAG status?
Can I order you a jacket?

OMG

I tried to tell my brothers this morning but they were obnoxious so I left the group chat

I'll order a jacket. You don't have to wear it for anyone but Alexei, in private

I can't believe you just typed that

If you haven't worn his jersey and nothing else yet, I highly recommend

Oh, I have

Okay, yes, order me a WAG jacket

———

Saturday morning

WYATT

Come back to the group chat and tell us your news

EMERY

Not until everyone agrees to mature about the fact that I have as much right to a healthy sex life as the next Granger

Shocker at the crickets

———

Sunday afternoon

EMERY

Hey Mom, just wanted to let you know that I'm flying to New York on Tuesday morning (and yes, we found a nanny)

MOM

I'm glad it all worked out

Alexei is being very supportive and excited for me

Of course he is

That was a leading statement

I don't understand

Nevermind

———

Monday morning

FORREST

Okay, we respect you as an autonomous adult who can make her own relationship choices

EMERY

You didn't write that yourself

FORREST

Lady friend helped

Does she know you call her your lady friend?

FORREST

It turns her on

Great

LOGAN

We're all ears

WYATT

I agree that lady friend makes you sound like a retiree, Forrest

FORREST

Nothing retiree about my game, brother

EMERY

Hey, focus!

CAMDEN

Yep, right, Emery's having sex and we're all cool about that, bring on the details

LOGAN

Hey

FORREST

Whoa

WYATT

Maybe no details, just the high level
news headline

Definitely no details

LOGAN

So you're seeing someone?

CAMDEN

Is it serious?

FORREST

Is it anyone we know?

EMERY

Shit, Inessa just… brb

———

Monday afternoon

FORREST

Does she know that brb means be right
back?

WYATT

Hope everything is okay over there

LOGAN

I called her and she sent back a do-not-
disturb text because it's nap time

CAMDEN

Speaking of which, I need to have a
nap, too

FORREST

You playing tonight?

WYATT

How do you not know our schedules?

FORREST

Unless you're on the other side of the
face-off dot tonight, it's irrelevant to me

LOGAN

They don't let you take face-offs

EMERY

Okay, I'm back, she's finally asleep

Oh, do you guys have to go? Is this not a
good time?

LOGAN

It's the perfect time

WYATT

We're all ears

CAMDEN

Tell us!

FORREST

Emery Granger, who are you banging?

EMERY

Your best friend (sorry not sorry, I actually
love him)

CHAPTER 47
ALEXEI

"How long do you think until he calls me?" I ask.

From where she's curled up in the crook of my arm, Emery shrugs. "Either immediately or not for, like, two weeks."

From the bedside table, my phone starts vibrating.

"Immediately it is," she says, crawling over me to grab it.

Which puts her ass in the air.

"Let it go to voicemail," I suggest, palming her bottom. "It's nap time."

She wiggles her hips. "Ooh, I like that, but—" She squeaks as I slip my hand up the loose leg of her shorts, squeezing the juiciest part of her ass just because I can, because it's mine, she's mine, and she's starting to tell people.

"Hang on," she gasps, laughing, then gasping when my fingers dip between her cheeks. "Alexei—"

"Get off my sister."

She hands me my phone, which she has answered and Forrest is on speaker—apparently.

"Hey bud," I say casually.

"Don't *hey bud* me. Why the fuck am I hearing about this from Emery?"

"Because she's your sister."

"And you're my best friend. You need to face me like a man."

Emery makes a gagging sound.

I put my finger to my lips. "Oh yeah? Why?"

"Because you can't just… I mean, she's going to kill me for this, but it's *Emery*, you know? She's sweet as fuck. And you're…"

"A filthy hockey player?"

"Exactly."

"But I have to respect her privacy, yes?"

That trips him up. "Well…"

"Forrest, I love your sister."

"I know, but—"

"Do you know? I've been in love with her for two years, man. And she wanted nothing to do with me. This isn't something casual. I *love* her." I'm talking to her brother, but I'm looking at Emery.

And she's smiling back at me.

"I knew she was trouble as soon as we met," I continue. "The best kind of trouble. And as long as she wanted that to be secret, it was going to be secret. Now, she wants you to know, so now you know."

"But Mom and Dad don't know yet, so you have to keep it secret with us," she adds, crawling on top of me.

Taking my phone and hanging up on her brother.

Putting my hands back on her ass.

"Trouble," I growl at her.

She gives me a smile that is brighter than the surface of the sun.

————

We go to bed early that night, because she needs to be at the airport in Toronto at four in the morning. My parents sleep upstairs, to be close to Inessa while I'm gone, in the room that was very briefly Emery's, but her place is in my bed now, and nobody questions that.

At three, her alarm goes off.

I drive her to the airport. The highway is pretty empty at this hour, and it doesn't take us long enough.

Before I know it, I'm holding her at the curb on the departures level.

And she's holding me back, so tight it feels like she never wants to let go. I know the feeling.

"I wish we'd had more than a few weeks together," she mumbles into my shirt.

"Sunshine." I cup her face. "We will. We're going to have the rest of our lives. Go. Text me when you're through security, and when you get on the plane. And when you land. Keep me updated, all day every day."

"No time for regrets," she whispers.

"Only hope."

"And anticipation..." She pushes up on her toes,

kissing me one last time. And then another, a bonus kiss to last us through the next week.

A week.

That's the same as me going on a road trip.

This is fine.

Hard, but fine.

"I love you," I say as she puts her backpack on. "I love you so fucking much."

She blows me a kiss, and then she's through the doors of the airport, her own *I love you* echoing back at me.

Time for me to head home, and go back to bed. It won't be long before Inessa crawls in with me, wondering where her Emmy is, because how do you explain to a two-year-old that her favourite person has something important to do somewhere else?

You can't.

We just have to keep carrying on, and distracting her, the same way we do when I leave on a road trip—and the next one is around the corner.

CHAPTER 48
EMERY

The first fun thing I do in New York is go to a hockey game. Not just any hockey game, but a PWHL game that one of my college teammates is playing in.

It's been a long few days of getting settled and meeting my instructors and fellow trainees, and there's something comforting about getting on the train to Newark and seeing the number of jerseys streaming towards the arena when I get off.

It's a sharp contrast to how out of my depth I feel at the culinary school—but I know I'm not alone in that. The learning curve is steep, because it's an intensive program, and I've already learned a lot in just a few days.

My phone rings just after I've scanned my ticket and gone through the gate.

I take a deep breath before answer.

"Hi, Mom. Sorry if it's loud, I'm on my way in to watch Cecilia play a game today."

"Who is Cecilia? That name is familiar."

I picture Alexei counting backwards, seeking patience, and I laugh under my breath. "Cecilia Lombardi, Mom." There's a blank pause. "We played together in college, and she's a pro player now. Anyway, what's up?"

"We just haven't heard from you all week."

"I've been busy."

"But not too busy to go to see a friend play hockey."

"You caught me," I say dryly.

"Emery, please. I'm trying to be interested in how it's going for you."

Right. Because I told her she should do that. "It's great. I'm learning a lot. I like my chef instructors." I dodge around a rowdy group and head for the escalator. My seat is up on the second level. "It's hard to be away from Alexei and Inessa, of course, but he's playing against New York next week, so I don't have to miss him for—"

I cut myself off, but I've already said too much.

My mom sighs happily. "I knew it."

Damn it. I step to the side of the concourse and lean back against the wall. "Mom, don't."

"But, Emery…"

I swallow hard. I wish Alexei was here to hold me as I say this. "Mom, you're never that happy for me in any other way, so please don't be that happy for me just because I've fallen in love. Trust me, I'm happy for me, too, but I was also happy for me when I was made captain in Boston and you didn't bother to come to my first game of the season. I was happy for me when I ran the Chicago Marathon. Do you even remember that? I was happy for me when I went to culinary school, and started my own business, and closed that business, and applied to this program. I will be happy for myself thousands of more times across my lifetime, but if it doesn't relate to an NHL player, will you even notice? I don't think so. Maybe you should think about why you're the last person to find out that Alexei and I are together."

"Oh," she says. And then she starts crying.

To her credit, she pulls herself together before I can complete the thought of, *really, Mom? Making this about your—*

"I'm sorry, baby. I will try to be better."

"I hope you will."

"Am I really the last to find out?"

"No, of course not. I haven't told Dad, either."

She sobs into a laugh. "Okay. Were your brothers Neanderthals about it?"

"No. I made them be mature about my sex life before I told them who it was with."

"Emery Granger!"

"Don't make me get specific, Mom. I will."

This time, her laugh is all giggle, no sob. "Is he good to you?"

"So good. He's very supportive."

"Good." She takes a deep breath. "Maybe I will ask him for advice on that."

CHAPTER 49
ALEXEI

Our last away game of the year is a quick overnighter in New York City.

The team plane touches down mid-afternoon the day before the game.

When we get to the hotel, we have a few hours of rest, followed by a team dinner—but Russ and I get excused from that because we're going to have dinner with Emery.

Or rather, we'll have dinner prepared for us by Emery, and her fellow trainees, at a pop-up tasting menu seating at the culinary institute she's training at.

She was so disappointed when she told me that she would be working on my night in the city. But I was delighted, and Rusty was more than happy to come with me, so I made a reservation for two through school's online system.

When we arrive, the person who I give my name to immediately recognizes me. And not because she's a hockey fan. "Chef Granger has picked your table out. She'll be out to greet you shortly. Can I start by bringing you still or sparkling water?"

We both ask for still water, and she leaves a bottle on the table for us.

Emery appears shortly after. She's wearing chef whites, and her hair is twisted back in four mini-French braids, two on either side.

She looks amazing. And the way her eyes flare when our gazes meet is all I need to be patient and wait to pull her into my arms, later.

"Welcome to our pop-up," she says professionally, setting a plate of bread between us, and a separate plate with two egg-shaped rounds of butter. "Each course today has been worked on by yours truly and my colleagues. Do either of you have any food allergies we should know about?"

"We do not," Russ says.

"You look great," I murmur. *I missed you. Sit on my lap. Feed me bread and butter and never leave my side again.*

Except that's not how life works, and Russ doesn't need to see the rest.

She winks at me.

She knows.

We've talked every day, and she'll come back to my hotel tonight.

"The butters today are ancho chili, nice and smoky, with a hit of flaky sea salt, and honey thyme, which is sweet and fresh. I need to work on a later course, so one of the other chefs will serve you the starter course. Do you have any questions?"

Is it too soon to ask you to marry me? I shake my head. "Not yet."

She points to the open kitchen, where people are working. "I'll just be in there."

We watch her set up at a station. Another chef comes over, who looks like the instructor, and they discuss something that is lost under the productive hum of diners and service.

Russ glances around. "How often do they do this?"

"Twice a week." I tell him what I read on the school's website.

He grins. "Does she talk your ear off about this stuff?"

I shake my head. "No. I read about it myself."

He gives me a surprised nod of approval. "Nice."

I don't want to talk out of turn about Emery's secrets, when Rusty is a family friend, but at the same time, I see an opening here to learn more about her early years. "She seems like the only foodie in her family."

"Yeah, I don't know where that came from. Maybe college. Until we reconnected at Camden's wedding last summer, I hadn't seen her in years. She's really grown into her own."

"Did you ever see her play hockey?"

He whistles. "Oh yeah. She was like lightning."

"I know."

Concern darkens his expression. "You can't push her—"

I hold up my hand. "No, don't worry. I don't want to

push at all. I just want her to be happy." I look back at where she's working in the kitchen. "This is a different kind of spectacular display."

He laughs. "You really are in love if you think that when all we've seen is bread and butter."

Except I'm not wrong, and it doesn't take long to prove that.

The first course is nice, some mushroom dish that wakes up our palate, apparently. But it's not Emery telling me about it, so I'm impatient.

She brings out the second course, though, and she's a complete pro.

"This is pan-seared black cod," she says, her voice steady and practiced. She pulls a note card from her pocket as she tells us about the presentation. "We marinate it first in blood orange and fennel, then sear it off to give it a really nice, crisp skin. It's served with charred scallions and a finger lime vinaigrette that brings a nice bright blast of acid on the finish." She sets the plate in front of me, then Russ. "Enjoy."

"Fucking will," Russ mutters under his breath, already reaching for his fork.

I elbow him, but he's not wrong.

As soon as our plates are clean, she returns. Her gaze flicks between us, gauging our reaction, but there's no need to worry—we're both blown away. "Are you ready for the main course?"

"Bring it on," I nearly growl.

She grins. Wide and familiar. "Shhh. Pretend to be normal customers."

I wave around us. "I'm pretty sure anyone would have the same reaction after that fish course. What's next?"

"Lamb shoulder," she says, twirling away.

And for all that I can see her influence on Inessa, that move is one my daughter taught her, I would swear it.

When she returns with the next plates, she doesn't even glance at her notes.

"I worked on this one," she says. "The lamb is slow roasted all day. The marinade is cinnamon, sumac, and date syrup. It's served with labneh and black garlic, and finished with orange wedges, pickled red onion, and fresh mint. It's complicated and sweet, like the best kind of memories."

That might be a line they're given by their instructors, but it hits me squarely in the chest because complicated memories are what sustained me in the two years between when she captured my heart and when I could finally give it back to her—but I didn't appreciate how sweet those memories were.

"It sounds perfect," I say.

"Enjoy." She squeezes my shoulder, and I catch her hand before she slips away.

Russ digs in. I wait until she's all the way back at her work station, but once I have my first taste, I don't stop eating until I've finished and my plate is completely clean.

There's dessert as well, but someone other than Emery tells us about it, so I'm only listening with half an ear as I watch her prepare more plates of lamb for other guests.

When her instructor asks her about something, she gives them her full attention. Crisp-sounding *yes chef* and *understood chef* responses filter through the noise and slide under my skin.

When we're ready to leave, she senses the shift in energy, and lifts her head. As if to say, *wait a minute?*

I nod.

She serves two more plates, then comes over. "Thanks for coming."

"Our pleasure," Armstrong says. "Seriously, Buzz. Very good stuff. Are you going to open a restaurant in Hamilton one day?"

She presses her lips together, pleased. "One thing at a time."

"It's a great idea," I say, just for her ears. "Let's talk about it tonight." And I slide one of my hotel room keys into the pocket on her chef's coat.

——————

There's a quiet knock before she taps the card key against the sensor and the lock whirs open.

I'm on my feet as she comes through the door, but I nearly fall to my knees when I see that she's changed out of her chef's clothes.

Her hair is damp from a shower and curling naturally, golden waves rioting in all directions, and she's wearing a white sundress with little purple threading on her tits—fucking innocent—and black leather boots that cling to her legs—not fucking innocent at all.

"I have to get up at seven," she says as I catch her in my arms and press her against the inside of the door.

Then neither of us say anything, because we're kissing.

And *God*, but she tastes good.

I fill my hands with her, squeezing her curves, the fabric of her dress crumpling in my fists.

"Missed you, missed you…" she pants against my mouth.

"It was so hot watching you work tonight. Love your white chef's jacket. Love this little white dress even more."

She laughs, and I bend my knees to kiss her neck, to feel that warm sound against my lips.

Then she pushes her hands against my shoulders. Making space between us and really looking at me. "Thank you for coming tonight."

"Of course," I say.

Because…of course.

Except I know that's not how it's been for her.

"Always," I add. "And I mean that."

"I know," she says.

And from the soft look in her eye, I know she means that, too.

She takes a deep breath and sinks to her knees. "Let me show you how much I appreciate you."

I plant my hands on the door above her and stare down. "You don't need to do this."

But my aching cock wants her to.

"I know." A bright smile. "I want to." She bats her

eyes at me. "Can I have a taste, Alexei? Can I taste your big, hard cock?"

Her words are filthy magic. "Who taught you to be so dirty?"

"You did."

"No, I didn't."

"Mm-hmm. You made me so curious about what it would be like to take your cock in my mouth, and then I didn't get to do that." Calgary. She's talking about Calgary. "So I thought about it in so…much…detail…"

Emery, on her knees, unbuckling my belt, is so sexy.

But once my fly is unzipped, she doesn't take me in hand. Not yet.

She strokes the front of my thighs, sliding her gaze from my straining bulge up to my face and back down again. "Do you know that I dreamed of this for two years? The feel of your cock in my mouth. The scent of your turned-on skin…" She leans and brushes her nose along the edge of my boxers. "The taste of your seed on my tongue."

"That's naughty."

"I'm naughty. But only for you. I'm your dirty, dirty girl." She hooks her fingers into my waistband, her knuckles grazing my bare skin, and I just about come from that touch alone.

There will be seed on her tongue all right. Real fucking soon.

But she's in no rush.

For all her erotic fire, this feels like worship. Reverence.

I have never had a lover look at me like this.

Fuck.

She smiles as she slides her fingers deeper and finally takes me in hand, pulling my cock into the open. "You smell good," she whispers. And then she licks around my flared tip with a soft, broad swipe of her tongue.

I squeeze my hands against the door and shudder.

She kisses the very tip, then looks up at me, her eyes bright. "You can hold my head." Another whisper. A smile next. "If you want. I'd like that, too."

I reach for her hair with one hand. Weave my fingers through it, finding her scalp. Curl my hands around her head and test bringing her mouth more directly onto my cock.

Fuck.

Fuck.

That. Feels. Incredible.

And then she swallows, her little tongue convulsing against the underneath as she takes a third of me into her mouth, and that's too fucking much. Just that. I spill into her mouth, pushing my cock over the mess I'm making, fucking into her even though it's too late, I'm already throbbing my release on her tongue.

Into her willing, gulping mouth.

"Mmmm." There has never been a more pleased sound.

I'm about to pick her up and kiss her mouth, wanting to taste myself on her tongue, when there's a knock at the door.

"Room service," a porter says on the other side.

Emery slides around me and bounces to her feet, patting me on the ass.

I'll let you get that," she whispers.

I put my dick away and zip up, then answer the door and accept the tray I ordered in case she was hungry, either now or later.

When I turn around, the door to the balcony is open.

I set the tray on the desk, then turn off the lights, giving us as much privacy as possible out on the balcony.

Doesn't stop her white dress from standing out against the dark like a forbidden beacon. The skirt flutters in the wind as she leans against the railing, looking out at the city.

I wrap my arms around her from behind and press a kiss to her temple. "Your turn."

She smiles at the millions of people around us who have no idea she's about to get railed in this pretty little sundress. "Out here?"

"If you want." My hands slide down her waist, gathering the light fabric of her dress in my hands, until my fingertips reach bare thighs—and quickly discover she's not wearing anything underneath the innocent white cotton.

I groan.

"I want," she whispers.

"Tell me you didn't walk here without any panties on."

"I took an Uber."

I growl and cup her bare cunt possessively. She's so hot between her legs, and I'm the only one who gets to hold her like this. "I should have met you at your apartment."

"And blow your curfew?"

"I'm a grown-up."

"You need to be the starting goalie tomorrow night. Imagine getting scratched because you were out getting laid." She laughs, but it dies into a sigh when my fingers push between her pussy lips and find her very, very slick.

"Did swallowing my cock make you wet, sunshine?"

"Mm-hmm."

"Say it." I press my face into the side of her head. "Give me more of that filthy dirty talk you practiced in this beautiful mind of yours when we weren't together."

She lifts her arms and anchors them behind my neck as I settle my fingers against her clit and start circling that sensitive bundle of nerves.

"Sucking you got me so turned on. I want you to touch me out here," she says. "Where anyone could see. Where I need to be…quiet."

"Mmm. You better be quiet. Or someone might notice how pretty you get for me when you come."

Her breath hitches. Her fingers dig into my neck.

"Can you be a good girl for me?" I ask against her hair.

"Yes."

"That's not quiet enough, Emery." I push my fingers deeper, seeking her entrance.

She squirms and presses her lips together.

"There you go… Don't cry out when I finger fuck you, okay? You have to swallow your horny sounds."

She nods furiously.

I thrust two fingers into her tight channel. My thumb slides to her clit, and the rock of her body pushes her ass against my cock, which is thickening for her again.

"Are you taking your pills?"

She shudders and nods again.

"Because I'm going to fuck you out here. As soon as you come on my hand, I'm bending you over this railing and pushing my cock into you." I grind against her. "Showing up without panties. Wet pussy. Leading me out onto the balcony…"

She whimpers.

"You are begging to get fucked."

"Yes," she bursts out. "I've missed you."

"Then you'll get me inside you." I pull my fingers out and slap her pussy, loud in the night air, even over the traffic and noise below. "Even if people can hear us." I shift her hips back, and she has to let go of my neck to fold forward, holding on to the railing. "Because I want everyone to know you're mine."

I flip her sundress up as she spreads her legs.

There's never been a hotter sight than Little Miss Sunshine tipping her bare ass back at me, her slim, strong legs clad in black leather, the rest of her barely covered by virginal white cotton.

I growl, low in my throat, and curve over her back, tugging her bodice down. Baring her tits, too.

"These are mine," I rumble in her ear as I fill my hands with her perfect handfuls. And I squeeze, because I can, because she's mine and in my arms, and I never want to let her go.

"Yours," she agrees, her nipples pebbling against my palms.

"Does the air feel good?" I thumb at one of the peaks as I curve my other hand back to her pussy.

"Mm-hmm."

Her clit is standing strong now, straining for my fingertips. I flick it and make her jerk in the tight confines of my arms. "This is mine, too."

"Everything is yours."

"Everything?"

I unzip and free my cock.

Bend my knees and bring us together, notching my tip against her slippery cunt.

She pushes back, bringing her tightness around my dick, and we both moan at the same time.

"Why does that feel so good?" she whispers.

I push as far as I can, then ease back, slicking my length with her arousal, before I sink all the way into her on the next thrust. "Because this is yours."

"I am yours and you are mine," she whispers.

"Touch yourself," I urge. "Rub your clit while I fuck you, because I'm not done claiming every inch of you."

She twists her head to the side, resting her blonde waves on the forearm stretching to the railing. Her other arm disappears into the shadows beneath her, but I feel it when she starts rubbing her clit. Her pussy clamps down on me, and blissful pleasure ripples across her face.

I swear under my breath and widen my stance.

Squeeze her hips and lift her onto her toes, adjusting the angle so I can get deeper, be more inside her.

"This is mine," I say thickly as I palm her ass again.

She moans. *Yes.*

I roll my thumb in, rubbing a light circle on her tight asshole. "Is this mine, too, Emery?"

Her mouth falls open and her eyes flutter shut.

Yes. Absolutely yes.

I press, giving her steady pressure there as well as deep inside her. She rolls her hips, fucking against my cock and my hand. Her rim squeezes against my thumb, kissing the pad before making a bit of space for me to push in.

Just a little.

Just the tip.

Just enough to make her knees buckle.

I catch her around the waist and hold her up as she comes on my cock and her fingers and my thumb.

And before she finishes, I pull out and turn her around, pressing her back against the glass door to the balcony, fitting my hips between her legs, holding her in my arms as I thrust into her again.

"Again," I tell her. "Come for me again."

She makes the sweetest whimpers.

I cover her mouth, tasting her trembling need.

Nothing has ever felt as right as moving inside Emery's body.

Her tongue is soft against mine, but as I snap my hips, the rest of her tightens up.

I find her asshole again, giving her that same double

penetration that got her off when she was bent over, and she clings to me. Riding me.

"I'm on the edge, Alexei," she whispers. "I'm so close."

"We're going all night tonight, moya polovinka. I want more."

"You're so deep."

And that just makes me bigger. That just pushes me deeper. My cock feels like it's wedged against her cervix, and even though I've come once already, I want to again, now. Right like this. I want to fill her up with my seed, the way I will when she's ready to give Inessa a little brother.

"What about your belly?" I demand, my lips at her ear. "Say that's mine."

"Alexei?"

"I want to give you a baby."

"Fuck." She twists her head and screams into my neck.

And around my cock, her body takes flight.

"That's it, sunshine. Yes, oh fuck, here it comes. Here's our baby."

She clings to me as I thunder inside her, shaking the glass door.

In the aftermath of our orgasms, all I can hear is traffic down at street level, and quiet, shaky breathing in my ear.

I hold her so tight she can't run away.

I drag in a deep breath, then hitch my arm under her ass and turn to carry her back through the open door.

As I lay her down on the bed, she tightens *her* grip on *me.*

"I'm yours," I remind her, easing onto my side beside her.

She looks down our bodies, then back up to my face. "The last time I was half naked on a hotel bed with you, I didn't get your pants open. This is progress."

I blink in surprise. "Pardon?"

She laughs. "Nothing. Um… So… babies?"

My pulse is so heavy in my neck. "Just came out."

She licks her lips, her gaze warm but searching. "Out of nowhere?"

"Not nowhere. I like the idea of making a baby with you." I slide a strand of hair off her damp cheek. "There have been times when I've watched you with Inessa that I wished she was yours."

She catches my hand and weaves her fingers through mine. "I love her."

"I know you're smart about stuff like that. But when you're ready—"

She closes the gap and kisses me. Firmly.

Later, much later, after she's licked herself off of my cock—and I've sucked her clit again, and she swears she can't come anymore, and I bring one more climax out of her, just to be sure—we're back in the same position.

Fully naked, our legs tangled together, both of us half asleep.

And I realize I haven't asked her an important question. "Are you coming to the game tomorrow night?"

She smiles slowly. "Absolutely."

"Are you wearing my jersey?"

"Of course I'm wearing your jersey," she murmurs.

"And I'll arrange my schedule to make the first home game in the playoffs, too. Shannon's getting me a WAG jacket made. I hear that players like those just as much as jerseys…"

So even though we're tired, we make love again. One more time, because it has to last us another week at least, maybe more.

CHAPTER 50
EMERY

In the next week, I pass my first plating assignment, learn three new techniques for glazing fruit desserts, and book a flight back to Hamilton for game three of the playoffs.

The Highlanders finish the season third in our division, right behind Miami.

It's going to be an exciting match up. Ty Connor played there for a decade, and they traded him because they thought they were going into a complete re-build. But then this season was an unexpected bounce back for them, and the fandoms are rabid over the way this has worked out.

Emotions are running high, and Miami has home ice.

The team flies south to open the series. Miami takes game one, just like everyone expects them to. But Hamilton steals game two, playing tight, disciplined hockey—and suddenly, the series is tied heading back to Hamilton.

I land in Toronto mid-afternoon. Alexei has a private car waiting for me, since he can't pick me up himself. By the time I get to his house, he's left for the arena already, but Georgiana, Maria, and Sergei are all happy to see me.

Inessa is a little unsure. She gives me a reproachful look, like, *where were you?*

I drop to me knees in the foyer and wait.

She hides behind Maria's leg for a beat, then runs at me, throwing her arms around my neck.

"Are we going to the game together tonight?" I ask.

She nods.

I squeeze her so tight, and I'm glad I'm home for three days. There aren't enough hugs in the world to fill the hole in my heart when I'm gone, but I'll stock up on the ones I can get in the time that we have.

I send a selfie of the two of us to the WAG group chat.

EMERY

I'm home! Cuddles with my girl and then we'll meet you all at Kiley's!

Shannon sends back a photo of my jacket on a hanger, on a rolling rack with all the others.

SHANNON

We're ready to make you official!

HARPER

I seem to remember a drunken wine cellar conversation about how much you really didn't want to be a WAG…

EMERY

Well, I was trying to pretend I wasn't in love with Alexei, so…

ANI

WHAT?

KILEY

That's amazing

BECCA

We need the entire story tonight

———

It's not only matching WAG jackets that I find at Kiley's.

The girls have made tiny sandwiches for us to eat, variations on the ones I developed for Ani's baby shower.

They have matching outfits for Inessa and Charlie, too, little hoodies with their dad's numbers on the back, and team-inspired badges down the arms—a Glengarry-wearing boar, red and black crossed hockey sticks, and "Mini Highlanders" in the middle.

"I love these," I murmur, my fingers tracing the mascot.

Shannon points to the grown-up quilted jackets. "We have the same badges on the inside."

"But you're only allowed to see that on after you tell us the whole story," Kiley says, holding on to the hanger.

"Well, it starts with asparagus sorbet…" I leave out the more private bits, but they get the gist of what happened two years ago.

As one, my friends all look to Inessa, who is happily playing with Kiley and Becca's dogs. "That same night?"

"The very same."

"Ooof."

"Mmm."

"So you just…"

"Blocked him. Moved on with my life. Kissed a lot of frogs. Got into culinary school." I blush. "And somehow, found my way back to them anyway. But I'm older and wiser now, and I know what I want."

"Cheers to that." Ani lifts her seltzer water. Then her eyes go wide and she puts her hand to her belly. "Oh."

"Oh?" I think we *all* said that at the same time.

She breathes carefully. "Just Braxton-Hicks, I'm sure."

A few more girlfriends arrive, and Ani doesn't report any more contractions, but as we head downstairs, and then pose in the lobby as a whole group, I know I'm not the only one watching our most pregnant friend.

"It's not time yet," she says as we settle into our seats for the game. "I timed this baby to come in the off-season."

As we wait for puck drop, I send a photo of my jacket to my mom. Not quite a peace offering, but I'm wearing it proudly, and I know she'll like it.

EMERY

Never thought I'd say this, but…had my WAG Jacket debut tonight

MOM

Does this mean Alexei will wear a chef's
jacket this summer when we visit?

I laugh. And then I drop a heart on it, because it's not just that she tried to hit the right note, but that she sent it back *immediately*. That says she's been thinking about what I said.

I don't send it to my brothers, but by the first intermission, Forrest has seen it on social media, and he sends a screen cap of that to the sibling chat.

FORREST

The Twittersphere doesn't like your WAG
jacket

LOGAN

Whoa, they're already jacket official?
Didn't they start dating two weeks ago?

CAMDEN

She's living with him, she better be jacket
official

Wyatt doesn't reply, because his team is also playing tonight.

I smile and mute the chat notifications.

———

Hamilton wins, and is now up two games to one in the series, and they have another game at home still.

Ani doesn't go into labour.

When Alexei gets home that night, everyone else is tucked in, and I'm waiting for him on our bed, wearing nothing but the WAG jacket.

He does like it.

A lot.

———

Game four is another clutch Hamilton win. That night, I fly back to New York on the last flight out, and the next day, Alexei and the team return to Florida up three to one in the series. They are one win away from doing what they couldn't do last year—clinch a playoff series.

That's when the wheels come off.

In Miami, game five is a must-win elimination game for the home team, and they play like it. I watch the game in New Jersey, with Cecilia and her girlfriend. Alexei has a rough game, and by the top of the third, it's three-nothing.

I can tell that the third goal is going to haunt him the most.

He gets a little horny on the poke check and goes down too low, leaving his shoulder wide open. It's an easy chip-in up top, a rookie mistake that he hasn't made all year. There's no way around it, it's a bad goal.

His teammates try to rally, and they score twice, bringing them within one, but it's not enough.

He gets pulled with three minutes left and has to watch from the bench as Miami sends one more into the empty net.

And the series heads back to Hamilton for game six.

"Are you okay?" Cecilia asks, wrapping her arms around me.

I realize I'm crying.

I swipe my cheeks. "I'm fine." I take a deep breath. "Just sad for my person tonight, you know?"

She pets my head and holds me while I compose myself.

Then I pull out my phone and buy a late afternoon ticket home in two days' time.

CHAPTER 51
ALEXEI

The buzz starts immediately. Is Makinen going to start game six? He's healthy again. I just got lit up in a must-win game.

It's only natural for people to ask if it's time to switch goalies after that bad loss.

But our coaches don't.

At practice the next day, I'm in the starter's net. At morning skate on game day, I'm the first one called off the ice.

Hale follows me off the ice. "Let's go, Arty. We've got a game tonight."

———

Ty scores a minute and a half into the game, a beauty of a shot. The crowd explodes. But there's barely any time to celebrate.

Miami comes right back down the ice and I do that

same stupid save again. I know it's a mistake as I'm going for the puck. I'm way too aggressive, and their video staff clearly did their job, identifying my weakness.

"Stupid fucking mistake," I snarl at my goalposts as the forwards line up at centre ice again.

The posts are quiet, too quiet. As if they're saying, *this is on you to fix.*

I look to the bench for a gut check. Makie's there. Coach could put him in.

But neither of them are looking my way.

I'm not getting saved here. This is my game to win for my team, I have to be better than that. And somewhere in New York, Emery is watching me, and I sure as fuck have to be better for her. I have to be better for Inessa, too. When she's older, she's going to be told over and over and over again how this game goes. Her dad's first playoff series. I want her to be proud of what she hears.

But most of all, my team in front of me—and my fucking self—deserves a win tonight.

We didn't go up three games in a series just for me to develop a case of the fucking yips.

I square my neck and hunker down, and I save every fucking puck that comes my way. Twenty-six of them by the end of the second period, an insane volley of shots.

And then, with three seconds to go before everyone gets a chance to catch their breath, Ty gets his stick tangled up with one of his former teammates, and it slices up and under the guy's visor.

A double minor penalty.

We'll start the third period on the penalty kill.

In the dressing room, we re-hydrate. We get refreshed. I put on a new undershirt and take a piss.

But it's not like any other intermission break. We are one period away from winning a play-off series.

And my teammates? They aren't fucking scared of being on the PK. They're *hyped*. Marsh draws up plays on the white board. Coach comes in, sees what we're doing, and just lets us cook.

Everyone is dialled in.

And then it's time to get dressed again, and get back out there.

They win the draw and get set up. Their centre falls back, looking for some space, and then powers up, suddenly gaining too much speed. And from where I can see the play, I know he's going to break through and get a shot.

I'm patient. I wait for it.

Don't read too much, just keep your eyes on the puck.

I catch it, a satisfying thump in my glove, and flick it away. Keep the momentum, keep the kill going.

They get another zone entry, there's another fast press, and again we hold them off. This time they don't even get a clean shot.

They fall back and do a line change. I don't have to look up at the display board to know we're nearing the two minute mark.

Their second penalty kill team isn't on for that long, maybe forty-five seconds, and then the first team comes back. We must be rounding the third minute.

And I start to think they're not going to get set up to do a third zone entry. I can feel the penalty kill ticking down, but then suddenly there's one last blast of energy, and there's a player in front of me.

Fuck.

I shove him aside, keeping my line of vision clear, and I plant my skate against the post. Stacked. Ready.

The puck snaps off a stick and zooms through the air. High. It's high. Shoulder maybe. Higher. Fuck.

I get my glove up.

Snap.

I've got it, I know I've got it, but there's no whistle, and then bodies are piling on top of me.

"It's in my fucking glove, right?" I scream the question. "I have it. Get the fuck off me."

I try to get my blocker up, using it to push with all my strength, and then the whistle finally comes.

But the pushing and shoving doesn't stop, even after I'm clear of the pile-up. Smash does his thing, flinging off his gloves and gesturing *come here* at one of the Miami bruisers, a big Russian guy named Petrov. Rusty grabs another one of their players, someone who is chewing on his mouthguard.

The last thing I see before I shove off the post and slide out of the melee is Armstrong shoving that guy in the chest, then snatching the mouthguard away.

I think that's the moment I know we're going to win.

The little squeak of indignation I hear before I float out of the mess, taking the brawl as a nice stretch break, over in the corner by myself.

Fans scream and pound on the glass.

I roll my shoulders and look up at the scoreboard.

The penalty is over. We killed it off, but with all the bodies being pushed toward the box by the refs, maybe a new one is about to begin.

I drag a deep breath into my lungs, then glide back to my net.

Let's fucking go. I'm ready.

———

In the end, once the penalties are read out by the ref, the forwards line up even strength for the drop, but four on four.

And then Calhoun scores.

For thirty seconds, Miami has a one-man advantage, but that means nothing to Hiro Watanabe, who tricks them into turning over the puck and scores short-handed for us.

After that, I don't see a single shot for most of the period. I have the best seat in the house for the most magnificent hockey I have ever seen played in front of me.

Haler scores. Connor scores.

The game is out of reach, but they still pull their goalie and now it's six on five, and then we called on a tripping that maybe wouldn't be called, except we're up six to two. And so now it's six attackers against four defense, and we're on the penalty kill, but there's only so many block shots that my teammates can take before the shots start coming at me. There's only a minute and a half left in the game, and I'm blocking shots and every time I get my glove on it, I have to put it down and stop it.

Which means there's face-off after face-off, ten feet away from me.

Miami is winning a lot of those draws, and each draw feels like a guaranteed shot to stop.

Glove.

Blocker.

Butterfly down. Knob up.

Until suddenly, the place slows down and the arena starts cheering.

High-land-ers, High-land-ers, High-land-ers

The horn goes.

We won.

We fucking won.

We're moving on to…

"Round fucking two," I scream, taking off for centre ice, throwing my hands in the air. "Round fucking two."

Dodaj is the first person to slam into me. Then Hale and Hooner.

Armstrong giving me a fucking bear hug.

Every single guy pours off the bench.

We're laughing and we're crying.

We line up for the post-series handshake with the other team.

Hale first, Connor second, because he spent a decade playing with a lot of those guys that we just beat.

I take up the rear.

It's the most surreal feeling. I'm tingling. The closest thing I've felt to this is holding Inessa for the first time. Like it's an incredible but mostly out-of-body experience.

Suddenly Petrov, the big Russian guy, is in front of me. He clamps his big hand on my shoulder and he says, in Russian, "You're a fucking legend, kid, you're a legend. Enjoy this run. It's gonna be the first of many for you."

"Thank you, my brother," I manage to say back.

He claps my helmet, then moves past me.

I shake hands with their goalie, then their coach, before the Miami team leaves the ice and we're alone at centre ice.

Someone from the team hands me my stick, which I left at my net.

We all raise our sticks in the air, recognizing the fans who are still on their feet. Our fans. Our home barn.

There are so many red and black jerseys in the house, it looks like a sea of Buffalo plaid. Like the Glengarry dicing our mascot wears.

And then one fan pops out of the crowd. Her jersey is a custom chef's jacket, and she's pressed up against the glass, a thousand kilowatt smile just for me.

CHAPTER 52
EMERY

two months later

I thought spending a week at the beach with a toddler would be stressful—worth it for the post-season getaway and uninterrupted family time, of course, but I was prepared for nonstop vigilance.

However, it turns out that sand is endlessly fascinating to Inessa, and with a bucket and a shovel, she's content to play in one spot for hours.

All I have to do is remind her to put her hat back on, and keep apply sunscreen.

By day three, she's remembering that herself, clever monkey.

"Emmy, my back," she says, running over to where I'm reading on a lounger under the cover of a cabana.

We're staying at a private villa just on the other side of the dunes, and we're the only family who has used this beach since we arrived. It's not completely private, but it feels like our own little oasis from the world.

I pick up the sunscreen tube and carefully cover every inch of her.

"Drink some water, too," I say.

She makes big eyes at me as she sucks on the bright pink straw the waiters put in her cup.

Alexei lifts the straw fedora that was covering his face and gives me a lazy smile. "I need some sunscreen, too."

He's totally angling for me to rub him all over.

I pass the tube to Inessa instead. "Go give this to your daddy."

She squeals and runs at him, throwing it hard at his chest.

He catches it easily and gives me a deeply amused look that I feel all the way to my toes, all hot and secret and fun. "Thanks, little one." He squeezes some of the sunscreen into his hands, then gives her the bottle. "You can give it back to Emery now. She'll need to do my back shortly."

Proud of her new job, she hustles it back to me. "This is Emmy's."

Then she tips her head to the side, thinking. She looks back to Alexei, then to me again.

"Papa. Emmy." She cackles like she's told a funny joke, but we aren't in on the punch line. Then she points at Alexei. "Daddy." She giggles and smashes her hand to mouth. Hilarious. She points at me. "Mommy."

My heart stops.

Alexei is looking at me. I hold very still and don't react.

But he sees me, he always sees me, so he scoops her up and strides down to the water as she shrieks in protest.

"Come for a swim," he calls me to over his shoulder.

I can't.

I'm crying.

They're happy tears, but I'm still crying. And my hands are covered in sunscreen, so if I wipe my eyes, they'll burn.

I blindly grab a towel to wipe my face, then I jog after them into the surf.

They're floating together in water that is mid-chest height on me. As soon as I get close, Alexei shifts Inessa to one arm, and uses the other to pull me in close.

"We love you," he says.

I breathe.

We float.

Inessa holds on to her dad's neck, super tight.

"I don't want to replace anyone," I finally whisper.

He smiles. "I know."

"I love her so much."

Inessa turns her face and smiles at me, dimples popping as she slaps her hand on the water.

I take her from him, lifting her out of the water, then splashing her down. Up and down. Up and down.

He wraps himself around me from behind.

"It's okay for you to be Mommy," he murmurs. "It

won't change the fact that Tatyana is her Mama. You aren't a…usurper? Is that the worry?"

I nod and sniffle and then smile at Inessa as we float in the waves.

His lips brush my neck, whispering against the sensitive spot behind my ear. "You'll be Mommy to her brothers and sisters, after all."

I turn hot inside, instantly.

"Stop," I whisper, not meaning it at all.

"No? You don't want to hear how I think about your belly swelling with our next child? I love being a father, Emery. You want to make me a daddy again?"

My tongue is tied and my heart is beating a mile a minute, but I'm saved from having to answer that immediately by Sergei coming down the path to the beach.

Alexei carries Inessa out of the ocean. As soon as they're on the sand, she wants to show her grandfather the hole she was digging. I stay floating in the water, watching them. After a few minutes, Sergei leads Inessa up the path, and Alexei strides back into the water.

I hold my breath, not quite believing this is my life— and my love.

"Deda is going to try to get her down for a nap, but we should head up there soon," he says when he joins me.

I wrap my arms around his shoulders as he lifts my legs around his waist. "And then a nap for us, too?"

"Absolutely." He takes my mouth in a slow, deep kiss that makes my toes curl and my thighs clench. Just us and the sea and the hot Caribbean sun.

His fingers slide under my bikini top, cupping my tit, his thumb finding my nipple with practiced familiarity.

We managed to squeeze a lot of sex into our long-distance relationship during the playoffs. And now that we're all in New York for the summer, I get him every morning. While the rest of the house sleeps, he wakes me up with his hard-on and his questing fingers and his hungry, hungry mouth.

Before I head out the door for a long day of chef training.

I'm not going to lie, I'm looking forward to getting back to a slower pace of life in the fall when we move back to Hamilton.

This week, though, we're on vacation, which means we aren't constrained to only morning sex. We can have afternoon and evening sex, too. We can, and we are. Often.

And the more we connect, the more Alexei wants to touch me.

But there's something extra about this, there's an intensity vibrating through his body that feels new.

"Are you okay?" I ask.

"I get a whole week with my girls, I'm perfect." He exhales against my neck before nipping me, gently. "I want to be inside you."

"Not in the ocean."

He pulls at my bikini straps. "Then get out. And I'll follow you."

I float away from him, topless now. He watches, his gaze hooded and hot, as I walk backwards out of the ocean, my belly and breasts jiggling for his eyes only. Then he follows, water sluicing off him, slicking the dark curls in the centre of his chest and on his legs.

He looks hungry and powerful, and I shiver as I turn and race for our towels.

"Can you be quiet here?" I jump when I hear him right behind me, a second before his arms scoop around my waist and he pulls me onto the lounge chair.

He pushes his swim shorts down, freeing his cock. Big, hard, and ready, it slaps against his wet belly.

I straddle him and he pulls my bikini bottoms aside, his gaze locked on my pussy.

"Pretty little cunt," he rumbles under his breath. "Needs to be filled up."

My belly clenches.

His thumb brushes reverently over my lips, then around my clit.

The clench eases into a warm, steady need.

I take him in hand, stroking him firmly. Bringing pre-come to his tip and slicking it around with my thumb. His cock throbs against my fingers, flexing and stretching. I love watching his foreskin slide down, revealing the dark pink crown fully.

And I love making that tip disappear inside me even more.

I lift up, then slide down.

Both of us gasping at the stretch, the way he changes the shape of me on the inside and takes up space. So much space.

"Lean forward," he rasps. "Feed me your tits."

I brace myself on his shoulders.

He squeezes my ass as he sucks on one breast, then the other, grinning up at me in between tastes. The pull of his mouth makes need coil tight in my belly, makes my body clench down on his shaft.

"You're going to give me little blonde babies, Emery. So many babies."

"Shhhhh." I brush my nipples across his mouth again, trying not to laugh and scream and say yes yes yes.

He takes my breasts in his hands, but keeps talking. "Need you to know how much I love you."

"I love you, too."

"How many babies?"

Now I give in and laugh. "I don't know. At least one more."

"A little sister for Inessa, hmm? Like that?"

"Yeah." I lick my lips as I sway on top of him, growing unsteady. "I'll give you little boys, too."

"Baseball players."

"Goalies."

"Same thing. Baseball in the summer, hockey in the winter. Triple threats."

"That's only two things."

"They're also lady killers."

I laugh and laugh and can't stop. I fall forward, flattening out on top of him. "You're terrible."

"You love me." He takes over and starts moving inside me.

"So much," I whisper before he finds my mouth with his.

———

When we get back to the villa and slip in to the primary bedroom through the patio, so we can shower off the sea—and the sex—before checking on the rest of the family, we both look at my birth control pills, sitting on the counter.

Alexei picks them up, his throat bobbing. "I want to throw these out."

I snatch them from his fingers and set them back in their spot for me to take one in the morning. "If you do that now, we might have a newborn during playoffs next year."

"I like your confidence that we are going to have another long run in the playoffs." He strokes my face. "I will hire you all the help."

"You will hire?"

"We will hire. I like keeping nannies busy."

I tip my head back and laugh.

He kisses my throat. "I didn't mean with sex."

I cling to his shoulders. "I was never your nanny."

"Disagree. You were my hottest nanny ever."

"EBUB only."

"EBUBs get full nanny credit if they get called on. Jerseys with their names on it and everything."

"Oh, that's…" I can't argue with that logic. "Okay, fair. I was your hottest nanny."

"But now you are my woman."

I laugh and nod. "I am."

"Marry me." He mumbles it against my skin.

"Is that a question?"

"I want you to take my name."

"Also not a question."

He leans over and reaches for my pills again, and I think he's going to literally toss them in front of me, but when he rights himself, it's only to step back and kneel down.

In his hand is a diamond ring.

Not my pills.

"Oh," I whisper.

His dark, glossy hair slides forward over his brow. I reach out to brush it to the side, because I can. Because this impossibly handsome man is mine to touch.

"I have a question I've wanted to ask you for two and a half years," he says.

Should I tell him now that I was prepared to say yes that very first night in Calgary? That he swept me off my feet from that very first smile?

No, I'll wait.

"Emery Granger, will you marry me? Will you take my name, and have my babies, and make me happy forever?"

"Yes," I breathe. "Yes and yes and yes and yes, always and forever."

EPILOGUE

ALEXEI

one year later

We get to the Basilica before the priest does.

"I told you we didn't have to leave the hotel yet."

I make a face at Forrest. "I didn't want to be late."

"We're almost an *hour* early." He taps my arm and points across the street. "Want to go find a drink?"

"That's not a bar, it's a…" I squint. "Real estate office, I think."

"No worries, I brought my own." He pulls a flask from the inside of his suit jacket. "Cheers, bud."

I laugh as he take a swig, then I accept it and tip back a small shot myself.

Why the fuck not? I'm getting married today.

As I hand the flask back, the door opens behind us, and we're invited inside. Guests start to arrive ten minutes later, which I pointed out to Forrest.

He offers me another slug, which I decline.

We mill at the entrance for a while longer, but as the church starts to fill up, we're led to a side chamber to wait for my bride.

As soon as we're shown the private room, though, my bride sends me a text message.

EMERY

Running late, I'm so sorry. It's not me, I swear.

ALEXEI

Is it my daughters?

The little one, yes. I needed to nurse her again, but I'm putting on my dress now!

We can come help, we are at the Basilica

No! You can't see me before the wedding!

I can't see her before… I laugh and show the screen to her brother. "Can you imagine?"

Forrest gives me a wide-eyed look I recognize from his sister. "Oh yeah, buddy. You can't see her."

"But she has both of our children with her!"

"And she has two moms, and a nanny, and a bunch of friends."

I frown.

Emery sends me a photo of baby Natalia, now sleeping her car seat.

And then another one of her big sister, dressed up in her flower girl dress.

Maybe you would be here faster if you
stopped sending photos

That wasn't me, that was Inessa

I love you so much. Please come here so
I can marry you.

We're leaving now! See you soon. I love
you too. So much.

Forrest reads that over my shoulder. He slings his arm around me. "That's very sweet."

EMERY

Late girls give the best blowjobs, though!

"And that's too much information." He pivots away from me as I double over laughing.

It's not that long before there's a knock at the door, though. It's Camden, who was tasked with driving his sister and our kids here. He has Talia in his arms, and she looks extra small against her oversized uncle.

"Delivering the littlest flower girl to you," he says.

I take my second daughter from him, nestling her against my chest before I shake his hand. "Is she nervous?"

"Talia?" He grins. "She's fast asleep."

I frown. "Emery."

He claps me on the shoulder. "Bud, she's the opposite of nervous. Literally dancing in the foyer. Get out there, and she'll run down the aisle to you. She's excited to marry you today, I promise."

We file out to the front of the church.

Emery's parents spared no expense on their only daughter's wedding. There's a string quartet, and fresh flowers, and a packed Basilica, probably the biggest cathedral in the entire state.

But I only have eyes for the woman hiding around the corner at the back of the church.

Our family comes down the aisle in a bit of a blur. My parents, her parents. Then her best friend from college, Cecilia.

And then Inessa, who looks so much older than her three years as she carefully walks and sprinkles flowers and keeps a steady pace the entire way.

The music changes.

I wipe my eyes.

Fuck.

No swearing at your wedding, Artyomov.

Fuuuck.

Her shadow falls at the entrance, and then she steps into view.

She's wearing white. And if I didn't know that her tits weren't usually that round, she would look every inch a virginal bride.

Golden sunshine.

My sunshine.

She walks herself all the way to my side, and then reaches out and takes my hand.

I still can't quite believe that a girl who had all the choices in the world chose to give me a second chance, but I couldn't love her more than I do in this moment. With our girls beside us and our families watching on.

"Hi," I whisper.

"Hi," she says back.

"Let's get married?"

"Oh yeah." And then she beams a thousand kilowatt smile.

We exchange vows about our family first. And then Camden and his wife step forward and take the girls back to sit with them in the front row, and I take Emery's hands in mine.

Her grip tightens around my fingers as the priest prompts us through our vows.

…to be my beloved… I promise to be true to you in good times and in bad, in sickness and in health… for all the days…

It's a dream.

It's incredible.

Then the priest intones, "May the Lord fill you both with his blessings. What God has joined, let no man divide. Amen."

And Emery steps in close and cups my face.

I pull her in close and dip her back as we kiss each other to make it official.

The priest clears his throat when we finish. "There was another part to follow that, but… newlywed excitement has taken hold, it seems."

Everyone laughs.

We kiss again.

And then he gets to say the other part, which is another blur. There's paperwork to sign, and then the girls join us again for the walk back down the aisle as husband and wife.

But most importantly, as each other's.

———

Turn the page for a bonus story about Emery and Alexei, fifteen years later and still very much in love (just with more kids, who all play hockey…)

THE SECRET ATTIC LIBRARY
ALEXEI & EMERY, FIFTEEN YEARS LATER

EMERY

"Okay, let's gather up!" I let my whistle drop as I push off, the ice biting under my skates.

The U-18 team I've brought to Switzerland for a co-ed tournament over the Christmas break is a talented, focused group. Some of them, whose parents played on the Hamilton Highlanders back in the day, grew up with my daughters and have called me Coach for more than ten years.

But they are talented in part because they show up and do the work, even when it's a reward tournament that feels more like a holiday than real competition.

"Really great practice today," I tell them as they circle around me, all bright-eyed and red-cheeked from exertion. "Good job on coming prepared and giving it your all. Enjoy the rest of the day with your families. Tomorrow afternoon, we play our first game at one p.m., so make sure you get a good breakfast in! Any questions?"

"No, Coach." A few kids say it in unison, but Nessa's voice is louder, stronger, more confident than the rest. There's a reason she wears the C on her jersey, and it's not because she's my daughter.

"Suck up," Talia snaps loud enough for everyone to hear.

In stark contrast to her older sister, it'll be a while before my second daughter earns the right to wear a letter on her jersey. At fifteen, she's one of the youngest kids on the team, and it's the first year that she's playing with her older sister. She's still pure impulse—and I'm sure there was something in there that her sister did to provoke the reaction, too.

For two kids who love each other more than life when nobody else is around, they find ways to constantly get under each other's skin as soon as there is an audience.

Teenagers.

I ignore the barb, because oxygen just makes fires burn hotter.

And they'll work it out themselves, they always do. Something Alexei taught me early on was that children act out with the people they love—parents, but siblings the most—because we're trusted, and we need to practice pushing back against the world. Learning to assert ourselves.

As my girls get closer to adulthood, I never want to do anything that makes them think they shouldn't assert the fuck out of themselves. If someone doesn't like it, they'll push back.

"Everyone is dismissed, then! Unless your family is joining us for free skate. We have the rink for another hour."

From behind me, there's a low, warm chuckle. "Might just be us, sunshine."

I pivot on the spot, the dismissed team forgotten. "Hey, handsome."

Alexei has our two younger kids, ten-year-old Lina and five-year-old Sasha, in tow. All three of them have their skates on, the kids wearing helmets with full face masks, too. Even for a fun skate, Alexei is a stickler for safety.

"How was practice?" He skates over to me, impossibly tall and lean. His thick hair is still glossy and dark, but his short winter beard has some grey in it now. Just enough to make him look stern as he looms over me.

His eyes, though, twinkle in a knowing way.

We're sharing a room with Sasha on this trip, because his older sisters don't want a five-year-old boy sleeping in their room, and the chalet where we are staying with the entire team is mostly made up of family rooms with three or four beds anyway.

It's fine, of course.

But I had my period last week before we set off on this adventure, and then we had a few days in France with Nessa's other mother. And neither of those things interfere our sex life, usually, but with the stress of travel and taking Christmas with us on the road, we just didn't get to it.

Especially because Sasha, unlike his sisters, is a morning kid.

Don't you know that's when your father and I bone? I have thought to myself more than once.

He does not, and for his sake, I hope maybe he never finds out.

For my sake, though...

"What are you thinking?" Alexei murmurs as he circles around me. "Are you horny?"

"Am I that transparent?" I grin up at him as he twirls me into a tight hug.

"I thought I might be projecting." He nuzzles my cheek. "Can I kiss the coach?"

"I don't see why not. Practice is over," I say breathlessly.

From somewhere else on the ice, there are a few whistles and claps, but there's also a familiar voice protesting that we should get a room.

"Lina," Alexei and I say at the same time, with an equal mix of adoration and exasperation.

Our ten-year-old is not a fan of PDAs. The two older girls never minded, and Sasha is a cuddlebug himself, but Lina...

He winks at me as we break apart, before he lifts his voice.

"Okay, Polina, let's race," he says.

Everyone loves racing their dad, because Alexei wears goalie skates, which are flat on the bottom and the sharp, pointed ends of the blades are a tripping hazard if he were to get out over them too far, like if he skated too fast. He could still beat a lot of people in them because he's an elite athlete—but his own kids? In regular skates? He's beatable.

And Granger/Artyomov genes guarantee that everyone wants to try.

Sasha takes off after them.

I turn around to see how the puck clean-up is going at the other end of the rink just in time to see a yelling match break out between the oldest two.

We all beeline for them, Alexei and Lina from one direction, me from the other.

"Nessa!" Talia carves a sharp line around her sister, who is apparently playing keep away with the pucks. "That's not *fair*. Mom!"

"*Mom*," Nessa mocks. "If you don't want me to take the puck from you, then *be better*."

"Jesus, she sounds like you," Alexei mutters under his breath as he comes to crisp stop beside me.

"I don't speak like that," I protest.

He laughs. "You do when you're playing your brothers."

"Oh." I sigh. "Well, yeah. But that's different. My brothers are savages who should know better than to try to beast-mode their way past me when I'll just…" I snatch the puck that was resting by Alexei's skates.

He throws his hands in the air as I pass it to Talia.

She catches it right on the tape.

"Soft," Nessa taunts.

"Shut up, Favourite," Talia snaps back.

"You're the one who—"

I get between them and blow my whistle, my most favourite thing to do. "Stop being exhausting, my darlings. You're setting a terrible example for your sister."

Lina zooms to a stop in between them, showering all of us with snow. "What's this about me?"

"Be glad that Mom decided to space the babies out more," Talia says.

"Ew!" Lina wrinkles her nose. "Don't say things like that."

And then right on cue, Sasha tries to do the same kind of stop that his older sister and dad did—and instead, he barrels into Talia's legs.

She loses control of her stick, Nessa snatches *that*, too, and suddenly there's actual shoving back and forth as all three girls tumble to the ice, Lina landing on top of Sasha.

I blow my whistle repeatedly.

Alexei laughs his ass off as he hauls them all to their feet.

"I don't know why I thought a family skate would be a good idea," I mutter, but I'm trying hard not to smile.

They are exactly like me. And while I wouldn't trade them for the world, Momma is definitely ready for some high-quality Swiss chocolate and a hot shower.

———

"Shower beer?" Alexei's hand appears around the curtain first, holding a cold bottle of German beer. Then his head follows, and he's got such a nice grin that how can I say no?

"Where's Sasha?"

"Passed out. Jet lag is still kicking his butt." He joins me in the steam and accepts the bottle back after I've taken a long sip. "A post-skate beer is the best part of retirement."

"I think being able to travel for two weeks at Christmas is a pretty sweet perk, too." I slide in against him and press my wet, naked body against his torso. "Did you lock the door?"

He nods as he tips the bottle back.

I push up on my toes and kiss his throat as he swallows. "Can you be quiet?"

"That's usually my question for you—"

Knock knock knock.

"Mommy, I need to pee!"

I exhale and step away from my naked husband. "Damn it," I whisper.

"Sorry." Alexei cups my face and kisses me quickly. "I thought he would stay asleep."

"It's okay." I squeeze his half-erect cock. "We'll find time…later?"

"Leave it to me." He tips the bottle. "You want more of this?"

I wave it off. "You finish your shower. I've got chocolate waiting for me."

I step out, wrap myself in the provided robe, and let Sasha in to use the toilet.

But this isn't over. We may have been interrupted, but

that just means that Alexei will be motivated to find another opportunity.

I grin to myself as I cross to the closet. I brought exactly the right outfit to provide that motivation.

———

After the nap-that-didn't-last-long, Alexei keeps Sasha awake, trying to push through the jet lag and get him to bedtime. They head off to explore the chalet before dinner before I get dressed, so Alexei doesn't see my white sweater dress and knee-high black boots until he finds me in the main dining room, where we're all going to gather for a group dinner.

But I feel his attention as soon as they return. As soon as he clocks that I'm wearing his favourite combination of innocent, soft, touchable white and sexy, not-so-innocent black boots.

After fifteen years, it's basically a short hand for *I want you inside me.*

Out of the corner of my eye, I see Sasha tart off to play with some of the younger siblings, and Alexei prowls my way.

"Hello, wife," he murmurs as he slides his arm around my hips.

"Hi," I murmur back. "We were just talking about..."

He nods along, but I can feel the tension vibrating in his hard body, and it doesn't take long for him to seize a pause and drag me away with an abrupt, "Sorry, can you excuse us?"

He turns us away and moves me rapidly into the hallway.

"Alexei!" But I'm laughing as he kisses me quickly before propelling me onward.

That worked better than I expected.

"Where are we going?"

"Somewhere you'll have to be very quiet." He pushes me up the wide staircase, chasing me up to the second floor, and then the third floor, where the hallway is open to the great room below, and the dining room just off that.

But up here it's pretty quiet. He kisses me again as he backs me into a nook, but it quickly becomes apparent this isn't our final destination—because this nook doesn't have a ceiling. Above us is an opening to a room, softly glowing with dim lights.

There's a rope hanging on the wall, and when he tugs it, it slides up, through his hands, and with a creak, a ladder descends from above.

"After you," he says.

I climb into the loft, wondering if he can see up my sweater dress the whole time.

But that thought disappears as soon as I get to the top of the ladder.

Alexei's found us a secret library nook strung with fairy lights, and there's an oversized bean bag chair covered in a soft blanket. He follows me up, then pulls the ladder up after us.

He secures the rope to a hook on the wall, then grins. "Now we can't be interrupted."

"But I still need to be quiet?"

"I sent Sasha and Lina up here early and I could hear them playing when I was out by the railing looking down, so…yes. The sounds might carry."

My eyebrows shoot up. "You used our children as a reconnaissance patrol for a sex spot?"

"Of course. You can thank me for my ingenuity on your knees."

God, I love it when my husband is brashly confident and demanding.

I sink to the floor as he unbuckles.

One might think that after fifteen years, I'd stop having that rush of excitement in the deepest part of my belly when I see Alexei's cock, but the thrill has never faded. It's the only adult cock I've ever held, or had in my mouth, in my pussy, in my ass… It's special, this cock. It's mine.

And it's so virile. So intense, the way it grows in my hand and pulses seed into my tongue.

"Look at me, sunshine," he rasps.

I blink up at him as I lick at his tip.

He groans.

I've never gotten over the thrill of that, either. Making him come undone with a little swipe of my tongue on his shaft.

ALEXEI

There's nothing in this world more beautiful than my wife, on her knees, worshiping my hard cock.

And even after fifteen years, sometimes I get so

fucking needy for her that I know I'll come too fast if she doesn't take the edge off.

"I want you to swallow my dick," I tell her roughly. "I'm going to come down your throat, and then we'll get to your needy pussy."

She's already gobbling me up, my hungry bride. My perfect girl.

I sink my hands into her hair and give in to the feel of her mouth, hot and wet and welcoming. She moans around my shaft, and that's so good, I can feel it in my balls. As if she can read my mind—or maybe because she's been curious about how to make me feel good for our entire marriage—she pushes my boxer briefs down further and cups my sac with her cool, clever fingers.

Jesus. Fuck.

"Shhh," she whispers against my tip before slurping me all the way into her mouth again.

Fuck.

"You're going to make me come," I growl.

"That's the point," she mumbles.

My eyes roll back in my head and all the muscles around the base of my cock clench up, but there's no stopping it.

She's got me off in record time...*again.* Always. She receives my release with practiced calm, waiting until I'm done twitching before she pulls off and swallows the entire load.

It's the licking of her lips after, as she looks fucking pleased with herself, that has me tumbling onto the bean bag and pulling her across my lap.

She's breathless as I grip her chin and stare at her.

"I was quiet," she says proudly.

I laugh and take her mouth with a savage hunger. I wasn't. I couldn't be.

But I'll do better now that she's taken the edge off.

I grab her hips and pull her down into my lap. "You wore those boots on purpose."

"They're good for snow," she lies.

"They're good for sin," I murmur, palming her soft, fluffy sweater dress and the lush ass underneath it. "You knew exactly what you were going to get when you put them on."

"You love that about me."

"I do." I kiss her again—slow and deep. The kind of kiss that says *we've done this for fifteen years and I still want you more than air.*

As we make out, she starts to grind against my thigh, rolling her hips slowly, and then she spreads her legs, clearly trying to get better pressure on her clit.

And I could let her come like this, rubbing against me slow and dirty—but while this is just enough friction to make her shiver, it's not enough to finish.

Also, I have something important I want to talk to her about.

Keeping my gaze on her face, I curve my hand over her belly, stilling the rock of her hips. "You finished your period a week ago."

Her breath catches, her eyes flaring wide. "Alexei."

"You didn't pack your pills."

To this day, Emery likes to be in charge of her own

birth control. I've told her that when we're done, I'll get snipped.

We aren't done yet.

She trembles, and I can picture her clit pulsing with need as she holds herself on the edge on top of my rigid thigh. Then she shakes her head slowly. "I didn't."

Fuck.

I push my hand down between her legs, up under her dress—and I find her bare.

Bare, slick, hot. Ready.

"Take your dress off before I rip it off," I growl. "I want you in the boots and nothing else. I want to fill you up and make you wonder how many babies I've planted in you for the rest of the trip."

She scrambles off me and slips the dress off, so she's standing naked in front of me, naked except for those fuck-me boots and a wet little cunt.

Holy hell.

I push forward onto my knees and grip her hips.

I kiss just inside her hip bone, then onto the soft pouch of a belly that's carried three kids for me. Decorated with little tiger stripes on the side.

She grabs my head as I circle one hand around her left thigh and tug that leg up and over my shoulder— balancing her on just one shaky boot heel.

I turn my head and kiss the inside of her thigh, just above the leather. Then higher. Higher again, to where she's slick and musky and perfect.

She gasps when I lick up the seam of her sex, slow and greedy, and she moans when I latch on to her clit.

I take my time. Work her over slowly, then faster, until she breaks apart with my name on her tongue, shuddering, one leg trembling against my shoulders, the other tensing up all the way to her lush, muscular ass.

Scooping my long arms up around her naked body, I urge her to relax into my hold, and she does.

A lifetime together has many advantages, and my wife reading my mind during sex is one of them.

I lay her on the bean bag.

She looks like the brightest sunshine and the ripest sin, limbs akimbo and her pussy all swollen for me.

My cock is already hard again for her. I push my pants down just enough and drop to my knees between her spread thighs, fisting it as I stare down at her slick entrance.

"You've given me everything, Em. But I'm still greedy. I still want this. Every time. Every chance I get, I want to put another baby in you."

I thrust into her slow and deep, and *fuck*, she's still so tight around me I see stars. Her whole body arches.

"You feel what you do to me?" I rasp. "Every time. Every goddamn time."

"Yes," she gasps.

I snap my hips harder. She cries out, and I catch it with my mouth.

"You gonna be quiet for me?" I growl. "Or do I need to put a hand over your mouth?"

"I don't know," she moans.

I pound into her then, hand at the side of her throat— not squeezing, just holding. My long fingers curving possessively up towards her mouth. Reminding her she's mine, and I will push her to the noisiest limits, but she needs to try to keep all that pleasure on the inside.

She comes again, legs locked around my waist.

And when I follow her, spilling into her with a groan and a litany of Russian curses, I collapse forward, kissing her temple, the corner of her mouth, her shoulder, and then as I hunch up, the tip of my cock so fucking sensitive now, I bow my head and kiss her between her breasts.

We stay like that for a long time. Messy. Happy.

But deep down, I know I'm not sated. Not by a long shot.

"You think anyone heard?" she whispers.

"Don't care." I drag in a deep breath. "Fuck, I could go again."

She hums happily.

"You like that?" I hunch up over her even more, my cock swelling again. "You like how I get so fucking hungry to put babies in you that I'll just keep coming all night, until you're swollen with my seed, so full it has to take?"

"Yes," she breathes. "God, Alexei, please…"

This time it's hard and fast and silent.

She shoves her hand between us and rubs her clit, getting there faster than I do. Good. I want her to come again and again.

I pull out and flip her over onto all fours, then mount her from behind and spit between her cheeks, giving her my thumb in her ass so she has no choice but to find another release.

Again.

Again.

And then I pound into her, finding my own third climax, filling her up once more.

I fall on top of her, and I wrap my arms around her, holding her safe beneath me.

"You're going to find all the private nooks in this chalet, moya polovinka. And we are going to use all of them to make sure that you leave here pregnant, yes?"

She rocks her hips back against me. "Yes. Always and forever, yes."

———

Thank you for reading *The Nanny Goal* and this bonus story!

If you haven't read the other books in the Off the Ice series, *The Playing Game* touches on the same delicious tropes as this book: second chance after a one night stand + a hero who falls first and hardest and *never* gives up— and supports the woman he loves in anything she wants. And *The Rebound Plan* is where we first met Emery!

I have another second chance romance, the first book in a small town series, written as Zoe York, that you might like as well. You can grab a FREE copy of *Love in a Small Town* via BookFunnel here, exclusive to *The Nanny Goal* readers: https://dl.bookfunnel.com/26birz4he3

ALSO BY AINSLEY BOOTH

Off the Ice

The One Night Mistake (prequel novella)

The Playing Game

The Scoring Secret

The Rebound Plan

Frisky Beavers

Canadian political romance, hockey adjacent

start with *Prime Minister*

Forbidden Bodyguards

erotic romantic suspense

start with *Hate F*@k*

Billionaire Secrets

rom-com

start with *Undercover Billionaire*

Secrets and Lies

erotic romance

start with *Tempt*

ABOUT THE AUTHOR

Ainsley Booth is a three-time *USA Today* bestselling author of erotic romance. Between her two pen names (she also writes contemporary romance as two-time *New York Times* bestseller Zoe York), she has published more than eighty books since 2013. Notable hits include *Prime Minister* and *Hate F*@k.*

facebook.com/ainsleyboothwrites
instagram.com/ainsleyboothwrites
tiktok.com/@ainsleyboothwrites
patreon.com/zoeyorkwrites

9 781998 523092